Praise for *How to Make a Life*

"Florence Kraut has written a sensitive and compelling multigenerational novel that begins with tragedy and ends with hope. Each chapter traces a family member who erases the scars of history's indelible mark with courage, determination, faith, and love. A wonderful read."

—Marsha Temlock, author of *The Exile* and
Your Child's Divorce: What to Expect; What You Can Do

"*How to Make a Life* is a novel about *family itself*—how to exist after unimaginable pain, acts of courage, secrets buried and revealed, that leave their glaring imprint on four generations of a Jewish family against the backdrop of history in the 20th century. Emotionally honest, rich, and deeply empathetic, this is a book for all of us nurtured in the tumult of the family."

—Marlena Maduro Baraf, author of
At the Narrow Waist of the World

"Florence Reiss Kraut has crafted a literary miracle. She's taken a century's worth of familial relationships and allowed the reader to enter into the emotional depths of her characters. Her experience as a family therapist is evident throughout the book, especially in her depiction of Ruby, whose struggles with psychosis and their impact on her family is as close a rendering of this particular challenge as any I have read—brilliant."

—Jill Edelman Barberie, MSW, LCSW, author of
This Crazy Quilt: Parenting Adult Special Needs One Day at a Time

"A moving novel of multiple generations of an immigrant family whose characters are so real I cannot forget them."

—Tessa Smith McGovern, author of *London Road Linked Stories* and host/producer of BookGirlTV

"A compelling and inspirational novel. Details have a way of creating potency, and the beautiful descriptions in Ms. Kraut's novel brings every character alive. Her images and painterly descriptions inspired me to write about my own family. I could not put this book down."

—June Gould, PhD, author of *The Writer in All of Us,* IWWG Writing Workshop Leader, consultant, and Master writing teacher

HOW TO MAKE A LIFE

HOW TO MAKE A LIFE

A Novel

Florence Reiss Kraut

SHE WRITES PRESS

Published 2020
Printed in the United States of America
Print ISBN: 978-1-63152-779-1
E-ISBN: 978-1-63152-780-7
Library of Congress Control Number: 2020908047

For information, address:
She Writes Press
1569 Solano Ave #546
Berkeley, CA 94707

She Writes Press is a division of SparkPoint Studio, LLC.

*In gratitude for my large, boisterous, and loving
extended family who shared their stories
and inspired me to create my own.
And to my husband, Allen,
who never stopped believing in me.*

Contents

"It doesn't matter what story we're telling, we're telling the story of family."

—Erica Lorraine Scheidt, *Uses for Boys*

"The strength of a family, like the strength of an army, is in its loyalty to each other."

—Mario Puzo, *The Family*

"Family is a life jacket in the stormy sea of life."

—J.K. Rowling, *Harry Potter and the Prisoner of Azkaban*

Family Tree

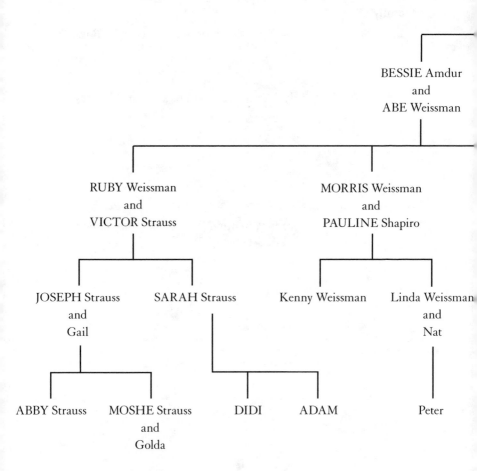

BESSIE Amdur
and
ABE Weissman

RUBY Weissman
and
VICTOR Strauss

MORRIS Weissman
and
PAULINE Shapiro

JOSEPH Strauss
and
Gail

SARAH Strauss

Kenny Weissman

Linda Weissman
and
Nat

ABBY Strauss

MOSHE Strauss
and
Golda

DIDI

ADAM

Peter

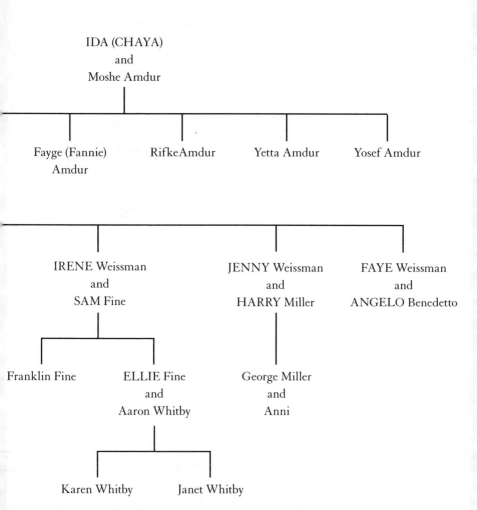

IDA (CHAYA)
and
Moshe Amdur

Fayge (Fannie) Amdur   Rifke Amdur   Yetta Amdur   Yosef Amdur

IRENE Weissman
and
SAM Fine

JENNY Weissman
and
HARRY Miller

FAYE Weissman
and
ANGELO Benedetto

Franklin Fine

ELLIE Fine
and
Aaron Whitby

George Miller
and
Anni

Karen Whitby   Janet Whitby

Prologue
Kotovka, Ukraine
1905

When the screams and crashes, the cacophony of clashing piano chords and splintering wood stopped, an eerie quiet came over the house. Chaya Amdur listened and cowered on the dirt floor of the root cellar clutching three-month-old Feige, who had nursed and fallen asleep. Ten-year-old Beilah crouched beside her and buried her face in her mother's skirt. In her free hand, Chaya held a shovel. If they came again, she would not go quietly.

She waited, hearing only her breath, shallow, fast. *Listen!* No more muffled thuds, no more footsteps on crunching glass. No laughter. Nothing. Silence. Her heart ticked, a clock. She counted seconds, minutes, ten, twenty. Then, trembling, she took in one last breath and crept upstairs toward the stillness. With the top of the shovel she pushed the hatch. It wouldn't budge. She heaved again and something moved enough so it opened a sliver. Dust motes danced in the light that filtered through. Her eyes wide open, she saw everything. The hatch dropped down. She gagged and cowered in the dark.

What had she seen?

Shattered blue-and-white dishes, her mother's splintered rocking chair, the overturned bookcase with prayer books spattered with blood. Beneath the piano a glimpse of her husband, Moshe, on his back, mouth gaping mid-scream, shirt and chest split, the white linen crusted with dark red.

She could not be still. Her legs trembled, jumped. Her heart hammered. Her stomach clutched. She crawled to a corner and vomited the little she had eaten before.

Before.

She had been nursing the baby. Beilah was rolling bedding into the corner, the others outside doing morning chores. Faint hoofbeats on the dirt road. Moshe raced into the house, shoving her and Feige and Beilah down the stairs into the root cellar. "They're coming. I'll get the others."

He never came back.

She took a deep breath, got up, pushed the hatch hard again. The table that had been lying on it fell over with a crash that stopped her heart. Still clutching the baby, she crawled out. Her mother, Channah, lay on her side holding a kitchen knife, benign in her hand. Her *shaitel*, askew on her forehead, showed short gray hair pressed in a puddle of blood. With first one step, then another, Chaya moved through the room. The feathers from her ripped comforter lifted into the air like red-and-white snow. She smelled smoke.

"Stay here, *mamaleh*," she whispered to Beilah. "Hold Feige."

"No." Beilah clutched her skirt, closed her eyes tight, shook her head back and forth.

"All right. Shush. Come."

Ignoring the roaring in her ears and her shallow, rapid breath, she forced herself to peek around the doorjamb into the yard and saw smoke rising in the distance. The doors to her barn were open, the horses gone. One of her black-and-white cats lay in a pool of its own blood.

In the yard was the body of twelve-year-old Rifka, her blouse ripped open, a gash down her chest. The bottom half of her body was naked, legs splayed, thighs streaked with blood. She leaned over and pulled Rifka's skirt down over her legs. Yetta and Yosef, ages six and four, lay on their backs near the barn, their chests red, a basket of broken eggs strewn nearby. Yetta's eyes stared sightlessly at the brilliant blue October sky. Yosef's eyes were closed as if asleep. They held hands.

Behind her Beilah was screaming, filling the air with her shrieks of terror. Beilah gagged, then vomited and screamed again. Chaya's legs gave way, and she sat on the ground. She opened her mouth, but no sound came, and she keened silently, rocking back and forth for a long time. She could not think clearly. There was a ringing in her ears. She was shivering, and she knew she could not stay in the yard, even though the road was quiet.

The road was quiet. Where had they gone, those men? Who were they? Would they come back? Terror gripped her throat again. Beilah lay sprawled on the dirt, her hands clutching fistfuls of it, her eyes closed. Her sobs had turned to soft hiccoughs. The baby began to cry. Chaya covered Feige's mouth with her filthy hand. "Beilah, come," she whispered. She grabbed Beilah's hand and pulled her to the door.

Inside she averted her eyes and with quick steps went to the cellar again. The comfort of the dark covered them. At the bottom of the stairs, she collapsed. Rocking Feige in her arms to stop her crying, she leaned against the cool dirt wall and closed her eyes, legs outstretched in front of her like a rag doll. The baby nosed her breast, and Chaya opened her blouse to let her nurse. Beilah crouched beside her, face against Chaya's shoulder. They sat like that, the silence a protective shield, broken only by soft skittering sounds of mice and Beilah's sniffles.

How long did they stay? Chaya's mind was a bottomless, black hole. Sometimes a picture flashed before her and she squeezed her eyes shut until it faded. The baby slept warm on her breast. Chaya handed the baby to Beilah and lay down on the floor, pillowing her head on her hands. They slept. She awoke to Beilah pushing at her shoulder.

"Mama, wake up. I have to pee. Where should I go?"

Chaya half sat up, stared at her daughter, and fell back down again.

Beilah shook her. "Mama, I have to pee." Chaya looked straight ahead with blank eyes. "Should I go outside?" Beilah waited for an answer. "Should I go? Where should I go?" She was wailing.

Chaya sat up as if coming from deep underwater. Her voice was thick. "In the corner. Go in the corner." She was about to lie back down, but Beilah thrust the baby at her and went to squat behind a barrel. The baby was soaking wet. She had nothing to change her with now. She put the baby down beside her, and Feige started to whimper.

"Mama, you have to take care of Feige." Beilah had picked up the baby and was holding her out. "Feige needs you. She's hungry."

Chaya looked at her daughter's grimy hands gripping the baby. She looked at Beilah's face, tear streaked, smudged with soot. She took a shaky breath and forced herself to her knees and then upright. "Give her here." She opened her dress and Feige latched on. She felt dry, realized she had not drunk all day. "Get me cider from the barrel." She drank, gave some to Beilah, shared a carrot, drank some more. She wondered how much time had elapsed.

Leaving the baby and Beilah in the dark of the cellar, Chaya crept up the stairs and pushed at the hatch. It was still daylight, late afternoon. She forced herself to look, but now she knew what she would see. She covered the bodies of her husband and her mother with a blanket and a Sabbath cloth stained rusty with dried blood. Taking bedcovers, she went outside. Beilah followed her mother and stood holding the baby, watching from the doorway.

She knelt weeping by her children. What should she say? Not Kaddish, the prayer for the dead—for that you needed a minyan, a congregation. The Sabbath blessing that was also a prayer? It was not

the right prayer, but it would do because she could not think of anything else:

May God bless you and watch over you
May God shine His face on you and show you favor
May God show you kindness and may He grant you peace.

She kissed their foreheads before she spread the blankets over
them.

Beilah was crying. "Mama. Come inside. They might come back."

Chaya looked around. The air was still. Nothing was stirring on
the road. She went back into the house, cleaned the baby, washed her
face and hands, and went to the cellar again. She was shivering. She
had no blankets. She'd used them all to cover the dead. She drank
cider, chewed a carrot, and stared at the barrels and baskets that
stored food for the winter.

Why hadn't they left earlier? They'd talked and talked, saved
money, pushed the date of departure further away. Never thinking.
Chaya hit her head with the palm of her hand. Dumb. Stupid. The
Tzar's October Manifesto had come, and then pogroms all over, but
too late they planned to leave. Too late. Beilah was sobbing again.
Chaya clenched her teeth.

Under the apple barrel Moshe had dug a hole to store a box. She
stood and shoved the barrel, scattering apples all around. She began
to dig with her hands. The dirt on the cellar floor was hard. She took
a deep breath, her throat constricted. "Get me the spade," she whispered to Beilah.

Beilah brought it over. With raging anger, panting from the
effort, she dug. Nothing. Leaning against a wall she wiped her sweaty
face and stared at the hole she had made. She covered her eyes with
dirt-encrusted hands. Deeper? She dug more. She scraped and shoveled. Then the dirt became softer, crumbly, and the spade stopped.

She pushed harder and there was a sound. She had found the box and inside was a burlap bag.

Sitting against the wall she opened the bag, counted the rubles, took out the gold necklace that Moshe had given her and her mother's pearls and gold earrings. She fingered the jewelry, warming it in her hand. Memories of her mother, Moshe, her children, threatened to crowd her brain. She would not cry. She shoved the money and jewelry back into the bag and breathed slowly, stilling her heartbeat. After a few minutes, she punched holes in the top of the burlap sack and tied it around her waist with a rope under her skirt.

Beilah sat like a statue, her eyes glass, her face stone. Chaya bent, kissed her filthy cheek, and took her hand. Carrying Feige, she went back upstairs and out to the road. She looked both ways and began walking.

A policeman rode by on a horse in the opposite direction. As he passed, he nodded. She stared at his back her mouth open. *Ah,* she thought. *It's over.*

All along the road was destruction. She saw a neighbor moving through the landscape, his eyes so blank he looked like he was no longer in this world. She saw that the synagogue was still standing, and as she got closer, she heard voices.

Inside, pews were overturned, and prayer books littered the floor. The room was full of people moaning, crying, praying. A neighbor clutched her shoulder, weeping. "My son is dead," he said. "I am a stem without my flower."

The rabbi stood by the Ark. He tried to talk. He whispered something, stopped. He put his hand to his mouth. He shook his head. His shoulders heaved, and he began to cry.

The smell of the blood had barely faded from her nostrils when she and her neighbors buried the dead from the catastrophe. The scourge had skipped houses and whole towns. Her in-laws had survived. Her sister's family was safe in the next town. She found her cousin Perel alive, a redheaded fury, known in the village as a *tayvl*, a crazy one. Perel had stood outside her door and screamed like one possessed. The murderers would not go near her, afraid of her demons. Cousin Perel's house was untouched, as if a wall had encircled it and made it invisible. In Perel's house, where they stayed for two months while they made plans to leave for America, Chaya could almost imagine the world was sane.

Her sister begged her to stay, but how could she? Each time she walked into the house, another shard would splinter off her broken heart until she would die. She had to close the door to Kotovka and never think of it again.

It was 1905. In early December, with her sister and in-laws saying, "Stay, stay," she left Kotovka for good. Chaya left behind her, buried in the Jewish cemetery, her husband, Moshe, her daughters Rifka and Yetta, her son, Yosef, and her mother, Channah. She left behind a prosperous life. Moshe had owned two horses and had a thriving business delivering milk and farm products to all the stores in the town. She left behind her own small business baking pies and bread to sell in Kotovka's market. She sold her house and land for half its worth to a gentile neighbor—maybe the one who had murdered her family—and traveled by train to Hamburg where she bought three tickets for the SS *Bergensfjord* to America. She put on the gold necklace under her dress and vowed she would never take it off. She embarked with her daughters, her mother's jewelry, and a sack of money tied to her waist under her skirt.

When the ship docked in New York harbor, they, along with the other people in steerage, were put on a barge and taken to Ellis Island. In Kotovka she had been Chaya Amdur, but when the clerk asked her name she said, "Ida. Ida Amdur." She changed her daughter's names as well, Beilah to Bessie and Feige to Fanny. They would be Americans now.

1

Ida

1906–1907

Ida spoke Russian, Ukrainian, and Yiddish but had only five words of English when she landed in New York: hello, goodbye, thank you, and please. She had a piece of paper with the name and address of her cousin, Hannah Cohen, written in Yiddish and English. Hannah had left Kotovka ten years before and ran a boarding house on Mulberry Street. Ida had used her name as her sponsor, but she didn't know if Hannah had received the letter she sent. She might be a big surprise to her cousin.

It was January, cold and gray. The wind blew up the street from the ferry terminal where they landed and waited on endless lines to be pronounced healthy and fit to enter New York. Ida, shivering in her woolen shawl, carried Fanny in one arm and a suitcase in the other. Bessie trailed next to her, hauling a large bundle with their bedding, some clothes, and her mother's candlesticks.

As they walked from the ferry up to Wall Street, Ida eavesdropped, hoping to find someone who spoke a language she understood. Most everyone was speaking English. The soles of her shoes burned. Her arms ached. Fanny was fussing.

"Mama, I'm so tired," Bessie said. "And I'm cold."

Ida ignored her. She stopped at the curb, shifted Fanny to her other hip, and picked up the valise again. A woman beside her smiled at Fanny. Ida took a deep breath, put the suitcase down again, and taking out the paper showed it to the lady. "Please?"

The woman nodded. She pointed and used her fingers to show how many blocks to the next turn. Ida bobbed her head and said, "Thank you."

She walked up Wall Street and repeated the process with anyone who looked approachable. In this way she got from Wall Street to Pearl Street to the Bowery. She and Bessie kept on until, exhausted, they came to a neighborhood where the streets were crowded, and they heard Yiddish. Even the smells were familiar. Ida began to breathe more easily. Here they could ask directions. Here they found what they were looking for, a brownstone four-story house—115 Mulberry Street.

Hannah Cohen was a large woman wearing a blue dress with circles of sweat under her arms. For a minute Ida and Hannah stared at each other, and then came recognition. Hannah grabbed her cousin in a huge hug, and Ida put her head on Hannah's bosom and closed her eyes.

But after they washed in the kitchen sink and used the hall bathroom, which was shared by two other apartments, and after Hannah fed them and the other boarders, soup and bread, and after Ida nursed Fanny, they sat on the horsehair sofa and talked. Ida knew this was not salvation.

"The apartment is full," Hannah said. "I have three boarders who take up the two bedrooms. I, myself, sleep on a cot in the kitchen."

Ida looked around the apartment, at the dining table in the living room, which was pushed to the side now that dinner was over. There were four hard wooden chairs, one armchair and a threadbare rug with big pink roses. There were pictures on the wall. Ida saw a photograph of Hannah's family in Kotovka, and recognized her aunt and uncle, long gone.

"I have no place to go. We'll sleep on the floor," Ida said. "Just until I get a job and a place for us."

Hannah took Fanny from Ida and rocked her, singing softly. Her eyes filled with tears. "You can stay until you settle yourself. You can sleep on the sofa, and we'll make a bed by the armchair and dining chair for Bessie. You'll be all right."

True to her word, Hannah let them sleep in the living room until Ida found a job and a place to stay. Ida had been a good baker in Kotovka, and through Hannah she found a job at Blumberg Restaurant and Catering Company. With her wages and some of the money in the burlap bag, she found two rooms in a tenement nearby, a fourth-flight walk-up with a bath in the hall shared with three other families. The corridor was dark and smelled of pee from the shared hall bathroom; it reeked of the garbage that stood outside people's doorways.

Ida worked at Blumberg's restaurant, baking the bread and pies. She also baked at home and sold her pies on the street when she wasn't at the restaurant. She made friends. She found Mrs. Schechter in the building, who helped her enroll Bessie in school and then babysat for Fanny while Ida was at work and Bessie at school. After school Bessie sat with Fanny in their apartment with strict orders not to let anyone in and not to go outside.

Everyone said what a beauty Fanny was. Flaxen hair, blue eyes, cheeks like roses. And smart. At one year she toddled to the door, banged on it and said, "I want go out!" Ida made her repeat it to be sure she heard right. Each day Ida came home, feet aching, and found Bessie and Fanny waiting for her. Fanny held her arms outstretched, and shouted, "Mama!" The pinafore Ida ironed and starched in the morning would be limp and stained with her lunchtime egg. There was a sweet milk smell in the soft creases of her neck. Ida would burrow her head in them and make her laugh. Fanny clutched her gold necklace in her hands so tight that after she fell asleep Ida had to uncurl the fingers one by one.

Sometimes Ida wondered if she loved Fanny best because she was the last, or because Fanny had no memories of before. Bessie had nightmares and would not let Ida forget, even though Ida pushed down the pictures that washed her dreams red. A mother is not supposed to love one child better than another, but she did. Fanny was beautiful, and Bessie was a tall and awkward eleven-year-old, whose eyes were sad.

After a year when they were well settled, Ida would help Mr. Blumberg for extra money when he was catering and needed her to bake the cakes for the party and stay and serve the dinner. Bessie babysat her sister. The instructions were always the same.

"Give her an egg for supper. Put her to bed at seven. Then I'll be back by ten. If you need help, call Mrs. Schechter upstairs."

One night in May, Ida dragged herself home after twelve hours on her feet baking and serving and cleaning. When she got to their fourth-floor landing, the door to the flat was open.

"Bessie," she called. "Bessie, where are you?" She raced into the empty bedroom, back into the living room. Now she screamed. "Bessie. Fanny." She ran up one flight and banged on Mrs. Schechter's door. The twelve-year-old son opened the door and Ida fell on him. "Where are they? Where is Bessie? Fanny?"

"They're at the hospital. My ma's there too, with them."

"Hospital?" Ida's eyes were wild. "Why hospital?"

"She got burned. Fanny."

The words barely came out. "Burned? How?" There was a rushing in her head. She grabbed his arms.

"Ow, you're hurting me. Let go."

Ida let go, steadied herself. "How?"

"Water."

"*Mit vasser*?" Ida whispered. "*Mein Gott. Mein Gott.* Which hospital?"

"Bellevue. A policeman took them. Bessie was screaming, and a policeman came."

Ida dashed down the stairs. The streetcar was two blocks away. Running, she stumbled on a crack where the sidewalk heaved, caught herself on the arm of a man in a brown suit, who glared at her.

"Whatchit, lady," he snarled.

"*Shuldich mir*," she whispered. Feet on fire, she ran, she pushed, she ran. The red house, the brown house, the butcher, the laundry. On the streetcar she prayed a singsong prayer. "*Gott, Gott, Gott.*" The streetcar stopped in front of the hospital and she raced in. Bessie and Mrs. Schechter were sitting in the waiting room.

Ida rushed to her daughter, put her face close and whispered, "What happened?"

"She pulled the pot down, Mama. Fanny wanted to see the egg, and she pulled the pot down on herself."

Ida tried to picture it. A little pot on the flame with the egg bubbling away. "How?" she asked. "Just the little pot? Not so much water in it."

"Not the little pot, Mama. The big one. The little one had the leftover soup. The big pot."

Ida could see it now. The big round pot with a long handle, Fanny stretching up. She slammed her fist into Bessie's arm over and over. "You let her? You let her pull the pot?" Ida pulled at her own hair. "What should I do, what should I do?"

"Nothing, Mama. They are taking care of her."

"Nothing? I should do nothing? Like what you did?" Ida yanked back her arm and smacked her daughter so hard across the face that Bessie's head snapped, and she stumbled backward. Mrs. Schechter gasped, reached out, and grabbed Ida's hand so she wouldn't hit Bessie again. But Ida was standing, arms limp at her sides, all the rage drained out of her.

Bessie was sobbing, her hand on her cheek. "I couldn't help it. She was so fast. On tiptoe she's tall enough. She reached up, and I couldn't get there to stop it. It was the big pot full of water." Her voice trailed off. She put her face in her hands. "I was so scared, Mama," she whispered. "I didn't know what to do. I wrapped her in a blanket. She was screaming. Her skin had blisters. I carried her."

"She came banging on my door. She was holding the baby, the poor thing. I took her and we ran outside looking for a policeman. They're in there," Mrs. Schechter went on and pointed. "You can talk to the nurse."

Ida couldn't talk to the nurse. She couldn't ask the questions that were in her head because there were no questions. All that was in her head was *Gott, Gott, Gott.*

If one could be said to turn to stone, that was Ida. She didn't move a muscle. Just fixed her eyes on the black closed door and willed the doctor to come out. She sat in a hard chair in the waiting room. She bunched her skirt in her hands, stared at her swollen feet, the ankles rolling over the scuffed oxford shoes. Bessie sat crying beside her, but Ida wouldn't look at her. Mrs. Schechter sat on Bessie's other side, patting her hand, whispering prayers.

Finally, the door opened and a tall man in a white coat came out. He looked so young, Ida couldn't believe he was the doctor, but she fell on him, clutching his arm. *"Mein. Mein tochter."*

"It's her daughter," Bessie said.

The doctor looked at them. He shook Ida's arm off, took long strides and went to the nurse's station, wrote something and then turned. "She's your daughter? With the burns?" Bessie nodded for her mother. "And who are you?" the doctor asked. "And what happened to your face?"

Bessie's hand flew to her cheek. "Nothing," she said. "Nothing happened. I'm her other daughter."

Ida stared at Bessie's swollen cheek. She was flooded with shame.

The doctor looked back and forth between them and shrugged. Then he said, "She's gravely burned. We will do our best but . . ." He shook his head. "It's in God's hands."

When Bessie translated, Ida's legs collapsed, and she sank to her knees on the floor. Bessie stood beside her. She pulled her mother up, led her to a chair all the while whispering, "I'm sorry, I'm sorry," until Ida turned on her. "Stop it. Stop crying. *Gay avek.* I don't want to look at you."

Ida sat still on the chair and waited. It was clear. God hated her. She did not know why, but it was clear. She sat like stone until the doctors let her in to see her baby for a few minutes. Fanny was bandaged so much Ida couldn't recognize her. She had second and third degree burns on her arms and chest and face. She went out and sat some more.

In two days, Fanny developed pneumonia. In two days more the nurse came out and, speaking softly, patted Ida on the shoulder. Ida did not understand the words, but she knew. Fanny was dead.

After Fanny's burial, after the shiva, which they sat in their flat, they moved back to Hannah Cohen's apartment for a while. Ida could not bear to stay in the apartment. All she took with her were two photographs—one of her family in Kotovka and the other of her, Bessie, and Fanny on the ship to America. She had paid a photographer to commemorate the beginning of their new life.

In Hannah Cohen's house, she sat on the sofa day after day, not talking to anyone. She sat through the night, barely sleeping. When Hannah Cohen asked her what she was doing, she said, "Nothing." Bessie went to school, came back, and found her mother sitting where she had left her in the morning. She would not speak to anyone.

After two weeks at Hannah Cohen's, Ida could not sit up anymore. She lay down on the sofa and fell into a deep sleep. She awoke, heart pounding from a nightmare she could not remember once she opened her eyes. She sat upright, reached up, and touched her cheek. Dry. She breathed deeply, in and out, in and out.

She held the photographs of her family and forced herself to remember. Moshe, with his bear hugs, his laugh that filled the room, his kisses and caresses in the dark, the smell of tobacco and horses. His chest split open with an axe. Her mother, always praying—and how had the prayers helped?—lying with her head pillowed in blood. Rifka, so smart people said she should have been a boy—with her skirt, a navy skirt, around her neck. And the little ones, Yetta and Joseph, always together, holding hands, pushed out of their babyhood by Fanny who was herself now cold in the cemetery among strangers. She saw everything.

She remembered Kotovka. She said goodbye to each street, each neighbor, the shops, the marketplace where she sold her bread and pies. She said to herself, *I will never look back again. If I do, I will die.*

Bessie was asleep on the chairs. Hannah Cohen was snoring on her cot in the kitchen. Ida put her two feet on the floor, slipped on her shoes, and stood. She shook Bessie awake and said, "Come. We're going."

Bessie rubbed her eyes. "Where?"

"To Orchard Street apartment."

"Now? Can't we wait until morning?"

"No. Now," Ida said. "We will go now."

Bessie put on her shoes and followed her mother. At the door Ida turned. She remembered her neighbor in Kotovka, the one who said, "I am a stem without my flower." She took Bessie's hand and looked into her eyes. She caressed Bessie's cheek and said, "Come. Let's go home."

2

Bessie

1931

Bessie was dreaming of her childhood in Kotovka when Ruby shook her awake.

"Mama, Mama, wake up! I'm scared."

"What?" Bessie sat up, snatching the fading images in her head. "What did you say?" Beside her in the bed, her husband Abe didn't stir.

"I'm scared." Ruby's eyes darted right, left. She turned behind her to see who was there. "They're coming." Her voice breathed panic. "They're going to hurt me, hurt everyone."

Bessie swung her legs off the bed and stood, grasping Ruby's shoulders to steady herself. "Who's coming?" She looked up at her daughter, at thirteen a head taller than she. She glanced at the clock by her bedside. A little after midnight. Maybe she was sleepwalking.

Ruby's face was slick with sweat, her long coppery hair a nest of curls around her face. She grabbed Bessie's hand. "Come with me. I'll show you." She pulled Bessie down the hall to the bedroom where she slept together with her sisters, Jenny and Irene. "See, see," she said pointing behind the headboard.

"No, mamaleh. There's nothing there. See, nothing. You're dreaming."

"No, I'm not." She turned her head back and forth, swiveling it until her whole body was shaking. "They're going to hurt us—me, you, Faye."

Bessie reached out and shook nine-year-old Jenny, who was sleeping in the bed she shared with Ruby. Jenny stirred and sat up, confused, rubbing her eyes. "Go to Irene's bed." Jenny trotted to the next bed, nudged her sister Irene, and snuggled in beside her.

Ruby was crying. Bessie held her, patting her back, settling her in the bed again. She peered at her daughter and her heart sank. Ruby had not been sleepwalking. It was one of her spells again. She was talking nonsense. *Oh God*, Bessie thought. *When will this stop?*

Smoothing Ruby's forehead, she said, "I'll stay with you, sweetheart. I'm here, I'll stay." She began to hum tuneless lullabies and gradually, even though Ruby still was agitated, Bessie was able to calm her. She pulled a chair to the side of the bed and sat watching Ruby sleep. Bessie breathed with her, in and out, and then her eyes closed, chasing a dream.

She startled awake, heart hammering, neck in a spasm. Even before she opened her eyes, she knew the bed was empty. She jumped up, knocking the chair backward. "Ruby, where are you, where are you?"

In the next bed, Jenny and Irene woke. Bessie ignored them and rushed out of the bedroom to the bathroom, the kitchen whispering, "Ruby, Ruby." She did not want to wake her mother, Ida, or two-year-old Faye, who slept in a tiny room behind the kitchen. She took frantic breaths as she ran, her bare feet sliding along the linoleum in the hall. In the hall mirror she glimpsed her face, eyes crusted with sleep, hair matted to her head. She was shivering in a flimsy nightgown.

In the living room, twelve-year-old Morris slept in the corner on a cot crammed behind two shabby sofas. "Morris, wake up. Wake up. Do you know where Ruby is?" He groaned, didn't answer. She banged on her own bedroom door calling, "Abe, Abe, wake up, wake up, she's gone. Ruby, she's gone."

They gathered in the living room. Abe, clutching his pajama bottoms, paced in bare feet; Jenny and Irene huddled wide-eyed on the couch; Morris, half-man, half-boy, stood by the living room window staring into the purple darkness. It was one in the morning, and the streets were deserted.

"Where could she have gone?" No one answered. "Oh God, she woke me with a bad dream, so I sat with her, and I fell asleep."

"She just went out? Nobody heard?" Abe asked, his six-foot frame slumping over tiny Bessie. "How could nobody hear?"

"We were sleeping," Irene said. "We didn't know anything was wrong."

Bessie's hand was over her mouth to keep herself from crying out loud, but tears streaked her face, and she shook her head back and forth. "Where did she go, where did she go?" She clutched her arms around herself, quivering with cold.

Jenny grabbed the crocheted quilt from the sofa, and wordlessly draped it over her mother.

"I'll look," Abe said. "Morris, come. Put on your pants." Morris followed his father and minutes later they emerged from the bedroom, pajama tops half tucked into trousers, carrying shoes and coats. It was late April, but the night air was chill, especially in the rain. Morris's hair, uncombed, stuck out around his ears, and Bessie reached up to smooth it.

"Where will you look?"

"I don't know." Abe kissed the top of Bessie's head and went to the door. "Don't worry, it will all be well," he said, closing the door behind them.

Bessie leaned against the door. For Abe, everything would always be well, but she knew different. She hurried to the window clutching the blanket around her shoulders and peered out. She watched Abe and Morris leave the building and walk down the street until she couldn't see them anymore. Then there were only slick, wet sidewalks and rain pelting the glass.

"Is Ruby going to be all right?" Jenny asked.

Bessie ignored her, stared out the window. "Maybe I should go out too."

"What for? Where would you go?" Irene said.

Bessie paced. Stopped. "Tell me again what you saw her doing that you were complaining about," she said to Irene.

"Which time? You mean when she was carrying on, talking to herself on the block, shouting as if there was someone there and there was no one there? And the policeman came and told her to move on. Or when I saw her take something from the candy store? Or when she took Faye to the park and left her alone there, and Mrs. Feigenbaum from downstairs brought her back? And Ruby said she told Mrs. Feigenbaum to watch her, and Mrs. Feigenbaum said no she didn't?" Irene crossed her arms on her chest and stared at her feet. "Why can't she just act normal? She's older than me, and I'm so tired of worrying about her, taking care of her."

"That's what families do . . . take care of each other," Bessie said. She started to cry.

"Oh, Mama, I'm sorry. I'm sorry. Don't cry." Irene came up behind her and put her arms around her mother. "Ruby will come back. She'll be fine."

Bessie rested her forehead on Irene's shoulder while Irene patted her back. She could feel Irene's breasts, already budding although Irene was only ten. She's so grown up. How had they all grown up so fast?

I take good care of them, that's how. I take care of all of them—five children, two adults. I watch them all and make sure they eat right and sleep right and don't fight, that they do good in school and Abe doesn't gamble and Mama doesn't get too tired or too sad remembering

Kotovka, and someone watches little Faye. Isn't that what happened tonight? I was taking care of Ruby. I was sitting by her bed. I was watching her.

Bessie's heart lurched. *But I fell asleep. I didn't watch. I'm so tired all the time.* She pushed away from Irene and began to pace again. *What if something happens to Ruby? Oh God, how do you live after that? How did Mama live after she lost them all?*

"Where is she?" Bessie asked, almost shouting, trying to distract herself from nightmare memories. "What will we do? Where is Abe? And Morris?" She sat down again and waited. Irene came out wearing a sweater and handed Bessie her bathrobe. The clock on the wall said two. Two thirty. Jenny was curled up on the sofa under the crocheted quilt. Time was endless. Three o'clock.

The doorbell rang. "Mama. It's me. Open up. It's so cold." It was a thin, frail voice. Ruby.

Bessie ran to the door, opened it, and after a startled second screamed, "My God!"

Ruby stood in the dark hallway, copper hair dripping on her shoulders, shivering in a flimsy nightgown that clung to her erect breasts, her nipples, belly, and thighs. Her bare feet were wet, her legs red and raw. In trembling arms, she held Faye, who was crying pitifully, dark hair plastered to her head, face shiny with tears and mucus.

Faye called, "Mama! Mama!" reaching pudgy arms for Bessie.

"Oh, my God," Bessie wailed again, snatching the toddler from Ruby. "My God. You had Faye? You took the baby? I'll kill you!" Bessie's voice rose to a high-pitched bleat. She pulled back her arm and although behind her, out of nowhere, she heard her own mother Ida screaming, "*Oy, Gott,* no!" it was too late. With all the force she had, she smacked Ruby across the face, watched her stumble as her head snapped back, saw Ruby grab at the wall, hold her reddening cheek, and crumple sobbing to the grimy tiled floor.

Bessie was crying too. She leaned against the doorjamb, her head spinning. She was drained of all strength, barely able to hold Faye who was wailing, hiccoughing, "Bubbie, Bubbie."

Like a bystander, Bessie watched as Ida took over, pulling Faye's trembling body from her arms and straddling the toddler on her hips. Where had Ida come from? She was not there before.

Ida shouted, "Irene, make a bath. Hot water. Hot." Her strong free hand gripped Ruby under her arm as Ruby tried to rise to her feet, and Jenny was on the other side, pulling her until she was upright.

"Come," Ida said. She carried Faye in one arm and gripped Ruby with the other, and with Jenny helping, they limped together into the bathroom, stripped the girls of their soaking nightclothes, and slipped them into the warm bath.

Bessie followed dumbly. She sat on the bathmat, back against the wall, legs splayed, limp. She let Ida slosh the warm water over Faye and Ruby, let her whisper soothing words to them while she soaped them with a cloth. Bessie could not move. She was stuck in a memory that all but stopped her heart, a memory of another slap, another baby, another daughter. She felt the black shadow of the blow from long ago on her own cheek, and she got up, kneeled by the tub, and reached out to touch the reddened swelling on Ruby's. "Oh, my God, why did you take Faye?"

Ruby, lying back in the water, eyes closed, said nothing.

Why didn't I check? Why didn't I go into Mama's room and check on them both? Stupid me. Pushing the black shadow away, Bessie said to Ida. "When did you wake?"

"I had to pee."

"Did you know Faye was gone?"

"I didn't look in the crib." There was a long pause and a sigh. "I had to pee. When I came out of the toilet, I heard the noise and saw you all . . . I had to pee."

Yes. We all have to pee; we don't look, don't hear, don't see. Terrible things happen when you don't watch. She clamped her eyes tight to shut out the memories. To stop the thoughts she asked again, "Ruby, why? Why did you take Faye?"

"They were going to hurt her. They said they would hurt Faye. I had to hide her," Ruby whispered. "So, I went out and I hid until they went away—just like you did in the old country when they came to kill you—and then I came home."

The blood drained from Bessie's face. She stared at her mother as she took a towel and lifted Faye into it. "How does she know?" she asked. "How does she know about Kotovka?" Ida was silent. "Take her to bed," Bessie said. "We'll talk tomorrow."

As Ida left the bathroom with Faye, Bessie turned to Ruby with another towel outstretched in her hands. She helped her daughter stand, wrapped her and rubbed her dry, listened as Ruby whispered, "I'm so tired, so tired." Finally, Bessie took her daughter, beautiful and broken as she was, and put her to bed.

She sat beside the bed again, as she had earlier that night. It was near dawn. She saw the sky lighten through the window behind the bed, a thin gray thread at first, then thicker and wider until the whole window was filled with morning. Abe and Morris had come home, and she heard them speaking softly to Ida. She watched her sleeping daughters.

All her life she had tried to make it up to her mother, taking her with her to the dances where she looked for, and finally found, a husband—tall and handsome Abe. She brought Ida with her to their home from the first day they married. She kept her with them always, wherever they went.

And she had named her children after their lost family in Kotovka. Had she done the wrong thing, keeping their memory alive like that? It must have been a reminder of the way they died. Was that why Ida had told the children stories about Kotovka?

A sob caught in Bessie's throat. Maybe she had tempted the

devil. Ruby named for her sister Rifka, Morris for her father, Moshe, Irene for her grandmother Channah, Jenny for Yetta. And finally, Faye—after Fanny the baby who had come with them on the ship to America and who had died because of Bessie.

Bessie remembered how, when her own Faye was born, she had handed her to Ida after she and Abe decided on her name. "Feige," she said, using the Yiddish. Then, "Faye." Her mother nodded and locked eyes with Bessie and took the baby as if she were a gift. Then she sang the lullaby about a little bird in the forest which she had sung to her own Feige when she was a baby. Now Bessie hummed it to herself, and watched her daughters, Ruby and Jenny and Irene, sleep.

Later that morning, Bessie got Morris, Irene, and Jenny off to school even though they were tired. "We'll be late," they complained. "We're tired. Why doesn't Ruby have to go?"

"She's sleeping," Bessie said.

"I wish I was," Irene said, sulking. "What should we tell them about Ruby?"

"Say she's sick," Bessie said.

Irene stared at her feet, a sullen look on her face. "She is sick. Everyone makes fun of her, calls her crazy."

"Then you defend her. You tell them to shut up," Bessie blazed. "She's your sister. No matter what, she's your family!" But as her children walked out the door, Bessie heard Morris say, "She's sick, all right. Crazy sick."

Bessie closed her eyes. Everything hurt—her feet, her back. Her heart hurt. She felt old, much older than her thirty-six years.

Abe and Ida were at the kitchen table, drinking coffee. Faye sat in a highchair eating a piece of bread and butter. Her eyes were bright, and she babbled about Ruby taking her out in the rain and the dark. Bessie leaned over to kiss Faye's cheek and then sat down.

She glanced at Abe, who was staring at the table. He had deep circles under his eyes. His usually tall and straight back was slumped. He was jiggling his leg, and she could feel the pulse on the floor. What had happened to the dashing man who'd spun her around the dance hall in the polka until she collapsed in a chair?

He'd called himself lucky then. Now he was worried about money. This Depression was a weight on everyone's shoulders, and it was even worse in Europe, where his mother and sister lived. He wanted to bring them here, but he hadn't saved enough. He even had to let the help in his hardware store go, and Bessie went back to work, leaving Ida to watch her family.

Bessie went to him, stood behind his chair, and put her hands on his shoulders. Abe reached up and patted her hand. "I have to go . . . open the shop." He stood and kissed her cheek. "You stay home today. I'll manage without you."

She wanted to say something to him. What? Be careful. It seemed so little. She settled on *"Zey gezunt."* He nodded and left the apartment.

Bessie and Ida sat in the quiet finishing their coffee. Ida drank hers in a glass, sipping it through a sugar cube, like she had in Kotovka. *"Nu?* What are you going to do with her?" Ida asked. Bessie said nothing. "I found out there is a place," she went on. "A hospital called King's Park Asylum—for people like her."

"What do you mean, 'people like her'? She doesn't need an asylum."

"Maybe yes, maybe no. You could look."

Bessie glared at her mother. "Last night, in the bath, she said men were coming to kill us. Where would she get such an idea?"

"It's her imagination. She was dreaming."

"Yes, you know she imagines things. And dreams? Dreams come from somewhere. I have dreams too. Nightmares. You told her the stories from Kotovka. What happened there."

"No. I never did." Ida's eyes shifted sideways, and Bessie didn't believe her. "I told her stories about good people and bad people. I tell them all the same fairy tales. Jenny and Irene and Morris. They don't go running out in the middle of the night with the baby."

"Well, to her fairy tales are true. She believes them, and now she's scared."

Ida turned away. "It's not my fault she's so flighty."

"It is your fault that Ruby took Faye out of your room, and you didn't stop her," Bessie shot back. "She could have killed Faye."

Ida's face collapsed in pain. "I was sleeping. I'm sorry." Her glass shook in her hand, sloshing the coffee over the top, and she put it on the table.

A hard knot formed in Bessie's gut. "Why? Why would you tell them those awful things that happened? Why do they have to know?"

Ida didn't answer. Faye had begun to whine. Bessie didn't know if it was because they weren't paying attention to her or because they were arguing. She stood up and took Faye out of the highchair. Holding her close, she whispered to her mother, "You won't tell Faye. If you want to take care of her, you won't tell her those stories." Bessie locked eyes with her mother, and after a minute, Ida nodded. She held out her arms and Bessie handed her the baby.

"Still," Ida said quietly. "You have to do something about Ruby."

Bessie often wondered why everyone described Ruby by comparing her to something else. For Bessie, Ruby was sometimes like a firefly, lit up one second, black the next, or a hummingbird, dipping here and there, flashing the brilliant red of her hair and the green of her eyes and then disappearing. Abe said she reminded him of a bumblebee, all gold and black and buzzing around, and occasionally stinging if you got too close and irritated her. Other people said she was the jewel, like her name, or red glass, sparkly and breakable. But

Irene said she was like a red fox—sly, untrustworthy, making a mess out of everything she touched.

Ruby wasn't easy, Bessie knew that for sure. Even when she was little, she was all over the place, never still for a minute. She was willful and determined. She had insisted they call her Ruby, even though Bessie and Abe had named her Rifka—Rebecca in English.

But it was only lately that Bessie had begun to worry. Just last month as she and Ida were peeling potatoes in the kitchen, Ruby had dashed into the room wearing a purple scarf around her head, and three lengths of beads around her neck. She danced around her mother and grandmother.

"I'm here," she sang. "I came as soon as you called." She grabbed a potato.

"Who called you? I didn't call you," Bessie said.

"Well I knew you wanted me," Ruby said. "I can read minds." She took a knife from the drawer and started peeling while she pirouetted around the room.

"Stop that," Bessie said, grabbing her arm. "You'll cut yourself."

"All right. I won't help," Ruby said. She threw the potato and knife into the sink and waltzed out of the room.

Bessie gave a little laugh. "She's a gypsy." She glanced quickly at her mother, who sat unmoving at the kitchen table, staring at the potatoes. Ida didn't look up. Her iron gray hair was pulled into an unruly bun, and her square jaw was clenched tight.

"I don't like to say," Ida said at last, and started peeling potatoes again.

"What don't you like to say?"

"I worry. She acts like a child. She's wild, like my cousin, Perel—the tayvl. She even looks like her."

"She's not crazy like Perel," Bessie whispered. She remembered her well. Even murderous hooligans were afraid of Perel. "She's just high-spirited—maybe immature."

"I worry," Ida said again, louder. "You remember you found her with the knife that time?"

Bessie's heart skipped at the memory. Something had frightened Ruby, and Bessie found her standing in a corner holding a knife in front of her as if warding someone off. She didn't protest when Bessie took the knife from her, but said, "Sometimes I have to protect myself."

"From what?" Bessie asked, exasperated.

Ruby shook her head and walked past Bessie, and Bessie thought, for the hundredth time, *Why can't she just act normal, like everyone else?* Then she was ashamed.

"She was pretending like always. Playacting," Bessie said, but she couldn't look at Ida. Bessie heard Faye calling her. "You finish. The baby is up from her nap."

Bessie left the kitchen to get Faye. But first she went to check on Ruby. She found her playing a record of a new song, "You're My Everything," on the Victrola in the living room and swaying in front of the mirror. *Not so bad*, Bessie told herself. *Mama's wrong. Plenty of girls dance like that.*

But Bessie couldn't ignore her mother's concerns. The thoughts kept niggling at her, and two days later, even though Ruby seemed fine again, and was back to school, Bessie went to see Dr. Marsh, just, she told herself, to talk. Dr. Marsh, a short and portly man with a mustache, had been their family doctor since they'd moved to Brooklyn. He knew them all, did all their check-ups, and had even delivered Faye at Brooklyn Jewish Hospital.

Bessie wondered later if he could possibly have understood what she was saying; she was talking nonstop, with barely a breath. "Ruby, she's so unpredictable. I never know what she's going to do. She took Faye out in the middle of the night because she said someone was going to hurt her—in the middle of the night, Doctor. We were so scared. We didn't know where she was. And she hid the knife, not that she would use it, but she took it anyway. And she talks all the time, fast, and sometimes I can't understand her." Bessie's voice faded, and she laughed. "I think I sound like her now, but it's only because I'm nervous. Maybe that's what it is . . . do you think she could just be nervous, Dr. Marsh? Maybe, she's just nervous."

Dr. Marsh nodded, and wrote some things down and then said, "So you are very worried about her?"

Bessie sighed with relief. "Yes. What can we do with her when she acts so crazy?" The word slipped out. "I didn't mean crazy," she whispered.

"When she gets so agitated?" Dr. Marsh asked.

"Yes. Agitated."

"We could give her laudanum. That would quiet her."

"And it wouldn't hurt? It would be all right?"

"Yes certainly. I wouldn't suggest it otherwise."

Bessie nodded. "Thank you," she said. Dr. Marsh stood up and Bessie realized he was dismissing her. She wasn't ready to go. Before she left, she had to ask. Her voice trembled and she said, "You ever heard of King's Asylum?"

Dr. Marsh pursed his lips. "King's Park Psychiatric Hospital?" he asked, leaning on his desk.

"Yes. That's it"

He hesitated for a moment. "I don't know if you would want to send her there. She's awfully young. Only thirteen. You could go look at it, if you want. It's out on Long Island, Suffolk County. In the country; but it's far and . . . of course if she's totally unmanageable . . ."

"No, I can do it. I can manage her," Bessie said.

"Well then. But maybe you should just look at it, in case, you know. Always good to have alternatives." Dr. Marsh walked toward the door of his office, handed Bessie the prescription, and she hurried out the door.

Bessie kept the bottle of laudanum in a drawer by her bed and, she told her mother, she would watch Ruby like a hawk, and the first minute there was anything to worry about, she would give her the medicine.

But in Bessie's head there was tucked away Dr. Marsh's suggestion, his "in case." She had been so worried since the night Ruby took Faye out of her crib . . . always watching, hyper-vigilant lest her oldest daughter hurt her youngest. When Ruby talked too much or too fast, Bessie followed her around, wondering if something was starting. She opened and closed the drawer with the laudanum, and then she watched Ruby some more.

Finally, Bessie decided she would go to Long Island herself and see. She asked Dr. Marsh to make her an appointment with the lady in charge of admissions at the hospital, and on a warm May morning, Bessie took the subway to the Long Island Railroad and the train to King's Park Station. There she transferred to the Kings Park Psychiatric Center spur, which delivered her directly to the hospital grounds.

It was immense—like a city with large and small buildings, some cottages, some small factories. And it was green, with lawns and trees, and in the distance, barns and pastures with black animals—*cows,* she thought. People walked on the paths, and Bessie was not sure who were staff and who were patients. It was not an alarming place, not somewhere that frightened her as she had expected.

The visit went smoothly. Mrs. Damrosh, a very tall, skinny nurse, met with her in her office, asked Bessie some questions, and wrote the answers in a notebook. After every answer, Mrs. Damrosh would nod her head and say, "Oh," and "My, that must have been difficult." And "Anything else?" And Bessie remembered more incidents when Ruby frightened her or worried her, and she told Mrs. Damrosh everything she could think of. She told her how Ruby muttered to herself, how she sometimes had loud conversations with imaginary people, how she talked fast and furious, how people pointed at her sometimes and whispered.

Then they toured the facility. The halls were clean, the staircases tiled white, the crowded common room was sunny and bright. She had not expected it to be so pleasant. Bessie supposed you would get used to the antiseptic smell in the hallways, the echoes of footsteps, the clank of iron when a door was slammed. The halls were full of people shuffling close to the walls. Bessie tried to imagine Ruby there, her hair flaming around her face, leaning against the wall. Her heart beat fast at the thought. Most of the patients were middle-aged or old. Bessie asked if there were any young people there.

"Of course," Mrs. Damrosh said. "They are in the cottages in the back of the property. They go to school and learn farming. It's very good for them. Would you like to see?"

They walked together down a paved path toward some small cottages, and Mrs. Damrosh talked all the time. "We keep them safe. You'll see. We have many troubled young people here. Your daughter will be safe," Mrs. Damrosh said. "She won't hurt herself or anyone else in your family."

Bessie nodded. "That would be such a relief," she said, and the minute she said it, she knew it was true.

There were only three teens in the cottage when Bessie and Mrs. Damrosh got there. They were sitting, two boys and a girl, at a round table with books and pencils, but none of them were reading or writing. They were staring, but Bessie couldn't see what they were looking at. She tried to imagine Ruby sitting there, but it was impossible to think of her sitting so still. "They are so quiet," Bessie said.

"Well, yes," Mrs. Damrosh said. "I told you we keep them safe."

Bessie nodded, but she didn't really understand how they got teenagers to be so still. She was afraid to ask and sound stupid, so she nodded again. At the end of the visit she took a booklet describing the hospital and promised to speak to Dr. Marsh about Ruby's admission.

On the ride back to the city, Bessie leaned her head against the window and let the rocking train lull her, keeping her mind blank. She even slept and woke at Penn Station after the car had almost emptied. It had been a long day, and she still had to take the subway home.

It was late when she walked into the apartment. The family was seated around the table eating supper. Bessie could not even hang her coat in the closet before she was accosted by the voices of her children, her mother, Abe. The words and the voices blended, chorused one on top of the other. "Mama, you're so late—Mommy, mommy, mommy!—Where were you?—Got to be hall monitor—Nu, what did you see?—senior play—baseball game." Bessie shook her head and plucked Faye out of the highchair before she sat down with her youngest on her lap.

"Shah! I can't hear you all," she said.

She waved away the soup her mother was going to serve her; she had a knot in her throat, and she didn't think she could swallow anything. She said, "I'll just take some tea." Jenny jumped up and poured her a steaming cup, but Bessie didn't want to drink that either.

She observed her family, her eyes moving from one to the next. Jenny was chewing her hair and needed a haircut, and Morris's shirt was getting too small. Irene must not have washed her hands before supper because they were dotted with paint and charcoal, and Abe looked gray and worried. Her mother was like a brown wren, hopping around the table, serving, but never smiling.

And Ruby? Ruby looked like an angel, bright green eyes darting around, looking at everyone. She was wearing purple, "The royal color," she said, because she had gotten a role as the queen in the Shakespeare play, *A Midsummer Night's Dream*. She was talking nonstop like a faucet that could not be shut off.

If I were a stranger, would I pick her out as odd? Would I notice anything about her except her beauty, her gaiety? I didn't see anyone happy like her there. What will happen to her if I send her away?

"So?" Abe mouthed. No one at the table noticed their silent conversation, except Ida, who looked up also, and stared at Bessie expectantly.

Bessie breathed a slow in and out. She looked from one to another of her children, marveling that they were there, and well, and good. Morris reached out and snatched an untouched piece of bread from Ruby's plate. Ruby smacked his hand and said in an imperious tone, "You can't take food from me. I am the queen." Irene rolled her eyes.

Bessie could feel Abe's eyes on her. Ida stared hard. The meal went on, and Bessie said nothing. She took a sugar cube and gave it to Faye, who sucked on it and then took it out of her mouth and put it in Bessie's with sticky fingers. Faye made an *mmm, mmm,* sound, like Bessie did when she fed her, and Bessie laughed.

Suddenly Ruby got up and took Faye from her mother's lap. She nuzzled her sister's cheek and waltzed around the kitchen with her. "You're the cutest baby in the whole world," she said. "I'm so glad we had you. How could we ever live without you?" And Faye giggled as Ruby tickled her under her neck and soon everyone was laughing, even Ida.

Bessie stood up, breathed deeply. She took Faye from Ruby's arms and kissed first one daughter, then the other.

Abe and Ida were looking at her. "Nu?" her mother said. Bessie kissed Faye again and shook her head. "No," she said. "No."

3

Abe

1932–1939

Late on a Saturday afternoon in February, Abe was sitting with Bessie at their dining room table drinking tea. They were reading his mother's latest letter from Poland begging—again—for passage money to America.

He watched Bessie get up, scrape the table free of crumbs from their lunch, and go into the tiny kitchen, leaving the stained cloth on the table. She came out again with a plate of *mandelbrot* cookies, a specialty baked by Ida. Abe could hear the children in the parlor in the front of the flat. Ruby was singing in her silvery soprano, "You're My Everything." Morris was teaching Jenny gin rummy with loud instructions. Faye was sitting on Bubbie Ida's lap with her doll, playing house. From Irene, the artist, there was no sound. She was probably curled up in a corner, drawing, but out of sight because she wasn't supposed to write on *Shabbos*.

Abe sipped his tea, took a bite of the cookie. The stubble of his black beard shaded his cheeks and he rubbed his hands over his chin. He did not shave on Shabbos, since it was forbidden. It was not that he was a religious man, but he believed it was unlucky to flout the laws, and he didn't want to do anything that would tempt fate.

"How was business this week?" Bessie asked.

Abe shrugged. "The Depression. People only buy what they need."

Bessie picked up the letter from Abe's mother. "What about your mother's ticket here?" she asked. "And your sister? Where will we get the money for that? All the time she said 'no' when we asked, and now, when there's no money, she wants to come."

"Be nice, Bessie," Abe said. "She doesn't want to stay in Molodycz now that my father's dead." Abe reached over and took his wife's hand. He turned it over and kissed her palm, rough from years of washing dishes and clothes for their five children. He tickled her wrist with his fingers, and she started to laugh. When she laughed, her face lit up, her hazel eyes became almost amber, and she was again the lively, pretty woman he'd met seventeen years ago.

"See," he said. "Am I still not your shining knight? Remember how you said I lit up the room when I came in? That you believed I would always take care of you? I will. I still will." Abe pushed her straggling brown hair off her face and lifted her chin. "I know you're worried, but it will be all right. We'll bring them. You'll see."

Bessie pushed his hand off her chin. "How? How will it be all right?" she said and turned away. "And what about Morris's bar mitzvah. At least we need a little something for a small *kiddush*."

"I don't have the money yet, but I'll get it." He was silent for a minute. "Could we go to your mother?"

The "No!" was out of Bessie's mouth before Abe finished his question. "We don't go to my mother for money. It's hers. She sold her farm for it. She broke her back starting a new pie business here to raise me. We don't take her money."

"All right, all right. We don't take her money . . . Maybe I could go to Gemilas Chesed again. They know I pay back fast. I'll get the tickets, and maybe a little extra for the kiddush."

"It's the Depression, Abe. The Ladies Free Loan Society doesn't have money to lend."

"I'll get it. I'll say it's for the business."

She got up, went back into the tiny kitchen and made a big show of washing the dishes and clanking the silverware, all the while Abe was talking. Her back was stiff. Bessie didn't argue, but Abe knew she was not happy. In truth he was not either, but he pretended.

Abe finished his tea, pushed the glass away, and stood up. He peered out the window and saw it was dark. The Sabbath was over.

"Don't go," Bessie said. Abe paused, waited. She came back to the table and sat, a shy smile on her face. "I'm expecting."

Abe sank into the chair. "Pregnant? Now?" Jenny was ten, Faye three. His mouth felt slack; his throat tight.

"Are you happy?" Bessie asked.

"Are you?" he asked back. She nodded. "Then I am." But his heart was beating hard and his stomach turned over. "You feel all right?" She nodded. He allowed a small smile to creep over his mouth. "Maybe it will be a boy."

"Maybe."

"Now we really need money," Abe said. He got up and kissed Bessie's head. "Does your mother know?" Bessie nodded. "Is she happy?

"Yes."

"Good," Abe said. "We should wait a little before we tell the children." He turned to leave.

"Where are you going?"

"It's Saturday night," he answered.

Bessie sighed. "You'll bet?"

"I don't bet if I don't know I have a good chance of winning. I'm not a gambler."

"You gamble plenty. Wednesday night with the pinochle and Saturday night fights, gambling with bookies. You could get into trouble with bookies."

Abe ignored her, wondering how she knew about bookies and

betting at the fights. But he turned his back and went into the bathroom to shave. He stared at himself in the mirror. His face was drawn. The Depression had been worse for the business than he let on. *Better get the loan from the Free Loan Society and use it well,* he thought. *Maybe double his money.*

Besides pinochle, Abe's other favorite pastime was the fights. Every Saturday night he went to the Velodrome in Coney Island, or the Broadway Arena.

"The fighters have guts," he once explained to Bessie. "They get knocked down; they get up. They have courage." At the fights, Abe's heart pounded with excitement. The crowd roared for blood, and the boxers stood their ground. The fighters seemed heroic to him. He thought that if he were younger and had been born in America, he would have become a fighter.

Sometimes he sparred in the living room with Morris, lightly tapping him on the shoulder or the chin, both of them laughing, giddy with the physical action. They danced around the chairs and tables, dodging the worn green sofas, knocking into the standing brass lamp and setting its beige fringed shade askew. Then Bessie would rush in waving her arms and shouting, "Stop it, stop it. You're making a mess! You'll hurt him!"

And sometimes Abe took Morris and his friend Sam with him to the fights. When they went to the fights they sat in the back rows, the cheapest seats they could get, and Abe placed his bets, with Morris helping him decide how to bet. They went over the odds on the fighters, their win–loss record, and Abe made what he called "smart bets." When Jewish boxers were fighting, he didn't look at the odds. Instead, he bet on them as a matter of ethnic pride, so he didn't always win. But win or lose, there was always that thrill of the wait, the elation at the win, the little twinge at the loss. Then he looked for the next bet, waiting for the rush.

Bessie didn't like it when Abe took Morris to the fights. "He shouldn't see such things," she complained. "Men knocking each other on the head. Jewish boys don't fight."

"Ha. A lot you know. There are a lot of Jewish fighters. And champions too. Slapsie Maxie Rosenbloom, Benny Leonard, Solly Krieger. And Morris loves the fights," Abe said. "He and Sam go to the settlement house—they teach boxing there. Soon, maybe he can even be in the Golden Gloves. Make him a man, put some muscle on him."

Morris was small for his age—a skinny kid, with a mop of dark brown hair that was always falling over his eyes, and a nose that he would have to grow into as he got older. He hadn't started his growth spurt yet, like his best friend, Sam Fine, who was tall and handsome.

"And it keeps him off the streets and out of trouble. He watches the boxers train." Abe started to laugh. "The other day he saw Jackie Fields training. He says Jackie called him the mosquito because he's always buzzing around. Imagine that. The mosquito!"

"And that's supposed to make me feel better?" Bessie said. She pushed her hair behind her ear. "He watches fighters? He punches other kids? What does he get for it? A bloody nose? That's a good thing?"

Abe waved her away. "All boys get bloody noses."

The Monday after Bessie and Abe's argument about money, Abe went to Gemilas Chesed. To his disappointment, they were not making loans because of the Depression. "It's temporary," they said. "Come back in six months."

He did not tell Bessie. He was thinking. He knew where he could get money. There were loan sharks on every street corner, Jewish and Gentile "businessmen" who loaned money at huge interest rates. It was risky, but it was money. He had done it once before and had bet half of the hundred dollars borrowed on a fight and won. He'd immediately paid them back with the interest they'd charged, and he still had more cash than he started with. He was lucky. He had always been a lucky man.

He was lucky when, with money from a bet on a donkey race, he left Molodycz, his hometown in the south of Poland—a place he called "a no-account village." He was lucky when he won his berth in steerage in an all-night card game in Krakow, and lucky again on the boat across the Atlantic when he won enough to enter Ellis Island with pockets heavy with coins. Back then he was called a "greener." He was a tall, skinny man who had big plans to make his fortune in America.

He had bought a pushcart with his winnings from the boat and later stumbled on the small building on Daniel Street near the Manhattan Bridge that would—with a large win in cards from the owner of the building and a small loan from Gemilas Chesed—become his hardware store. He had met the dazzling Bessie Amdur at the Galicia Association annual ball for Polish immigrants, where she had come with a friend from Poland. He saw other young men who tried to surround her, jostling and pushing for a spot at her side. But he had been the one who made her laugh so hard at his silly jokes that she spilled punch all over her lavender dress, and she whirled around the dance floor with him in a wild polka, her brown curls bouncing around her heart-shaped face, while his underarm sweat slid down his side in a long, slow tickle.

He had promised Bessie he would take her away from the crowded Lower East Side and charmed her with stories of the life they would live together afterward, a life with servants and pearls and music and plays. But lucky as Abe was with his bets and his cards and hard as he worked, with Bessie and her mother at his side, the life with servants and pearls had not materialized. "Yet," he said. He and Bessie lived with their five growing children and his mother-in-law in a railroad flat in Brooklyn, where rent was cheap, and he was still chasing his luck.

—

At supper one night that week, Abe listened to Morris rave about the fighters and the trainers at the gym. Abe sat at the head of the big dining room table, all five children and his mother-in-law strung out along its sides. Bessie bustled in and out of the kitchen making sure everyone had what he or she needed. There was soup with bones from the butcher, potatoes and onions and carrots, crusty rye bread. Bessie ate afterward, first making sure there was enough for everyone else in the family.

Abe watched his children, gabbing away in English. He was so proud of them and the way they talked "pure American." Sometimes they talked so fast he had trouble keeping up with them.

"Did you know there's a Jewish policeman at the gym, Pop?" Morris said. "He's one of the trainers. I didn't know Jews could be cops. Did you know that?"

"I didn't," Abe said.

"So what? This is America," Irene said. "There are Jewish artists and musicians and movie actors. John Garfield, Edward G. Robinson. Jews can be anything."

"Yeah, well, there's plenty of anti-Semites. I think its swell that a Jew is a cop," Morris said.

"I hate cops," Ruby said. Everyone stared. Ruby pushed her red curls behind her ears. "Yesterday one of them shoved me. He told me to get on my way."

"What were you doing? You must have been doing something bad," Bubbie Ida said.

"I wasn't doing anything," Ruby said. "I was just walking and . . ." Her voice trailed off.

Irene narrowed her eyes. "And singing. I bet you were singing."

"What if I was?"

"And dancing too . . . the other day I saw her performing in the middle of the block . . . acting like she's on the stage . . . and people had to walk around her. It's crazy, singing in the street . . . who sings and dances on the street? Only in the movies," Irene said.

"*Meshuggeneh*," Bubbie Ida said under her breath.

"I'm not crazy. Why do you keep saying that?" Ruby jumped up and bumped the table, so the soup sloshed out of her bowl.

"Shah," Bessie said. "Sit down, Ruby. Of course, you're not crazy. Don't say that, Mama."

"Stop the noise! Leave Ruby alone," Abe said in his loudest voice. Abe exchanged looks with Bessie, as Bubbie Ida walked into the kitchen. "I like it when she dances," he went on. Ruby grinned. Sometimes, Abe waltzed around the living room with her, the way he used to with Bessie, dipping and swirling her and then romping up and down the hallway. Abe was closest with Ruby and Morris. After them, there were just too many children. *And now*, he thought with a little dread, *another one*.

Everyone was quiet, bent over food. No one argued with Abe.

"Well I like cops," Morris said.

"I suppose now you want to be a cop?" Irene said. "That's what Sam told me." She took a piece of rye bread, tore it and dipped it in her soup before placing it in her mouth.

"Irene's in love with Sam," Jenny told everyone.

"Shut up," Irene muttered.

In the silence Morris said, "Can I have more soup, Ma?"

Jenny shoved her bowl in front of him. "Here, you can have mine. I don't want it."

"You never want food. You look like a chicken neck," Bessie said. "You better eat."

But Morris had already taken Jenny's bowl and poured the soup into his own. "Thanks," he said. "Maybe I will be a cop," he went on. "Or a fighter. Eddie says I'm good."

"Who's Eddie?" Abe asked.

"Eddie. The cop." He turned to his father. "I'm learning a lot from Eddie. How much the guys have to weigh to fight in a class; who's the best fighter; what the managers do; how to figure the odds."

"Don't be a bother to him," Abe said. "But it's good to have a cop, a friend."

"I don't bother him," Morris said. "He likes me." That put a period at the end of the discussion. Dessert was homemade applesauce, and afterward Irene washed and Jenny dried the dishes, and Bessie picked at some leftover potatoes before she sat down to put her feet up for the first time all day.

Abe paced the hallway, a half-formed idea in his head. That week he acted.

The next Saturday night, Abe left the house for the fights. Because Morris had a good report from school, Abe took him and Sam with him. That night the fight was at the Broadway Arena. They rode the subway from Brooklyn to Manhattan, and as they sat, rocketing through the black tunnels, Abe's insides churned in excitement. He wondered if any of the other men on the subway were going to the fights, wondered if they all were feeling the mixture of feverish anticipation and a little fear.

The crowds streamed in at seven thirty to watch two new fighters battle against each other. Abe hustled the boys to the back of the arena for the pregame warm-ups. He was jumpy and scared. He was trying to pay attention to Morris badgering him, whispering that he had a tip that couldn't be ignored. Abe bent low to hear what his son was saying. Bernie "Kid" Steiner was a young fighter with an unproven record, but Morris and Sam were sure he was going to win. He was fighting Daniel McDougal, and the posted odds were ten to one for McDougal for a knockout.

"Pop. We have to bet on Kid Steiner."

"But he's ten to one to lose."

"Steiner's Jewish. You always bet on the Jews."

Abe fingered the bills in his pocket. He had a wad. It was frightening money. It wasn't really his, and he had to be careful how he used it.

"This time I don't think I should. McDougal has the odds and a great record."

"Yeah, but it's fake," Morris whispered. "The fights were all made."

"What does that mean? Made?"

"Fixed."

"How do you know?"

"I know. I heard it. They fixed his fights. Everyone he fought threw the fight. So he's the favorite by a lot, but tonight he's going to lose so they can make a killing on their bets."

"Who is they?"

"The managers. The mobsters."

Abe looked down at his son. Morris's eyes shone in eagerness. He could barely stay still, dancing around in excitement, pulling at Abe's sleeve. He held his father's eyes without wavering. "Who told you this?" Abe asked.

"No one told me. I heard it."

"From who?"

"Eddie."

"The cop, Eddie?"

"Yeah. We heard him talking. He was saying the odds are sometimes fixed so the mob men can make a killing."

"Sometimes?" Abe asked.

"Yeah, but I'm sure this is one of those times." Morris looked at Sam for corroboration.

"It's true, Mr. Weissman." Sam spoke with authority. "That's what he said. All the other fights were made." Sam dropped his voice so that Abe could barely hear him. "Morris and me, we're sure tonight McDougal is going to take a fall. We think if you bet on the Kid, you'll win a lot of money."

Abe shut his eyes; he felt the surge. All his life he'd trusted it, and he'd come out ahead. Why shouldn't he bet on the Kid? He was lucky. The Kid was a *landsman*, a Jew. Morris and Sam were sure.

He took a deep breath and didn't think anymore, heard only the roaring of the crowds, saw only the lights in the ring. Even the well-dressed spectators sitting ringside faded into the background. He went to place a bet and stood wondering. He thought, *How much*? He fingered the bills in his pocket. *Half? Half.* That seemed good. If he won, he would have enough for the boat tickets and the payback. But all—if he bet all of it, he could have the tickets, the payback and the interest and have some left for the business.

He wavered, his heart hammering.

"Come on, come on. There are other people here," the bookie said.

Abe took a breath. He took the bills from his pocket and peeled off all but three tens and placed it all on Kid Steiner to win. Then, feeling a little nauseous, he walked back to his seat.

Morris and Sam waited for him there. "Did you do it, Pop, did you do it?"

"Sit still," Abe said. "We'll see if what your big shot cop Eddie said is right. That the Kid is going to win."

Sam and Morris looked at each other. "Yeah, he's going to win, we say he's going to win. It's going to be easy."

The Kid came out with his handlers, wearing bright blue silk trunks. McDougal wore blinding white. At the first bell, they came out punching. The Kid's footwork was fast, but McDougal was faster. Abe watched intently. It did not look easy to him. The more he watched, the harder it was to watch. A sick feeling was rising in his stomach. McDougal was punching the Kid's middle and the Kid's hands flew between his gut and his face, as if all he could do was protect himself. The crowd was yelling, "Kill him, kill him!"

Abe jumped up to see better, and the man behind him yelled, "Siddown there!" Abe sat. McDougal landed a hard punch to the Kid's chin, and then backed him against the ropes, hitting him again and again. Even from where they sat, Abe could hear the *thwack* of leather on skin. Blood poured out of the Kid's nose, his mouth. The bell rang. The round was over.

Abe turned and looked at Morris and Sam. They were staring at each other, at the floor, at anything but the ring below them.

"What's happening?" Abe whispered.

"It'll be all right. You'll see. Like you always say. It will all be well."

But it wasn't. The second round was a repeat of the first. The sick feeling in Abe's stomach turned to panic in his chest. In the third round they watched McDougal batter the Kid like he was a punching bag, and in a matter of minutes the Kid was down.

"Get up," Abe screamed. "Get up, goddamn you!" But the Kid didn't hear him or anyone else in the crowd. He was on his knees, and then he toppled over and lay there as the referee called a long slow count to ten. He was out. McDougal had won by a knockout in the third round.

For the rest of his life, Abe would remember that moment. How he looked down at the ring, balled his hand in a fist around a worthless piece of paper, and walked out of the arena with the boys trailing behind. How he didn't stay for the main fight, didn't say a word. On the subway platform, waiting for the train, Morris kept saying, "I'm sorry, Pop, I'm sorry. The Kid was supposed to win. We thought he was supposed to win."

Abe was collapsing inside under the weight of his loss. It was not like any other. He tried to still the nausea, but he couldn't. He kept swallowing the bile that rose in his throat, then turned to a corner of the platform and vomited, coughing and retching. Waves of shame washed over him. His throat burned. Morris and Sam were standing behind him, patting his back, in imitation of their mothers when they were sick. The train came. Abe found a seat and rode home in silence, eyes closed. When they got to Brooklyn, he walked the boys to Sam's apartment and told Morris to stay there. Then he went home.

The house was silent. The girls and Bessie were asleep. He sat on his bed watching his wife, his head hanging, his arms between his legs, waiting for her to wake up, waiting to ask her to help him figure out what to do. But she slept hard. The early weeks of pregnancy always exhausted her. He reached out and touched her hair, but she remained still. The taste of his vomit remained on his tongue, but he did nothing to refresh his mouth. He sat looking at Bessie until early in the morning.

At the store the next day, Abe's hands shook with every penny transaction. He looked in the cash box, counted, figured the difference between what was in the box and what he owed Georgie Lieber. Georgie the *Gonif*, they called him. He had a week and they would be there, asking for the money, plus the vig.

As the days went by, Abe's mind swirled but he had no answers. On Friday afternoon, he closed the shop extra early, thinking he would avoid Georgie. He looked furtively around. He did not see Georgie anywhere. He walked quickly to the subway, blending in with the crowds. He had a dizzying sense that he would be lucky again tonight.

But then Abe felt his elbow grasped hard, and someone was walking step by step in tandem with him. "What's the hurry, Abe?"

"I have to get home . . . for Shabbos," Abe stammered. He looked down on Georgie. Short, barrel-chested. His grip was strong. Abe was shaking.

"Oh, yeah, of course," Georgie said, his voice like satin. "But you owe the money today. Friday. Better pay up before Shab-bos." Georgie's voice leaned hard on the word.

"The money's at home," Abe said. "I'll bring it tomorrow."

"On Shab-bos? You'll bring it on Shab-bos? I thought you were a good Jewish boy. And tomorrow night's a new week. And you'll owe the vig for the whole next week."

"It's okay, it's okay. I'll get it for you," Abe said. "I'll have it, I promise."

"Promises. Promises. Tomorrow. Money." Georgie let go of Abe's elbow abruptly, causing Abe to pitch forward, almost fall, and the loan shark disappeared into the crowd.

Abe hardly breathed the whole way home on the subway.

That night, after everyone was asleep, Abe crept out of bed and went into the tiny bedroom behind the kitchen. Faye was sleeping in a ball in her crib. She was covered with a blanket and he couldn't see her face. He tried to imagine another baby coming soon. He couldn't. He shuddered. He reached down and touched Ida on the shoulder. She was snoring quietly and didn't move. He shook her. She sat up, startled, saw him and finally nodded. In minutes she followed him to the kitchen table, pulling her bathrobe tight around her.

"What?" she asked sitting.

A deep breath. "I need money."

She didn't say anything for a long time. She got up, put the kettle on the stove and took out two glasses for tea. She waited until the water boiled, put spoons in the glasses and then tea, poured the water and let the tea steep as she stood there.

Abe waited, watching her. He had always admired his mother-in-law. She was smart, tough. She never faltered no matter what life threw at her. He thought she respected him as well—until now. But now he was scared of what she would say.

"Money for what?"

"I owe three hundred dollars."

"So much? Why so much?"

"For my mother and sister's passage here. For Morris's bar mitzvah. For the business."

Ida nodded. She spoke slowly. "So, we'll pay it back. They understand at Gemilas Chesed."

"I didn't get it from them. They're not giving loans now. They have no money. They said come back in six months."

Ida's eyes widened. "Where then? Where did you get it?"

Abe stared at the wall behind the stove.

"From where?" she insisted.

"From Georgie Lieber."

"Who?"

"Georgie the Gonif," Abe whispered.

Ida stood in stunned silence. She knew who he was. "Give it back. You didn't spend it yet. You owe the interest? I'll help with that."

"I owe all of it *and* the interest."

She was slack jawed. He could see her mind going fast. "Where? Where did you spend it?" He didn't answer. "Gambling," she said. "You stupid, stupid man." She turned away, stirred the tea in the glasses, put them on saucers with a small sugar cube, and brought them to the table. She sat down, blew on the tea, and sipped slowly.

Abe didn't touch his. "Will you help me?"

"Where would I get such a fortune?"

Abe stared at his hands, clutched together on the table. He knew Ida had money. She had come with money. Bessie had said so. She had come with jewelry. She could give him some. "Can you loan me any? With the baby coming?"

Ida shook her head. "You have no shame."

Abe looked away. "I have plenty of shame," he said.

"I'll help," she said at last. "Just so you don't get your fingers broken. But not for the passage for your mother and sister, or the bar mitzvah, or the business. Only for the loan shark. And you pay me back."

Abe took a deep breath. It felt like he hadn't breathed since he'd come into the kitchen. "Thank you," he whispered.

"Don't look at me like that. Like my sick cow. You'll pay me back. With interest—not like them." She pointed with her chin to the street. "Not like the bums out there. But some."

"And we won't tell Bessie?"

"We won't tell Bessie. And until you pay me back, we're partners in the business. You ask me before you do anything." Abe nodded. "And no gambling. No pinochle, no fights, no betting. Nothing."

He would promise her anything. There was no other way.

Life went on. One morning Bessie woke with blood on the sheet. Abe scurried to the kitchen and brought Ida to the bedroom. She sat for a long time with Bessie on the bed, rocking her back and forth, whispering reassurance. Abe held Bessie's hand while Ida got her sanitary pads and sat her in the rocking chair. She stripped the bed after the children went to school and soaked the sheets in the bathtub in cold water.

"It happens," Ida said. "I had two miscarriages in the old country. My sister too. You'll be all right." They had not yet told the children about the baby, so there was no announcement. Jenny was the only one who seemed to notice anything. She kept asking Bessie, "You look so sad. Is everything all right?"

The shine was out of Abe. He kissed Bessie's cheeks, but he never tickled the palm of her hand or reached for her waist to whirl her around the kitchen. He held her in bed, breathed her familiar sweaty scent, but when he tried to sleep in the softness of her arms, he thought she shrank back from him as if she could not trust the solidity of his body. He thought she didn't know about the money, but maybe she did. She and Ida were very close.

She only once asked, "No pinochle tonight?" And when he said he wanted to save money, she didn't ask again. There were no questions about why he didn't go to the fights anymore. He held his money close to him, wanting to pay Ida back as soon as he could. He took a second job, working nights doing the books for his neighbor who ran a dress shop. By the time the debt to Ida was paid, he was relying on her in the business and kept going to her for advice. She was a good partner.

Abe had written to his mother and sister. They would have to wait to come until he saved the money. He did not hear from them for five worrying months. When he heard back, everything had changed. His sister had married a widower, a man from the village with a two-year-old, and they had decided to stay in Molodycz. Abe's mother would live with them. They sent a wedding photo of Malka and her new husband, who looked very round, very prosperous. Abe's mother looked satisfied. He still wanted to bring them to America, but it wasn't so urgent now.

Over the next five years, letters came with pictures of the growing family. They stared out at the photographer, wearing their finest clothes, their faces bearing serious expressions. The last picture Abe received showed his mother—wispy gray hair in a bun—his sister and husband and three little children, the youngest, a boy, on Malka's lap. It had all turned out well, she wrote. They were not worried about the rumblings of trouble in Europe; they lived in Molodycz, a no-account village in the middle of nowhere. What could hurt them?

On September 1, 1939, when the Nazis marched into Poland, they were still there. Abe never heard from them again. Night after night he dreamed, reversing time: He didn't bet. He bought them tickets, they came to America, he saved them all. But when he woke, he faced his life. And sometimes, in the middle of the night, Abe imagined how things would have been different if the Kid had knocked out McDougal that night at the Broadway Arena, the way he was supposed to.

4

Jenny
1940–1942

In October 1940, on the morning of Irene's wedding to Sam Fine, Jenny found Ruby sitting on the toilet seat in the bathroom, her red curls lying on her shoulders, her lap, the sink, the floor, like spirals of blood. She had taken their mother's kitchen shears and hacked off her hair.

"What have you done, Ruby?"

Ruby gasped as if coming up from a deep underwater dive, and shoved Jenny hard against the towel rack. "Leave me alone!" Her hand clawed the scissors.

"Ruby, shush, it's all right."

"No. No." Her head swiveled back and forth. "She has no right. It should be me." Ruby's hair was sticking out every which way and there were patches of scalp showing through. Her face was mottled with tears.

"What are you talking about," Jenny asked. "Why did you cut your beautiful hair?"

"That's what brides do. They cut their hair. They wear a wig," she wailed. "I should be the bride."

"Oh, Ruby, Ruby. We don't do that. Only very religious people do that."

"She's only nineteen. I'm twenty-two. She should have waited. I should be first."

Jenny crouched beside her, knees butting up against the sink. The bathroom was so crowded her heels hit the tub where a wooden drying rack stood draped with socks and panties and brassieres. She patted Ruby's shoulder. "It doesn't matter, Ruby. Shush, it doesn't matter."

"I don't know what to do," Ruby whispered. "I don't know what to do."

Jenny took the scissors from Ruby, led her from the bathroom to the bedroom, and laid Ruby on their bed. Then she went to her parents' bedroom to get Bessie, who was fussing over Irene's hair. Jenny stood in the doorway and beckoned her mother, who followed Jenny into the hall. Jenny pulled Bessie's hand and led her to Ruby.

Ruby was supine on the bed, her arms stiff by her side. Bessie's jaw dropped. She covered her mouth, so she wouldn't cry out loud. She knelt and whispered Ruby's name and touched her ruined hair. Jenny had never seen Ruby quite like this before. With her hair chopped off, her eyes staring at the ceiling, she looked like a mad woman.

Jenny whispered, "I didn't know what to do."

"Go to Irene," Bessie whispered. "Don't let her come in here."

Jenny nodded and went back to her parents' room. She sat on the bed watching Irene dab her cheeks with rouge, blot her mouth with lipstick, comb her hair into an upsweep, place the veil on her head.

"How do I look?" Irene asked, standing up.

"Beautiful," Jenny said. And Irene did look lovely. Her hair, a deep chestnut, was piled on her head, and a wreath of flowers was wound in and out of the curls. "You are just beautiful." But Jenny's face was ashen, and she could not summon a smile.

"What's the matter," Irene asked. "Is something wrong?"

Jenny nodded.

"What?"

"Ruby's having one of her fits."

"Of course." Irene dropped onto the bed. "What happened?"

"She cut off her hair," Jenny said. "She just chopped it off every which way. She looks awful."

"Oh, my God, why does she always ruin everything?" Irene pulled the veil off her head and threw it on the bed. Now the upsweep was lopsided, hairpins sticking out.

Jenny couldn't look at her. "She can't help it."

"Maybe not, but Mama and Papa could." Irene paced up and down, her feet in high-heeled slippers pounding against the wooden floor. "They pretend she's normal, and she isn't. The only one in the house who ever speaks the truth about Ruby is Bubbie Ida, and Mama doesn't listen to her. Ruby always does this." She took one shoe off, threw it across the room and started to cry. "It's my wedding day, and she's ruining it!"

Jenny put her arms around Irene and held her until she stopped sobbing. "Your mascara is running," she said.

Irene sat down in front of the mirror, wiping her tears and the black mascara leaking around her eyes. She took a tissue and started to repair the mess, but then stopped. "She was supposed to be my maid of honor. I never wanted to ask her, but Mama made me." Irene threw the tissues on the vanity. She looked into the mirror at Jenny standing behind her. "Will you do it? Be my maid of honor?"

Jenny nodded. She began to fix Irene's hair, but Irene pushed her hands away. "I'll do it. You go get dressed."

Jenny left her parents' bedroom and went to her own. Bessie was still there, patting Ruby's hand, but Ruby lay, eyes fixed ahead, unblinking.

"Mama, you have to get dressed," Jenny said.

Bessie sighed. "She can't come," she said, nodding her chin toward Ruby. "I gave her the laudanum, and I sent Morris to ask Mrs. Feigenbaum if she would sit with her." She got up and walked to the door. "I'll get dressed now. You do too. Then help Bubbie Ida and Faye."

Jenny put on the pink silk dress she had borrowed from her best friend, fixed her hair so it was smooth on her shoulders, dabbed on a little lipstick, and, ignoring Ruby, walked out of the room into the tiny bedroom that Faye and Bubbie Ida shared. Eleven-year-old Faye was sitting primly on her narrow bed, trying not to mess her freshly ironed blue dress. Bubbie Ida was already wearing her navy silk dress. Around her neck was the gold necklace she always wore. In her hands was a string of pearls. "They were my mother's," she said. "Give them to Irene to wear."

Jenny nodded and took the pearls. "Ruby's sick. She can't come."

"What? What's wrong?"

"She cut off her hair. She's having one of her fits."

Bubbie Ida rushed from the room, and Jenny grabbed Faye, who started to follow her. "Come with me to give the pearls to Irene. They don't need you asking questions."

The family gathered in the living room, waiting for Mrs. Feigenbaum to come and sit with Ruby. At the wedding they tried to have a good time, but the formal photographs show the family standing in a line, dressed in their finest clothing, and there is not a smile on anyone's face.

After Irene's wedding, Ruby spiraled down. Irene and Sam went on a two-week honeymoon to Niagara Falls and Canada, and the rest of the family watched Ruby. She barely got out of bed for three days, and she wouldn't eat. Bessie tempted her with her favorite foods. She made Ruby soup, gave her the white meat from the chicken, baked lemon cookies, hovered over her cajoling her to eat. Bubbie Ida was irritated and Jenny heard her say, "Leave her. Stop fussing over her. It makes it worse."

Ruby sat at the dining table mumbling to herself, keeping her eyes downcast. When Jenny leaned over to listen to what she was saying she realized it was Hebrew—a prayer—or part of one. Over and over Ruby whispered, "*Baruch attah Adonai, Baruch attah Adonai. . . .*"

Abe pushed his chair back from the dinner table and, almost shouting, said to Bessie, "It's too much. She has a *dybbuk*. You have to do something!"

"It's not a dybbuk. She's praying," Jenny said.

"It doesn't matter. We have to do something," Abe said.

"All right, all right, I'll talk to Dr. Marsh again."

This time Dr. Marsh sent them to a psychiatrist, Dr. Franklin, whose office was in the back of his large house on Ocean Avenue.

In Dr. Franklin's consultation room, Bessie, Abe, and Ruby sat in hardbacked chairs while he talked to them. Jenny had come with them, another set of ears to help them understand any complicated medical information. The room smelled of cigarette smoke, and there was an ashtray, overflowing with butts, on the doctor's desk. Jenny stood behind her mother's chair, hands behind her back, and watched the doctor talk to Ruby, whose eyes were downcast. She whispered her answers to his questions. Jenny could barely hear.

"I'm prescribing phenobarbital," Dr. Franklin said. "She says she's not sleeping. This will calm her down, help her sleep better."

"Dr. Marsh said laudanum," Bessie said.

Dr. Franklin pushed his glasses up on his sharp nose. "Laudanum is addictive. Phenobarbital will help with her anxiety. It will be better." The family nodded, waited for more instructions. "And I think you should take her to the country. The air will do her good." Dr. Franklin bent over his desk, scribbling on a pad; his fingers were stained yellow from nicotine.

"How . . . how will going to the country solve anything?" Jenny whispered to Bessie.

Dr. Franklin heard her and looked up from his pad. "It will get her away from everything," he said. "All the things that upset her in the family."

Bessie looked with alarm at Jenny, at Abe. "I don't think it's the family that upsets her," she said. "It's just the way she is."

"Yes, well, you said this started at her sister's wedding. Getting her away will help." He spoke with such authority that Bessie, Abe, and Jenny just nodded, afraid to protest. "If it doesn't, we will have to look into hospitalization at Kings County Psychiatric Center."

Bessie said quickly, "I saw it. I went there to look. I don't want her to go there."

Dr. Franklin nodded. "Take her to the country. Then we'll see."

Bessie and Abe sent Jenny with Ruby to the country for a week, to Gold's, a small family-run hotel in Lakewood, New Jersey, where the dining room offered three meals a day. It was off-season, not crowded. There were a few older couples there, and one scholarly looking gentleman who sat at a table in the dining room alone, reading. From the porch of the hotel, there was a distant view of a small lake. It was the end of October, and the weather was surprisingly warm. The trees behind the lake were every color of red, gold, orange, and maroon. Champagne-colored reeds lined the opposite shore, and ducks paddled, dipping their heads to fish while two enormous white swans drifted through the water.

Their bedroom had twin beds with white chenille spreads and rag rugs on the floor. Jenny and Ruby had shared a bed for so many years that they slept together here too, leaving the other bed empty. Jenny would close her eyes and smell Ruby's hair on the pillowcase, feel the soft warmth of her skin without touching it.

They took long strolls between meals. At first, they walked in silence, and then they sang together, Jenny harmonizing with Ruby's silvery soprano. They sang "Stardust," and "All the Things You Are" and "You're My Everything." Jenny thought the music soothed Ruby, but afterward when Ruby started to talk, she wondered.

"Everything is out of kilter," she said. "It's like I'm crooked inside. Sometimes I feel like snakes are crawling up my arms. I'm bad. I keep telling them I didn't do it, but they don't believe me."

"Who?" Jenny asked. "Who doesn't believe you?"

"Them, them," she said. "They tell me things,"

"What things?"

"They told me to cut off my hair—shame myself—because Irene was marrying Sam." Ruby reached up and touched her head, grimaced.

Bessie had cut Ruby's hair into even ringlets and most of the bald spots didn't show. "Your hair looks nice," Jenny said. "It suits you. And there's no one telling you things," she repeated. "It's your imagination."

"No." Ruby said. "It's like there's an animal inside me." She stared at Jenny and the pupils of her eyes were so dense they almost eclipsed the green. "It's trying to get out, but I can't let it. It will tear the world apart. That's why I pray. I pray all the time, but it doesn't help."

Jenny knew that arguing with her would not help. She linked arms and kept walking.

Ruby went over and over the things she had done wrong. "I'm the oldest and I didn't help Mama. I spent too much money. Did you know I lied to Papa about where I got that red silk scarf? I stole it." She stopped by a tree and leaned her forehead on the rough bark. "I'm bad, Jenny. Bad . . . and I kissed all those boys."

"What boys?"

Ruby stared at Jenny. Her face hardened. "How come they sent you with me?"

"What . . . what do you mean?"

"You don't want to be here. Why did you come? Mama should have come." Ruby turned and walked away, head down.

Jenny watched her back receding down the path. *Ruby can always read my mind*, Jenny thought. It was true. She did not want to be here—she had come, taking time off from her classes at Brooklyn College, because everyone expected her to, because family came first. A shiver of anger rippled through her chest, but she pushed it down; she swallowed hard and ran to catch up with Ruby.

That night at dinner Ruby suddenly said, "I have to get married." She pushed the potatoes around on her plate, making designs in the gravy. "I'm being punished for all the bad things I did. That's why Irene got married first."

"That's crazy," Jenny said.

"Don't call me crazy!"

"I'm not calling *you* crazy," Jenny said, grabbing Ruby's hands. "I'm saying nobody is punishing you. Sam and Irene got married because they've loved each other forever, since they were little kids." A hard look settled on Ruby's face. Arguing with her was useless.

Jenny looked down at their clasped hands. Ruby's nails were bitten down, the cuticles pulled and reddened. It was like she was eating herself. The sleeve of her sweater was pushed up to just below the elbow, and Jenny saw light red lines on the inside of her arm. They looked like cuts. Jenny took a deep breath. "How did you get those?"

Ruby pulled her arm away. "They're nothing. Leave me alone." They ate the rest of their dinner in silence.

On Sunday morning, Jenny and Ruby took the bus back to New York City and the subway home to Brooklyn. Ruby settled into her bedroom and seemed all right. Bessie and Abe got the report from Jenny about how Ruby had been, and although Jenny said things had gone pretty well, she was apprehensive. She didn't tell them about the strange marks on Ruby's arm. Let her mother see them herself.

Irene and Sam came back that evening. They were going to stay with Sam's parents until they saved enough money for an apartment of their own, but they came for dinner to her parents on their first night back. They were holding hands, their faces glowing. They couldn't stop looking at each other, touching each other. The minute they entered the apartment, Ruby fled the room.

Bessie turned to Jenny. "Why did she go?"

"Seeing Irene and Sam together upsets her." Jenny sighed. "She wants to get married. She thinks she needs to find a husband, like that will make it all right."

"Maybe it will," Bessie said.

Jenny just shook her head.

Jenny could never remember exactly how it happened. There were whispered conferences at the table between her parents and Bubbie Ida, punctuated by long silences if anyone came into the kitchen. She knew her parents hired a *shadchan*, a Jewish matchmaker. Jenny had seen her several times, sipping tea with Abe and Bessie, a skinny, sharp-featured woman, who wore her head covered in a cloth wrap as a sign of her piety and who held her teacup with her pinky crooked in the air. All spring in 1941 the shadchan worked to find the perfect match.

There were dinners where one or another young man mysteriously appeared at the table, and Ruby sat quietly as if sedated, her black pupils huge. Sometimes she went to the movies with them. Each time she wore the new dress that Bessie had bought for her and Bubbie Ida's pearls. But nothing happened. At the end of some evenings she shook her head no. Sometimes the young men came back once and then disappeared. Nothing was working.

And then, in June 1941, Abe brought home a widower and refugee from Berlin named Victor Strauss. For almost a year, he had been a clerk in Abe's hardware store in downtown Brooklyn, but except for Bessie, who worked there also, no one in the family had met him. Bessie told them that he was twenty-nine years old, had been an engineer in Berlin, and had escaped Germany after Kristallnacht in 1939.

The night he came, Bessie fussed over Ruby. "Now remember, be still, and don't talk too much. Smile. You have a beautiful smile."

Jenny watched her mother brush Ruby's hair, which had grown out into a halo of light that shone around her face, saw her slip a silky lavender dress over her head.

"Another new dress?" Jenny asked.

"Oh, just this time," Bessie said. She smoothed the shoulders. Then she touched Jenny's arm. "Isn't it pretty on her?"

Jenny walked out without answering.

When they went into the living room, Victor was there, sitting on the brown sofa, leaning against the lace doily behind him. His hands lay on his lap, and he was opposite the wooden rocking chair where Morris was rocking back and forth in the silence. He jumped up immediately and bowed slightly to Bessie, to Ruby, to Jenny. He was of average height with thick brown hair that fell on his forehead and eyes that were so dark they were almost black. He had a mustache that marked two sharp, slanted lines above his mouth. *Just like Clark Gable*, Jenny thought. He had the sweetest smile she had ever seen.

At dinner, at the crowded table, Jenny was quiet, not trusting her voice. Ruby didn't talk, following her mother's advice, but Morris and Faye peppered Victor with questions about Berlin. Jenny thought they were being nosy. After all, he didn't know what had happened to his family in the past two years. They might be dead.

Jenny saw shadows flicker over his face when he mentioned his parents or talked about his wife, who had died shortly before he left Germany. She marveled at his almost perfect English, which he spoke with a slight emphasis on the letter S at the end of his words.

"We would have left together long before Kristallnacht, but she was too sick to go," he said, explaining why he left Berlin so late.

In the awkward silence that followed, Jenny could not take her eyes off him. She watched him lift his water glass and sip slowly. She saw his tapering fingers play with the soup spoon, noticed the slightly worn cuffs of his shirt showing from his jacket sleeves. His nails were short, clean, buffed.

"Did you ever play the piano?" she blurted.

"Yes," he said. "Why do you ask?"

With a shaky voice Jenny said, "I . . . I don't know exactly, but your fingers are so long they look like they should play the piano." She felt her cheeks redden, and then a distinct pinch on her arm. Ruby, who was sitting next to her, glared.

By the end of the evening, it was clear that everyone liked Victor, Ruby most of all. Over the next months he came often to the Weissmans' house, playing chess with Morris, taking Ruby to the movies on Saturday night, bringing flowers to Bessie when he came for dinner each Sunday afternoon. Some summer Sundays they went to Coney Island, and Ruby came back sunburned and happy from sitting on the beach, or excited from riding the Wonder Wheel. All through the fall and into the early December, Victor was a constant presence in her life. He had a calming effect on Ruby, and her occasional startling outbursts did not seem to faze him. Life seemed serene, going in a predictable direction.

The Japanese attack on Pearl Harbor changed all that. Suddenly the United States was at war with Japan, and everyone knew it was only a matter of time before there was war with Germany as well.

Over the next months, lives suspended, Morris and Sam waited, talked about joining up or waiting for the draft, listened endlessly to the news, wondered what they should do. In the end the waiting was too much, and they both enlisted in the Army. Victor talked about enlisting too, but Abe convinced him that he would do better to stay with him. He needed him in the store. And in early February 1942, Ruby and Victor announced that they would marry.

Bessie and Abe beamed. There were congratulatory cries of "*Mazel tov, mazel tov*" from everyone around the table. Jenny sat with her mouth open and finally dipped her head, nodded, and mumbled, "Congratulations," glad that no one seemed to be looking at her except her grandmother.

Jenny got up and began to clear the dishes from the table and Bubbie Ida followed her. "You don't like him?" she asked.

"No, of course I like him. He's a wonderful man." Jenny scraped the remains from the dishes into the garbage pail while her grandmother filled the sink with hot water. "I just don't see how he can marry her," Jenny burst out. "Does he know?"

Bubbie Ida shrugged. "I didn't tell him."

"Someone should," Jenny said.

"It won't be me."

"Mama thinks getting married is going to solve Ruby's problems. It won't."

"How do you know? It might make things better."

Jenny shook her head. "No, it won't. Maybe it will for a while, but it won't last. He doesn't know what he's getting into. Someone has to tell him."

Bessie poked her head into the kitchen. "Come," she said. "We're toasting them." Jenny and Bubbie Ida went into the dining room.

Right now, Jenny thought, Ruby looked and acted perfectly normal. She wasn't talking fast, her laugh was not too loud, not too wild. If Jenny hadn't seen for herself how unseen spirits and voices could possess her sister, she wouldn't have believed there was anything wrong with her.

Ruby hugged Jenny and said, "There you are, little sister, my best friend in the world. Aren't you happy for me?"

Jenny could only hug her back and whisper, "Of course I am." But that night she could not sleep, and in the morning, she went to Bessie in the kitchen and said, "Mama, did you or Papa tell Victor about Ruby?"

"Tell what?"

"Don't be like that. You know what. How she gets sometimes."

"Papa talked to him. He understands she is high-strung."

Jenny was exasperated. "She's more than high-strung. You know she is."

"I know that she will be happy and calm when she becomes a wife and mother. And you . . . " Bessie glared at Jenny, "mind your business." She walked out of the room.

But Jenny could not let it go. Jenny knew Victor could not possibly understand about Ruby. If he did, he would never marry her.

One Thursday afternoon in late February, when the streets were slushy with snow that had fallen that morning, she waited outside her father's shop in lower Manhattan, watching the last customers come out of the store with their packages. It was already dark out, the streetlights shining on the wet pavement. Jenny huddled in the doorway of a ladies' dress shop. She hadn't dressed warmly enough. She scrunched her toes in her shoes trying to warm her cold, wet feet; she was wearing stockings and pumps to be fashionable and now knew how silly that was. She should have worn slacks and socks. Victor would never even notice. She watched her breath in the cold air, like a mist in front of her face. Everything looked blurry.

At six o'clock she saw her father leave the store, and she ducked inside the dress shop until he passed so he wouldn't see her. Then she stepped quickly outside again. In a few minutes Victor came out, locking the door behind him. He was wearing a worn camel coat with the collar turned up against the cold, his hands jammed in his pockets. He must not have gloves, Jenny thought. He wasn't wearing a cap like all the other shopkeepers, but had a brown fedora pulled low over his brow. He looked like a businessman. Taking a deep breath, she stepped in front of him.

"Jenny! What are you doing here?"

Her tongue felt thick and she couldn't speak. She bit her lip.

"What is it? Is everything all right?"

She swallowed, nodded. "Yes, of course. But—I just wanted to talk to you—to make sure you . . ." she stopped. She suddenly didn't think she could do this.

"Yes? Make sure . . ." he prompted.

Her heart hammered. "Make sure you knew, understood about Ruby." The words hung between them.

He reached out, touched her cheek. His hand was cold. "I do," he whispered. "I know. You are very kind to worry, but you do not need to. I understand."

"No, really," she rushed in, the words tumbling fast. "Do you know? How crazy she is sometimes? How could you know? You haven't seen her. She's wild. She says she has a dybbuk, snakes inside; she steals sometimes, she tells lies . . . we can't trust her. She hears voices and does what they . . ."

"Stop, Jenny," Victor interrupted. "I know."

Jenny searched his face. His brown eyes held hers, never wavered. "You don't understand," she said, her voice dull. "You can't, or you wouldn't marry her."

"Yes, I do understand."

"And you'll marry her anyway?"

He nodded. "Yes. I told your father I would."

Jenny closed her eyes. "Well," she said, "all right then. As long as you know. I've said it." She began to walk away; her feet dragged through the slush. There was a sick feeling in the pit of her stomach.

"Jenny," Victor called.

She turned and waited. He stood there, looking at her. Then he said, "Thank you for worrying about me." He came to her and kissed her cheek. She felt his warm breath, his mouth, the bristles of his mustache. Her heart lurched. She felt a rush of warmth below her belly. She closed her eyes. There was nothing more to do. She had to get away before she cried.

At home Ruby was waiting for her. She'd been shopping for her trousseau, and Bessie had bought her two lace-trimmed nightgowns in pastel colors and a deep purple jacket with a velvet collar. "Look Jenny." Ruby showed Jenny her new jacket. "Purple, my favorite color."

She waltzed around the room, grabbed Jenny by the waist and sang to her, "Somewhere over the Rainbow." The silver of her voice pierced Jenny and sent chills up her arms. "I was waiting for you. I want to show you something. Look." She held out an antique cameo pin. "Victor gave it to me for a present last night. He can't afford a ring, so he bought this. Isn't it beautiful?"

Jenny fingered the cameo. The pale apricot of the shell was translucent, and the face carved in it was delicate perfection. "It's beautiful," she said, her voice thick.

"I'm going to wear it always. I'll never take it off." She pinned it back on her dress, turned to Jenny, and hugged her. "I want you to be my maid of honor."

Jenny stared. What? She should stumble down the aisle in a pink dress again, sick in her heart for them all? She had nothing to say. She didn't want to be Ruby's maid of honor or go to the wedding and watch Victor marry Ruby.

There was a black taste in her mouth, like shame. "I have to go to the toilet," she mumbled, and ran to the bathroom, locking the door. She sat on the lid of the bowl with the lights off and waited for the nausea to disappear. She closed her eyes and said, "It's over. Forget it now. It's over."

Four months later Ruby and Victor were married. Soon Victor took more responsibility at the store, almost like a partner to Abe. And Ruby settled down.

"See," Bessie said. "I always knew. She only needed the right man and she would be fine."

Jenny struggled with her feelings. One evening when she was helping Bubbie Ida prepare dinner, she felt her grandmother's rough hand on her arm.

"You're not happy are you, mamaleh?"

Jenny's eyes filled. "I can't help it, Bubbie. I want to be happy—for her, for me—but I'm not."

Bubbie Ida sighed. "You think you're in love with him, but you have to let go. They're married. He's your brother."

Jenny shivered. The thought that Victor was now her brother made her feel sick.

5

Jenny
1942–1945

Morris and Sam finished their Army basic training in August 1942 and shipped overseas. Letters were read aloud at the dinner table. War news was discussed endlessly. The family prayed daily for the boys' safety. But otherwise life at home went on the way it always had.

Irene worked for a company that made hand-painted trays and lamps where she was one of the star artists. She moved back into her old room, and thirteen-year-old Faye, a freshman in high school, slept there too, taking Ruby's place in the bed with Jenny.

Jenny attended her classes at Brooklyn College and, along with Bessie, helped out at the hardware store. The business was doing very well despite the rationing of metal. Victor, with his engineering background and his ability to fix almost anything, had opened a side business. People brought their broken tools to him, their old radios, record players, small appliances, and he fixed them. Soon he was buying, for a small sum, items that were beyond repair and swapping out the usable parts to fix other products, for which he charged a tidy amount. For the first time the family was financially comfortable, and Jenny thought it was because of Victor's ingenuity.

Jenny loved the time she spent in the store because when he wasn't looking, she could watch Victor work, see how he charmed the customers, fixed their precious tools and electrical appliances, improvised for parts. Jenny always made sure she was home every Friday night when Victor and Ruby walked from their apartment to Bessie and Abe's for Shabbos dinner.

Everyone watched Ruby carefully, but she seemed fine. She was married. She had not had a spell since the day she met Victor. For the first time in years, Jenny was not responsible for Ruby. She was independent, the weight off her shoulders.

In November 1942 Ruby announced she was pregnant. At first, she seemed thrilled at the prospect of motherhood and began decorating part of the bedroom for a baby, with a crib and a bassinet and a stroller, buying a layette in yellow and green, saying, "It will be fine for a boy or girl."

"It's bad luck to prepare for a baby before it's born," Bubbie Ida said, but Ruby wouldn't listen. She went on one buying spree after another. Bubbie Ida shook her head. "She's high again. I don't know what will be."

Joseph was born in late June 1943. Ruby came home from the hospital, they had the *bris*, the ritual circumcision ceremony, and right after that Bessie began going to Ruby and Victor's apartment every day to help out.

"Ruby isn't acting right," she confided to Jenny. "She's putting all the yellow and green clothing in piles to give away. She says, 'I need blue. He's a boy! We have to have blue.' I ran out and got a blue-and-white layette, but it didn't work. She's still hysterical." Bessie passed her hands through her hair and sighed. "I'm so worried. When I bring the baby to her to nurse, she says her breasts hurt, or he just nursed, he can't be hungry again. She takes no interest in him. She just sits in a chair, looking out the window. I'm afraid to leave her alone with the baby."

One evening Bessie called Jenny into the kitchen. It was August, stifling in the apartment. The room smelled from the onions Bessie had fried for supper, and the tablecloth was stained with the night's dinner spills. Bessie had been crying. "Jenny, we have to help Victor," she said. "I was there today. The diapers, the mess . . ." Her voice broke.

Jenny felt a stirring of panic. "Mama, I can't. I have my own life now. I have school. I have to study. I can't take care of Ruby."

Bessie nodded, but tears continued to slide down her cheeks.

Jenny's voice got louder. "Everything is always about Ruby. What am I supposed to do? What?" She sat heavily on a chair. "I'm sick of it."

Still Bessie said nothing. Jenny could hear the ticking clock. She could hear the radio in the living room. The war news was on. The Allies had landed in Sicily. Faye came into the kitchen, looked at them, and walked out quickly. Jenny followed her into the bedroom and sat beside her on the bed.

They held hands. "It's bad, isn't it?"

Jenny nodded, looking at Faye's worried face. Faye was fourteen now, and no one ever asked her to help. She was the cherished baby, studying hard, writing almost daily letters to Morris to keep him up to date on the family. Although Irene was living at home again, she was working, so no one bothered to ask her to do anything either. Jenny was still considered Ruby's watcher, even though she didn't want to be.

"It will be all right," Jenny said to Faye, and stood up. She couldn't stay in the bedroom. She breathed deep to stop the churning inside her stomach, paced the living room crammed with the two couches, their arms dirty and worn from years of grimy hands. Bessie had thrown lace doilies on them, but they were askew, and one had fallen to the floor. Jenny bent to pick it up and placed it back on the couch. In front of one of the sofas was the scratched coffee table where Jenny used to play gin rummy with Morris and Steal the Old Man's Bundle with Faye. She could not find anywhere to put herself, so she went back into the kitchen. Bessie was sitting with Bubbie Ida, not talking. Drinking tea.

"I hate this, you know," Jenny said. "When do I get a life?"

Bubbie Ida put her glass in the sink. "Maybe your life is this. For some of us, that's the way it is. We do what we need for family. In the end, it's all we have." She turned away.

Jenny took a deep breath then went to the window. It had begun to rain lightly. She walked back to the table and forced the words out. "All right. What do you want me to do?"

"Come with me. Now," Bessie said. "We'll clean up. Help him put the baby to bed."

Victor opened the door when they arrived, holding Joseph in his arms. Behind him Ruby sat stony-faced on the sofa. The little kitchen sink was stacked with dishes. In the bathroom the diaper pail was overflowing, and the smell of ammonia made Jenny gag. Without a word they set to work.

When Jenny held Joseph, a scrawny, pale baby, her heart was heavy. The baby's spastic arm and leg movement frightened her. Bessie told her it was normal, to hold him close, swaddle him in a baby blanket, and when Jenny did that, he calmed down somewhat, but he rooted around for a nipple, opening his mouth wide, trying to latch on to her arm. Sometimes it made her laugh, but mostly she ached with pity for the tiny boy.

Bubbie Ida said that some new mothers had "baby blues." Ruby would get over it. But Jenny didn't believe it, and she didn't think Bubbie Ida did either. She and Bessie took turns staying at the apartment with Ruby in the daytime until Victor came home from work. They made formula for all Joseph's feedings; Bessie took on the sterilizing of the bottles and the boiling of the water to mix with the evaporated milk. She soaked the diapers and scrubbed them by hand in the bathtub, hanging them as she had her own babies' diapers, on clotheslines strung out the back windows.

Ruby sat alone. If she noticed that they were there too often, she never said anything. Her eyes sunk hollow in their sockets, and her clothes hung on her. She was biting her nails again, tearing the skin around her cuticles. When Victor came home, Jenny was there, after work or school. She heated up the food her mother had prepared and then cleaned up the kitchen while Victor bathed Joseph and put him to sleep. She watched how gentle he was. Ruby was always shut away in the bedroom. After Joseph was asleep, Jenny left for home.

One day, after she cleared the dishes and was about to leave, Victor came out from the bedroom and said, "Stay, Jenny. Stay a while." They sat side by side on the sofa, Victor with his arms on his knees. Jenny noticed a twitch in his left eye.

"I don't know what to do anymore, Jenny. She's not getting any better. I took her to Dr. Franklin. He told me about a new treatment for this kind of depression. It's called ECT. Shock therapy. I don't know if it's right to do to her."

"What is it?"

"They put electricity to her brain and shock her."

Jenny gasped. She couldn't speak.

"It sounds horrible, I know. But Dr. Franklin says it works in the worst cases."

She looked down at Victor's hands. The cuffs on his shirt were frayed, but his long tapering fingers lay gracefully on his trousers. She wanted to touch them. She had an urge to put her head on his shoulder, smell the starch on his shirt. Her heart was hammering. She looked away, ashamed.

"I don't know what to do," Victor said again. He followed her to the door as she was leaving. "I should never have agreed to marry her," he whispered. For a second Jenny wondered what he meant by "agreed to marry her," but then she knew. They stared at each other, the words he had said like a weight between them. She reached out and touched his cheek and then pulled her hand away.

"Talk to Papa or Bubbie Ida. She's smart." It was the only thing Jenny could think of. Then she turned and ran home.

Victor consulted Abe and Bubbie Ida. Was it cruel to attach electricity to Ruby's brain to give her a seizure? Could it kill her? What would happen if he didn't try it? In the end he had to make the decision, and in desperation he gave his consent.

It was a miracle. Ruby came home that fall like her old self. She sang. She laughed. She shone with her former brilliance. Bessie and Jenny didn't have to go to the house all the time. Through the winter and spring of 1944 all seemed well. Even when, in November, they discovered that Ruby was pregnant again, Jenny was the only one who said it was a terrible idea.

They had been hopeful after the Normandy invasion in June that the war would soon be over, but it slogged on and stalled that bitter winter at the Battle of the Bulge. In late January 1945 Irene received the news that Sam had been wounded there, burned on his torso in his foxhole, and was being treated in a hospital in England.

Over the next months, while they prayed for Sam's recovery, Ruby went through her second pregnancy with very little drama. Sarah was born in June, just after victory was declared in Europe. By August, after the bloody battles of Iwo Jima and Okinawa were won, and the war with Japan was finally over, the Weissmans were faced once again with Ruby's slide into blackness. She couldn't cook or shop. When toddling Joseph tried to climb on her lap, she stood up, letting him slide to the floor, and walked into another room.

This time Jenny didn't have to be asked to help. Bessie went to Ruby's in the daytime and Jenny, who had graduated and was working full time at a publishing company in Manhattan, went in the evening. And this time Victor just took Ruby back to the psychiatric hospital for shock therapy. When she came home, Ruby's eyes were not quite so bright, and her smile was forced.

As soon as she came home Ruby said, "I want to see my babies." Jenny went with her into the bedroom. Joseph was sprawled on his bed, sleeping deeply, his pale gold lashes feathering his cheeks. Sarah lay on her stomach in the crib. Ruby sat between the two children and sang softly the lullaby Bessie had sung to each of her five children. Neither Sarah nor Joseph stirred. Ruby's voice was silver as always, and Jenny closed her eyes in relief.

But things were not really better. Ruby tried hard. She dragged herself out of bed. She watched while Joseph played around her and Bessie prepared their meals in the kitchen. She stayed in a corner of the living room, looking at the wall while Victor put the children to bed and Jenny cleared the dinner dishes.

On a rainy Tuesday in early September, Victor came to the family's apartment, his face chalky. He was clutching Sarah in his arms, and two-year-old Joseph hid behind his father's leg. Jenny could just see his auburn head peeking out behind Victor's gray trousers.

"Ruby?" Bessie whispered

Victor handed her the baby. His voice was hoarse, thick. "I don't know where she is . . . she's disappeared. They were alone when I came home from work. I have to go look for her."

In the hours that followed, Jenny and Bessie and Bubbie Ida busied themselves with the children. Jenny was heartsick to think of the children alone in the apartment. What if something had happened? Bessie cried in a chair in the corner of the living room, rocking Sarah who slept fitfully. Joseph lay curled in Jenny's bed. Jenny thought what life would be like if Ruby didn't come back, wishing it, hating herself for wishing it, then wishing it again. Bubbie Ida was watching her. Jenny was sure Bubbie Ida knew what she was thinking.

When Victor returned hours later, he had Ruby beside him. She was shivering, dripping wet, her hair hanging about her face. She stared vacantly ahead of her. Without a word Bessie took her by the arm and led her down the hall into the bathroom. They heard the water running and Bessie's soothing voice as she helped undress her and put her into a hot bath. It was like the night so long ago when Ruby had disappeared with Faye. Nothing had changed. Everything had changed. Jenny got up and put the kettle on for tea.

"Where was she?" she asked.

"Sitting on the stoop. I looked everywhere, and then, when I had given up and went home, there she was sitting in the rain, shivering on the steps in front of the house." He closed his eyes. "I don't know what to do . . . will she be like this always?"

"Maybe," Jenny said. "I don't know."

The next day Ruby went back to the hospital for more treatments. It was up to Bessie and Jenny and Bubbie Ida to take care of the children. Jenny held them, fed them, and sang them to sleep. She tried not to think about Ruby.

It was the children she focused on, the softness of their skin when she toweled them dry from their bath, Sarah's first smile when Jenny leaned over the crib, Joseph's comments on how he liked to eat dinner with everyone and listen to the radio together. In those weeks Jenny daydreamed they were her children.

One night, Bubbie Ida said to her, "They're not yours. You're their aunt."

Jenny flushed with shame. How did Bubbie Ida always know? "I know. It's just a wish. A daydream. It can't hurt."

"It can hurt plenty. What do you think will happen when Ruby comes home?"

Jenny hesitated, then said, "They'll go home with her. Things will be fine and then they won't be."

"Yes. And you can throw your life away wanting what you can't have, but you can't change anything for Ruby and Victor."

Jenny nodded and took a deep breath. The war was over. Morris, and all the other soldiers, were home or would be soon. They would all go on with their lives. She could have her own life. She could look for a better job, go out at night with friends. Surely somewhere she would meet a man who would make her forget Victor. Somehow, even if there wasn't a new road for Victor and Ruby, she could find one for herself. She was not going to throw her life away, watching over Ruby. Bubbie Ida said all we have is family. Jenny didn't believe it. She was going to have more than her family. Much more.

6

Morris

1946

"Morris! Where the hell have you been?"

Morris looked up. *Sam*. He watched his brother-in-law slip into the seat opposite.

"Here I am," Morris said. He was sitting in a booth in the Strand Tavern in Brooklyn, where he had been all afternoon, nursing a beer, smoking one Lucky Strike after another, and trying to keep his mind still.

"Yeah. But where is that? You disappear. No one knows where you are. What's going on with you?"

"Nothing."

"Where've you been?"

"Around," Morris mumbled.

"Don't give me that shit. You sound like a twelve-year-old. Your mother's going nuts. She said you haven't been home in three nights." Sam reached over, took the pack of Lucky's, shook out a cigarette and lit it, closing his right eye against the smoke. He inhaled and blew two perfect smoke rings.

"I've been staying with Frank."

"Well at least call her and tell her where you are," Sam said.

"God, she makes me feel like a kid again. Always wants to know where I'm going, when I'm coming home. I can't stand the apartment. It's so full all the time."

"What's new about that? It was always full."

"Yeah. But now Ruby's kids are there most of the time. She can't take care of them, so the rest of them do—Mom and Jenny and Bubbie Ida and Faye. It's a three-ring circus."

"Well your mother's worried about you. We all are. What's going on?"

Morris reflected on his friend and brother-in-law, Sam. He was a very handsome man: six feet tall, thick blond hair, and gray eyes. Morris himself was barely five foot ten, and his hair and eyes were plain brown. "Just taking some time off," Morris said finally.

"Enough with the time off. You need a job." Morris was silent, so Sam went on. "Irene told me to ask you to dinner tomorrow night."

"I don't know. I might have plans."

"Don't be a shmuck," Sam said. "If your sister asks you to dinner, you come."

Morris thought about it. He didn't really have plans—just the possibility of plans with Pauline. Morris wondered what Sam would say if he met Pauline, with her thick black upswept curls and green eyes, sharp as a needle—and the small brown mole two inches below her naval that seared his mouth when he kissed it. *What will happen to the mole when the baby Pauline has told him she's growing expands that tight smooth stomach into a round globe? Will the mole spread? Grow?*

"Okay, I'll come," he said, abruptly, not wanting to think what he was thinking.

"Good." Sam looked around the bar. "This place is still a hole. It stinks in here."

The tavern had a dense smell, dank and fusty from decades of booze spilled into the cracks of the wooden floor, smoke yellowing the walls, no ventilation. Two fans spun from the tinned ceiling, and the bar on the side of the room was crowded with early evening drinkers.

"You need to get on with your life."

Morris nodded. "I am." *I'm trying*, he thought.

"Where? How?" Sam asked. "Your father said you don't want to work in the hardware store with him. Why not?"

"Why not? I should compete with Victor? He's got a lock on the store since he married Ruby. That was their deal. You know that. I'd be a clerk instead of the owner's son."

Sam nodded. After a minute he said, "Come work with me then. At least for now, until you decide what you want to do. I need the help."

"I'm no good at plumbing," Morris answered.

"How do you know? You never tried it," Sam said.

"Yeah, I did." They both laughed at the memory of a minor flood he had caused in the bathroom when he was fifteen and had insisted he could fix the leak in the toilet.

"Okay, so no plumbing. But what about the police force? That's what you always said you wanted."

Morris nodded. "I still want it, but I got a few things I got to take care of before I sign up."

Sam fixed Morris with a steady gaze. "What? Why won't you talk to me anymore? You spend all your time with Frank. I know he's your buddy and all, from the war, but I'm your family."

Morris breathed deep, took a sip of his beer. Warm. Why didn't he talk to Sam anymore? He used to share everything with him, but now he and Sam were living in different worlds. Morris was only a few months out of the service. Sam was married with a baby; he had been home for a year, ever since he was brought back from Europe with a million-dollar wound . . . burns over his chest and arms from a firebomb in his foxhole. He had a Purple Heart and an honorable discharge.

Morris didn't think Sam would understand him anymore. Would he get it if Morris told him how he wanted to take his discharge money, buy a car, and travel across the country? Would he get Morris's hunger for the wideness of the world instead of the confines of Brooklyn? Would he get why Morris didn't want a job just now? Not as a plumber. Not as a cop.

Morris took a drag of his cigarette and said, "It's funny. A little while ago Frank offered me a job too."

"Doing what?"

"I don't know," Morris said. "Odd jobs."

Frank had said, "Come work for my uncle. Do odd jobs. Easy work. Good money."

"Sounds funny to me. Good money for odd jobs."

"Nothing funny about it," Frank said. "My uncle pays good money."

"I don't know. I can't seem to decide anything. I don't know what I want to do."

"I thought you wanted to be a cop?" Frank lit a Camel with his silver Zippo. "Not that I think that's such a great idea, but if that's what you want, do it."

"Sometimes I do, but then I think I just want to travel around the country for a while."

"So, go."

"Everything's simple for you. For me there's always complications . . . Pauline's pregnant."

"Tough." Frank whistled, shook his head. His thick black hair fell over his eyes. "So take care of the business with Pauline and go."

"What do you mean, take care of the business with Pauline? What . . . get rid of it?" When Frank nodded, Morris sighed. "I wouldn't know where to go, who to trust. And it takes a lot of money. And anyway, it's illegal. I'm sure Pauline wouldn't go for it."

"You want me to help you? I will. Whatever you want. Money's no problem. I'll lend it to you. You need a doctor? I know a good one. We're brothers." He smiled.

Morris smiled back. Blood brothers—that's what they called each other. Morris had met Frank Tedeschi in Fort Dix, New Jersey, where they went for basic training. Frank was a Brooklyn boy who had grown up two neighborhoods over from Morris. They attached themselves to one another like long lost brothers. The rhythm of their language—pure New York—was so comfortable. They laughed at the same jokes, liked the same movies. They played poker, and Morris—the better card player by far—beat Frank routinely, racking up his winnings against Frank's debts, and then forgiving them so they could start playing again, even. They were both avid Dodger fans and listened to the baseball games on the radio or the fights, making side bets on their favorite boxers. They were first sent to Africa and then, in the summer of 1943, they got to Sicily, inseparable, finishing each other's sentences, sharing rations, packages from home, foxholes, rubber parkas in the rain, and metallic-tasting canteen water in the heat.

And it was hot then, blazing July. In Sicily they became a threesome, adopting Willie Barden, a green recruit from Iowa. He was terrified at first, his pale farm-boy face stony. They took him under their wing and swore they'd make him a tough New Yorker by the time the war was over and teach him not to be afraid of anything.

The truth was even Morris felt safer with Frank near him. Frank was always cool, his brown eyes in a perpetual squint, assessing, deciding. He could talk the lingo too—Sicilian was his first language. Morris and Willie depended on Frank.

The Italians were supposed to be haphazard soldiers and taking the town of Agrigento a cakewalk for the Allies, but no one told the Sicilians. They defended their city fiercely, building by building, killing as many Americans as they could and disappearing into doorways that opened into dark warrens of hallways hiding anything or anyone.

The men scuffed up stone dust as they slid along the narrow streets, keeping close to white buildings. Dust coated their faces, rimmed their eyes with a gray white powder. The platoon split into twosomes, going into doorways, searching the rooms. Morris and Willie slipped into one house. The room was black, and Morris couldn't see. Sweat slipped down his back like crawling bugs. He waited a minute to get accustomed to the dim light and then ran quietly first into one room—empty—then the next.

Behind him, Willie tripped on a piece of rubble, his boots clumping hard, as he caught himself on the doorway. "Shit," Willie said, loud.

"Shut the fuck up," Morris hissed, turning to look at Willie. And when he turned back, he found himself staring into the eyes of a young Italian soldier, who had come from nowhere and who was now pointing his rifle at them both. Willie and Morris froze in cold terror. Then they raised their rifles in surrender, and the Italian quietly took their rifles with one hand and motioned them to move ahead of him with the other.

Fuck, fuck, fuck. We should have shot him. Why didn't we shoot him?

Morris and Willie walked with the muzzle of the Italian's rifle jammed first against Morris's back and then against Willie's. When they came to a wall they stopped and turned to face him. He was no more than seventeen with the small slim body of a boy, first fuzz on his cheeks.

He's just a kid, Morris thought. *Fuck it all. And where the hell is Frank?* After the thought, there was a shadow, and the shadow became Frank coming up behind the soldier, saying something in Sicilian. Before the boy could turn, Frank reached in front of him and slit his throat. The boy's eyes opened, startled, and his legs buckled as he fell at Morris's feet.

But first there was blood. It spurted onto Morris's face, his feet, his hands, leaving them red and sticky. Willie was covered too.

"Shit," Morris said. "There's so much fucking blood." He wiped it from his cheek with his forearm and stared into Frank's cool and steady eyes, marveling at Frank's guts and his swiftness in slitting the boy's throat. He could hear Willie gag.

Frank grinned and held up his hands, which were bloody too. "Yeah. We're all blood brothers now."

Morris nodded. "I owe you for that one," he whispered. "We both do."

"Ah what the hell," Frank said. "This shithole of a war will go on and on, and you'll both have plenty of chances to pay me back."

After Agrigento, Sicily had been easy. With the enemy falling away before them, they marched across the island to Palermo, Frank's ancestral home. Frank showed them the neighborhood where his grandfather had grown up, where his grandmother's bakery had been. "Here's the cathedral where my father was baptized," he said, laughing. "All these people could be my cousins. We're all connected." And he winked.

When they landed in Naples, they were hardened veterans and sauntered casually up the road, rifles at the ready. Or they walked fanned out with the rest of their platoon across fields, through woods. They were tired, Morris and Willie, even a little sloppy some days. But Frank, he was always ready. It was like he had a sixth sense about danger, had sharp ears, could hear the whistle of incoming mortars before anyone else, could see the slightest shiver of the trees or bushes that told him the enemy was waiting.

One day their platoon was walking down the road alongside a wooded area, laughing, wisecracking. Willie was in front of them carelessly tossing his head back to say something to Morris, when Frank shouted, "Watch out, Willie, take cover!"

In that instant it was too late. Willie either didn't hear him or waited a fraction of a second too long before diving into the trees. As the air shattered with mortar fire, Frank had already jumped on Morris shoving him out of the way and beneath him into a ditch. Morris's head slammed the earth. Pebbles, dirt sprayed his cheeks, his eyes burned, the tinny taste of blood filled his mouth. His shoulder and hip throbbed. When Frank and Morris untangled themselves in the ditch, they saw Willie lying on the road, a mess of blood and scraps of filthy uniform.

"Oh God, oh God, fuck, Willie, fuck, fuck, fuck!" Morris could hardly breathe.

Frank inhaled. He turned Morris away from Willie's body, shoving him into the trees, with hardly a glance back. His face was marble, his eyes hard. Around them the rest of the platoon scrabbled to get under cover.

"We got to take him with us," Morris said. He turned his head again to look at Willie.

Frank pushed him forward. "No, we got to get out of here, or we'll be the next ones on the road."

Morris still hesitated. "We can't leave him."

"Okay," Frank said, his voice cold. "Choose. A dead body in the road or your own life." He moved deeper into the bushes. Morris followed him.

Morris heard Sam say, "Talk to me," and tried to shake himself back to today, the bar. "Talk to me," Sam said again, studying Morris with a steady gaze. "I asked you what kind of odd jobs you would do."

"I don't know. He didn't say."

Sam shook his head. "He's probably in the mob. That's why he didn't tell you."

"No, he's not in the mob." Morris was annoyed. "Not all Italians are in the mob. It's his uncle's business."

"You're not going to work for him, are you?"

"No, but I got to do something. There's this girl, her name is Pauline. I might get married."

"You know you're making me crazy? First, you're going to take a job with the mob. Now you're getting married. I never met her, and you'd marry her just like that?" Sam stood up to go to the bar. "I got to have a drink. Then you'll tell me where you met her."

When he came back, Sam gulped down half his beer before he asked, "Where'd you meet her?"

"Frank introduced us," Morris said.

"Who is she?"

"Pauline Shapiro. She lives in Bensonhurst. Her father's a doctor."

Sam whistled. "Sounds great. What's the problem?"

"She's pregnant."

Sam stared at him. "God, Morris. That was fast. Do I need to explain the facts of life to you? Didn't you use a skin?"

Morris hesitated. "Every time except the first two." He watched Sam shake his head, push his glass around the table.

"What are you going to do," Sam asked.

Morris passed his hand over his face. "I don't know. Maybe fix it—you know—get rid of it. But I don't have the money."

"Do you love her?"

"I suppose."

"You suppose. If you love her you can't fix it. You got to marry her."

"Maybe. I don't know."

"What choice do you have?"

Morris heard Frank in his head. *There are always choices.*

"What are you going to do?" Sam asked again.

Morris shrugged. "Frank offered me money . . . but . . . it doesn't feel right."

Sam grabbed Morris's arm. "Shit, if you need money, I'll get it for you."

"I know. I know you will. I just don't want to ask." He got up from his seat in the booth and moved to leave. "I got to go. I have to pick Pauline up in an hour," Morris said. "I'll see you tomorrow night." Without looking back, Morris walked out of the bar and into the dim light of July dusk.

He caught the bus down Bay Parkway and walked two blocks to Pauline's house on Stillwell Avenue. She lived in Bensonhurst, the same neighborhood as Frank, in a three-story brownstone with white stone stanchions in front. The first floor was her father's medical office. The family—Pauline, her parents, and her younger brother—lived on the top two floors. Morris climbed the staircase and pressed the bell. Pauline opened the door immediately, like she'd been waiting behind it for Morris to come.

Morris caught his breath when he saw Pauline. She was wearing a sleeveless white gauzy dress for the hot July evening and white high-heeled pumps. Morris saw the softness of her body beneath the flimsy fabric of her dress. She looked tan, almost bronze, and he knew she had been at Coney Island this week, toasting in the sun, her skin slicked with baby oil. Her hair was down tonight, curling gently over her shoulders, and when she tossed her head, it shimmered in the light. The first time he had seen her in the smoky cellar club in Frank's uncle's red brick house in Bensonhurst, she had been wearing a green taffeta dress to match her eyes, her hair was in an upsweep, and she was smoking a cigarette, looking sultry. Tonight, she looked like an innocent angel.

He couldn't help himself. He leaned down and kissed her cheek and she smiled at him. "My parents aren't home, so we can just go. They said you should have me back early."

"I will," he said, feeling like a hypocrite, pretending to be watching out for Pauline's safety, when he had already done the damage.

Pauline and Morris walked down the street. "My mother likes you," she said. "I think it's because you're Jewish. My father hates that I hang out with the Italian crowd. He calls them Wops. He never wanted to be there when Frank picked me up."

Morris stopped and looked down at her. "Frank never told me you and him went out." Did he imagine it or did Pauline blush?

He tried to remember what Frank had said when he mentioned Pauline. "There's this girl I want to fix you up with. She goes to Brooklyn College, and she's really cute. And Jewish too." He never said he dated her.

Pauline hesitated a second. "We didn't exactly go out. Only one or two times. We were more like friends." She smiled at him and tilted her head flirtatiously. "Are you jealous?"

"No," Morris said, but he felt uneasy. Maybe he was jealous, or maybe he didn't understand everything. He didn't know how to tell her what he was thinking. He was not even sure he knew what he was thinking. He could remember how he felt when he danced with her the night he met her. It had been so long since he'd had an American girl in his arms, a girl whose language was his own. There had been women in Rome, when the GIs marched in as victors, women who threw their arms around his neck and kissed his mouth, smelling of hunger. They were bony, as if their bodies had hardened into a shell to protect the soft inner core. Pauline was soft all over, her curves pressing against him. It had been a revelation.

Now Morris pushed the unease out of his mind and took Pauline's hand. His was sweaty; hers was cool. He took a deep breath. "You want to get a bite?" he asked.

"I'm not hungry," Pauline said. "We got to talk. To decide."

Morris nodded. "Let's get coffee or something."

They went to the luncheonette three blocks from her house. The front of the store was busy with a steady stream of customers buying cigarettes and gum and chatting with the counterman. They took a booth in the back where it was quiet. An older couple, dressed up for dinner and maybe a movie, occupied one other booth.

Morris and Pauline ordered two Cokes. When the drinks came, neither touched them. Morris couldn't look at Pauline. He was staring at the elderly couple, watching them silently shovel the food into their mouths. They were eating the "special" advertised in the window— chicken soup, meatloaf, and mashed potatoes. Their forks clacked on the plates. The round-faced lady delicately wiped her mouth with a paper napkin.

"Morris," Pauline said, shaking his arm to get his attention. "What are we going to do?"

Morris still didn't want to look at her. He lit a cigarette. "Frank knows this doctor." Pauline's mouth dropped open. "You told Frank?"

"Well, yeah. He's my friend. I ask him advice."

"Who else did you tell?"

"Just Sam."

"God, Morris. I didn't know you had such a big mouth." Morris started to say something, but she waved him away. A little shudder visibly went through her body. She stirred the Coke with her straw. She was looking down and Morris could only see the top of her hair. "I don't want a doctor," she said. "At least not the kind Frank's talking about."

"Look at me," he said. But he had to tip her head up with his finger under her chin to look into her eyes. Her eyes were teary. "Please don't cry, Pauline."

"I can't help it. I'm scared. I don't want an ab . . . abortion."

"Well what do you want to do? Get married? I don't have the money to get married." Morris felt his voice getting louder. He looked around the luncheonette. The round-faced lady was staring at them. His face reddened. "Let's get out of here," he said.

They got up and Morris walked quickly to the cashier to pay. Pauline trailed behind. Outside, it was getting dark.

"Where are we going?" Pauline asked.

"The playground. It has benches."

—

They walked the two blocks in silence, their bodies carefully separate, not touching. Pauline was crying quietly. Morris handed her his handkerchief.

They settled on a bench, and Morris looked around the park. He felt as if the ghosts of all the kids who played punch ball and basketball and Johnny on the Pony were swirling around him. He remembered shooting marbles with Sam in the corner of a park just like this one when he was eleven years old. It seemed he could feel the cement of the ground on his bare knee as he kneeled and leaned in to shoot his favorite black-and-white aggie to beat Sam in the perpetual game that went on all summer long. There were kids there now, bent over their marbles, and across from them four boys were shooting baskets.

Morris took a deep breath. He couldn't stop thinking how she said her parents didn't like it when she went out with Frank. Frank had called her a little wild, a little bit of a party girl. Now Morris wondered if he had tried out her wildness before he offered her to Morris and switched his allegiance to Dolly, a voluptuous blonde who could barely carry on a conversation and snapped her gum incessantly.

Morris and Pauline first had sex in the rear seat of Frank's Chevy when they parked at the water at Sheepshead Bay. Morris laid her back, and she lifted her hips, splayed her legs. He entered her, slick and swift, and she only cried out briefly, and so softly he wasn't sure he heard her. He had wondered then if anyone had been there before him.

He had to ask. "I got to ask you something, Pauline. Don't be mad."

Pauline stared up at him. Her silky black eyelashes were stuck together in triangles from her tears. "What?" she said. "Ask me. I won't be mad."

He waited a minute, then said, "You sure this is my baby?"

He couldn't read her face. Her mouth was open slightly, her wet eyes staring into his. Her breath was ragged. "Why would you ask me that?"

He spoke very fast. "Because you went out with Frank. Because it's all too soon. Because I'm just too convenient."

She took a long time to answer and when she did her voice sounded dead. "It's your baby, Morris. But if you don't believe me, I can't force you to."

Pauline stood up and faced the monkey bars. "I used to climb those when I was a kid." She pointed to the swings. "My favorite swing was the one right in the middle. My mother used to push me on it and recite Robert Louis Stevenson's poem to me. Do you know it?"

Pauline kicked off her high heels, sat on the middle swing and started to pump, bending her knees. "Oh, how I love to go up in a swing, up in the sky so blue," she recited, in time to the rhythm of the swing. "Oh, I do think it the pleasantest thing that ever . . ."

"Stop it, Pauline. You'll hurt yourself."

". . . a child can do," she continued. "Up in the air and over the wall, till I can see so wide . . ." and on the upswing she jumped off and landed, graceful as a dancer, on the cement in front of Morris. "I knew I could still do it," she said.

"You're crazy," he said. He took her shoulders and turned her, shook her and her shoulders seem to collapse. "I'm sorry," he said and pulled her toward him. He smelled the shampoo on her hair. He felt words form in his mouth . . . *Okay, we'll get married, we'll do it.*

He couldn't say them.

He stepped back. "I thought you would want to graduate college."

There was a slight flicker on Pauline's face and Morris felt he had hit on something. "You're smart. You have one more year to graduate." The words rushed out. "Your parents would want you to graduate."

Pauline narrowed her eyes. The tears had dried now. "I can go to school after."

"No you can't. You'll be drowning in diapers and formula."

Pauline turned her back. "You don't want to take responsibility."

"I do. This is the responsible thing to do. Not getting married. I can't. I just can't. Look Pauline, I'll go with you, I'll hold your hand, I'll pay. No one has to know. . . ." He reached out and took her shoulder.

"No one except Frank and Sam and Sam's wife, whatever her name is. And probably your other sisters." She shook his arm off her.

In Morris's head something was hardening. *I don't want to get married now.* He started to pace. Why wouldn't she just agree? He hardly knew her. She hardly knew him. Why wouldn't she just say yes?

"You want me to let you off the hook, don't you? You want me to just go along with you. You're a selfish bastard. You don't care about me at all. I have a friend who almost died from an abortion."

"Well, she probably didn't go to a real doctor. Frank knows a real doctor who can do it. I can get the money from him."

"If I want to get rid of it, I can get the money from Frank myself. I don't need you."

"Come on Pauline. Don't be like that."

"Like what?" she asked. She stepped into her pumps and turned to leave the park.

He ran after her, grabbed her arm stopping her. "It'll be all right. You'll see, it will be all right."

She didn't answer and in truth he didn't know what he was saying. What will be all right? It will be all right to be married? To be a father? To make Pauline get an abortion? To be a cop? To throw it all up and buy a car and escape to California? He still had to choose.

Pauline was waiting. His hand grasped her elbow. Finally, she pulled away, and walked toward the gate of the chain link fence.

"Wait," Morris said. "I'll walk you home. Your parents won't like me anymore if I let you go home alone." He was trying to keep it light, make her feel better, make her believe he still cared about what her parents thought of him.

She turned, eyes blazing. "You think so? You think they like you now? My father told me last night I shouldn't see you anymore. He knows about your sister Ruby. My father says mental illness runs in families." Pauline walked quickly out of the playground and down the block. Morris stopped following her.

He felt smacked in the face. He watched Pauline walk away, her back straight, her black hair tumbling around her neck. Did she mean that? They were afraid of him because of his sister Ruby? Well it was too late for that if Pauline was pregnant with his baby. She turned the corner and disappeared. Then Morris walked back into the playground to sit on a wooden bench and think.

7

Ruby
1954

Last night it came again. They call it my dybbuk, but I call it The Voice. It starts with fullness in my head, the way it feels when I'm diving too long or swimming deep in the lake, and water gets in my ear, clogging it. Then there's a whisper, then a buzz. I slap the side of my head over and over, but the buzzing gets louder, so I sit up in bed. I swallow and swallow, the way the doctor told me to, but there is not the *pop* that I hope for. I am alone in bed and remember that Victor is in the city.

My bare feet are cold on the linoleum as I go to the window. Yes, I'm in the country where it's supposed to soothe me; but sometimes when The Voice comes, it's so fast that the only way I can still my heartbeat and my brain is to do what it tells me to do.

I try to calm myself. The beat when I sing and dance works. Swimming is good too—count, stroke, count, stroke. But the sky is so black, and I don't know what I will find in the dark if I go to the lake to swim, or dance on the green part of the lawn in front of the bungalows. Maybe the snakes that The Voice warns me about will be waiting in the grass.

Yesterday, before I went to bed, Jenny came to make sure I was okay. She said, "Victor told me he'll be back tomorrow afternoon." Right away The Voice said, *How does she know when he'll be back?* I narrowed my eyes and stared at her, but all I saw was innocent Jenny.

"And he knows I'm right next door, and Pauline is on the other side. You can come knock on our doors if you get nervous. You're sure you're all right?"

I grabbed her hand to stop her from patting my shoulder. "Yes, I'm fine."

"Why don't you turn the radio on for company?" She turned the knob on the RCA portable on the kitchen table and the room filled with static as she whirled the knob, and then settled, and I heard the music of the Coke commercial: *"Coke in the bottle . . . naturally."*

I snapped it off. "I will later." But now the song was in my head, over and over, The Voice singing it: *Coke in the bottle, naturally. Coke in the bottle, naturally.* I shook my head. No use. It didn't stop.

"You can go," I said. "I'm okay." *Coke in the bottle, naturally.* I breathed in and out, in and out. I had to speak quietly, or she would never leave. When I get excited, she hovers over me, watching, and The Voice says, *Watch out or she'll put you away.*

Pretty Jenny went to the door and stood with her hand on the knob. How did she keep her figure after miscarriages and her pregnancy with "the miracle of George?" *He's no miracle, just an ordinary kid like the others.* Sometimes The Voice is so calm and reasonable I think I'm listening to my own thoughts. But then The Voice gets snide and snaps nasty things at me. *And she is nothing but a whore.*

"Knock if you need me," Jenny said.

"Okay," I said. "I will." *Go, go, go. Gogo, gogo. Coke in the bottle. Natur-ally.*

But when she left, my head was full of warnings, instructions, orders. I was filled with urges that I felt I must follow, like an itch I had to scratch. The Voice said, *You are dirty. You must check yourself.* My fingers moved under the waistband of my shorts, my panties.

They hovered just above my slit, in my happy place. I balled my hand and rubbed while my heart pounded and whorls of feeling made me tremble, tremble, up, up until it was over. I began to cry and rushed to the bathroom to wash and wash, while The Voice hissed, *Dirty, filthy thing.*

I lay in bed and brought the Coke song back to drown out The Voice, and then I counted until I finally fell asleep. But in the middle of the night I awoke, my heart pounding, my ears stuffed, and then The Voice again: *It's time, it's time to check yourself.* I was barely awake but reached down inside my panties, stuck my fingers into my privates and they came away wet. In the bathroom the toilet paper showed brown smears. *Disgusting. You are so dirty, disgusting.*

Now I don't know what to do. I stand at the window. The sky is velvet black, and I can see the bright stars peeping at me between the branches of the trees. *You stink, you stink, you stink.* I smell my skin; I'm afraid to breathe. Something rotten is inside me. I breathe through my mouth. *Outside, go outside.*

Down the porch, the pebbles on the path cut into my feet, the slippery grass feels dewy, cool. I lie in the circle of the lawn and stare at the starry sky. There are no lights in any of the bungalows. The stars are moving overhead. I see faces, dogs, snakes, an eye. I see words. *Eye. Fly. Die.* My eyes are heavy, my throat dry. I pluck at the grass, press handfuls of it to my nose and breathe the green smell. *Count. One two three four in and out breathe one two three four breathe. One two three four in and out breathe.*

When I awake the sun is hot on my face, and I sit up and stretch. I remember why I am on the grass.

Mike Ratner is sitting on the porch of his bungalow sipping a mug of coffee. He is big, and his white T-shirt stretches over a large stomach. "Taking a snooze?" he asks.

"It's hot inside." My head is clogged again. *You stink, you stink, you stink. See if it's blood inside you. Old blood rots inside you. Old blood.* I want to touch myself again to see if I am dirty down there. My hand drifts down, down. I grab one hand and hold it with the other. I can't touch myself. Mike is looking. I breathe through my mouth so as not to pollute my nostrils.

"Funny place for a campout."

"Who you talking to?" Mike's wife Emily comes onto the porch. She stares at me. "Oh, her."

I don't like Emily. She doesn't like me either. Last week I was in a sing-y mood. I was wearing my new purple bikini and halter top, and I was waltzing through the colony singing Paul Anka's "Put Your Head on My Shoulder," which was my background song all that day, when I spotted Mike sitting on his porch reading the paper. He is out of work and always sits on his porch. I could see Jenny and Pauline watching me, but I didn't care. I felt like dancing. I grabbed his hand and pulled him down the steps. He was laughing in embarrassment, looking behind him, but he followed me down the stairs and we danced on the grass while I crooned in his ear, bumping and grinding my hips.

"Mike, what the hell are you doing?" Emily came out, stood, hands on hips, frown on her face.

"Oh, don't be such a party-pooper," I said. "We're only dancing." But Mike pulled away and went back up the stairs.

"Who do you think you are?" Emily said to me. "Dancing half naked in that disgusting bathing suit. Flaunting yourself. I could have you arrested."

"Have me arrested? I'll have my brother Morris arrest you, you stupid bitch."

Emily pushed the screen door open and shoved Mike into the bungalow. I could hear her loud voice all the way outside. "You stay away . . . she's crazy, don't you know that?" I couldn't hear the rest of the conversation, but I could imagine it. People have called me crazy my whole life.

Pauline came over and patted my back. "It's all right. Dancing's good. I like to dance too." We polkaed around the lawn laughing. I love Pauline. She doesn't always shake her finger at me the way Jenny and Irene do.

Jenny used to be my favorite. I chose her when we were children, instead of Irene—even though Jenny was almost five years younger— to sleep in my bed with me, listen to my stories, be the one I brought my presents to. She looked up to me then, but no more. Now I don't like the way she looks at me. And I don't like the way she looks at Victor. The Voice says, *Watch her, the bitch, the whore. Watch out for her.*

I go up on the porch of Pauline and Morris's bungalow and knock on the door. She's feeding cereal to her two kids. I miss my kids as babies, even the mess on the table and the Cheerios under the chairs. Joseph and Sarah are big now—eleven and nine—and they're at sleep-away camp for a month. In their baby days, I was in and out of the hospital, wires attached to my brain. I don't remember. I don't remember so much of that time. The Voice says, *There is a hole in your head, and the memories drain out.*

"You're not dressed yet?" Pauline asks.

I look down at my nightgown, wet and clinging. "Can I have some coffee?"

"Sure." Pauline pours me a cup, brings me her bathrobe and slips it around my shoulders. I shrug it off, afraid if I wear it I will ruin it with my smells.

I touch the silky black hair on four-year-old Linda's head and cup her chin. "I love you," I croon, waiting for her to say *I love you* back. But she doesn't. She picks up Cheerios from her bowl and pops them into her mouth, and then she flips her head to push my hand away. *She smells you; you stink.*

"Pauline," I say, "it's starting." Pauline gets still when I speak; I can see she's listening, and I like that.

"The Voice?" I nod. "Did you take your medication?"

I shake my head. "It makes me dopey."

"You can stay with me today . . . Victor will be back this afternoon."

"I'm all right," I say. "I don't need Victor." The Voice does not like it when I call on Victor. The Voice gets loud, vicious, spits words: *chicken, whore, pissant, wimp.* I jump up to leave. "I'll get dressed now."

"Come right back," Pauline says. "Put on your suit. We can go for a swim."

I nod. The words jumble in my head. *Go for a swim, suit on. Swim, swim, put on suit can go on off suit swim.*

The smell follows me. In the bungalow I strip, shower. I scrub my skin with soap, then, dripping wet, run to the kitchen, take butter and dried herbs, tarragon and basil, make a paste and bring it back into the bathroom with me. I rub it on my skin and all over my private parts, but the smell is there anyway.

I should have gone to the ritual bath, to the *mikvah*: I told Jenny and Pauline that, but Jenny said, "Why are you getting so religious all of a sudden?" and Pauline said, "That's for the old country. We don't do that anymore." But they are wrong. The Voice says: *You need to do that.* I start to count. *You have to have seven clean days before you go to the mikvah, and then after that you can be with Victor.* I did not have seven clean days. I keep bleeding little bits of brown on my panties and the toilet paper. I am *niddah*, unclean. I smell.

The Voice tells me, *Swim far, far. Don't come back.* I put on my violet bathing suit over the mash of butter and herbs and walk down the hill to the lake.

Are people calling my name? I look around. No one is there.

I step into the lake, squishing toes through the muddy bottom. Green weeds and algae and brown dirt swirl around my feet. *Swim.* I strike off, charge my arms forward. The lake water is soft, silky, smells fresh, cold. I reach the raft, climb the ladder and stand arms high above my head looking back to the beach. No one is at the lakefront, but at the top of the hill are two figures, waving and shouting at me. I turn my back on them, strip off my suit and dive naked into the black cold water. Then I stroke for a long time until my arms ache.

"Ruby!" They are calling me, running down the hill. I stop and turn. *Watch out, they are getting the rowboat! They'll stop you.* I turn and stroke, pull, stroke, pull. My eyes are open, I see shadows below me. Fish? Turtles? Seaweed? The water swirls over my skin, and in my openings down there, cleaning me. *That's right, clean all your openings.* I open my mouth. I swish and spit like a whale. Then I take the water and I swallow.

I'm tired, but I shouldn't stop. I lie on my back. I can feel my middle collapsing, sinking. I want to float down, down. I could drift forever.

"Ruby, Ruby."

I open my mouth and swallow, open it swallow again, sink down, snort, try to get my breath, gag, flail, pump my arms. *Too late now.*

But it isn't. Jenny is in the water. Her hands grab me, tugging my hair. Pauline pulls me, scraping me over the side of a rowboat. Jenny climbs in beside me, panting, crying. I lie in the bottom, coughing, spitting, sputtering. Jenny rows sobbing, and Pauline cradles my head, crooning, "*It will be all right, itwillbeallright.*"

Jenny gives me pills, but I press my lips together, clench my teeth, shake my head. She persists. "All right," I say. *Stupid, stupid. Don't take them, poison, watch out for them.* But it's too late. I swallow.

I drift in and out of a deep pool. I dream of water, I dream of baby Sarah swimming with me, and I get tired and let her go in the lake, thinking I will grab her before she sinks, but I watch her float below me, waving chubby arms, white skin shining in the water. I try but she is too far below me and I can't reach her. I sit up, gasp for breath. The sun slashes lines on the wall. I squint. I can't breathe in the heat of the room. Sweat slips down the side of my face, under my arms.

There are voices in the other room. *Listen.* The voices are Victor's, Jenny's. But I can't make sense out of what I hear. *Listen, listen.*

I slip out of bed, dizzy, weaving. The Voice says, *Quiet now. Quiet. Make yourself small, hunch over so they can't see, slide along the wall, peek around the corner. What is that jumble of arms and legs? Don't look, don't look. You have to hide, they can't see you, get back to the bedroom, jump under the covers! Lie like a snail with covers over your head, eyes scrunched shut so you don't see what you have seen.* What did I see?

The bedclothes cover me. I am breathing my stink, but I must hide. *You are so stupid, you smelly bitch, you know what you saw. Shame. Their shame, your shame. Never tell. Never tell anyone what you saw. Swear, you will never tell.*

I swear I will go to my grave and never tell another soul.

8

Jenny
1954

Jenny called Victor to come up to the lake the afternoon Ruby almost drowned. She waited for him in Ruby's bungalow, while Ruby lay in her bedroom, twitching and mumbling in her sleep.

When Jenny heard the car drive up and stop on the gravel in front of the porch, she tiptoed out, making sure the screen door closed quiet on its latch. Without thinking she ran straight into Victor's arms.

He patted her back. "What happened? Tell me again."

"I don't know if she was trying to drown herself or just swam too far," Jenny whispered. "Pauline saw her go down to the water, and Irene stayed with the kids while we went down to the lake. She was on the raft and next thing we saw, she'd pulled off her swimsuit and was swimming as far out to the middle of the lake as she could get. By the time we rowed out, she'd disappeared underwater. Oh, Victor, I was so terrified. I dove in and searched underwater until I saw her hair. Thank God for her hair. I pulled her out by her hair."

Jenny closed her eyes. She could see the murky water, the weedy bottom of the lake and the white arms of her sister, with her red hair waving behind her.

"When we pulled her out, she was coughing and gasping so I knew she would be all right. When we got her to the shore, Pauline had to run up to the bungalow for a towel to cover her. She was stark naked. We got her up here and I made her take the Valium, even though she didn't want to, and then I called you. She's dozing in the bedroom."

They went inside together and sat side by side in the kitchen drinking sweet iced tea. They were talking in whispers, trying to figure out what to do with Ruby.

"I don't know what to do anymore," Victor said.

Jenny drew lines on the frost of the iced tea glass. "What about the ECT? It helped before. Couldn't you do it again?"

He shrugged. "I don't know. I actually read about a new chemical treatment—a drug called lithium; it's used in Europe, but it's not approved here. It's sort of a poison."

Jenny shuddered. *Horrible*, she thought. *Poison or shock.*

Victor closed his eyes, leaned back. "Everywhere is a dead end."

Victor was unshaven. He had a heavy beard, and Jenny wished she could touch his cheek, rub her hand against the stubble. She wondered if he used an electric shaver like her husband, Harry, or a razor, and wished she knew. He seemed to sense her looking at him, and he took her hand and held it loosely in both of his. A jolt went through her; goose bumps shivered up her arm at the thought of touching his face. It was such an old longing. It shocked her that it had emerged again.

Victor stood up, walked to the window, came back and sat down again. Jenny's eyes followed his every movement. "I remember how you and your mother came to our apartment after Joseph and Sarah were born. You came every night to help me with the diapers and the laundry and the cooking. And you were so kind and gentle with the children, and I didn't know what to do with them. I wanted you so much, and you were so far away."

"I would have done anything for you," Jenny whispered.

Victor put his hand under her chin, raised her face and leaned in to kiss her mouth. They kissed for a long time, and then Victor pulled back saying, "We can't do this."

Jenny wanted to. She leaned over to kiss him again and heard a noise. She looked up and there was Ruby, standing unsteadily in the doorway of the bedroom. Her eyes were bleary, her long red hair matted like a bird's nest. She looked like she was in a stupor, and before either Jenny or Victor could say anything she went back into the bedroom. Jenny thought, *I don't think she saw us. She can't have seen us.*

"You better go back to your bungalow," Victor said. Reluctant, Jenny left with a longing for Victor mixed with a deep, sick feeling that she recognized as shame.

Harry would be coming up tonight. Handsome Harry, whom she had met right after the war, whom she'd spotted at a party at a friend's house because at six foot two, he towered over almost everyone else. They'd married five months later because she liked him, because it was time for her to marry, because she could never have the man she wanted, and she had to move on with her life. But she had always wanted Victor, and now she knew that Victor wanted her too. That changed everything.

The next morning Victor took Ruby back to the city to see her doctor. He didn't say good-bye to anyone. The summer season ended a week later, and Ruby was hospitalized.

Jenny did not see Victor again until she visited Ruby in the hospital a week after she returned to the city. It was raining hard. She took the crosstown bus from the upper West Side to Lexington Avenue and then walked under her umbrella to Lenox Hill Hospital. When she got to the door, she took her time, shaking the raindrops off her umbrella, closing it carefully, wiping her feet so she didn't slip on the marble floors in the lobby.

She tried to ignore her extreme nervousness when she entered the hospital, wondering how Ruby would greet her, what it would be like to see Victor again. She needn't have worried about Ruby, who looked like an automaton, walking stiffly through the halls, eyes focused straight ahead. She couldn't carry on a conversation. Irene had told Jenny that when she was there, Ruby was shuffling through the halls of the psychiatric ward with her hospital gown open and no underwear. After that the psychiatrist upped her medication significantly, which explained her stupor.

Nor did Victor look Jenny in the eye, and he barely spoke to her. She thought that Victor almost breathed with relief when she walked out the room. But she didn't leave the hospital. She waited just inside the front door watching the cars drive through big puddles, their windshield wipers rhythmically swiping side to side, their headlights reflecting in the street. Finally, she saw Victor come out of the elevator and walk toward her.

"I thought you left," he said.

"I waited for you."

Outside they simultaneously opened their umbrellas and began walking side by side, toward Madison Avenue.

"How is she doing?" Jenny asked.

"She's gone from being manic to being depressed. They may do ECT again, or maybe just try medication. They're debating."

Jenny's mind was racing. All she could think about was asking the one question that had been on her mind from that day in August when she had last seen Victor. Do you want me as much as I want you? She could not bring herself to ask. Instead she said, "Let's go for coffee."

They ducked into a small café, took a table and sat silently, waiting for the waitress to bring their drinks.

Victor said, "I don't think Ruby knows."

Her heart hammering, Jenny asked, "Knows what?"

"That I love you."

Jenny closed her eyes, nodded, and reached across the table to take Victor's hand. They sat like that for a long time.

Later that day they found a hotel room. What she remembered afterward was hot, wet kisses, frantic hands ripping, unbuttoning clothing, stumbling together to the bed, as if they were famished. An unstoppable urgency had overtaken them, and they grunted, making soft animal sounds. It was fast, furious lovemaking, and they were finished almost before it registered in her head what they were doing.

In the next weeks, while Ruby was hospitalized, they kept on meeting. They found out-of-the-way motel rooms in Connecticut and New Jersey where they could have a quick lunch in a nearby diner and then slip into the room and out of their clothes to make hasty love. Afterward they scurried to their respective cars and back to their ordinary lives. The smell of sex followed Jenny, and she would race into the shower, washing and washing herself, all the while regretting that she couldn't hold onto the tangible fragrance of Victor's aftershave. She would start dinner for Harry and two-year-old George, and sometimes Harry came home early and nuzzled her neck, whispering he couldn't wait until George went to bed. And later Jenny made love again, only with Harry this time, and it was long and leisurely, and even though she had always enjoyed lovemaking with Harry, and he was a sure and considerate lover, she found her mind drifting to Victor, imagining she was with him.

Jenny hated her life. Victor was in her mind, a constant thrum in her head. Below and under everything she did was the thought of him. She felt jumpy. She went from euphoria to black shame.

When Ruby came home from the hospital in early October, Bessie called Jenny to be at the apartment and help settle Ruby. It was the last thing Jenny wanted to do, but she showed up anyway. She busied herself in the kitchen, putting the groceries she'd bought into the cupboards and refrigerator. She took Ruby's suitcase and unpacked it, sorting out the dirty clothes from the clean ones. Did she imagine it, or did Ruby's gaze follow her around the apartment as she did these chores? Did her eyes dart from Victor to Jenny as they moved around the room, avoiding each other? Irene came over in the afternoon, and Jenny left an hour later, feeling that Irene, too, was watching.

Jenny didn't see Ruby or Victor for the next two weeks except at dinner on Friday night at her parents' where the family had gathered to welcome Ruby back. The following Monday, Irene barreled into Jenny's apartment, slammed her purse on the dining room table and said, "This has to stop."

"What are you talking about?"

"You. Victor. Whatever is going on has to stop."

Jenny wanted to say, *I don't know what you're talking about*, and she started to speak the words, but mid-sentence she couldn't go on. She sat at the table and stared straight ahead. "How did you know?"

"It doesn't take a genius. All you have to do is look at the two of you together. You don't talk to him, you avoid each other, but you can't help looking at him."

Jenny wondered if Irene had any sympathy at all for her. Why should she? Everyone thought she lived a perfect life, with perfect Harry and a perfect son. Jenny took a deep breath. "I don't know what to do," she said.

"What do you mean you don't know what to do? End it."

"It's not so easy." Jenny walked to the sideboard and looked at the photographs crowding the top. There was the one of Irene and Sam's wedding. Everyone was in it except Ruby; that was the day Ruby had her first paralyzing depression. But then there was another picture of Ruby in a satin wedding gown with the skirt draped in a perfect circle at her feet; Victor stood behind her, holding her hand. Jenny thought how beautiful Ruby had been when she was young, and how like a movie star she'd looked.

Jenny whispered, "It's like she's owned me all my life. . . . I was always the one to take care of her. When she needed me, I came. But I can't do it anymore. I just can't."

"You don't have to. I understand a lot more than you give me credit for."

Jenny stared at Irene. She'd always thought Irene was so conventional, even though she was an artist. She was first a housewife and mother. She and Sam had been a couple since they were children. Jenny was sure Irene had never thought about another man.

Irene was still talking. "I understand that you think you're in love with Victor, but it doesn't matter. You have to end it. If you keep it up it will ruin everything—the whole family."

"It has nothing to do with the family," Jenny said.

"It has everything to do with the family." Unexpectedly Irene put her arms around her sister and held her. "Oh Jenny, I'm so sorry. You don't have to take care of Ruby, but you do have to stop seeing Victor. You won't be able to hide it much longer. Ruby's weirdly intuitive, you know."

"Do you think she knows?"

"With Ruby it's hard to tell. She's always saying things."

"Like what?"

"Like the other day she said to me, 'You never were my friend, Irene. Jenny used to be my best friend in the family, but now I love Pauline better.'" Irene waited, but there was no response. "She's your sister, Jenny. You can't betray her like this. . . . You're married to the best man in the world. Victor doesn't hold a candle to him. If you aren't careful, Harry will find out. Maybe he knows already."

"No. I don't think he does." Jenny closed her eyes and thought of the way Harry acted around her. He was so loving, kissing her and holding her and telling her that she was his Jenny. "No. I don't think he suspects anything." Jenny looked at Irene. "You don't like Victor much, do you?"

Irene shrugged. "Like I said, he doesn't hold a candle to Harry. Victor takes care of Victor."

"How can you say that? He suffered so much . . . he lost his first wife to cancer and then his whole family to the Nazis, and then he gets married again and has to take care of our crazy sister and their kids!"

"Ruby is sick, not crazy! And now he's deserting her for you, just like he left his sick first wife so he could save his skin and come to America."

"What are you talking about? She died before he came."

Irene looked away. "I don't think so. She was dying, but she wasn't dead."

Jenny was stunned. "That can't be true. How do you know that?"

"I know. I know because Bubbie Ida told me. When they made the *shidduch,* he had to prove he wasn't still married. He showed them a letter from his parents telling him that his wife had died, and it was dated after he came to America. He said his wife told him to leave and save himself—but even if she did, I know I would never have left Sam or the rest of you to save myself. Never. And neither would Mama or Papa, or Bubbie. Harry would never leave you."

Jenny sat down hard on the sofa. *Was that true? Would she leave Harry, or Harry leave her? How do any of us know what we would do when we are desperate?*

"And then," Irene was still talking. "He bargained really hard with Papa. He only agreed to marry Ruby if he got half of the store. That's why Morris never went to work there. He told Sam he'd never be more than a clerk. . . . So, no. I don't feel sorry for Victor, and I don't like him very much. He knew exactly what he was getting into."

Jenny did not know what to think. She was exhausted. All she wanted now was for Irene to go away, so she could sort out what she had been told. She said what Irene wanted to hear. "I will stop. I don't know how, but I will."

—

It was almost as if Ruby did it for her. A few days after Irene's visit to Jenny, Ruby mixed up her new pills and when eleven-year-old Joseph came home from school, he found his mother lying on her bed barely breathing. Afterward, Ruby was hospitalized again for two weeks, just to straighten out the medication. She insisted it had been a mistake, and everyone wanted to believe her.

Jenny and Victor knew it had to be over between them. They met one last time in the same coffee shop where they had started their brief affair. Jenny could not bring herself to ask Victor about any of the things Irene had told her, but she found that she was looking at him differently now, and when they agreed to break off their relationship, it was almost a relief.

The hardest part was going on as if nothing had happened. Jenny stayed away from Victor except in large family groups, but she worried that everyone would notice that her relationship with Ruby was strained. The weight of her secret was like a stone.

Then an odd thing happened. Shortly after Ruby came home from the hospital that second time, she asked Jenny to call her every day to make sure she was all right. If Jenny didn't call her, she called Jenny. "Just checking in," she would say. "I'm feeling good today." Or, "I'm feeling down, Jenny. Can you visit me today or tomorrow?" And sometimes she would say, "I have a secret to tell you," but when Jenny came, she said she forgot what it was.

And gradually Jenny became her caretaker again, as she had been when they were young and lived at home. She watched out for Ruby's ups and downs, watched for her outbursts and tried to avoid them. She saw her manipulate and torment Victor and the children with her histrionics. Jenny soothed her when she flew off the handle, took her to the doctor, encouraged her when she was depressed. Ruby again filled in the spaces of Jenny's life.

Victor and Jenny circled around each other, hardly speaking, paralyzed to change things. And their memories—Ruby's and Victor's and Jenny's—remained, filling the silences with secrets that they could not share with each other. But maybe that didn't matter. Maybe their secrets were the same.

9

Faye

1959

When Bubbie Ida died at age eighty-three, Faye was more devastated than she had been when her father died the year before. All through her grandmother's long slow decline, Faye had come directly home from her teaching job in the Bronx to help Bessie nurse Bubbie Ida, to watch her skin yellow and her flesh melt away from the cancer that spread from breast to liver. It was devastating to watch her suffer.

Knowing that she had come to her last days, Bubbie Ida called Faye to her side and gave her an envelope. When Faye opened it, the gold necklace her grandmother had treasured her whole life spilled out into her hand.

"It came with me from over there. I want for you to have it, Faye . . . Feige."

Faye put the necklace on, felt it warm against her skin. "I'll wear it always," she said and leaned over to kiss her grandmother. Bubbie Ida put her calloused hand against Faye's cheek. Faye sat with her while she slept.

—

A few weeks after they buried Bubbie Ida, Faye announced to her family that she had decided to move to the Bronx to be near her school. She had been thinking about it for a long time.

Each morning, after she moved into her apartment on Pelham Parkway, she took a ten-minute bus ride and then walked four blocks to her school, past Ruben's Grocery, Kaplan's Fruit and Vegetable Emporium, Bardeen's Butcher. There were dress shops and pharmacies, candy stores, and bakeries. It reminded her of her neighborhood in Brooklyn, but this felt different. It was the Bronx. It was hers.

She met Angelo Rosario Benedetto a few months after she moved. Every morning on her way to work she stopped to buy an almond horn to go with her brown bag sandwich lunch. The store name was lettered in fancy gold leaf: Angelo's Italian Bakery. The window was filled with tarts, cream-filled cannoli, cheesecake. She loved the smell of yeast and vanilla and sugar. It reminded her of her childhood, when Bubbie Ida made mandelbrot or apple strudel.

One day, after she'd been coming into the bakery for a while, the owner, Angelo, came out of the back holding a white paper bag with a tissue wrapped pastry.

"I know you like these," he said. He was wearing all whites—T-shirt, pants, sneakers—and as he handed her the bag, he lifted himself up and down on his toes, as if to make himself taller.

Angelo was thirty-nine, she found out later, five feet nine, with a black moustache and a head of curly black hair. Faye thought he was very handsome.

She tried to think of something clever to say, but all that came out was, "Thank you. These are the best almond horns I've ever tasted."

Each day Angelo came out from the back carrying the white paper bag, and they made small talk, and after a few weeks, Angelo asked Faye to go out with him. He lived in New Rochelle, not too far from her, and he said he'd pick her up Saturday night at seven and they would go to the Loew's Paradise Theater.

As she walked toward school, she felt emancipated. She was going out with Angelo, an Italian Catholic. It seemed brave. Independent. Freedom, she decided, was a heady thing.

They began to go out every weekend. They talked incessantly, about where they'd gone to school, foods they liked, their favorite baseball teams. They both loved movies, and in the beginning, they went to the Paradise on Saturday night and then out for coffee where they would dissect what they had seen. They both liked *Ben Hur* and *North by Northwest*. They talked about the Catholic Church after watching *The Nun's Story*, with Audrey Hepburn, and they both cried during *The Diary of Anne Frank*. It made Faye very happy that Angelo had such tender emotions and was willing to show them to her. She watched him in the movie theater when they saw *Some Like It Hot*, watched his belly move as he laughed out loud. When he saw her watching him, he took her hand and squeezed it.

After a few dates they went out for dinner at Mario's, on Westchester Avenue, where she ordered chicken Parmesan, feeling very daring because she had never eaten cheese with chicken. Angelo ordered them each a glass of Chianti wine. Faye felt her cheeks redden with each sip.

"I'm a cheap drunk," she said.

"Nah," Angelo said. "You're just not used to it."

For dessert she ordered Italian cheesecake, but Angelo said it was not as good as the one he sold at the bakery.

"It's different from Jewish cheesecake," Faye said. "This is more lemony and fluffier."

"Yeah. It don't taste the same because we use ricotta cheese. Jewish cake uses cream cheese."

Faye nodded. Her mother put a whole brick of Philadelphia cream cheese in her yellow mixing bowl and beat it hard so that the flesh on her upper arms swung back and forth with the effort. "My mother loves to bake," she said. "My grandmother made all the desserts for a catering company when she was young, and she taught my mother. That's how she supported them when they came here."

"Oh yeah? I'd like to meet her. We could compare recipes," Angelo said. Faye said nothing, not wanting to tell him that Bubbie Ida was dead, and then wondering how she would introduce Angelo to her Jewish mother.

After a while he took her ballroom dancing at Roseland. She bought patent leather Cuban heel shoes so she would not be as tall as Angelo, and a navy-blue silk dress with a swing skirt. She had decided against a red dress, thinking it was too garish for her, but when she looked at herself in the mirror she wondered if she had made a mistake. Maybe red would have set off her curly brown hair and eyes. As always, she wished she looked more like her sister Ruby with her dramatic red hair, or Jenny and Irene who were petite and small breasted. Instead, at five foot six, she had the ample chest of her Bubbie Ida and the plain brown hair of her mother. But the navy blue was slimming, she decided, and it showed less cleavage of her breasts than the red dress. When Angelo picked her up, he smiled and said, "You look great!"

She was not a very good dancer, but somehow Angelo was so light on his feet and propelled her around the floor so easily, she felt graceful.

"You dance like Fred Astaire. I never knew I could like dancing," Faye said, breathless, when they stopped for a Coke.

"What's not to like?"

"I always feel awkward. I never was a natural."

"That don't matter," Angelo said. "Just follow me, that's all you have to do." Faye tried not to wince at his grammatical slips. If he tolerated her lack of grace dancing, then she would not bother about his using "don't" instead of "doesn't."

One Saturday afternoon, after they'd been dating for four months, she went with him to six o'clock Mass at St. Gabriel Parish.

They sat in one of the back pews. He'd asked her to wear a hat, but she didn't have one. She found a green-and-yellow plaid silk scarf, which she tied around her hair. She'd seen a lot of teenage girls going to Mass on Sunday with scarves on their heads.

As she sat and listened to the solemnity of the Latin Mass, the splendor of the music, she was transported. She'd never had a connection to religion. On the Jewish High Holidays, she went to the little neighborhood synagogue, a storefront where the women sat on one side with a white curtain that separated them from the men. She went because her mother asked her to. Bessie was fervent in her prayers, and when Faye stood next to her in the women's section of the synagogue, her mother would sometimes weep, especially during Yizkor, the prayer for remembrance of the dead. During the community confessional on Yom Kippur, she struck her chest hard for each sin recited, as if she herself had committed each offense against God. At the end of the day of fasting and prayer she said she felt renewed. Bubbie Ida did not go to the synagogue with Bessie on Rosh Hashana or Yom Kippur, and when Faye asked her why, she simply said, "What I want to say to God, I do in private." Faye thought Bubbie Ida didn't really believe in God. Faye didn't know what she herself believed.

The church felt very different from the synagogue. She saw small wooden booths on the sides of the cathedral, which she knew were confessionals. This was not the first time she'd been to church. She'd gone into the Holy Trinity Roman Catholic Church in Brooklyn with her Irish friend, Mary Alice, while she said confession. As she watched, she imagined kneeling on the side of the confessional, talking to a disembodied voice: *Forgive me, Father, for I have sinned.* She blushed as she thought the words. Mary Alice, who lived down the block from her, had told her all about it. She had said that Faye should cross herself and put holy water on her forehead, but Faye refused, thinking at the time that it was a sacrilege. She wondered what it would be like to be forgiven for everything bad you ever did. Was that what her mother felt at the end of Yom Kippur?

Her mind wandered even as the music and the Latin swirled in her head. Her mother never approved of her friendship with Mary Alice. She didn't say why, but Faye thought it was because she was Catholic. For some reason her mother didn't like Catholics.

What did Faye know about Catholics? They didn't eat meat on Friday. Mary Alice called that a fast day. They couldn't divorce. They had to do what the Pope said. There were even some movies they weren't supposed to see and books they weren't allowed to read. The Virgin Mary was very important to them. They prayed to a lot of saints. Faye watched as Angelo filed up the long aisle to take Holy Communion from the priest. She saw him put out his tongue and the priest placed a wafer on it. What does it taste like? The body of Christ. She shivered with the strangeness. Could she ask what it tasted like? Faye looked around the cathedral at the alcoves on the sides. Statues of saints, hands outstretched, were surrounded by candles and flowers. She had seen people kneeling and crossing themselves in front of the statues. Did they think the statues were Gods?

When they came out of the church, they stood on the steps and Angelo lit a cigarette and blew out a stream of smoke. Faye took off the scarf and let her curly hair loose around her face. The street in front of the church teemed with Saturday evening foot traffic. Faye supposed people thought she was a Catholic coming out of Mass. It made her feel odd.

"What did you think?" Angelo asked.

Inside the church Faye had a million questions. Now she hesitated and finally said, "It felt strange."

He nodded. "I would probably feel funny in a synagogue," he said.

"You're not kidding." They laughed.

He had invited her back to his house afterward for spaghetti and what he called gravy, which she called sauce. It was the first time she'd been to his house, a small ranch on Webster Avenue. The first thing she noticed—hanging in the front hall—was a picture of the Virgin Mary holding the baby Jesus in her arms. They had huge haloes around their heads. Over the living room sofa was a large cross and a picture of Jesus. Angelo noticed her staring. "I keep meaning to redecorate. My mother was very religious."

They had supper in the dining room with Chianti wine, and Angelo put a Frank Sinatra album on the record player. That was the night that they finally made love.

He had been coming to her apartment after their dates, and they would sit on her beige sofa, kissing and making out for a long time. Faye liked the feel of his arms around her, his mouth soft, the push of his bristly mustache against her lips. She thought she could go on kissing forever, but Angelo didn't. That night, in his house, his kisses became more insistent. He opened his mouth, she felt his tongue, his hands wandered over her body, up under her sweater. She had goose bumps on her arms.

"Come on, Faye. We're not kids you know." He kissed her neck, pulled her bra strap down so her breast came free; he stroked her nipple. She felt her insides spasm.

Faye was nervous, but she nodded. She had not dated much in school, and after college, when she was twenty-four, she'd had a brief, uninspiring affair and lost her virginity to a boy named Lenny, whom she thought she might be able to love. It was fast and unsatisfying, and after three or four more dates he stopped calling. "I don't think I'm very good at this," she whispered, and she told Angelo about Lenny.

She focused on Angelo's eyes, brown, thick-lashed, the pupils black. "It'll be okay," he said. "You'll see. You'll like it."

And she did. Not at first, but a few weeks later, when they were used to each other, when she wasn't afraid of the starkness of his uncircumcised penis, his hairy chest. The first time she had an orgasm she tried to keep quiet, kept her lips pressed together, but found herself saying, "Oh, oh, oh," loud and breathy.

Afterward they laughed at her surprise. "I never knew," she said.

He looked at her curiously. "Don't you ever—you know—touch yourself?"

Faye blushed. "Yes, but it isn't like that."

"No." Angelo laughed. "That was the real thing." He lit up a cigarette and leaned back against the pillow blowing thin streams of smoke. "I told you you'd like it."

She nestled her cheek against his chest, felt the softness of his breathing, stroked the curly hairs. "I do," she whispered. "I do like it." *I like you. No*, she thought, with a sense of wonder, *I love you*.

Angelo turned to face her, leaning on his elbow. "This is nice," he said. "I was supposed to get married about eight years ago, but Theresa—that was her name—decided she didn't want to marry a baker. Not good enough for her or something."

"She must have been crazy," Faye said.

Angelo smiled and lay back against the pillow. "Now I'm glad it didn't work out."

"Me too. You smell nice," she said and inhaled a mix of tobacco, vanilla, and sugar.

He always wore a condom. One time when they were lying in her bedroom, she said, "I thought Catholics don't believe in birth control."

"They don't. But we're not married, and I don't do all the stuff the Church says anyhow."

Faye nodded. Would it be different if they were married, she wondered? Would he wear a condom then or want her to get pregnant? She pulled the blanket up to her neck and closed her eyes.

"Why do you always do that?" Angelo asked.

"Do what?"

"Cover yourself right up afterward. It's like you're embarrassed or something."

"I don't know—maybe I am," Faye mumbled.

"Why? You're beautiful."

Faye made a face. She turned her head and stared at the window where just last week she had put up venetian blinds and green café curtains to match her bedspread. She liked the way they looked.

"What, you don't believe me?"

"I'm not beautiful. I'm fat, my nose is too big. . . ."

Angelo stripped the blanket off and pulled her up. He stood her in front of the mirror, which hung over the dresser. "Look at yourself." First, she squeezed her eyes shut in embarrassment. Then she looked. She was almost as tall as Angelo, with a long neck, and full breasts and hips. She was curvy, but—maybe not fat. Her brown hair waved down her back, loose from its clips. In the mirror she caught Angelo's eye.

He kissed her neck. "You're not fat. You're beautiful." Angelo said. "Like Jane Mansfield or Sophia Loren. I love the way you look." He turned her and took her face in his hands. "I love you. I want to marry you."

Faye could hardly breathe. But she didn't hesitate. She just said, "Yes." And then, a sense of panic flooded her, and she thought, *What am I doing?*

She went to tell her mother the next day, a Sunday. Instead of taking the bus, she walked from the subway, thinking. She could hear her dead father on his soapbox. Do you know what they did? They murdered us, that's what they did. She could argue: It wasn't Angelo. It was the Germans, not the Italians. But he would say it was the Italians. The Italians and the Poles and the French and the Dutch.

And she knew all the facts. Hadn't she just wept through the movie *Anne Frank*? She knew why the State of Israel was established. There had been endless conversations about it at her mother's house, at Morris's house. Her own sister, Ruby, had married a refugee from Hitler's Germany. Faye also knew that the Nazis murdered all her father's relatives in Poland. She had seen pictures of the survivors, skeletal wraiths, in the concentration camps.

As she rounded the corner to her mother's apartment building, she grew more anxious. She didn't know how to tell her mother.

She found Bessie, in the kitchen rolling out pie dough. There was flour on the table, on her face.

She kissed her mother's cheek and sat at the table. "Who are you baking for?"

"You," Bessie said. "I'm making you pie. You always like my pie."

"I like it too much," Faye said. "That's the trouble." She almost said "that's why I'm fat," but then she remembered how she had stood naked, looking at herself in the bedroom mirror through Angelo's eyes, how he thought her beautiful. She took a deep breath. "Ma, I'm getting married."

Bessie paused, rolling pin in midair. Once, Faye knew, she had been so pretty. Now she looked tired, older than her sixty-four years. Her hair was graying; her eyes were faded. Faye thought her mother missed Abe and Bubbie Ida very much. Her mother's voice was full of surprise, even wonder. "Who? Who are you marrying?"

Faye said his name slowly. "Angelo Benedetto."

Bessie put the rolling pin down. "Angelo," she said carefully. "What kind of name is that?"

"It's an Italian name."

"So, what? You're going to marry an Italian now?"

"Yes. I'm going to marry an Italian Catholic." Her mother's mouth looked bloodless. She sat down heavily on the kitchen chair.

"Mama, I'm . . ."

"*Shah.*"

"Mama . . ."

"No."

Faye kept quiet, let her mother absorb her news. The window was open to let in the fresh April air. In the silence, Faye heard the kids on the street bouncing a ball and playing "A, My Name Is Alice . . ."

Finally, Faye said, "I know you don't approve, but . . ."

"You know nothing," Bessie said. "Nothing. You are marrying a stranger. A stranger with a stranger's ways. You'll see."

Bessie stood, turned her back on Faye, who had to strain to hear what her mother was saying. "Do you know why we came here, to America?"

Faye thought of the stories her grandmother had told her. They would sit for endless hours together while Bubbie Ida told her about the old country, how they lived outside of the town of Kotovka and had two horses and a cow, chickens and cats. How she had a garden and her husband was a carter. Had she ever said why they came here? Once, she said it was getting hard for the Jews in Europe. But that was all. Now all she could think of was that they must have been poor. Weren't all immigrants poor? She said, "You were poor. You wanted a better life."

"No. We weren't poor. My father, he was a carter, he had horses and wagons, he had three men working for him who delivered for all the merchants and farmers, from one town to the next—a Jewish neighbor and two Gentile boys from nearby. He paid them all good wages. We had a house. I had three sisters and a brother and two cats. We even had a piano."

Faye sat down. Her mother had a brother. Sisters. A piano.

"We lived in Kotovka, Ukraine . . . near Odessa." Her mother was silent.

"I always thought you came from Poland."

"No. That was your father. We came from Kotovka, near Odessa, Ukraine." Bessie turned to face Faye. "You ever hear how the Gentiles said we killed their children to use their blood when we baked matzah?"

"That's ridiculous!"

"You think so? They didn't. The pogroms started with that. In Kishinev, right after Easter Sunday. They came straight from church and began to murder the Jews. There was talk that it would happen again the Easter I was ten, and my father said we had to save and leave for America. We put money away, only maybe not fast enough. Nothing happened that Passover, but on October 20 it happened.

"They had already been murdering in Odessa and the small towns around it for two days. On Friday, before Shabbos, they came to Kotovka. My father must have expected it. He told my mother to hide with me and my baby sister Feige in the root cellar. My father said he would bring the rest of the family, but the murderers came before he could bring them. We lay in the root cellar behind the potatoes while they murdered my father and grandmother and brother and sisters. The whole time Bubbie Ida had her hand over my mouth, I shouldn't cry. She kept nursing the baby, so she wouldn't cry either. We peed on ourselves. We stayed there until there were no more sounds in the house, or outside; five hours we stayed there. And when we came out, we found them all, blood everywhere, furniture broken, dishes smashed. My sister Rifka was naked, her neck slashed. My little brother and sister, shot. Even the cats were dead. They had thrown one against the wall and the other in the well. The only ones who survived were Mama, me and the baby—Feige—who you're named after."

Faye could hardly breathe. How had she not known this? "Who . . . who did it?" she whispered.

"Who? Who?" Bessie was shouting. "Them, them. Our neighbors, who we thought were our friends. The good Catholics from the church. The people we smiled at and wished a good Christmas to when we passed them on the street in December. Maybe even the two boys who worked for my father. October 20, a Friday, before Shabbos, they came out to murder the Jews." Bessie was breathing hard. She was staring at Faye. She sat down at the table. Before her were two unbaked pie shells and the cut-up apples in a yellow bowl, glistening with sugar and cinnamon. She pushed them away.

Faye stood up and went to her mother, kneeled beside her. "I didn't know that, Mama. I didn't know any of that." She wondered if her brother and older sisters knew . . . Ruby, and Irene and Jenny. No one had ever said anything to her about it. Even Bubbie Ida, with all her happy stories about life in the old country, had never told her a thing.

She patted her mother's back. There were so many things she wanted to say, but she couldn't open her mouth. She wanted to say, *It isn't like that here, Mama. We're in America.* She wanted to say, *Angelo isn't like that, Mama. He's a sweet and gentle man. He cried when he saw the movie,* Anne Frank. She wanted to say, *Mama, I'm so sorry that happened to you. But it was a long time ago, and this is now. And I love Angelo.*

"So, now you know." Bessie took a deep breath. "And will it make a difference to you?" She looked into Faye's eyes. "No, it won't. You think things are different now."

Faye looked away, stood up, sat down again. She swallowed. "Yes."

"They're not. Only fifteen years ago it was Hitler, and in the whole world, no one would take Jews, not even here in America. Your father's family in Poland couldn't get out. They were marched into the woods and murdered. Shot. Even the babies. The whole town."

Faye couldn't speak.

Bessie straightened her shoulders, stood up, and lifted the rolled pie dough into the pie pan. She poured the apples into the pan and put the second round of pastry on the top, pinching all around to make a fluted edge.

Bessie didn't say any more. She didn't try to talk Faye out of marrying Angelo, didn't threaten, didn't cajole. She baked the pie, made some tea, and they sat at the kitchen table sipping and eating like they always did. Faye talked about her students. Bessie told her about all the grandchildren.

When she was ready to leave, Faye asked, "Will you meet him at least, Mama? Can he come?"

Bessie shrugged.

"You'll like him, Mama. He's a good man."

Bessie closed her eyes. "We'll see," she said. "Bring him."

Faye and Angelo came the next Sunday for supper. It was threatening rain, the sky dark and cloudy, and along with an umbrella, Angelo carried a large bunch of daffodils and purple irises. He was dressed in a new blue suit with a white shirt, a red striped tie, and a gray fedora. He looked like he was going for an interview. Faye had worn her navy silk dress and the gold necklace that Bubbie Ida had given her. She touched it for luck.

When Bessie opened the door, Faye saw that her mother had dressed up too. She wore light blue, which set off her eyes. Her hair was in an upsweep, and she had rouged her cheeks and mouth and put mascara on her lashes. Faye had not seen Bessie looking so pretty since her sister Jenny's wedding. But her face was like a mask. She could not figure out what her mother was thinking from the look on her face.

Mouthwatering smells came from the kitchen . . . brisket and roast potatoes, sweet carrots, and a fresh loaf of bread. The house was very quiet, but Faye's heart lurched. Behind her mother stood the whole family. Ruby and Victor, Morris and Pauline, Irene and Sam, Jenny and Harry. And behind them their children milled in the living room, craning their necks to get a view of Angelo.

"Well," Faye said. "I . . . I didn't know . . . you didn't tell me you invited them all."

"I thought he should meet the whole *mishpochah*," Bessie said.

"All right then." Faye turned to Angelo and took his hand. Hers was sweaty. "Angelo Benedetto, I'd like you to meet my family—the Weissman clan."

Angelo smiled, extended his other hand to Bessie and said, "I'm pleased to meet you, Mrs. Weissman. I'm pleased to meet you all. Faye's told me all about you."

"Come in," Bessie said and stepped back to let Faye and Angelo pass, taking the flowers to put in a vase. Within minutes the family had surrounded them. Faye hardly saw Angelo. He was talking to Morris, he was talking to Sam, Jenny and Harry were sitting with him. At dinner the family peppered him with questions. Where did he live, what was his family like, what did he do for a living? Jenny smiled encouragement to Faye, and once she whispered in her ear as she cleared the dishes from dinner, "He's very sweet."

The evening passed in a blur. Faye thought everything was going well when Ruby said, in her loudest voice, pointing at Faye, "Isn't that Bubbie Ida's necklace? I didn't know you got it. How come you, and not Mama? Or me? I'm the oldest."

"I don't know why. She . . . she gave it to me," Faye stammered.

"Well it's not right; you're the baby of the family."

"It was Bubbie Ida's to give to who she wanted," Jenny said.

"It's not right." Ruby's green eyes were darting around the room as if looking for another target. She landed on Angelo. "Tell me, Angelo, is Faye promising to raise your children Catholic?"

"Ruby, stop," Victor said.

"Well, that's what everyone wants to know . . . everyone's been asking each other, so I thought I would just ask him. And was his family back in Italy Fascists? Did they like Mussolini? And . . ."

Victor put his hand on Ruby's arm. "That's enough, Ruby. Let Angelo alone."

"No, why should I? Everyone is always trying to shut me up." Ruby jumped up and pushed her chair back. "I'm just asking what everyone else is thinking."

"No, we're not thinking that," Morris said. "My best friend besides Sam is Frank. He's Italian. He introduced me to Pauline."

"It's all right," Angelo said. He directed his answers to Ruby. "I don't mind answering. My family, back in Italy—a lot of them were killed by the Germans. Then my brother died in the war, in the Philippines. I was 4-F. I had bad ears and flat feet. I felt like a bum, not being able to fight. My father never got over Tony's death, and one year later he died of a heart attack. I stayed home and took care of the bakery with my mother. When she got cancer three years ago, she went to be with her sister in Jersey. She died there. I got it all. That's my story." He smiled at Ruby.

"So, you're rich?" Ruby asked.

He laughed. "Not rich. I have the house, the bakery, some money. But it feels like nothing when you're alone. I love Faye too, just like you do. I'll be good to her, I promise."

Victor was pulling Ruby out of the dining room. She was protesting.

"But what about their children? He didn't answer about whether he's making her promise to raise their children Catholic."

"Enough!" Victor said. His voice was loud. "You're being rude." He turned to Angelo and spoke with his European courtesy. "I apologize, Angelo, for my wife." Then he said to Ruby, "Now I think we should go."

"I don't want to go. We haven't had dessert yet," Ruby said. Her cheeks were red and her eyes fiery. She began to talk very fast, "I don't want to go, why is everyone always shutting me up, I want to stay and have dessert, I want to be with the family." She turned and walked into the living room. Victor came up on one side of her, Jenny on the other. Both talked softly, in soothing voices; Ruby shrugged Victor's arm off her shoulder and walked away from him. She let Jenny sit with her in the living room while Victor came back to the table. His face was stone.

Faye looked around the room for her mother. Where had she gone? She waited a bit, in case her mother had gone to the bathroom, but then she walked down the hallway and knocked on the closed door of her mother's bedroom.

When she entered the room, she half expected to see her father lying on the bed in the last week of his life, struggling to breathe with his lungs filled with water from the failure of his heart to pump. She had sat with him, holding his hand, stroking his arm, listened to him mumble how sorry he was that he had lost the money, asking unseen spirits for forgiveness. And then it had been Bubbie Ida, struggling for breath as she told Faye how much she loved her.

The bedroom was full of ghosts. Bessie was sitting on the edge of the bed, staring at a photograph.

"Mama?"

Bessie looked up. "I thought I could do it," she whispered.

"Do what?" Faye asked. Her stomach dropped, knowing.

"Accept. Say it's okay. But I can't. Papa might have. But not Bubbie Ida and not me."

Faye's legs were weak. She felt sick to her stomach. "Bubbie wouldn't have?"

"No."

"How do you know?" Faye whispered.

"I know."

They sat in silence for a while. Then Faye asked, "You never liked my friend Mary Alice, did you?"

"No. I didn't trust her."

Faye nodded. She wondered how her mother had known. She had

never told her how Mary Alice, in a game of jump rope, when she was forced to be an ender and turn the rope, had yanked it when it was Faye's turn to jump, tripping her and yelling, "Christ killer!"

Faye had run upstairs, crying, her knees bloody, into the waiting arms of Bubbie Ida who had comforted her, cleaned her wounds, and in the end said, "Stay away from them. Just stay away." She hadn't said who "they" were, but Faye had known she meant the Catholics. Maybe Bubbie Ida had told her mother about Mary Alice.

Faye asked, "What will you do? Will you come to the wedding?"

"I don't know if I can." There was a long pause. "You do what you want. I'll do what I can. Each of us chooses. Maybe in time." Bessie got up and walked to the door. "Come, it's time for dessert."

Faye waited, stood in front of the mirror, looking at herself. She missed Bubbie Ida. She thought if Bubbie Ida were here, she would feel more secure. She wondered if her mother was right. Would Bubbie Ida have disapproved? Would she have left Faye her gold necklace? Or would she have given it to Ruby or Bessie? She thought of the terrible story her mother had told her of their coming to America.

Faye ran her fingers over the necklace. It felt cold to her touch. She had a feeling that she had betrayed something, but she didn't know what. She looked at herself in the mirror. Her face was red, and her throat and chest were flushed. After a minute, her heart hammering, she unclasped the necklace and slipped it into her pocket. Then she went back to the dining room.

Bessie was cutting the pie and making tea. Angelo was talking to Morris and Pauline. Ruby was sitting with Jenny in the living room. She was crying, and Jenny was whispering to her. Sam and Irene and Harry were putting out the plates for dessert and the teacups. The kids were playing Monopoly. Faye felt as if she were standing outside a window, looking in on someone else's family.

She could not know how things would work out. She would have to wait and see. They would all wait and see.

10

Irene

1964

Irene felt like a disembodied spirit. She sat on the traditional wooden box, lower than the visitors seated on the sofa and chairs, staring ahead into the middle distance. Her feet were in slippers. Over her black dress she wore a black sweater, torn by the rabbi just before the funeral. She never took it off, clutching it close over her arms, shivering within it. Everything was a blur. They were sitting shiva for her beloved Sam, and she felt as if her own life were over.

Later she remembered certain things. How the night when Morris came to tell her about Sam, with a blue uniformed policeman behind him, she and her children, Franklin and Ellie, had clutched each other on the sofa, sobbing. How it had been standing room only at the funeral home, with friends, neighbors, business colleagues, and family filling every seat and leaning against the walls, and how there were so many people at the gravesite spraying shovelfuls of dirt on the lowered coffin that there was nothing for the gravediggers to do at the end. How at the shiva they had covered the mirrors with her blue-and-yellow flowered sheets and how silly it looked, almost like they were decorating the house for a party. How the table was heavy with food and how the people who came to visit the mourners ate and drank like they were at a celebration.

She was so tired she could barely talk, barely respond to any of the visitors or even her family members, but her brain was a scramble of thoughts. She saw a neighbor; why was he here? Sam never liked him. There was a water stain on the ceiling; Sam had promised to paint it. Should she have worn her best black silk dress? Did it look like she was going to a party? Sam hated her in black. Franklin needed a haircut. She clenched her eyes shut trying to squeeze her brain quiet. And below all the other thoughts was a thrumming question. *What will I do now? What will I do?*

Irene's brother and sisters were crowded on the sofa, looking through old photographs and talking over one another competing to tell stories from their childhood. Morris, as Sam's best friend, was passing around picture after picture of him—in knickers, in his tux at their wedding, in a bathing suit at the beach, flexing his muscles like a weightlifter, in his army uniform.

"I think he used up all his life," Morris said suddenly in a lull in the conversation. "I mean he always lived so intensely, so on the edge. And he had so many close calls . . ." his voice trailed off. "He had a lot of close calls in the war."

Irene thought of when he came home in 1944, his body scarred from the flames of a firebomb that flashed through his foxhole, killing his two buddies and nearly ending his own life. He had third degree burns on his torso and arms and spent months recuperating in an Army hospital. He was so badly burned that he never uncovered his chest in front of anyone but Irene. And he was afraid of fire. But it was not fire that killed Sam. It was water.

The *New York Times* article, buried on the third page under city news, read:

GOOD SAMARITAN DIES WHILE TRYING
TO SAVE DROWNING MAN

Samuel Fine, 46, drowned Wednesday while rescuing Charles Conyers, 22, from the Hudson River at 79th Street. Bystanders reported that they saw Conyers struggling in the choppy water and calling for help when Fine ran in to save him.

Lawrence Ellis, 54, a bystander, described how Fine dragged Conyers to the pier where others pulled him up, but then Fine was caught by the current and disappeared underwater before anyone could help. Police boats combed the area and found Fine's body within hours. Police said the water was especially high because of a full moon and the waves were choppy and cold because of an oncoming storm.

The family tried to hide the newspaper articles about the drowning from her, but she roared, her voice hoarse, "I want to read them! Every last one of them!"

Irene read the *Times* article over and over and put it in her pocket, fingering it as a last connection to Sam. Who was this Conyers? Why had he been in the water? Why had Sam rushed to his rescue? She sat through the week, barely talking but listening to them all lauding Sam—about what a generous man he was, a buddy who loaned money to friends and family whenever they asked, a hero who had received a Purple Heart and a Bronze Star for valor in WWII, who had once saved a little girl from drowning at the bungalow colony, a man everyone wanted to spend time with—until she couldn't stand it anymore and had to get up and walk away.

He always did everything large. He filled the room with his loud voice and laugh, and sometimes his anger. Every pronouncement he made was definite. There was no arguing with Sam. She could hear him in her head. Pronouncements about politics . . . what President Johnson was doing right or wrong. What was wrong with today's teenagers. And how he had laughed at the book, *The Feminine Mystique* by Betty Friedan, which Faye, who was always trying to get her sisters to be more assertive, had given Irene as a birthday present. Women working? That's a man's job. And to Irene's hesitant thoughts that she enroll in Brooklyn College, he had roared his disapproval. Why do you have to go to college? What are you going to do with a college degree? Faye insisted that he just didn't want Irene to be more educated than he was. He was afraid she would outshine him. Irene had wondered if that were true.

Irene stood by the table staring at the food, thinking how Sam would have loaded his plate full and eaten with gusto. Sam had an enormous appetite. He loved his mother's garlicky brisket, his wife's Italian meatballs and spaghetti, and when he ate out, he would order a Reuben sandwich, relishing the pastrami and sauerkraut and cheese combination, even though it wasn't kosher. He slugged down quantities of Pepsi-Cola with every meal. Irene looked at the table in the corner that held the drinks. For a minute she panicked. Where was the Pepsi? There was Coca-Cola, 7-Up, Tab. No Pepsi.

Irene was on the verge of panic. "There's no Pepsi. We have to have Pepsi."

Jenny was coming out of the kitchen. "Shush, of course we have some. I'll get it. Everyone is drinking the Pepsi because they know that was Sam's drink. Don't worry. I'll get it." Jenny hurried back into the kitchen. Irene waited, clenching her hands.

It was an eternity before Jenny came out with a bottle held aloft. "See, here, I found one. And I'm sending Harry out for more."

Irene watched as Jenny's husband, Harry, put on his overcoat, kissed Jenny's cheek, and slipped out the front door. The sight of Harry stroking Jenny's brown curls before he left pierced Irene's heart.

Her head drooped, and she was crying again, her shoulders heaving. Jenny pulled her close and held her, but she didn't say anything.

Irene felt fractured. Her bones hurt. She struggled moment by moment to continue or finish whatever task she was on but then forgot what she was doing. In conversations she would begin speaking and stop midstream, as if she were learning all over again how to put a sentence together.

After the week of mourning was over, the family still came. Her mother, Bessie, brought her soup to eat, but she pushed it away. "I can't swallow," she said.

"You have to eat something."

"I can't. There's a lump in my throat. I can't swallow." She wondered if she had a tumor in her throat but was afraid to go to the doctor.

They were there, all the time. Bessie and Pauline, and Faye and Jenny and Ruby. Irene wished Ruby would stay away, but she insisted on being there like everyone else. She talked nonstop, cried all the time, wailing as if Sam had been her husband. Irene remembered bitterly how she had ruined her wedding, carrying on that she was the eldest and should marry first.

"Make her go away," Irene whispered to Jenny. "I can't stand her around me right now."

Jenny nodded. She got up and encircled Ruby with her arm.

Ruby flung her arm off. "Don't do that to me. I want to help."

"You can help more if you go in the other room and make sure the kids are okay. See if they need anything."

"They don't need me. Faye is there, and she acts like she's their mother, not Irene."

"Stop it, Ruby. You're upsetting Irene."

Irene turned her back, closed her eyes, and put her hands over her ears. There was Ruby's intuition again, hitting the mark on things nobody else said. Irene was dimly aware that her children were suffering, that sixteen-year-old Ellie especially was grief-stricken because she'd had a fight with her father two nights before he died, but Irene couldn't muster the energy to reach out to her. She'd let Faye, Ellie's favorite aunt, comfort her.

Jenny came back to Irene and touched her arm.

Irene recoiled. "Even my skin aches," she said. "I feel like I have flu. Everything hurts."

Jenny nodded. "All right, I won't touch you, I'll just sit with you in case you need something."

Irene knew she was supposed to get on with her life, but she didn't know how. Each night she lay in bed, tossing and turning, unable to sleep. Each morning she got out of bed, went to the kitchen, and sat at the Formica breakfast table, letting her coffee get cold, pushing the cup around and staring into space. She wore Sam's bathrobe, a soft flannel plaid that he'd had since they were married. She held it close around her. She walked around the house and found herself in their bedroom closet, pressing her nose to Sam's jackets. Sometimes she spilled a little of his Old Spice aftershave lotion on a tissue and held it in her hand. It felt like he was trailing after her.

She closed her eyes, and she could almost feel the bristles of his beard on her cheek. She lay on their bed, imagining Sam spooning her back. How would she live her life without his kiss, his muscled legs around her body? She would drift into sleep and awaken with a start, not knowing where she was.

Then it would be afternoon, and Jenny or Faye or Pauline would come over to stay with her, make dinner for her kids, encourage her to eat. She could barely get anything down. She lost weight. Her face was gaunt, her eyes sunken. She didn't recognize herself in the mirror.

Irene had always comforted herself with her artwork. Her pictures hung all over the house. Still lifes with apples so red and slick you thought you could bite them, portraits where the skin on the faces called out to be touched. Her work was modulated. Exact. The likenesses were perfect.

Jenny said she should go back to painting. "You'll feel better with a brush in your hand. You always said you could lose yourself in your pictures. Go down to your studio and paint."

Irene shook her head. "I can't. I haven't painted in months. Even before Sam di . . . passed."

"Why not?"

Irene didn't answer at first. She hadn't told anyone, not even Sam, about what happened. "This teacher told me I had no talent."

"Which teacher?" Jenny looked shocked. "How could he say that? Your paintings are wonderful."

Irene gulped a big breath. "Not according to Larry Hatcher." After a minute she added, "He didn't exactly say I had no talent."

"What exactly did he say?"

Irene began to talk. She'd taken his class on the recommendation of the woman she had been studying with for years. His was a huge studio. Easels crowded every available space. Some students were painting in a style called abstract expressionism, which Irene admired but didn't wholly understand. She watched them wield their paint-laden brushes and listened to Hatcher hold forth in a bombastic voice about color and space and the emotionality of the brush. She stood on the side, intimidated, afraid to paint anything.

Finally, she positioned her easel with a group of students who were painting from a still life of apples and bananas. Trying hard not to look at what others were doing, she set about drawing exactly what she saw. After about an hour she looked up to find Hatcher staring at her work. He was a tall man with wiry, iron gray hair and deep creases on either side of his mouth. He seemed to be musing on what to say. Irene watched him, barely breathing in anticipation.

"You know," he said. "You have some talent. You obviously can paint what you see." He paused. "But can you do anything else?"

Irene looked at him and back at her painting. "I don't know what you mean."

"This is pretty but there's nothing there. It's imitative. Conventional." He seemed irritated. "Is there something more you can do?" He waited for her to answer.

She struggled to find something to say. "I don't know what else to do. Is there something else I should be painting?"

Hatcher shook his head and shrugged. "If you don't know, I certainly can't tell you." He waved his arm at the other students. "Look at them. I don't tell them what to do." Then he turned his back and walked away.

Stunned, Irene looked around at the work of the students clustered around the still life. None of their pictures looked like hers. They reminded her of paintings she saw at Museum of Modern Art and in galleries. Some painted exaggerations of the apples and bananas on a blue plate; some used smudges of color as mere suggestions of what they saw. One painted the apple cobalt blue and the bananas fuchsia, like the cloth on the table. At the end of the session, Irene packed up her paints and canvas, glanced at Hatcher surrounded by animated artists, and left. She didn't go back to the class the next week. She didn't tell Sam what happened because she didn't want to repeat what Hatcher had said to her. Sometimes things didn't seem real until she said them to Sam, and she didn't want Hatcher's words to be real. Instead, she stopped painting altogether.

When she had finished her story, Jenny said, "Irene, it's just one man's opinion. And he said you have talent. Everyone thinks you paint beautifully. Forget what he said. Go down and do your own thing."

Irene didn't respond. But the next day she went to her studio and sat on a chair in the middle of the room. She looked at the finished and half-finished canvasses that lined the walls. After a while she thought she knew what Hatcher meant. The paintings were pretty.

They were good likenesses, but nothing more. They didn't make her think or feel. Meaningless, she thought. She fled upstairs to her bed and lay there for a long time.

The next day she went again to the studio and picked up her palette. The remnants of her oil paints from the last time she had painted were dried gobs of color. She scraped them off with a palette knife and then wiped the palette clean with turpentine. She took her tubes of oil paints and began to lay out the colors, squeezing large worms of them in a circle on the palette: alizarin crimson, cadmium yellow, titanium white, cobalt blue. She took a blank canvas, propped it on the easel and stared. She had no idea what to paint.

Never before in her life had she touched a canvas with a brush, not knowing what she was going to paint. Now the empty canvas shimmered before her. How did abstract painters know what to do?

She took a deep breath and dabbed her brush into the shiny crimson paint on her palette. With the brush held aloft she closed her eyes and slashed it across the blinding white canvas. She stared at it. Her heart jumped and she shuddered. It looked like blood.

She loaded another brush with blue and scrubbed at the red. Now it was purple. She took yellow and rubbed it into the white spaces, and dabbed green in one corner. In a frenzy of activity, she covered every inch of the canvas until it was awash with color. She painted almost in a trance, her heart hammering so hard she thought it would burst, utterly out of control. It terrified her, but at the same time it excited her. Was she going crazy? Was this what Ruby felt in one of her spells?

She was exhausted. She dropped her paintbrushes on the palette and turned her head away, covering her eyes and stilling her breath. Then she looked again at the canvas. She had no idea if it was good or bad or nothing.

She fled upstairs to her bedroom, lay on the bed, and covered herself with the blanket. Maybe she slept. She wasn't sure. She heard her daughter, Ellie, calling her but didn't answer. About five o'clock Irene got up, stumbled out of bed and downstairs to the kitchen. Jenny was there and had just put a meatloaf into the oven.

"Ah, you're finally up, Mom," Ellie said. "I wondered where you were, and then saw that you were in bed, napping." She hesitated a minute. "I was just about to tell Aunt Jenny. I went downstairs to the studio to find you and I saw the strangest thing."

Irene's mouth hung open. Her heart was pounding.

Ellie said, "Was Aunt Ruby downstairs the last time she was here?"

Irene couldn't answer, so Jenny said, "Why do you ask?"

"Well there was a painting on the easel. It was nothing like what you paint, Mom. I just thought maybe it was Aunt Ruby."

Irene opened her mouth, closed it again. "No. It was me. I was just trying something out—for fun. It didn't mean anything."

"Oh. That explains it. It was just so wild. I didn't know what to make of it."

"Was it terrible?"

"I don't know. I'm not an art critic."

Now, sitting with Jenny, Irene looked at her hands. They were shaking. She took a deep breath, pushing down the waves of nausea. "I can't paint anymore," she whispered.

"Of course, you can," Jenny said, misunderstanding. "Give yourself some time."

Irene was silent. But she thought, *No, I can't paint any more. I'm not an abstract painter. All I paint is pretty pictures. I'm not an artist. I don't know what I am. I'm nothing.* She fell deeper into despair.

One gray November morning, two months after Sam drowned, Irene was sitting alone at the kitchen table when the doorbell rang. The second time it rang she got up and shuffled to the front door. When she opened it, a young man stood there, his arms by his side. Neither spoke for a moment.

"Mrs. Fine, I'm . . ."

"I know who you are." Irene clutched the bathrobe closer against the chill, suddenly aware that she was wearing only a flimsy night-gown underneath. She shivered and stepped back to let him in.

They stood in the foyer staring at one another. Charles Conyers was a lanky six-footer. He had a shock of sandy hair that fell over his brow, intense brown eyes, and a strawberry birthmark on the right side of his cheek. He was wearing a gray woolen overcoat whose arms were so short that his wrists dangled below the cuffs, and his hands, red from the cold, were balled into fists. He started to speak several times but couldn't get the words out. Each time he opened his mouth, his right hand flew to cover the red mark on his cheek. Then he stut-tered, "I . . . I'm . . . s . . . so s . . . s . . . sorry." His shoulders heaved and he began to cry.

Irene grit her teeth. She took her fist and struck him on the chest. Then, as if the floodgates had opened, she hit him again and again, pummeling him with both fists and shouting, "Why? Why? Why?"

He reached around her and pulled her to him, whether to stop her from punching him or to comfort her, Irene couldn't tell. But in seconds, both were sobbing together, her forehead butted against him. They stood crying like that for a long time, and then she pulled back and looked up at him. Through the blur of her tears she recog-nized how young he was, how his face had the raw, unformed look of a teenager, even though the paper had said he was twenty-two. Now, her hand hovered near Charles Conyers' cheek, near the raised birthmark, not knowing if she wanted to caress it or slap it. Then, without a word she turned and walked into the living room. He followed.

She sat on the sofa. He pulled up a chair opposite and sat so his knees butted up against hers. His long fingers were flat in his lap and

Irene saw his nails were bitten raw, to the quick. She felt the salt lump in her throat but choked out one word: "Talk."

The thing was, Charles Conyers could barely talk.

"Why did you come here?" Irene asked finally.

"T . . . to ap . . . pologize." He took a long, deep breath and seemed to steady himself. Listening to him was agonizing. The words came in bursts, or else he landed on a letter and repeated it until, with a force of breath, he moved on to the next word. He told her that he had been depressed for a long time, maybe his whole life. He was an only child, and his mother had been in her forties when he was born, his father even older. Both of them had died in the last year, his mother of cancer and his father of a heart attack. He thought he was responsible for his father's death. Before the heart attack he had confessed to his father that he thought he was homosexual. His father's face had turned red, and his eyes had bulged. He'd shouted to Charles to get out, and Charles had fled, never to see his father alive again. His father had died a few days later. Now he was alone.

"No aunts or uncles? No cousins? No friends?" Irene asked. After each question he shook his head. Irene steeled herself. She would not let herself feel sorry for this boy—this man, she corrected herself. Let him feel sorry for her. She looked at him. What did they call them? Fairies? She didn't know if she had ever met a homosexual. No one ever talked about it.

"I had thought . . . about suicide . . . but I'm chicken. Afraid of everything. But that . . . day . . ." he began. "That . . . day I felt calm. "I was at the pier at Seventy-Ninth Street looking at the water and the boats, and I just walked off the pier into the water." He had been caught by the current. The waves were wild that day. "I . . . tried . . . to swim . . . but I couldn't." The water had soaked his woolen coat, pulling him down. And then he realized he didn't want to die. "I called, 'Help! Help me!' and your husband came." He had struggled to stay afloat, swallowing water. "It was . . . cold, so . . . f . . . freezing." Charles took a deep breath and his head sank on his chest.

Her head was throbbing; she rubbed her temples. "Go on."

He went on. He felt at first, when Sam pulled him by the hair and put his arm crosswise around him that Sam was trying to drown him; they were both sinking and swallowing water, so he had fought. But Sam was stronger, and he got them both above the water. To Charles it seemed that Sam had heaved him toward the shore, toward the pier. "These guys leaned over and pulled me out. But your husband was still in the . . . water and I saw him, he . . . drifted away and the waves were . . . bad, and he sank."

In the stillness that followed Charles' excruciating recitation, Irene started to shake. She thought she could see the whole scene: the other people on the pier watching Sam drift and sink and doing nothing; Charles, like a statue on the pier, staring at Sam's disappearing body.

Finally, she said, "You can go now. You've told me. Get out."

Charles stood up, scraping the chair back. She heard his footsteps go toward the door, hesitate, and walk again. The door closed. Irene took a deep breath. She was shaking, full of hate for him. This boy—this man—who looked like a starving poet—was out of her life. She never had to see him again and be reminded that he was the reason she would never hear Sam's laugh again, never smell his Old Spice aftershave on her own skin after she had kissed him, never feel his soft mouth nuzzling her neck.

She walked back and forth to the kitchen and then went to the living room window and looked out. Charles was still standing, looking up at her house. He stood for a long time, his shoulders hunched, his arms hanging limp. She watched him. He seemed to be aware of this. He waited, but she didn't move. Then he turned and began to walk away, his body slumped forward.

He's probably going to try it again, she thought. *Good riddance.*

She turned away from the window and walked to the kitchen. *Oh God, he might do it again!*

She raced to the door, flung it open and ran down the street after him, her slippers slapping against the pavement, her bathrobe clutched in her hands. "Charles!" she shouted. "Charles, wait!"

He turned and waited. She reached him, breathless from the run. "Promise me. You have to promise me you won't do it again. Promise. Or he died for nothing. Nothing."

He gulped. She watched his Adam's apple slide up and down in his throat as he swallowed. He shook his head. "I won't. I . . . promise."

"You won't what—say it. Say it."

"I won't . . . kill myself."

The words, laid out flat like that, were what she wanted to hear, but empty somehow. This man was a shell. He had nothing inside. Irene stood, helpless. "Do you know why you won't?" she finally asked. "Are there things you want to live for? Like my husband did? Things you love?"

He stared his face blank. "I won't try again. I . . . promise," he repeated.

"You didn't answer me. What do you love?" she shouted. "What?"

He shook his head. He had no idea what things he loved in this life.

"You must love something. You cried out for help. And Sam came. There must have been a reason."

A neighbor pulled up beside them in a gray Chevy. He leaned over, rolled the window down and asked, "Is everything okay?"

"Yes, yes. It's fine," Irene said. She looked down at her bathrobe and slippers, realized how strange she must look. How strange they looked together. What was she doing here with this man? There was tumult in her head. She couldn't think straight.

A voice came into her head—Sam's—and the words were as clear as if he had whispered them to her: *If you save someone's life, you are responsible for that person forever.*

Not me, she thought. *Not me. I didn't save his life.*

You are responsible for that person forever, the voice said.

How long?

Forever.

And how long is forever? Until he makes a friend? Finds a person to love? She shuddered, clenched her fist. *He can go to hell*, she thought. She turned her back and started to walk away. Someone would have to teach him how to love, but it wouldn't be her. She had not saved his life. She was only the one who had lost everything because of him.

But he has no one. Someone has to teach him.

She stopped walking. She was crying. She felt Charles standing a few feet behind her, breathing hard. She turned to look at him again, a skinny, pathetic boy/man who didn't know what to do with his life. His arms dangled from too-short sleeves. His eyes were like black holes, fierce with pain. His mouth was slack, his shoulders slumped. She could not believe what came into her mind next. She could see him on a canvas, a long, tall canvas, all grays and blacks and a few red strokes for the strawberry mark on his cheek. "Pain," she would call it. She shook her head. The picture disappeared.

She breathed slow and steady, turned and took a few more steps. She couldn't walk any farther. *This was crazy, reckless.*

But she did it anyway. She reached out her hand to him, said, "Come. It's cold out here." She walked to the house and he trailed behind her, holding tight to her hand. And it was like she was not alone, but was with Sam, pulling this lost boy out of the water toward the shore and toward the safety of her house. God knew what she would do with him. But maybe she could help him. And God only knew how, maybe he could help her too.

11

Sarah

1969

When Sarah stepped off the bus in Monticello into the driz-zle that had been falling on and off since the night before, she almost tripped over a grimy man and woman who sat chanting, bowls in front of them. The man plucked her long, orange-and-pur-ple flowered skirt.

"Can you help us, miss? We're hungry."

She paused and rummaged through the bulging blue sack she carried and put a coin in each of the bowls, thinking of how her mother Ruby always gave away her loose change to the beggars on the street.

Sarah looked around. She was headed to the Woodstock Music Festival but was not sure how to get there. The driver had told her this was the closest she could get by bus; after that she'd have to walk or hitch.

"How do I get to Woodstock?" she asked the beggar.

"Follow them," he said, pointing down the road to a group of people walking.

"How far?"

"About ten miles. It's in the next town, Bethel."

Her heart sank. She could see that hitching was impossible. Traffic wasn't moving. People swirled around the cars, trying to walk to the music festival, but the road was muddy, and the rain felt chilly, even in August. Sarah abandoned the idea. She walked across the street to the café.

In the doorway of the café, she stood looking into the crowded room. The waitresses wore pink dresses and lacy aprons, and one bustled from table to table holding a coffeepot and topping off each cup before the customer had drunk it halfway. There was a counter in the back with red leather stools and a glass case featuring three different pies. She saw there were no free tables, but there was a seat at a table where a man was pointing his camera straight at her. He waved. The flash went off.

"Why are you taking pictures of me?" she asked, coming over to him. "Do I know you?"

"No. You don't know me—yet. I'm a photographer. Herb Morrison. I'm taking pictures of you because you're beautiful."

Sarah was flattered and blushed. He put out his hand for a handshake but didn't stand up. "What's your name?"

She considered not answering him, but then took his outstretched hand, nodded, and said, "Sarah Strauss."

She plopped down on the chair opposite. "I was going to the concert, but I found out you have to walk there. And it's ten miles. I can't walk ten miles, especially in these shoes." She stuck out her legs showing him her Dr. Scholl's sandals with a wide leather strap and wooden soles.

"I couldn't walk there either." He stuck out his leg, which wore a metal brace. He tapped it lightly with his cane.

Sarah observed him. He was handsome, with blue eyes and black hair; he was tall and slim, and except for his leg, you might call him a catch. She finally asked, "How did that happen?"

"Polio. When I was three."

"That's too bad." She wondered if she should say she was sorry.

"Did you buy a ticket to the concert?" he asked. "Because they're not even taking them anymore. They pulled the fences down—too many people trying to get in. Everything's free now."

"Well I'm glad I didn't buy one, then. I . . . I'm supposed to meet someone there. He's a drummer in a band. I think they're playing today. The Wandering Winds, they're called." She looked embarrassed. "Have you heard of them?"

Herb shook his head.

"His name is Lochinvar. Lochinvar Kramer." Herb laughed. After a minute she did too. "He changed it."

"No kidding. What is he—your boyfriend?"

"No, just a guy I know. He's from California."

"And you like him?"

"Yeah. But not so much that I'm going to walk ten miles to see him." There was a beat of silence. "I think he was full of hot air anyway. I didn't see his name on the list of performers."

"No, I never heard of him," Herb said.

"I'm really unattached," Sarah went on, feeling pressure to explain herself to him. "I was married once, but I'm divorced now, and I have a three-year-old daughter, Didi . . . well her real name's Dianne. I left her home with my Aunt Jenny." She paused and looked down at his hands, which were clutching the camera. "You married?"

Herb shook his head. "I was once. But no more."

Sarah nodded. She was folding a napkin into a fan, and then unfolding it. "When I got married, my parents went nuts. They didn't like Hank, thought he was a bad choice—they were right—but I was pregnant, which made them more hysterical. We had just graduated from college, Hank didn't have a job, he wasn't Jewish. . . ." She looked up at him. "Are you? Jewish?"

"No."

"It doesn't matter. Anyway, my mother took one of her emotional nosedives. She was always up and down all through my childhood, and finally my father said we should get married and he would give Hank a job in his store, which is funny because that's just what his father-in-law—my grandfather—did, when he got married, gave him a job in his store. Hank really didn't want to be a shopkeeper, but he figured he'd go along with it, and he did for a while but then . . ." She had been talking very fast, but she stopped abruptly. "I'm talking too much, aren't I?"

"No, I like it. Go on."

All around them were clanking noises of dishes, the hum of people talking, a baby crying in the background. Herb just kept looking at her.

So Sarah went on. "When Didi was a year old, he left me, and I moved in with my parents, but that didn't last because my mother was—is—such a nutcase, so my Aunt Jenny said I could stay with her and Uncle Harry for a while, so that's what I did, and that's where I am now. I've been there for almost a year—well more than a year." She was suddenly silent. It was like she had come up for air after a long dive. She unfolded the little fan she had made of the napkin and smoothed it on the table. "I know I'm talking too much," she said again. "I always do when I'm nervous. Do you have a pen or pencil?"

Herb reached into his pocket and gave her his pen. "Why are you nervous?" he asked, as she took a fresh napkin from the dispenser on the table and started drawing faces of the people around her with quick strokes. He craned his neck and tried to look at the drawings, but she stuffed them into her bag.

"I shouldn't have said that," she said.

"What?"

"That my mother is a nutcase. She isn't a nutcase. She has highs and lows and living with her is hard. So when Didi and I moved in with my parents, it was one thing after another. Sometimes she drinks. She disappears for a few days, and everyone is frantic until she comes back—she's done that since she was a teenager. Finally, I couldn't stand it anymore. But she isn't a nutcase. She just has problems, but me too . . . who am I to talk? I feel bad I said that."

"That's okay. Don't worry about it."

Sarah was looking around the café, restless. "You haven't told me why you're here," she said. "You obviously weren't going to walk to Woodstock." She blushed.

"No. No, I wasn't. I drove . . . I'm a photojournalist. Well, not for a living, but that's what I want to be. I work in a camera store. I thought this would be a great chance to write a story on all the musicians and celebrities here, maybe get to interview a few, take some pictures, sell it freelance if I was lucky."

Sarah nodded to encourage him.

"I got stuck like everyone else in a massive traffic jam on the highway. So I parked off the side of the road and started walking; I thought I would hitch a ride into town with my backpack and tripod . . . and my cane." He picked up his wooden cane and showed it to her. "But there were no cars moving. I did interview some of the other people who were walking. Maybe I can do something with it."

"That'd be good," she said.

Herb asked, "Do you want something to eat?" She nodded, and he called the waitress over and ordered a tuna fish sandwich for her, two coffees and what was now the last slice of blueberry pie.

Suddenly she jumped up. "I have to call and check on Didi. Do you have a dime? I'll give it right back. I'll reverse the charges. I gave all my change to some homeless people."

He fished out a dime, and she went to the back of the store where there was a pay phone. In a few minutes she came back and put the dime on the table. "No answer. I hope everything's all right."

The sandwich came and she ate fast, cramming her mouth with bite after bite. "I didn't have any breakfast," she said after she'd finished, and wiped her mouth with the back of her hand. He gave her a fork, and they shared the blueberry pie. She ate most of it. Then she said, "Now what?"

That's how she met Herb. They made their way back to his car, Sarah carefully slowing her steps to Herb's, carrying his tripod, and then it was an easy drive south to Manhattan. The traffic north was at a crawl, and even though Herb knew he was missing a story, he said he was glad to be out of the crowds.

He hardly spoke; she talked nonstop. Her father had been born in Germany, she'd studied art at Pratt, she worked in an advertising company, she wanted to travel to Europe, drive across America, but she had a kid, maybe she would anyway and visit with her older brother, Joseph, who was going to law school in California. He had been all over the world, in the Peace Corps in Tanganyika, then back to the States, working in the civil rights movement, registering voters in Mississippi, and finally applying to law school last year and moving to San Francisco where he was now. "I'm so jealous of him," she said. "He's so free, and I'm so not free. I'm like my aunts, stuck in New York with unexciting lives. Two of them are already widowed. Aunt Irene and Aunt Faye. Both their husbands died so young, it's really sad. Only Aunt Jenny—she's the one who's taking care of Didi—still has her husband. And my mother, of course. She's the oldest sister." Sarah stared out the window, silent now, as they rolled down the parkway and toward the bridge.

"Where's your aunt's apartment?" Herb asked when they had crossed the George Washington Bridge.

"I don't have to go home yet," Sarah answered. "My aunt's not expecting me until tomorrow evening." She stared straight ahead. Her heart was pounding.

"You want to come home with me?"

"Okay."

After they parked the car three blocks from his apartment, he limped, and she walked beside him carrying his tripod again. In the lobby they waited side by side for the elevator, staring straight ahead like the two strangers they were.

His apartment was a large one-room efficiency on the lower East Side. It had great light which reflected off the white walls from a huge north-facing window, and an inside bathroom that he said he used as a darkroom. There was a Formica table and chairs in the corner, a futon on the floor with a red bedspread, and lots of his hanging photos. In the corner was his vinyl record collection, stacks of albums leaning against the wall.

Sarah and Herb were both mud-spattered and sweaty. Once inside the apartment, Sarah was a whirlwind. She pulled a jumble of clean clothes from the blue bag, went into the bathroom to shower and change, and then she waited while he showered too. When he came out of the bathroom, she was looking through the albums, pulling out Joplin, Baez, Guthrie, Jefferson Airplane, The Dead.

"Ah great, you're finished. Do you have anything to drink?"

"Beer? Soda?" he asked.

"Vodka? Scotch?" she asked.

"Beer or soda."

"Okay, beer." She turned to the albums she was holding. "Let's listen to these. It'll be like we're at the concert."

Herb got a beer from the refrigerator and put the stack of records on his changer. Then they settled on the futon.

Sarah took two long swallows of beer and put the can down. "You smoke?" Sarah asked.

"Sometimes."

She rummaged around in her bag, rolled a joint and offered it to him. While Joplin played on the hi-fi, they passed the joint back and forth. Sarah held the smoke deep and long before she blew it out in a haze in front of her. She could feel the high. It slowed her, settled the churning, and she relaxed, closed her eyes, let the music swirl. They talked softly, exchanging information. They had both grown up in Brooklyn, loved Nathan's frankfurters, preferred Pepsi to Coke. They talked about Vietnam. They both had friends serving there, and Herb's childhood friend had been killed in the Tet offensive the year before. They both loved Star Trek and talked about space travel, extraterrestrials, and Neil Armstrong walking on the moon, which had just happened the month before. Sarah felt profound.

"You know," she said, "when I was a kid, we used to say about things we never thought would happen, 'That'll happen when a man walks on the moon.' Now that a man walked on the moon last month, what are we going to say?" She giggled.

"When the moon turns blue."

"Once in a blue moon."

"When the moon is made of cheese."

"Blue cheese." She laughed, thinking she was funny.

Later they drank more beer and ate take-out Chinese and ice pops from his freezer. Then, while they were washing the dishes, he leaned over, brushed her hair lightly off her forehead, and kissed her mouth. His was colored red from the cherry pop. He tasted sweet.

As they moved from the sink to the bed, strewing their clothes around, laughing and stumbling to get the metal brace off his leg, she stopped suddenly. "Do you have . . . " she paused delicately. ". . . something? I'm off my birth control pills."

He nodded and held up a small plastic covered square. "I'm a Boy Scout. Always prepared." His skin surprised her; it was so smooth; he smelled faintly of sweat and cologne. She liked the way their bodies fit together, the rhythm they struck, the way he almost hummed, "Oh my, oh my" as he came. Later she fit perfectly into the curve of his arm, her head resting on his shoulder. She saw that he was drifting in and out of sleep, but she talked anyway—about all the men she'd been with since high school. She went into great detail about a Paul and a Matt and someone named Brady whose room smelled of sweaty clothes. It was a catharsis, spilling all her stories to someone who was only half hearing her. Then she told him about Hank who had gotten her pregnant.

"He had incredibly big thumbs, and I wondered if what they said was true. About big thumbs and big penises." She giggled. "It wasn't." She nuzzled his neck. "You smell nice," she said. "Old Spice." She giggled again. "I rhymed. I'm a poet and I don't know it." She paused to look at him. He was breathing very regularly, as if in a deep sleep. She sat up abruptly and looped her hands around her knees. The movement jarred him, and he opened his eyes and said, "What?"

"I think maybe I shouldn't have slept with you so fast; that was dumb."

"No, no," he said. "Don't feel that way. I'm glad you did."

"I'm glad too."

Sarah lay back. "Sometimes I'm so lonely," she said. "But I don't feel lonely with you." Sarah hooked her arm around his neck and kissed him sweet and long.

She felt him stirring against her, but she turned on her side and yawned. In a few minutes her breathing slowed, her eyes were closed, and she was sleeping.

The next morning Sarah was up first. She was clanking pots, looking for coffee, but really wanting to wake Herb. When Sarah finally saw him sitting on the edge of the bed she said, "I thought you'd never get up. I've been up for hours. I'm looking for your coffeepot. I'm desperate for coffee."

He looked at the clock, which read 6:45. "When did you get up?"

"I don't know. I couldn't sleep," she said. "I had bad dreams. I showered and everything." They made coffee and toast with peanut butter. They made love again, and afterward when she was sprawled under the red cover, he started snapping pictures of her.

She began striking different poses. She had a natural grace and was not at all self-conscious about her naked body. She flung her head back, tucked her face down, put her hands on her waist or held them behind her like a Degas ballet dancer.

After he shot a roll of film, they got dressed and went out. It was cloudy, threatening rain, the air muggy the way it is in a New York August. They spent the afternoon following Sarah's impulses. They walked around the Village, ducking into first one, then another little shop where she bought an Indian print scarf and a throw for her bed. They watched the chess players on the stone tables in Washington Square Park and the kids jumping in and out of the big oval fountain. There were musicians playing guitar on the benches with buckets in front of them, and the park was full of hippies, homeless, drunks. Sarah continually asked Herb for coins so she could give them to all the beggars she passed.

"I feel so sorry for them," she said. "I can't help giving them something. My grandmother says charity is the most important thing. Charity and family. Do you think I'm stupid?"

"No. You're sweet," he said. "You make me want to take care of you."

Every now and then he would hug her, and she would smile up at him. Once she reached out and ruffled his hair. Another time she kissed his cheek.

"Could we stop for a coffee?" he asked after a while.

Sarah looked at him and saw he was white with exhaustion. She felt embarrassed by her thoughtlessness. "I'm an idiot," she said. They stopped in one of the coffee houses on MacDougal Street. The coffee revived them, and Sarah again was sketching faces on the napkins. Then she said, "What time is it?"

"Almost five."

"Do you want to come home with me? Come. I want you to meet my Aunt Jenny and Didi." They took the subway to the upper West Side. Aunt Jenny and Uncle Harry's apartment was in one of those block-size prewar buildings. It had long hallways with room after room edging off each side, with high ceilings, moldings, and parquet wood floors. "It was Uncle Harry's family's apartment forever, and he inherited it. Uncle Harry's pretty rich—he's a big-shot lawyer." She paused for a breath. "That's why I can live with them. They only have one kid—George, he's seventeen. They don't need all the room. The place has six bedrooms and three bathrooms."

When they got to the apartment house, Sarah stopped before going inside. They were standing in a courtyard in the front of a U-shaped building. Kids were playing ball, jumping rope, their parents watching.

"Don't tell them where we met," she said.

"What?"

"Don't tell them we met at Woodstock."

"Why?"

"Just do it, please. Say you met me at Marjorie's—she lives in Pittsfield, Massachusetts. I told Aunt Jenny I was going to Tanglewood with Marjorie—you know, classical music. Aunt Jenny approves of classical music. That's where I was supposed to be. You were coming back to New York, so you gave me a ride."

"I don't understand," Herb said.

"Just do it, please," Sarah repeated. And he agreed.

Aunt Jenny answered the door. She was frowning and looked worried; her slim body seemed strung like a wire. When she saw Sarah she burst out, "Where have you been? I've been trying to reach you. I finally called Marjorie, and she didn't know where you were." The edge to her voice got stronger. "She didn't know anything about you being there. Where did you go? How could you just disappear like that?"

Sarah could see she was mad. "Is Didi all right?"

"Didi's fine." As if on cue, a tiny replica of Sarah in a bright red pinafore came barreling down the long hallway, sliding and screaming, "Mommy, Mommy! I ate ice cream."

Sarah caught her in a big hug and swung her around. "This is my friend Herb," she said as she walked into the apartment. Herb followed. "Is it my mother?" Sarah asked Jenny.

"Yes. She's been gone since yesterday. You just missed your father. He wanted you to go with him to look for her."

Sarah dumped Didi on the floor.

"Oh God, Aunt Jenny. I knew this was coming. I knew it." Sarah's heart hammered.

"You knew and you left?" Jenny said. "You're just like her."

"I am not like her. How can you say that?"

"You're exactly like her. She disappears. You disappear. Neither of you tells anyone where you're going."

"This was the only time. . . ."

"Your father comes for your help, and no one knows where you are. You leave your baby with me, just like she did. Who do you think took care of you and Joseph when she disappeared? Me. That's who." Jenny threw her hands up. "Well you're back now. Didi will be happy." She went into the kitchen.

Sarah turned to Herb and said, "I'm so sorry. I shouldn't have brought you."

Didi was peeking out from behind her mother's legs. "Why is your leg in a cage?" she asked, pointing to his leg and his brace, which stuck out of his pants and went around the bottom of his shoe.

"That's not nice, Didi," Sarah said trying to shush her.

"It's okay," Herb said. He smiled. "It's not a cage. It's a brace." Didi touched his leg, so he took her hand and swung it gently.

"Does it hurt?"

"Not at all," he answered.

"I can skip." She did an awkward hop and put her other foot down and hopped again. "Can you?"

"No, I can't," Herb said.

"Because of the cage?"

"Yes."

"I can run, can you?" She ran down the hallway and back again, stopping in front of him, her face upturned.

"I can't run very fast," he said.

Sarah said, "I'm sorry. She's only three. She doesn't understand." Her head sank down on her chest. "Let's get out of here," she said suddenly, so he turned to follow.

"Where are you going now?" Jenny asked coming out of the kitchen.

"My mother's missing. I'm going to look for her." Sarah turned to Herb. "She does this. She disappears. I told you she's a nutcase."

"Don't say that," her aunt said.

"She is. I can't help it." Sarah was walking around, punching her fist against the palm of her hand. "She's crazy, and she's driving my father and me crazy." She sat on the sofa and put her head in her hands. "I'm sorry, Aunt Jenny. I'm sorry I went away and left you to deal with it. But I could feel it coming. She was calling me every day, even at work. I would hang up, and she would call again. I could feel it building up, and I just wanted to get away."

Jenny sat on the sofa beside her and took Sarah's hand. Didi climbed on her mother's lap and patted her cheek. Sarah hugged her.

"You couldn't have done anything anyway," Jenny said. "I know how you feel. It's a burden. My mother used to say, 'Take care of Ruby, she needs you.' And I would, but I resented it. I resented it so much." She sighed. "They'll find her. They always do. She's probably giving away all her money and clothes to the homeless people." Both Jenny and Sarah were quiet.

"Maybe I should go," Herb said. "I'm sorry about this trouble."

"No." Sarah almost shouted. "Don't leave. I want you to stay. Aunt Jenny, can he stay for dinner?"

—

At dinner the conversation felt stilted. Harry and George came in, and George, who studied clarinet at Music and Art High School, kept talking about the Woodstock music festival in upstate New York. "It's the greatest festival of all time," he said.

Sarah was afraid to speak, afraid she would give away where she had been the past two days.

Harry disagreed. "Just a bunch of hippies camping out, doing dope, from what I understand." He and George argued, the way teenage boys and their fathers often do. The chicken was moist and flavorful with an apricot glaze, the rice pilaf a pale orange with saffron threads through it and crunchy almonds. Jenny brought out vegetables and salad and crusty bread.

Sarah kept glancing at Herb, who was eating with gusto, shoveling the food into his mouth. "This is delicious," he said. His cheeks reddened. "I haven't had a meal like this in ages."

When the phone rang Harry answered. He came back to the table a few minutes later and said, "They found her. She was at the Brooklyn Bridge with all those homeless people there. Your father's taking her home. He asked if you would go there and bring Didi. He thinks that will settle her down more."

Sarah nodded. Tears streamed down her cheeks. "Okay, I'll go," she said.

Herb thanked Jenny and Harry for their hospitality and went to the door with Sarah and Didi.

In the elevator Herb leaned against the red enameled walls.

"I'll take a cab," Sarah said.

"I'll go with you."

Her head snapped up; her mouth opened. "Why?"

"I don't know why," he said. "I just will."

On the main floor they walked to the street. Two boys were playing catch in the courtyard in the twilight, even though it was starting to drizzle. Didi was practicing her skip as they walked. Herb followed

Sarah, but he couldn't keep up. She turned and faced him, a good twenty feet away. It was like he had asked her a question and she was answering.

"I just wanted to go to Woodstock; I met this guy and I thought it would be fun to spend a weekend just listening to music, and I didn't think Aunt Jenny would babysit for that, but she likes Marjorie, so I figured she would let me go see her, so I made up the story about visiting her. I don't disappear like my mother. My mother is fine some of the time, and then she goes off, starts racing around and takes money, gives it away, drinks with the people she meets. That lasts for a while and then she gets depressed, and we start all over again." She whispered, "I'm not like her. I'm not."

Herb limped closer to her. The drizzle mixed in with her tears. She was crying.

"I don't know why," he said, "but I have lousy luck with women. Are you going to be one of them?"

"No, I'll be good luck. I promise." Sarah pressed her forehead into his chest. His chin was on the top of her head. He held her and rocked her. She felt really safe.

Sarah wondered why he was with her—him with a gimpy leg, and her, a kook with a crazy family and a three-year-old kid. It didn't bode well. They stood like that for a while and then something whizzed by them. It was the ball the boys had been tossing. It was rolling and bouncing past into the street. Just behind it was a flash of red.

Sarah felt Herb shove her aside. She watched as Herb lunged toward Didi's red dress. He ran. His legs clomped, slapped, clomped, slapped. But he ran. Horns blared, brakes squealed. Rain shone on the macadam. Sarah watched as he grabbed the edge of the red skirt and pulled Didi into his arms, crashing onto the pavement. His elbow, knee, hip, and cheek hit the ground. His face was bleeding. He held the squalling girl in his arms. He was laughing wildly, and he hung on and on.

And Sarah, watching from the sidewalk, thought that he was a man she would want to hold on to forever, just the way he was holding Didi.

12

Joseph
1973

Joseph was running away again, wanting to be anywhere but near his mother, Ruby. Ever since college he'd been escaping from her—first to the Peace Corps in Tanganyika, then to Mississippi to fight for civil rights, and finally across the country to law school in San Francisco. He'd thought he and his girlfriend, Gail, would be able to settle down there, but when they graduated, she wanted to go back to New York to be near her family; being near his was the last thing Joseph wanted. So he'd left Gail and everything he knew, to try out life in a new country.

He arrived in Israel in late June, exhausted from fourteen hours on the plane. The dry heat hit him like a wind from an oven when he stepped out of the terminal building. He looked around at the swarms of people clustered about the entrance, and within minutes he was able to identify his cousins. They were waving a sign with his name on it, but he would have found them anyway, stunned by the family resemblance. Alfred looked a lot like Joseph's father, Victor, and spoke with the same clipped English. Alfred's son David, who was a few years younger than Joseph, stood beside his father. He was just over six feet with dark brown hair and eyes and full red lips. Joseph felt he was looking at himself in a slightly skewed mirror.

They crammed into the small dusty kibbutz car and drove two hours from the outskirts of Tel Aviv to Tiberius and then around the Sea of Galilee and up the winding road, lined with banana trees and date palms, to Kibbutz Etz Hadas where his cousins lived.

After just two days, Joseph knew he loved it. It was like a scrim of gray had been peeled from his eyes. He was dazzled by the color, the freshness of the air, and the brightness of the sun. He felt he was on a perpetual vacation. From the hilltop where Etz Hadas sat, he could see the Kinneret, the Hebrew name for the Sea of Galilee. Small cottages rimmed a large green in the center of the kibbutz; flowers grew every-where, and the myrtle tree, for which the kibbutz was named, dripped its profuse pink-and-purple blossoms. The kibbutz offices and the *chadar ohel*, the communal dining room, stood under tall trees that had been planted over fifty years before when the kibbutz was settled. There was a recreation field with volleyball and basketball courts, a ping-pong table, and an empty swimming pool that gleamed with aqua paint.

The first Friday night Joseph was there David said, "We're going swimming . . . want to come?"

Joseph was hot and sweaty, and the thought of a swim was entic-ing. "Love to. Where do we go?"

"The swimming pool."

"You're kidding, right? It has no water in it."

"Put on your bathing suit and come see," David said, laughing. He led the way down the path to the swimming pool and even before he got there, Joseph heard splashing and shouting. He stood before the sparkling water staring like it was a mirage.

"How?"

"Every Friday we fill it," David said. "We swim all Shabbat, and on Sunday we empty it, and the water fills the pipes for the drip system in the fields."

Joseph shook his head with admiration. "Ingenious."

"Yes," David said. "We do much with little."

It was just one of the many innovations Joseph saw as he worked in the kibbutz that summer. The *kibbutzniks* made something of nothing and repaired things, as they said, with rubber bands and safety pins.

Joseph lived in a cement house with the other volunteers and worked with them in the date orchards. They came from every country in Europe and included many Scandinavians, who stood out with their white-blond hair and ice-blue eyes. "Sun seekers," David called them. "They love it here because it is so warm and beautiful. Because of them, most of us speak English. We learn in school and practice with the volunteers."

David's girlfriend, Shoshanna, who had grown up with him in the kibbutz, could not stop staring at Joseph when she first met him. "You are like brothers," she said, looking from one to the other.

"So you must think him very handsome." David turned to Joseph. "She loves me since she is four. She chased me all the time and made me promise to marry."

Shoshanna laughed and shoved David away with a playful push. "I chased you? No. You chased me."

"Until you caught me," David said and raced backward as she ran after him. Then he stopped short, grabbed her slim waist and swung her around and around. Her streaked blond hair flew out behind her, and her laughter was like a song. It pierced Joseph with envy to see the way they loved each other.

David worked in the kibbutz office, managing the books for the many profitable businesses of the kibbutz, which included a factory that produced coasters and paperweights made of wildflowers enclosed in plastic. Shoshanna was a teacher of the three- and four-year-olds. Kibbutz Etz Hadas was one of the first to abolish the twenty-four-hour-a-day children's houses, and now the children slept in small cottages with their parents and ate with them in the dining hall. They came to the children's house only when their parents were working. That made it possible for Shoshanna to live with David. They shared a room in the single adults' house.

Life was not hard at Etz Hadas. Because two meals a day were provided in the kibbutz dining hall, there was time for leisure. There were long afternoon naps, easy evenings with campfires and dancing. People visited from cottage to cottage, dropping by without an invitation.

"We are not formal here," Alfred's wife, Miriam, said to Joseph the first week he stayed at the kibbutz. "Come by whenever you want."

Miriam had a broad smile. She was, he knew, roughly the same age as his mother, but she looked older, her face lined with sun wrinkles, her hair peppered with white. She did not wear a speck of makeup. One Monday afternoon when he dropped by, Miriam emptied a can of peaches into a bowl and served it with a box of crisp sugar cookies. Another day she put out crusty bread and olives, sliced a red tomato on a blue plate and served it with cheese and tea. It was as delicious as any meal Joseph had ever had.

"So," she would say by way of greeting each time he came into her house, "have you decided to join us? We need young people like you."

Joseph would smile and always say the same thing: "I'm considering my options." He tried to imagine what it would be like to live his life in the confines of a kibbutz. There were many things he loved—the way the young people were together, always walking with their arms around each other's shoulders, the peace and beauty, the support they gave one another. But there were irritations too. Life was provincial here, with everyone knowing everyone else's business. He thought it might get boring after a while.

One thing that was not boring was the talk when they sat around the kitchen table. It was loud and lively with political arguments

"You Americans are all so spoiled," David said one day.

"Everything comes easy. You buy everything you see on the television."

"Depends who you are," Joseph answered. "If you're poor that's not true."

"What do you know about being poor?"

Joseph was annoyed at the tone, the assumption that all Americans were rich. He sat back, wondering how much to say about his life, before and after college. "I lived with poor people," he said. "When I was in the Peace Corps, I lived in Tanganyika for two years digging wells so the people could have clean water. There was no electricity, and the women were going down to the river and carrying pails of water a half mile back to their huts. Your kibbutz is like the Ritz compared to where I lived."

"Yes, but that was Africa," David said. "I was talking about America."

"Well, in America I lived with poor black people too. I worked voter registration in Mississippi in 1965. I lived in a shack, just like the blacks did. None of us had much. And it was dangerous. We were scared all the time because of the white Southerners—the year before they had murdered three civil rights workers."

Shoshanna looked perplexed. "Why did you do that if it was so dangerous? You have a choice. Not like us. We have no choice. *Ayn breyra.*"

Joseph had heard that expression many times. The Israelis used it constantly. Ayn breyra they had to come to Israel, ayn breyra they had to fight the Arabs, ayn breyra they could not give back all the land they conquered in the Six Day War. "There are always choices," Joseph said.

"Yes? So why do the black people stay there? Do they have choice? No. And we don't either. Where would we go? Who would have us? There is no choice." Shoshanna's cheeks were red, and her eyes blazed.

David jumped in. "And anyway, they are not your people. Why do you not come here and fight for your own people?"

Joseph stared at them. "But they are my people. They're Americans. Don't we have to stand up for all oppressed people? Especially us? Especially after what happened to our family and no one spoke up?" There was thick silence around the table. "And I don't understand how people like us, who were discriminated against, can talk the way I sometimes hear Israelis talk about Palestinians. Like they aren't as good as us." The words reverberated, and Joseph was embarrassed.

Miriam interjected. "Some of them are good. Just different." And she changed the subject.

One Saturday in July, he was hiking with David and Shoshanna in the hills above the Kibbutz when they came upon a boy squatting in the road, his bare feet the color of dust. He was not wearing a shirt, and his ribs showed under his skin like a precise line drawing. Behind him Joseph saw the crags and stubble of white rocks on the hills. The crooked olive trees had gnarly arms laden with gray green leaves. They were ancient olive groves owned by the Arabs who had once lived there.

Joseph, David, and Shoshanna spread a cloth under a tree. They had brought bread—large crusty loaves baked fresh that morning in the kibbutz bakery—and white crumbly goat cheese, and olives—brown and green and black. The tomatoes were fresh from the kibbutz garden and burst with red juice in Joseph's mouth; he could taste the sun. There were figs and dates from the kibbutz orchard and huge globes of Jaffa oranges, left from last winter's harvest. David peeled one in a long single loop.

As they were eating the boy came closer, standing under the tree, looking with sullen eyes at their picnic. Shoshanna offered him bread and cheese.

He shook his head.

Shoshanna had brought a bag of small, black and white *garonim*, sunflower seeds, which both the Israelis and Arabs were fond of. She held out the bag to the boy. He took a handful and began eating them and spitting the husks on the ground.

"Joseph," David said. "Look. You can see the kibbutz from here." He pointed to the land below them, green and dense with growth.

The boy's eyes narrowed, and he said something in Hebrew. He spit a husk onto the blanket.

"Go home," David said. "You are bothering us."

"What did he say?" Joseph asked.

"He said that was his land."

"What does he mean, his land?"

"Nothing. He doesn't know what he's talking about." David turned again to the boy. "Go home!"

"No, let him stay. He's an Israeli Arab, isn't he?"

Joseph shrugged. "Yes. But it doesn't matter. He should go."

"Does he speak English?" Joseph asked.

David looked at the boy suspiciously. "Maybe a little."

"Where do you live?" Joseph asked.

The boy pointed behind them to a village Joseph could barely make out in the hills. The Arab villages were hard to see during the day, built to merge into the rocks. At night, the electric lights of hundreds of them twinkled on the hills. The boy seemed to be waiting for something.

"Should I give him some money?" Joseph asked.

"No!" David said. "You will make him a beggar." He turned to the boy. "I told you to go." The boy took a few steps backward. He stooped and picked up a rock. David got up and, fists clenched, moved toward the boy who turned, ran a few yards off and stood watching them.

The lunch was ruined. "Let's go," Shoshanna said. They began to pack up and as they left the cool shelter of the tree to move onto the path, they turned their backs on the boy. Then Joseph felt a rock hit his leg, and another splatter in the dirt in front of him.

David started to run after the boy, but he had already disappeared into the trees. "Shit," he said with disgust, turning back. "Little terrorist."

As they walked back to the kibbutz Joseph felt sick to his stomach. "I don't understand what just happened. I don't get Israeli relationships to the Arabs," he said. "Your mother brings food to the families of the Arabs nearby when their mother is sick. The ambulance from the hospital in Tiberius goes all over the Galilee—Jews and Arabs, it doesn't matter. The doctors even make house calls to the Arab villages. And the Arabs work in the kibbutz. They seem like they are your friends. You wouldn't do that if they were all terrorists."

"Yes, well we know them for years," Shoshanna said. "And they are our neighbors. Of course, we help them."

"But still they resent us," David said. "You see how he throws rocks. I told you, don't trust them. You always have to watch them."

Joseph shook his head and kept walking, deeply puzzled. He did not understand the mix of hatred and compassion the Arabs and Israelis felt for one another—neighbors and enemies.

On another Shabbat, David borrowed the kibbutz car and took Joseph to Jerusalem. He showed him the huge new plaza in front of the Western Wall where the Israelis had made an outdoor synagogue after the Six Day War in 1967. Joseph folded his own little paper prayer and lodged it into a crack in the wall.

"When the Arabs were here, this plaza was a *shuk*, a marketplace, in front of the Wall. It was dirty. They didn't care that it was our holy place. We weren't even allowed near it. We had to look at it from there." David turned and pointed up to the King David Hotel. "The 1948 armistice line was right in front of it." Then he turned and looked above the Western Wall to the Dome of the Rock, where a golden dome glittered in the sun. "And there is our Temple Mount where our ancient Temple was, and they have a mosque there, and we have to protect it and let them in to pray there. They never protected our holy places or let us in to pray." David's voice was full of resentment.

"Why do you care?" Joseph asked. "You never pray."

"No, but it is my right if I want. Let's go up."

"I thought they don't like us to," Joseph said.

"Who? The Arabs? Who cares what they like? They can't say anything. We're in charge here now." He glared. "My best friend, Tal, died here in the Six Day War. He didn't die so I am afraid to walk up this hill."

Joseph took David's arm. "I'd rather not go there. Let's go into the old city." David hesitated, but followed.

They walked aimlessly through the narrow winding market streets of the old city, which were filled with shoppers—Israelis, Arabs, Europeans, and Americans on holiday. The Arab shopkeepers, who all spoke English, held up their goods: brass pots, wooden boxes made from olivewood inlaid with mother of pearl, earrings and necklaces and all kinds of clothing and fruit and vegetables. Joseph smelled spices and coffee and heard a gaggle of languages. He tried to imagine it before the reunification of East and West Jerusalem. It probably was the same—just no Jews there before the Six Day War.

"Tell me about Tal," he said to David.

"Nothing to tell. We grew up together on the kibbutz. He was funny. He made me laugh." David wouldn't look at Joseph. They passed a vendor selling fragrant pita bread and he stopped to buy some, tearing it into pieces and offering some to Joseph. They kept walking while they chewed. "He was a paratrooper," David said eventually. "He was with the brigade that reunified Jerusalem, but he was killed by a sniper."

"I'm sorry," Joseph said.

"Yeah. Me too."

"Did he have any brothers or sisters?"

"There's a younger brother, but he has Down's syndrome. And then, after Tal was killed his mother got pregnant again and had a baby girl. She's four years now."

Joseph was silent. *How could they risk it?* he wondered. "Weren't they worried they might have another kid with Down's? Or another war?"

David looked at him oddly. "Ayn Breyra. We need to make more people. And there won't be a war again."

Joseph raised an eyebrow. "You sound pretty sure."

"I am. They won't fight because they are afraid of us."

"I don't blame them," Joseph said. "I'm afraid of you too."

David laughed and threw his arm around Joseph's shoulder. Joseph put his arm around his cousin's neck, and they walked like that together back to the car.

September came with little change in the weather, but everyone was preparing for the High Holidays, the stores decorated with fruit and horns of plenty. There was a festive mood all over the country. Rosh Hashanah was in late September, and Joseph, David, Shoshanna, and their friends went to the beach in Tel Aviv. The weather was gorgeous, the beach full of young partygoers and vacationing families who were not religious. They swam and played volleyball and camped on the sand.

A week later, October 7, everyone was at home. No Israeli traveled on Yom Kippur, the holiest day of the year, and no cars were on the road. But by mid-morning it was clear this Yom Kippur was different. In some of the cottages on the kibbutz, men who were in the elite army and air force units received telephone calls and disappeared with their gear.

"Don't be scared," David told Joseph. "It is just maneuvers." But Joseph saw the kibbutz members standing in groups, worried looks on their faces, whispering to each other. The Israeli radio station, which was usually silent on Yom Kippur, had begun to broadcast. Portable radios were brought outside, and everyone clustered around listening to the call-ups. Numbered codes told the reservists where they should go to meet their units. Joseph knew it was more than just maneuvers. He could hear explosions far away and saw trails of jets flying overhead.

Huge city buses appeared on the roads. They parked in front of each kibbutz in the region and waited for the men who swung out of their houses wearing khaki uniforms with their Uzis slung over their shoulders. The family members hugged them good-bye, pressed packages of food on them, and watched them enter the buses and disappear.

David and Shoshanna clung to each other, and then David climbed the stairs to enter the bus and join his fellow reservists in the Golan Heights. He reached out the window, waved to Joseph and his parents, and touched hands with Shoshanna. Then they stood back and waited until the bus disappeared down the road.

Everyone reassured Joseph that everything would be okay. They would push the Arabs back in a few days as they had in 1967. But Joseph was frightened. Like most Americans, he had never been in a war. When he went down into the town, he saw the rush of people in the grocery stores, buying everything off the shelves, picking them clean. He realized that most of the Israelis had lived through many wars in Europe and the Middle East, and they did not want to go without.

His parents called the kibbutz office, and when he finally was able to speak with them, they begged him to come home. "The news we hear is terrible," Victor said. "It sounds like the Arabs almost overran all the borders."

Joseph knew that in the first days, the Syrians had overrun the border on the Golan Heights, and in the south, the Egyptians had advanced and taken the whole Sinai Peninsula. It had looked grim at first, but now the reports were more optimistic. The Israelis were pushing back hard, and after one week had regained most of the land they had lost.

"I think we'll be all right," he said.

Victor told him that Ruby was crying hysterically every day. "She says she keeps seeing you lying bleeding somewhere, dead."

"Tell her she's imagining things."

Victor snorted. "You try telling her. She says she sees the future."

"Well it doesn't matter. I can't just walk away when everyone here has to stay and fight."

"It's not your fight," his father said to him. "You're not an Israeli."

"I'm a Jew. I'm one of them," he said. But in the end, he promised that if the American government advised its citizens to leave, he would go home.

Most of the European volunteers left. The kibbutz was short-handed, with all the able-bodied men, even the older ones, called up to serve. Alfred was assigned to guard duty at a local jail. With the volunteers gone and the Arab workers afraid to show up at the kibbutz, Joseph was one of the few men around. He worked hard but he was unskilled. School was out for several weeks—there weren't enough teachers. There were blackouts at night, but it was Succoth, the fall harvest festival. There was a full moon, so he was able to walk with the bright moonlight to guide him down the road to visit friends and neighbors.

After the first week, casualty reports started coming in. A soldier from a neighboring kibbutz was killed. Etz Hadas kibbutz members visited his family, bringing food. And then two and a half weeks into the war two Israeli Defense Force officers appeared at the gate of Etz Hadas. The kibbutz members, knowing that the Israeli Army notified families in person of the death of a soldier, watched as the two men entered Alfred and Miriam's cottage. Someone rushed to call Shoshanna out of the children's nursery, but she stood like a statue on the path until Alfred came out of his cottage and, weeping, walked toward her holding his arms out.

Alfred and Shoshanna half carried each other back inside the cottage. Their kibbutz neighbors parted the way for them, touched their shoulders and whispered words to them. Joseph slipped into the house and sat in the kitchen with a few other close friends listening to the two Army officers talking in the living room. It seemed that David had died defending his comrades with a machine gun in a crippled tank on the Golan Heights, until finally the Syrians had exploded it with a bomb. He would receive a medal for his bravery.

Little by little the room filled with neighbors. When Shoshanna finally looked up and saw Joseph she rushed into his arms and her head knocked against his lip. He tasted blood. He had no words.

For two nights he lay sleepless in the empty volunteer dorm room, thinking. On the third night, the door to his room creaked open and a shadow crept in. It was Shoshanna, shoulders hunched, her face carved with anguish and streaked with the tears that had been flowing since she first heard the news.

She stood by his bed and whispered, "Hold me." Her breath smelled from coffee. Joseph reached up and drew her down beside him, folding her in his arms, moving his body against the wall to make room for her in the bed. The odor of grief was on her. Her unwashed hair was rank, and her body smelled of stale sweat. Her breasts pressed against his chest. He stroked her curls, kissed her forehead. Her brow was sheened with sweat. She burrowed closer to him, her shoulders heaving with sobs. His mouth moved from her forehead to her closed swollen eyes, and he tasted salt on her wet eyelashes.

He knew she just wanted the comfort of a human body—to feel life again. She did not want him. But as she continued weeping and he continued stroking her back, she moved closer to him. His hands moved over her shoulders and toward her breasts. She did not stop him. He kissed her and against his open lips she murmured David's name. And again, "David, David."

Joseph drew back; shame flushed his face. "I'm sorry," he whispered. He pulled himself up so he was sitting against the wall, and she was leaning against him, her head on his chest, her tears wetting his shirt.

"I am sorry too," she said. "It is my fault. I just want to be held."

"I miss him," Joseph whispered. And he started to cry, his shoulders heaving. Shoshanna stroked his arm. He rubbed his eyes. "I'm not used to crying. Men don't cry much in America. I only saw my father cry once in my whole life."

"How sad, not to be able to cry. Why did he cry then?"

"I was very little when I saw him. I remember I just had my fourth birthday, so it must have been 1947. We were at my grandparents' house, and they were all sitting at the dining room table—Bubbie Ida and Bubbie Bessie and Zeydie Abe, and my parents. My father was holding a letter. He said, 'They are all dead. They must be all dead.' I didn't know what he was talking about, but he was sobbing. That's why I remember it. I had never seen him cry before." Joseph shifted against the wall.

"Years later I figured it out. They were looking for their relatives, the ones they left behind in Europe. My grandfather had a sister and her family in Poland, and my father's whole family was in Germany except for Alfred. They were writing letters, searching lists, and I guess that day my father realized that his whole family was dead."

They were silent for a long time. Then Shoshanna said, "What did he do?"

"Nothing. He went on." Joseph heard the in out, in out of Shoshana's slow breath. "What do they do here, all the people who lose someone? Do they marry again, the widows?"

"If they can find someone." Then she said with characteristic Israeli bluntness, "Are you asking me if I will find someone?"

"Will you?"

"I hope so. I can't think of it now, but some day. And I will have a child and name him after David."

"Aren't you afraid? That there will be other wars?"

"Yes. Now I am. But we go on. That's what we do."

"I don't know how you do it," Joseph said.

"Ayn breyra." Shoshanna said. "No choice."

"I'm afraid. Afraid to have a child."

"You?" Shoshanna was shocked. "What are you afraid of? From America, the big land of safety, of wealth."

He didn't want to answer. Some fears you don't say out loud. But then, in the darkness, with the warmth of Shoshanna on his chest, he said, "I'm afraid I'll have a child who is crazy like my mother."

"What do you mean, crazy?"

"Mentally ill," Joseph said. "My mother is mentally ill." It was the first time he had said it out loud.

There was a big intake of breath from Shoshanna. "But is it better to have no child at all?"

The question hung in the air for a long time. Shoshanna fell asleep with her head on his chest while Joseph lay with his hands over his eyes thinking.

He stayed at the kibbutz after the fighting was over, through the winter rains, into January and then February when an occasional day of soft air brought the promise of spring. The Arab workers returned. Even though Joseph didn't think any of them had fought in the war, there was great anger against them, but it eventually faded. He even saw one of them speaking softly to Miriam, his hat in his hands, his head bent—offering condolences, Joseph thought. Miriam patted the worker's shoulder and shook his hand.

Joseph watched how the kibbutz members went on and supported each other. Shoshanna walked through the kibbutz, doing what she always did, eating with her friends and taking care of the children, acting as if she did not have a huge hole in her heart. Miriam sent food to her Arab neighbors. There were two babies born on the kibbutz that winter. No one questioned why. "Ayn breyra," they all said. Joseph did not understand the matter-of-factness, the simplicity, the bravery and fatalism of ayn breyra.

The question Shoshanna had asked him reverberated in his head. Is it better to have no child at all? Was the risk of Ruby's mental illness and the chaos he had known as a child worse than the loneliness he felt now? He could not answer that question, not while he was in Israel, where people were mending their broken lives all around him and going on and starting over.

One night, over coffee and cookies Alfred said bluntly, "You are going back to America, aren't you?"

Joseph was startled. "Why do you say that?"

"You look lost. Unhappy." Alfred nodded toward Miriam. "We have been talking. We feel you are separate from us."

Joseph nodded. "I think I have discovered that I am more American than I realized."

Miriam said, "Not everyone is made for the hard life in Israel."

It sounded, Joseph thought, like he was a weaker species of man than they were. He wondered if he was.

On one of the first spring days, he kissed Shoshanna good-bye, hugged Miriam and Alfred, took his duffle bag and his backpack and caught the bus to the airport and the plane back to New York.

He thought about what he would find there. There would be his father, who could tell him, if he asked, how he had lived his version of ayn breyra. For sure there would be Ruby, creating her particular chaos; there would be his sister Sarah with her daughter Didi, who, he admitted, showed no sign of any mental problems. There would be his girlfriend, Gail, if she still wanted him. There would be the law, where he might address some of the injustices that he saw around him. There would be his future, waiting for him to start again and find a way to make a life.

13

Morris

1977

The last time Morris drove cross-country it was 1946, and he had left New York and his pregnant girlfriend, Pauline, and set off for California in a haze of confusion. He was driving a used Chevrolet that he had bought with $250 borrowed from his friend Frank. After three months of camping, of exploring the Badlands of South Dakota, Yellowstone Park, and Yosemite in California, he had awakened one morning in San Francisco and realized that he wanted to go home. The doubts he had felt before he left on his trip—that he was too young to marry, that it was too soon to have a baby, that maybe the baby wasn't even his—had disappeared in the loneliness of traveling solo for so long. He wanted to marry Pauline and go to the Police Academy and settle down near his family and Sam and Frank, his two best friends, and raise kids and live a normal life.

And here he was, thirty-one years later, pulling an RV trailer in his brand-new Chevy, with that same Pauline beside him. It was two o'clock on a Monday afternoon in early July. The sun was shining. He and Pauline had a long wide road ahead of them and a reservation at a KOA. He felt lighter, freer than he had in a long time. Morris started to whistle.

—

The sign said KAMPGROUNDS OF AMERICA, in big black print on a sun-yellow background, and it was a model of order. Each trailer or RV was assigned a cement pad to park on, with a wooden picnic table and a metal barbecue. There were waste pumps and water stations, a small grocery store, and a swimming pool full of splashing kids. In the campground office there was a list called Rules of the Road—things like "Don't make noise after ten o'clock" and "Keep your campsite free of garbage."

Morris would have preferred someplace a little more rustic, but Pauline was comfortable here. It was a good start to his trial plan, to see if they liked this vagabond life. He had put in thirty years on the job. Enough. The past two years his blood pressure had been through the roof, and he'd noticed the beginnings of a potbelly. He had vowed he would get back in shape now that he was retired. Maybe even start running, like their boy, Kenny, had—Kenny, who was tall and slim, handsome and smart. And gay. Morris still didn't understand how that could be. He was trying, but he didn't really get it.

As soon as the trailer was squared on the pad, Pauline introduced herself to the woman at the next site who offered to take her to the grocery store. The woman Pauline befriended had a large rear end that swayed in her navy polyester pants as she walked. She reminded Morris of Bubbie Ida, who always carried too much weight on her backside. He was stabbed with a pain of longing. Weird, he thought, to miss his grandmother after all these years. He was fifty-nine years old, for God's sake. She'd been gone nearly twenty years. Then he thought of the other people who were gone—his father, Sam, Angelo. Life went far too fast.

Morris took a can of Schlitz out of the fridge, two folding beach chairs from the trunk of his Chevy, and a cigar from his pocket. He lit up, puffed two perfect smoke rings, and settled into his chair. Time, he thought, to make decisions about the next twenty years of his life. He'd had close calls during these years as a detective on the job. It had hardened him. Made him cynical. He was glad he'd reached this day with his health and a few dollars in his pocket. He thought that if he were a religious man, he would say a prayer of thanksgiving, but he was not, so he simply stretched his feet out before him and breathed the country air.

And over the next few days, as they got into a routine, he saw that it was good for both of them. Morris loved the trailer, the ingenuity of the layout, the way the cooktop sat on the refrigerator, the dishes fit neatly into the cupboards, and the sink had a pump-handled faucet. He felt completely self-sufficient. Pauline said it was a little like playing house.

During the day it was sunny with blue skies—great driving weather. The scenery changed as they moved westward through Pennsylvania, Ohio, Michigan, Illinois. Every night, they settled into a new campground, had a beer with their neighbors, and after dinner sat around a campfire, drank coffee, and swapped stories.

They'd been on the road for five days when they left the Badlands of South Dakota for Yellowstone National Park where Morris wanted to see Old Faithful erupt. Ranches dotted the landscape, the towns were spread further apart, and finally the sides of the roads were densely forested. The weather turned cloudy when they reached Wyoming, the landscape wider, the sky bigger. The one radio station they got in the car played country music. Everything felt a little deserted. Pauline said it was spooky.

Morris was anxious to get settled for the night so, after checking his maps, they pulled off the highway toward a National Forest campground about one hundred miles outside of Yellowstone National Park. Pavement turned to gravel and then dirt, and as they bumped along, Morris saw something lying by the side of the road about two hundred yards ahead. The light was low, dusky, but as he got closer the shape of a body, sprawled in the dirt, became clear. He slowed the car and came to a full stop a few feet from a man.

"My God," Pauline said. "Is he dead? What should we do?"

Morris rolled his window down. He felt uneasy. His cop instincts told him something was not right. What was a man doing lying in the road, in the middle of nowhere? There was no car, no means of getting there. Could he have been hiking and come out to the road and passed out? No sign of a backpack, but the guy was wearing heavy boots. Did someone drive him and dump him out of the car? The man was lying on his stomach, one arm out, the other under his body. His face was turned away.

"Aren't you going to see if he's dead?" Pauline said. "Do something? You can't just leave him here."

"Hold on a minute," Morris said. He leaned out the car window, yelled, "Hey," but the man didn't stir. Morris opened the glove box and took out his Smith and Wesson .38 caliber revolver. He didn't have a license to carry it outside of New York, but he knew that if a cop stopped him and he showed his police ID, nothing would happen. There was that brotherhood. Now he said to Pauline, "Just a precaution. Don't you move out of the car."

He opened the car door and stepped out. Bending over the inert body and fishing around under the man's chin he found the pulse. "He's alive," he shouted. He rolled the man onto his back. As he did so, Morris's stomach turned over.

Shit," he said, as a gun came up in the man's hand and was jammed beneath Morris's chin, too fast for him to position his gun, which in a second, the man knocked out of his hand. "Easy guy," Morris said. "Easy."

The man stood up and motioned for Morris to get up, taking the gun from where Morris had dropped it and shoving it into his own pocket. *Shit, shit, shit,* the word repeated over and over in Morris' head, as he scrambled around for a solution. *What a fucking stupid,*

rookie mistake. I should have wrestled him. I should have gotten the
gun from him. I'm losing it. Losing it. Flashes of the other time he'd
reacted slowly . . . in Sicily. If it hadn't been for Frank, he'd be dead.

Morris's eyes shifted to the car, and he shook his head to Pauline.
Don't get out. "Hey man, I was only trying to help," he said.

"Shut the fuck up," the man said, shoving Morris with the gun
hard against his neck into the woods.

Morris turned to see the man's face. He was tall, wearing a dirty
khaki jacket and camouflage cargo pants. He had a red bandana tied
around his head and his hair stuck out around his ears and neck,
greasy and brown. He looked about thirty years old and was breathing heavily, his mouth open, and he was missing one upper front
tooth. He was heavily bearded, with grime lines around his neck. His
eye sockets look purple and bruised, and his dark brown eyes were
rheumy. He smelled from sweat and unwashed hair. He was mumbling something.

Morris said "What? What'd you say?"

The man poked him with his gun. "Shut the fuck up. You don't
do the talking. I do the talking."

"Okay, okay," Morris said, and he kept walking with the gun
pressed against his back. He felt nauseous. He was washed with
shame, jolted with self-disgust. He could not bear to think how this
happened, so he concentrated, trying to figure out where they were
walking. He focused his eyes down and saw the scuffed dirt of a well-
worn path. That was good. It calmed him a little. He could find his
way out.

After about fifteen minutes they were in a small clearing in the
woods. He was shoved against a tree, his back and head slammed
against hard wood. He was forced to sit. The man, still holding the
gun, backed up and fished behind him, never taking his eyes off

Morris. He reached a rope and tied Morris to the tree, using his mouth as a third hand to hold one end of the rope. Morris tensed his arms, hoping the man, handicapped by holding the gun in one hand, would not notice and that the tension would leave him with slack in the rope when he relaxed his arms. The man backed off, grunted approval and sat against a tree opposite Morris.

Morris looked around. It was a campsite. Beside a khaki army tent was a pile of trash—Pabst Blue Ribbon beer bottles and empty cans from Chef Boyardee and Spaghetti-Os were littered around a small, rock-rimmed campfire pit. Two pails of water sat by a tree. Morris could hear a brook running nearby.

The man took a fresh beer, popped the top, and fished a pack of Lucky Strikes from the pocket of his jacket. He had his revolver by his side, and across his lap was a rifle, which had been leaning against the tree.

Morris stared, assessed. The man was dangerous, possibly psychotic, but maybe not—maybe just a criminal. "Where are we?" he asked.

The man shook a cigarette out of the pack, put it in his mouth, and lit it with a Bic lighter from his pocket. "Nowhere . . . my home sweet home." He was sneering. "Near your fucking village."

What village? What the hell is he talking about? "What's your name?" Morris asked.

The man stood up, came closer and loomed over Morris's head. "You don't ask the questions. I ask the questions."

Morris nodded, was quiet.

"Hammerman," he said suddenly. "They call me Hammerman."

"Hammerman," Morris repeated, noting the 'they.' He waited.

"You want to know why . . . because I'm a goddamn hammer." He lifted his rifle and made as if to hammer Morris on the head. Morris flinched. Hammerman laughed. Then in a burst, he said, "You have Angel. I want to trade."

"Who's Angel?" Morris asked.

This enraged Hammerman. He took the rifle and knocked it across Morris's chin, banging his head back against the tree. "Who's Angel? You know goddamn well who Angel is. You fucking gooks always pretend to be ordinary people, but every fucking one of you is VC." He turned away and started to pace, mumbling to himself.

Morris's head, chin, and neck were all pounding pain. He closed his eyes against it. *Fuck. The guy was hallucinating. Psychotic. He's a fucking psychotic Vietnam vet—the war's been over two years, and he's still reliving it.* Morris tested his jaw, moving it back and forth. It didn't seem broken. He moved his tongue in his mouth. No blood. *Think. Think. He thinks he's in Vietnam. His buddy was captured by the VC, and he's looking for him, and he thinks I know where he is.*

Above the trees the twilight was deep lavender. It wouldn't be long before it was full dark. Hammerman was pacing now, around and around the unlit campfire, muttering to himself. Morris watched him carefully.

Suddenly Hammerman was at his side again, with a rifle against Morris' head. "Where is he? I ought to shoot your chickenshit brains all over this fucking jungle."

Morris opened his mouth to talk.

"Shut the fuck up. Don't say nothing. My finger is twitchy. I could shoot you now and not worry about a thing except for Angel. Where is he?"

Morris swallowed, his eye on the rifle that Hammerman was pressing against his head. He focused on Hammerman. *Don't shoot,* he prayed to a god he didn't believe in. He felt his stomach clutch, prayed he didn't piss his pants.

"Stop staring." Hammerman shoved the rifle harder against Morris' temple. "Where? Tell me." Hammerman nudged him again. "Tell me, motherfucker. Tell me now before I blow you away. Now."

Morris closed his eyes. *Not now, not now, not now.* His breath was ragged, then steadied. "I don't know," he said. "I swear I don't know where Angel is."

"Ah, Fuck it." Hammerman moved away to get another beer. Morris almost gagged in relief.

Morris thought Hammerman was one of the craziest people he'd ever dealt with, and he'd dealt with a lot, starting with his own sister, Ruby, who could really go off when she heard the voice in her head. The people he'd arrested, people he'd talked down . . . once he'd talked a man off the ledge of an office building. Calm. Encouraging. He didn't think that would work here. Hammerman was too psychotic. One thing he'd learned. Never contradict a psychotic in the midst of his psychosis. When he was a rookie, he'd tried to convince a psychotic woman that he wasn't a zombie, and she'd taken a knife to him, almost killing him. He'd never do that again.

Hammerman took another beer. He sat and leaned against the tree, his rifle across his lap. After he finished his beer, he got up, lit the fire, and then took two cans of Chef Boyardee from the stockpile, opening them with a can opener. He seemed so calm now. The man who had rifle-butted Morris was gone. Disappeared.

Hammerman gave a can to Morris —spaghetti and meatballs— no fork, no spoon. Morris ate slowly, with his fingers. The meatballs were grainy, the sauce, cold and gelatinous. He was not hungry, but he ate anyway. He wondered why Hammerman hadn't tied his hands, just his body, and figured it was because he had the rifle trained on him the whole time.

The darkness beyond the small glow of the campfire was pervasive. He could see Hammerman's shadowy figure on the other side of the fire. He looked undone. He was mumbling to himself.

"Angel's a good friend to you," Morris said, as if he knew Angel.

"Goddamned fucking-A right. We been together since we got to this asshole country."

"Best friend I ever had was Frank, my buddy from Baker Company. We slogged through Sicily together."

"Where?"

"Sicily. In World War II. It rained and rained. Our feet were wet. Everything was wet. My feet nearly fell off."

"Yeah. I never dry out. Everything's hot and wet. Did you ever get foot rot? The crud? Jeezus, you never get dry." Hammerman pulled out paper and tobacco, rolled a joint, and pulled hard on it. The smell of marijuana wafted toward Morris. "Fucking country."

"I don't know where Angel is," Morris said, "But I think I know how you feel. My buddy was captured by the Italians in Sicily and I had to rescue him . . . just like you want to rescue Angel."

"Yeah?" Hammerman narrowed his eyes. "How? How'd you do it?"

Morris started to talk. Slowly, calmly, making things up as he went along, conflating fact and imagination to meet what he thought Hammerman wanted to hear. "Frank was captured. I followed them, just like you're trying to. I lay in the trees. The Italians weren't so smart, just like the gooks aren't smart. I watched them."

Morris went on with the story, half-truth and half fantasy. How his buddy Frank had been captured in Agrigento, where they were fighting in Sicily. How he had followed them through the woods, crawling on his belly until it was dark. How he'd come up behind the guard and slit his throat before he could do anything, and how he and Frank had hightailed it out of there.

All of which had more or less happened, but it had been the other way around. Frank had rescued him. Even now, thinking about it, he felt the same mix of awe and pride and shame he had felt that day. Killing someone at a distance was one thing—he'd done plenty of that as a soldier. Slitting someone's throat was another story altogether. You could smell their sweat, their breath; they were real, alive one second, dead the next.

"We need to find them, where they have Angel," Morris said now. "Then we can figure how to get Angel out."

"How do we do that?" Hammerman asked.

"We wait. Move out at first light. Trust me. We'll find him."

Hammerman grunted. Finished his beer. Took another. "Why should I trust you?"

"Look at me," Morris said. "Do I look like VC to you?"

Hammerman stared at him, seemed to find a moment of lucidity, a flash of reason. He nodded. "No, you don't look like a gook. You look like an old guy," he said.

"That's right. An old guy from another war," Morris said. "And besides, you have the gun."

That seemed to satisfy Hammerman for the moment. He drank two more beers. He didn't talk, but the rifle was still trained on Morris. After a while Hammerman's head dropped. He snapped it up, looked wildly around. Then, satisfied that Morris hadn't moved and nothing had changed, he took another sip of beer. Again, and again, his head lolled, and again and again he pulled it up. The fifth or sixth time his chin rested on his chest. The beer slipped out of his hand. Morris waited. Soon the rifle dropped down. Eventually Hammerman's fingers loosened. Hammerman had passed out. Ten minutes passed. Twenty minutes. Hammerman didn't stir. His snoring grew loud.

Morris pushed his arms sideways and worked the rope until it was loose enough for him to move one arm through. Quickly, silently he untied himself, stood, and moved toward Hammerman. Very slowly he bent down and picked up his Smith and Wesson lying beside Hammerman and trained it on him. Then he moved the rifle slowly off Hammerman's lap, ready to yank it away if he woke. Hammerman didn't move. Morris took the revolver and rifle with him into the tent, glancing back at the motionless Hammerman several times.

In the tent he found four more weapons and stacks of ammunition.

Quickly and methodically he emptied bullets from the guns and took clips from the rifles. He saved one loaded rifle and revolver from Hammerman's stash and took them with a flashlight he found in the tent. Training the rifle on Hammerman, he backed quietly out of the clearing into the dark of the woods.

Switching on the flashlight, he found the path. It was amazingly easy to see the scuffed leaves and packed-down dirt. He walked about one hundred feet away and stood behind a tree, peering out every few minutes, to see if Hammerman was still sleeping.

Morris took stock. He breathed in and out, in and out. His head still hurt. His pulse was pounding. He could stand here until morning, betting that Pauline got help and they would be coming soon. She probably had. She must have driven into the park to get a ranger to help. Thank God she was a good driver. Pulling the trailer wouldn't faze her. All he wanted now was to see her again and tell her how much he loved her. He could walk out now and try to get help himself or he could wait here.

In the end he walked back into the clearing, picked up the rope and looped it around the legs of the sleeping Hammerman, then around his middle, then around his neck, tying it as tight as he dared without waking him, and then attaching the end to a nearby tree. That was as much rope as he had. It wouldn't hold Hammerman forever, but if he woke, it would give Morris some time.

Morris retreated to the edge of the clearing and, with the flashlight pointed at the well-trodden path, he walked quickly and quietly toward the road, leaving Hammerman passed out, sleeping, and unaware a few hundred feet away.

Just before first light, when the blackness grayed and he could see the edges of the trees in front of him, Morris heard them. He waited as three men in uniform approached. Morris put his finger to his lips and pointed behind him toward the clearing. He handed one of them the Smith & Wesson and rifle and followed them back down the path until they came to the clearing and surrounded Hammerman. Morris leaned back against the tree and closed his eyes.

They shook Hammerman on the shoulders. He stirred, mumbled, opened his eyes. They closed, then opened again. "What the fuck!" He looked around with disbelief, tried to get up and then, as the rope restrained him, let out a howl of pure pain. His wild eyes searched for Morris. He yelled, "You motherfucker."

Morris turned away. He trudged behind Hammerman and the police, trying not to listen to Hammerman scream obscenities at him. He wanted to tell Hammerman to shut the fuck up. He'd lost all compassion. Hammerman was just another crazy guy in a crazy world, left hollowed out and unmoored by another terrible war. Morris wanted to be done with him and all the other guys like him.

When he got to the road, he saw Pauline, her small figure pacing on the side of the road, the only woman in a sea of men. He didn't know how she had done it—how she had gotten help, found the place to enter the wood, led the sheriff and his men to him and Hammerman. He always knew she was a smart woman, smart and loyal and utterly wonderful. She was wearing a red sweater, and it flashed toward him like a beacon. He turned and walked into her waiting arms.

14

Sarah

1984

The first two or three days of the shiva for Ruby, everything was hushed with the shock of her suicide. Their neighbor Maryanne Goodman, a large, mouthy woman with iron gray curls, was the one who had called the police the day Ruby died. She came the first night and sat with the family in groups of twos or threes. As soon as she had finished speaking to one group, another took its place. Sarah heard her whispering to them about what she had seen.

"I saw it all, you know. I had to tell everything to the police. I just happened to be looking out the window of my living room, and I'm on the fourteenth floor, just one floor above the roof of Ruby and Victor's apartment, you know?" She waited until her audience nodded in understanding.

"I noticed that Ruby was on the roof," she went on, "and she was pacing back and forth. I called to my husband, 'What do you think that Ruby is doing on the roof of her apartment?' And he came over and looked with me. I was about to open the window and yell out to her when I saw her start running, running and she took a leap over the side and she was flapping her arms like she was trying to fly . . . . I screamed and screamed, but it was too late. I saw her lying on the ground. It was awful." Maryanne covered her mouth as if she wanted to take the words back.

Sarah walked away, not wanting to hear anymore. She looked around for Aunt Jenny and saw her sitting with Bubbie Bessie. So old, so confused. Jenny was patting her mother's hand, whispering soothing words. She looked up when Sarah came over, put her finger over her mouth in warning. *Don't say anything to her.*

Bessie was plucking her skirt. "She took Faye. I was frantic. Frantic. What makes her do such things?" She looked with watery eyes at Jenny who just shushed her. Bubbie Bessie was living with Jenny and Harry now, but she lived in the past, remembering every single detail of before, and nothing of now. How did Jenny do it? Jenny, the constant caretaker.

Irene came over to sit with her mother, and Jenny rose and put her arm around Sarah's shoulder. "Come sit with me."

Sarah sat with Jenny, the question in her mind, out of her mouth before she could think. "Did she . . . did she call you? Before?"

"Before what?"

"Before she did it? Jumped? Did she call you like she used to? Again, and again?"

Jenny stared for a minute. "Did she call you?"

"Yeah. A few times. I tried to calm her down. I thought it worked," Sarah said.

"I was out all day," Jenny said. "If she did call, I wasn't home."

Sarah nodded, but jumped up after a minute or two. Thoughts were intruding, and she didn't want to think them. She went to sit with her father and Joseph. Victor was responding to all the visitors with his usual grave and courtly manner. "I can't breathe in here," she said to them as she sat down. "I wish they'd all go home."

"Most of them are family," Joseph said. "They're sitting shiva too." And Sarah realized that was true. Ruby's brother Morris and his wife and kids were there and Aunt Irene and her family, Aunt Jenny and Uncle Harry and their son, George, and his wife. And of course, Joseph's wife, Gail, and their two kids, and her own daughter, Didi. Even Herb had come. They had been divorced now for two years, but he was part of the family and was there almost every day. It was a lot of people. Not nearly as many as had been at Irene's husband's shiva. Sam had been popular, a hero, with friends all over the city. Ruby had very few friends outside of the family. *Maybe there are street people she knew, and people at the bars where she hung out, but they would never come to a shiva,* Sarah thought.

"I'm going to open a window," she said, getting up from her seat.

The dining room table was full of food. It seemed everyone who came wanted to eat, and there was a continual spread of bagels and lox, cream cheese and salads, and coffee percolating and reheating in an electric pot and filling the air with its burnt smell. Sarah took a pastry from the table and bit into its buttery crust. She leaned against the wall near the window and breathed the air coming from outside. The July heat was sticky with humidity.

Didi came over to her and put her arm around her mother. Sarah laid her head on Didi's shoulder and Didi patted her back. It was good to see her. They didn't see each other enough now that Didi was in college.

Sarah was raging inside. *Who can breathe here?* Sarah thought. *All these people, talking and visiting and laughing. It's like a goddamn party, not a shiva. And the way they talk about her. Like she was a saint, like she was this gorgeous, funny woman—telling stories about how wonderfully she sang, and do you remember how she liked to wear orange and red together, and how artistic that was—and blah, blah, blah.*

Ruby had been impossible to love, and yet they all said how they loved her anyhow. *And,* Sarah thought, *it was mostly lies. She wasn't lovable. She used up everybody's time and energy taking care of her. It wasn't because they loved her. It was because she was crazy. Her last*

act had proved it. Leaping off the roof of her twelve-story apartment
building, flapping her arms like some kind of cuckoo bird!

The thought pierced Sarah like a white-hot needle. *Was there a*
moment of terror when she realized that her flapping arms were not
wings? That she was dropping like a stone? Was she sorry? Sarah's
stomach turned over at her thoughts. She shut her eyes tight, but it
came anyway. *I could have stopped her.*

When it was finally over, Sarah went downtown to her apartment in
Chelsea and settled into the thick silence around her. She was dry-
eyed and hollow, and the same question reverberated in her head.
What now? What now?

When she divorced Herb, Sarah had thought she wanted soli-
tude, but she'd never really gotten it, always having her mother to
fill in the spaces in her life. And there had also been her daughter,
Didi, to take care of until she graduated from high school and left for
college last year. And her job as an artist in an advertising firm, and
a few friends to go to museums with . . . not enough to fill her time.
What would she do now?

She looked around the apartment, took in the dingy, rain-spat-
tered living room window overlooking 16th Street, the striped curtains hanging limp. The rug was frayed, and dead and dying plants
stood by the wall, their dried leaves scattered around the floor. She
had once wanted to have an indoor garden, but there was never
enough light, or she forgot to water the plants or mist them like the
plant lady said on television. Her unfinished canvasses were stacked
against another wall. She never had time to paint the way she wanted
to. Sarah had always wanted to organize herself, make the apartment
beautiful, but she never did.

Herb used to say, "If you just make a small plan, and then take tiny
steps to make it happen, it's like magic." She found it so irritating, so

holier than thou. But Sarah knew he was right, so she tried anyhow. She would write down her plan on a piece of paper and then lose it in the chaos of the apartment. And nothing would change. "I'm lousy at planning," Sarah said. That became her mantra.

She went into her bedroom to undress and take a shower. She had to get the smell of mourning off her—all the food heaped on the tables in the dining room, the musty odor from being closed in the house with all those people for a week. As she stripped off her clothes, she saw the little black mourning ribbon still pinned to her blouse. And right beside it was the antique cameo her father had given her this morning, just before she left his house.

Victor had said, "I want you to have this now. There's other jewelry to give out, but you know this was my engagement present to her—instead of a ring. We couldn't afford one then."

Sarah had fingered the pin, looking at the face carved into the apricot colored shell of the cameo. There was a small crack in the background. "I remember when the background cracked, that time she sat on her jacket lapel," Sarah said. "She was so upset."

Her father nodded as he pinned it to Sarah's blouse. "I don't think it ruins it though," he said. "The face is still beautiful. Your mother really loved it."

"Thank you, Dad," she had said, kissing his cheek. "I always loved it too."

Sarah took the cameo off and put it on top of her bureau, next to her gold earrings. Then she went into the bathroom to shower.

After Sarah got dressed, she stood in the middle of the room. The question reverberated in her head. *What now? What now?* A familiar pulsating anxiety rose in Sarah's throat. She felt as if she were suffocating. She remembered her mother opening all the windows in their house, even in winter, saying, "I can't breathe in here. Why is there no air in this apartment?"

She saw herself reflected in the mirror, a pretty woman with even features and vivid coppery red hair. Sarah had begun coloring her hair to cover the streaks of gray and thought it made her look much younger than her thirty-eight years, but she had not realized what a change it made in her appearance. All through the last week, people had commented on her resemblance to her mother. They said she even had her laugh.

Sarah was outraged. "I don't think I sound like her or look like her at all." She didn't want to be like her mother in any way.

Remembering this now, her anxiety grew stronger. She had to leave the apartment. She took some cash from her wallet, stuck the money and her keys in the pocket of her jeans, and closed the door behind her.

Outside it was drizzling, and the air was heavy with the heat of early July. Droplets of water surrounded the streetlights like halos, and the road reflected them back. How many nights like this had she and her father searched for Ruby, trolling the streets in Brooklyn, peeking into bars or looking under the bridges at the slumped bodies of passed out drunks.

It seemed to Sarah that it had been going on her whole life. She used to think that everything would be fine if only her mother would just act normal. She bargained with God, she prayed to God, and then finally, as she grew older and recognized her mother's erratic behavior—her rants, her lows, her use of alcohol, her suicide attempts—she just gave up and called her mother "crazy," the way everybody else seemed to.

But Sarah still did what she had to—watched her, took her to her doctor's appointments, made sure she took her medicine, looked for her when she went wandering the streets. And at the end it hadn't been enough. She had not done what she needed to do to save her mother. And now a thought peeked out behind her rage and grief: *What a relief it was that it was over, that she didn't have to do it anymore.*

Sarah walked fast, head down until she reached the middle of the block on 13th street where the fluorescent sign for Morley's Bar and Grill glowed green. She had walked there without thinking. She often went there for a drink, and she liked the familiar smoky interior, the smell of booze, the icy blast of air conditioning. She nodded hello to Stan, the bartender, slipped onto a stool, and ordered a martini with an olive.

On the side of the L-shaped bar, a large woman with stringy platinum blond hair and heavy makeup caking her cheeks was expounding to anyone who would listen. She held a tall glass of gin tightly, and her nail polish was chipped. She didn't look at all like Ruby, but there was a buzz about her that reminded Sarah of her mother. As Ruby had aged, she drank more, and she had become sloppy like that, wearing bright orange lipstick, the color smeared and bleeding into the fine lines around her mouth.

Ruby hadn't always been like that. Sarah had a distinct memory of standing in the doorway of her parents' bedroom when she was very little, watching her thirty-year-old mother shimmying her shoulders and moving close to her father, enticing him to dance with her. She had been so beautiful with her red hair and white skin. Her father had bent down to kiss her, and Sarah felt like she was watching a movie.

Now, Stan, a barrel-chested man with curly brown hair, put the martini in front of Sarah and moved a dish of peanuts nearer to her hand. She took the first sip of the drink and felt the warmth of the gin spread down her throat. She began to calm down.

"Hot enough for you out there?" Stan said conversationally.

"It's never hot enough for me," Sarah said. "I love really hot weather."

"Me too," a man two seats down at the bar said to her. "I don't know how New Yorkers stand the winters here."

Sarah pulled the olive off the toothpick with her teeth and

chewed. She looked over at the man and said, "Oh, we just bundle up and keep our heads down against the wind."

"You live in New York?" When Sarah nodded the man went on, "If you like hot weather you should come down where I live." The man was very good looking, in his twenties, with a tanned skin and slicked black hair. He was tall, with wide shoulders and muscled biceps, which showed under his white T-shirt.

"Where's that?"

"Guess," he said.

"Florida? California? Arizona? Mexico? Puerto Rico? Hawaii?" Sarah fired off the place names too fast for him to answer.

He laughed. "Whoa," he said. He looked straight at her, and his eyes were bluer than hers. Sarah felt a little jump inside her.

"Where then?"

"California," he said.

"North or south?" Sarah asked.

"South. Way south. Practically in Mexico."

"Are you Mexican?"

"Do I look Mexican?" he asked, a little edge to his voice.

She tipped her head. "Maybe. I'm not sure what Mexicans look like."

"Well I'm not," he said. "I'm pure American."

"Whatever that is," Sarah said. She sipped her drink slowly. What was she getting so huffy about? They were just making casual conversation.

"I've never been to California," Sarah said. "My brother used to live in San Francisco, but I never visited him when he lived out West. What's it like?"

"Well, San Francisco's different from Southern California. Where I live it's warm, and the ocean's great. You should come," he said. "It's beautiful. Always great weather . . . except for the earthquakes." He laughed, and his teeth were very white.

"Well there's always something with the weather. We can have bad hurricanes in New York," Sarah said. The man reminded her of someone . . . who? She couldn't think of anyone.

"I was in New Orleans in August of sixty-nine when Hurricane Camille hit," the floozy yelled from her corner. "The winds nearly blew my house out from under me."

"Yeah—Camille—I remember that," the man said and winked at Sarah. He took a swig from his bottle of Budweiser.

"You no more remember that than I do," Sarah said to him. He laughed. But she did remember the month and the year. August 1969. That was when Sarah had met Herb—at the Woodstock Music Festival. She remembered how he had just picked her up in the café by taking her photo as she walked in the door. He'd bought her a tuna sandwich, and they'd shared a blueberry pie. It was raining that day too. Now she said, "August of sixty-nine was Woodstock."

"Yeah, Woodstock," he said. "I heard about that too."

Sarah laughed. "Do you really remember that?" She was feeling better. She swallowed the last sip of her martini.

"Everyone's heard of Woodstock," he said.

"I guess so," she agreed. "It was a pretty big deal. How old were you then? Fifteen? Sixteen?"

"Fourteen. By the way, my name is Mark."

"Sarah."

They got comfortable. The conversation at the bar swung from one topic to another. Mark told her about being in an earthquake and bought Sarah a second martini. She asked him about growing up in Southern California, while she sipped the drink slowly. They ordered hamburgers and shared fries. She ate the fries one at a time, dipping them into the ketchup he had poured on the side of her plate.

On the third drink, Sarah felt her lips and her tongue getting numb as she sipped. She wondered what it would be like to go to bed with this guy—this Mark. She felt adventuresome, wild almost.

She and Mark kept talking, a casual conversation about what was going on in the world. They agreed that it wouldn't matter at all that the Soviet Union was boycotting the summer Olympics in Los Angeles that month, but they had a heated debate about whether Vanessa Williams should give back her crown as Miss America because she had posed for nude photos published in *Penthouse*. Sarah defended Vanessa Williams. "There's nothing wrong with showing the female body," she said.

"Want to show me yours?" Mark said. He grinned down at her. "I bet you're as gorgeous as she is in the altogether."

"Oh God," Sarah groaned. "Is that the best you can do for a line?"

"Pretty bad?"

"Yes," she said. But she had a familiar riffle inside, like she used to get when she was in high school and college and she'd experimented with sex with a dozen boys in a relentless drive to first lose her virginity and then find the man of her dreams.

Sarah was staring at Mark's mouth as he chewed the French fries, watching how careful he was, dabbing the corners of his lips with his napkin. It was very sexy. She was feeling a definite attraction but declined the fourth martini, afraid she would slip over from feeling good into a state of drunkenness, which she did not want.

What she wanted, she decided, was sex. She was starved for sex. It had been way too long. Two years since she and Herb had split, and during that time there had been only infrequent sexual encounters. More often than not she was left satisfying herself in her big, empty bed. And Mark was attractive—very attractive.

She pushed away the uneasiness that she had felt when they first were talking about Mexicans. She would bet they were on opposite sides of the political spectrum. But what did that matter? She wasn't marrying him.

"Where do you live?" she asked finally.

"Live? I told you, California," he said.

"No, I meant here," she said.

"Oh. I'm visiting my sister for a few months. She lives uptown. Where do you live?"

Sarah hesitated and then thought, why not? "Two blocks away . . . this is my neighborhood."

For a minute they stared into each other's eyes, and then Sarah cocked her head. "Why don't you walk me home?"

It was easy after that. They linked arms, as much to help her steady herself as to be friendly and walked the few blocks to her apartment. When they got there, she opened the door and he followed her in.

The sex was good. She was giggling as she lifted his T-shirt over his head, admiring his biceps, running her fingers over his chest. They wandered into her bedroom, strewing the rest of their clothes as they went. Afterward they lay in her bed, and Mark told her again about California and how beautiful it was.

Sarah was enchanted. She suddenly knew that outside of New York there was a world of possibilities. She felt her skin tingle with them. Talking with Mark had opened a window. Somewhere else there was warm weather, maybe a small house in a beach town, a simple job that would leave time for her to paint. Ruby would never need her again. Her daughter, Didi, was in college now, and her father could get along without her. They would all get along without her.

She closed her eyes and remembered all at once who it was that Mark had reminded her of. It wasn't any of the boys in high school or college who she dated or went to bed with. It was a young George Hamilton from *Where the Boys Are*, the movie she and all her friends had seen over and over the summer she was sixteen. It was the beach and the boys and the sex and all the possibilities of being young that she had wanted. She drifted off to sleep wondering if any of it was still there.

She woke in the middle of the night, feeling fuzzy-headed. Her mouth was dry. The room was dark, with only a slight glow from the outside streetlights. She remembered the whole evening, the sex, the fantasies she'd had as she drifted off to sleep, about living in paradise and waking up with Mark and spending the day together. She reached out and touched the sheets beside her. They were empty. She felt deflated. He hadn't said good-bye; she didn't know his last name. She would probably never see him again.

But something wasn't right. She sat upright with a sense of unease and, as her eyes focused, she saw him. He was rummaging in her bureau drawers pulling out clothing. The jewelry box on top of her bureau was lying on its side, empty. With the blood pounding in her head she jumped up. "What the hell do you think you're doing?"

He held his hand out in the warning signal of *Stop!* Her pearls, her gold earrings, the cameo, were bunched in his fist.

"Give me that," she said.

He started backing out of the room, his arm still outstretched. She raced toward him, grabbed his arm and struggled to get the jewelry from him. With his other hand he slammed her hard in the face, and she crumpled to the floor. She lay crying in a heap, her mouth throbbing, feeling a loose tooth, holding her mouth, tasting blood.

He loomed over her and stared. "I wouldn't get up if I were you," he said. He turned and sauntered out of the apartment, slamming the door behind him.

Sarah lay in a heap, her body shaking with sobs. Suddenly she felt sick, needing to throw up. She ran to the bathroom and vomited into the toilet again and again, retching until her throat hurt and there was nothing left within her. Afterward she sat for a long time on the tile floor, her arms embracing the bowl, her cheek resting on the cool porcelain. *What now? What now?*

She knew she should call the police. But she couldn't imagine what she would tell them. She thought how it would sound . . . she had brought this stranger into her house, gone to bed with him, he'd beaten her up and disappeared with her jewelry that was conveniently left on her bureau. She couldn't call them. It was too humiliating.

She went back into the bedroom and sat on the bed, head in her hands. In the mirror opposite she saw herself: pathetic, unkempt, lost. Her cheek was swollen, her eyes dull.

Suddenly she had a memory of her mother looking just like that. She'd been out on the street all night, probably drinking, but that time she had come back on her own, disheveled and bleary-eyed. She must have fallen or gotten into a fight because her face was bruised and her arms scratched. She had come into the house in the early morning and sat on the sofa, head drooping, just as Sarah's was now. Her red hair was in disarray and her clothes were askew. At the time, Sarah remembered looking at her and thinking, with a flash of absolute conviction, that her mother had been with a man. But she had pushed the thought out of her mind, refusing to believe it. Now she was sure it was true.

And she, Sarah, was just like her mother. She started to cry. Waves of disgust engulfed her. Once she began, she could not stop. She wept then for the loss of her childhood, her marriage, her father's pain, her mother's anguish, her own shame, and finally, the theft of her mother's cameo. She lay down on the bed, covered herself with blankets and cried until she had no tears left.

It was her fault, she knew. Her fault that her mother had died. Ruby had called and called. Each time, Sarah had tried to assuage her hysteria. Each time her mother had seemed calmer and hung up, only to call again five minutes later. And again, five minutes after that. Until finally, Sarah had shouted to her, "You're making me nuts. Stop calling me." She had slammed the receiver down on the cradle, and before it had a chance to ring again, she had taken it off the hook.

She lay, ashen on the bed. *What now,* she asked herself over and over again. She had no answer, only emptiness.

15

Jenny
1986–1988

Jenny came out of the bathroom after her morning shower and looked over at the bed where Harry lay, eyes closed. She wondered if he was still sleeping. She put her hand on his cheek and caressed it. His eyes opened, and he smiled a lopsided grin. "Goo mor-ing," he said.

"Want to get up now?" she asked.

He nodded. She began the laborious chore of helping him into his wheelchair and going through his morning washing. His hands and arms were weak, and he could no longer hold or maneuver the toothbrush, so she brushed his teeth for him and wiped his mouth. Then she pushed him down the apartment's long hallway to the dining room.

Jenny loved their apartment. The floors were covered with old Persian rugs and runners, and Jenny had decorated the house in warm reds and blues to match. She had painted the walls rich creamy colors and hung prints and paintings in every room. It was a beautiful home, one many of her friends and family envied, and she herself felt blessed to have lived in it for her entire married life. Especially now, with Harry needing a wheelchair, the apartment's one floor made it so much easier for her, and she was grateful for that as well.

In the dining room she poured Harry's liquid nourishment into a glass with a straw and helped position it, so he could sip. She could see it was getting difficult for him to swallow, and sometimes he would take too big a sip and go into spasms of coughing.

He can't go on much longer—or could he? He isn't getting enough calories. Is a feeding tube next? Would he even want one?

She blinked hard and breathed deep. "Patrick will be here in a few minutes," she said. "He'll help you get dressed. And George and Anni are coming again tonight."

"He's a goo son," Harry said.

"He is," Jenny agreed. "Do you have any thoughts about what you'd like to do today?"

"Wha the wuther?"

"What's the weather like?" Jenny asked. Harry nodded. "Mild, I think. Perfect May day. Maybe a nice walk by the river or a visit to the Metropolitan or the Guggenheim?"

"Me-ropo-tan," he said.

"Okay, Metropolitan Museum it is," she said. "I'll get dressed and when Patrick comes, you'll get dressed and we can leave. We'll get a taxi. Are you okay here? Want the paper?" He nodded. She positioned the *Wall Street Journal* in a special reading rack that she had designed and placed it in front of him on the table. "You read the front page, and I'll come back when you buzz to change the page." There was a manual buzzer attached to the armrest of his wheelchair, and he could buzz it by moving his elbow and pressing on the button.

Jenny patted his back, kissed his head and went quickly into the bedroom to dress. She was used to interruptions in her daily activities, but it was still hard to take. Pull on her slacks, go out to turn the page, give him a sip through the straw, button her blouse and comb her hair, answer the doorbell and let Patrick in. After that, Patrick took Harry into their bedroom to help him dress. It took a long time, because Patrick let Harry do as much as he could. Jenny tended to step in and do it for him. She didn't have the patience to wait while Harry struggled with his increasing inability to manage his body, while Patrick was trained to. Lou Gehrig's Disease was rapidly winning the fight.

It had been little symptoms that finally led them to Dr. Paul Winter, the neurologist recommended by their GP: a weakness in his legs, a slight loss of balance, an occasional trembling in his arms and hands. They told each other that it would turn out to be nothing but the aging process. But when she thought about it now, she realized that those first symptoms had not only been about his physical condition, but they already signaled the end of the self-confident, take-charge man he had been his whole life.

After her mother, who had been living with them for five years, deteriorating from Alzheimer's and diabetes, died, they had gone to Spain to celebrate their fortieth wedding anniversary. Early in the morning on their first day in Toledo, they walked from their hotel, up the hill into the old city through winding cobbled streets so narrow only carts could go through.

The houses leaned precariously. They had beautiful ironwork balconies with women leaning over and talking to neighbors below. Jenny tried to make out the words from her rusty high school Spanish, but she could not understand what they were saying.

Except when she heard a woman standing above them on the hill, shouting and pointing, "*Mira, Mira. Dios! Mira, Mira.*"

Jenny and Harry raced up the hill following her pointing finger and stood at the crest staring at a yellow stucco building with a black wrought-iron balcony on which a woman staggered, blood pouring from her neck, which was slashed open from ear to ear. She bent forward and back like a pendulum, the weight of her body throwing her over the railing, and as she tumbled to the ground, her long black hair floated in front of her and one single brown leather slipper fell from her foot in an arc. The sound—*thwump*—reverberated as she hit the cobbles, and she lay splayed on the ground, arms and legs outstretched.

A crowd assembled around the body; someone was crouching over it, and people were chattering to one another. No one seemed to be doing anything. Harry was staring up at the glass door behind the balcony. "There he is," he said, pointing.

Jenny just saw a blurry shadow of a man, and then he was gone.

"He's going out the back," Harry said. "I'm going to get him—the bastard." He turned to run up the street that wound behind the house with the balcony.

Jenny was terrified, but there was nothing she could do. It was so like Harry to act as if he were still a major in the Marine Corps, taking charge during emergencies. Why did he always do this? She peered around the corner but saw nothing. Her heart was pounding. She could just see the body of the dead woman between the legs of two men who were standing guard. Jenny heard the two-toned siren of the emergency cars and looked up to see the police running down a side street, waving their arms and shouting at the crowd. Where was Harry? She was so frightened. What would she do if anything happened to him?

It seemed interminable before he came, limping slowly around the corner, his head down, shoulders hunched. She ran to him, clasped his arms. He held her tight, burying his head in her hair. She reached up to stroke his cheek.

"Did you see him?" she asked.

He shook his head. "No," he said. "I don't know what I was thinking. I'm an idiot!"

Jenny patted his shoulder. "No, you're not." He looked so vulnerable and sad, she wanted to comfort him. "You just wanted to help," she said. "The police are here now. Leave it to them. They know what to do."

Harry turned and together they watched as the police pushed the crowds back away from the body, gesticulating, yelling instructions. Two orderlies trotted up with a stretcher between them and moved the body onto it. Police were moving among the crowd, talking to the bystanders. One came over to them when he spotted Harry and Jenny.

"We don't speak Spanish," Harry said before the policeman could ask anything.

"Ah," the policeman said. "Yes . . . *Si.* I speak little English." He hesitated, trying to put words together.

Jenny rushed in. "We saw a man in the window," she said, pointing.

"You saw a man?" he repeated.

"Yes . . . in the window."

"*Por favor,* can you describe him?"

Jenny and Harry looked at each other. What exactly had they seen? Jenny wanted to be helpful but could not remember anything except a shadow.

Harry said, "It was fast, blurry. We only saw him for a second. But he had dark hair, was wearing a green shirt, and he looked big." Harry held his hands out, describing someone fat.

Jenny was amazed. How had he seen that? All she had seen was a shape; she squeezed her eyes shut, imagined the scene again. Was there really a blur of green and a dark-haired man? It must have been. Harry was good at that kind of thing.

The policeman nodded, thanked them, asked for their names and the hotel they were in and wrote it all down. Then Harry and Jenny were left alone. Not knowing what else to do, they continued their walk, holding tight to each other's hands for comfort.

They were sitting at a tavern drinking icy beer when she asked him how he remembered a big man with a green shirt. "It must have been your old Marine Corps training in observation. I didn't see anything but a blur."

He took time to answer, then shook his head. "I'm a fake," he said.

"What are you talking about?"

"I told you I didn't see the guy—the murderer—when I ran around the corner, but I did. I saw him. He was coming out of the building. He was wearing a green shirt with blood all over it. He was a big guy like I said to the police, with dark hair, but I didn't know that when I saw him from the street. I could only describe him because I saw him run out of the building with blood all over."

Jenny stared at Harry. "And then? What happened then?"

"Then? I chickened out. My hand started to tremble. I couldn't stop it. I saw him, and I knew he was the murderer, and I was shaking. He was big and young and stronger than me, and I don't know the language, and I'm sixty-seven years old, for God's sake. I started after him, but I just couldn't do it."

Jenny blew air out of her mouth, reached over and touched his hands. "No, of course you couldn't. I'm glad you didn't go after him."

Harry pulled his hand away. "You don't understand. I wanted to stop him. I started after him. But I was scared. Me. Scared. My hand was trembling and then I . . . I stepped forward and I fell. My legs just went out from under me."

"You fell? So that's why you were limping. So okay, you tripped. Did you hurt yourself?"

"No, no," he said. He sounded exasperated. "I didn't trip. My legs just couldn't hold me. They collapsed under me."

Jenny stared at him, uncomprehending. "Are you all right now?

"I don't know," he said. "I can't believe my arm was trembling like that. I've never been scared like that. Not since the war."

The waiter came and asked in Spanish if they wanted another beer? They shook their heads, no. She shifted in the chair. Her heart was pounding.

Harry's face was gray. "It's not the first time," he said.

"What isn't the first time?"

"The shaking. The weakness . . . I almost fell last week, but I stopped myself . . . I feel . . . strange."

"Strange? Like sick?"

"No. Not sick. Just strange."

They went back to the hotel, both caught in their own dark thoughts. For two more weeks they traveled, and they didn't talk about it, but Jenny watched him. She noticed that he tired easily when they toured, that he held the bannister for balance when he went down the stairs, that he had trouble standing when he rose from a chair. By the time they went home to New York they both agreed that he should go for a check-up. Their GP sent them to Dr. Winter.

"I'm sorry," Dr. Winter had said after a series of tests. "I think you have amyotrophic lateral sclerosis." Jenny and Harry looked confused. "You don't know what that is?" he asked. They shook their heads and Dr. Winter took a breath. "You ever hear of Lou Gehrig's disease?"

Jenny sat motionless. Then Harry said, "Who hasn't?"

Dr. Winter nodded. "That's what you have; Lou Gehrig's, or ALS." The shock stopped Jenny's breath. Time pooled around them.

"Are you sure?" Harry asked after a long time.

"The early stages are hard to diagnose. But yes, I am sure that is what it is. You have ALS. I'm sorry."

That's how their education began: what amyotrophic lateral sclerosis did to muscles, the vagaries of its progression, the different ways it manifested in different people, the adaptations they had to make in their daily life to the losses that were chipping away at Harry's six-foot, muscular body, the timeline of the long, slow decline to the respiratory failure that would probably end his life.

With Harry the losses started in his legs. For a while he carried on as he always had, making sure he walked close to the wall, so he could catch himself if he lost balance. Soon he accepted the three-prong cane Jenny got for him, and he walked leaning heavily on it—to his law office, to restaurants, shows, concerts, museums. Deliberately they continued to live the life they had always lived. When, after ten months, the cane wasn't enough, he moved to a walker, then a wheelchair. He did it with a grace and lack of whining that made Jenny's heart swell. It made her ashamed of her own frequent and secret resentment of her caretaker role.

They had known, when they looked ahead, that there was inevitability to where this would end. Harry characteristically didn't talk too much. He made sure his will was up to date and he left clear instructions for his end of life care. "I don't want any extraordinary efforts just to keep me alive," he said. He talked to the doctor about whether he wanted feeding tubes for nutrition and hydration, about quality of life. Jenny was always with him. She thought she knew what all his wishes were.

But she was surprised one afternoon, when he wheeled himself into their bedroom, his face mottled with anger. "I'm so fucking sick of being nice to everyone," he raged. His voice was still strong then, and he spoke with power. "If I hear from one more person, that 'everything happens for a reason,' like there's a silver lining here, I'm going to tell them to go fuck themselves. Everything doesn't happen for a reason. Sometimes it's just goddammed bad luck!"

Jenny was stunned. Are people still so stupid, she thought? She remembered friends saying those very words to her each time she had a miscarriage before finally getting pregnant with George and carrying him to term. She remembered her rage then and how she stopped her mouth when she wanted to scream at them. They were so smug, so patronizing.

She remembered that Harry had spoken for her, saying to one particular friend of theirs, "Since none of us can fathom why Jenny is suffering so much, perhaps it is best not to make reference to the reasons." His tone had been withering. The woman had slunk away. Jenny couldn't remember who she was now. But she did remember how grateful she had been to him for sticking up for her that way.

"Who said it to you?" she asked now.

"It doesn't matter who said it. I'm not going to listen to it anymore. And I'm not going to lie to people and tell them I'm fine when inside I'm cursing my luck. I have too little time left on this earth to spend it making people feel good about themselves."

Jenny crouched beside him. "Of course," she said. "You can say anything you want."

"I'm so sick of all the niceties, the way we gloss over things and don't speak honestly." He was quiet for a minute, then said, "We do that too, Jenny, don't we?"

"What?"

"We don't speak the truth."

Jenny was silent, considering. She looked away afraid he would see in her face her own resentment at what her life had become.

"I don't want us to be like that anymore," Harry said. "I want us to tell the truth to each other. To say everything we haven't said in forty years. I want the time I have left to matter." Harry looked straight into Jenny's eyes. "I'm counting on you, Jenny. Nothing left unsaid."

She nodded, stroked his cheek. "Can I sit with you?" she asked. She didn't wait, but curled up on his lap, her head against his chest. His chin rested on top of her head. She felt his chest move up and down as he began to cry, silently at first, then louder. In minutes she was weeping too, then realizing that if she were going to tell the truth, she would howl with pain. She let loose and Harry did too, and soon they were crying as loud as they could, and finally, with great heaving sighs, spent with the emotion, they stopped. They looked at each other. Jenny saw Harry's tear-streaked face. She leaned and kissed his cheeks and licked his salty tears. She sobbed again, and the sob turned into a laugh, and then they were both laughing together until that was done too.

She sat nestled on his lap, unbuttoned his shirt, rested her cheek on his bare skin, and felt the soft hairs on his chest. After a long silence their breathing synchronized.

"Remember, Jenny," he whispered. "Only the truth."

She nodded. But she wondered if she would be able to keep this promise. There were some truths she had never told him. Why would she want to start now?

They went on with their lives. Friends came over. Jenny, who loved to cook, made scrumptious dinners for them, and Harry presided at the table, and the conversations were as lively and interesting as they had always been. As the disease traveled up his body, he couldn't manage his fork anymore, so Jenny would feed him earlier, and he would sit and talk to the guests. He was using an electric wheelchair now, so he didn't have to push the wheels with his hands.

Harry and Jenny didn't change the frequency of the conversations they had together, but they did change the topics. One of them, usually Harry, would say, "Tell me something I don't know about you, something you never said to me." And Jenny would dig back and tell him stories. Her stories were about the early years with her sisters, particularly Ruby—sweet, funny stories. How she had adored Ruby when she was little, the things they had done together, how they sang together and harmonized. And then, because Ruby had chosen her as her favorite sister when they were growing up, Jenny had become the responsible one, the one who cared for her all the years, as she got sicker.

"You've always been the caretaker, haven't you?" Harry asked.

She nodded and looked away. "It seems like there's one in every family."

"Don't you resent it?"

"No," she said, too quickly.

"Jenny? We promised."

Jenny forced herself to look back at Harry. She swallowed. "Sometimes I do." Her heart was pounding. "Sometimes I feel like screaming, 'Why me? Why do I always have to be the one?' But then I look at you and I'm so ashamed. You didn't ask for this either. Who am I to complain?"

"You have a right to complain. We can bitch and moan as much as we want to. Go in the bathroom, close the door, and holler." Harry started to yell over and over, "Shit, fuck it all! Why me?" As he yelled his face got redder, and the vein in his forehead pulsed.

Jenny almost laughed it seemed so contrived. "Be careful, Harry. You'll have a stroke."

"So what?" Harry stared at her, eyes blazing.

Jenny stared back. She was suddenly terrified of what she would say: *You'll die. I want you to die so this will be over!* She ran into the bathroom and began to scream. She pounded the wall, crying, cursing. There was a deep black pool of rage that she had never touched; it was bottomless. She slid down and sat on the cool tile floor and cried until she hiccoughed, filled with a mixture of shame and relief. It was a familiar feeling—one she'd had after Ruby committed suicide, when she realized that under all the caretaking and worry, she had wished her sister dead.

After a while, calmer, she washed her face and went back out to Harry, who had wheeled himself to the window and was looking out. She stood behind him, not touching him.

Some days Harry would tell her stories. Jenny was amazed at what she didn't know about him after all these years of marriage. His war stories were particularly poignant to her. The details he remembered of the men he had led into battle in Iwo Jima and Okinawa, the fear and the blood and the death, touched her. He would cry sometimes when he spoke of those years, and then, embarrassed, say, "Dr. Winter said I would sometimes laugh or cry for no reason. It's part of the disease."

"But this isn't for no reason," Jenny said. "Your stories are wonderful. You should write them down."

He raised an eyebrow. "If I could hold a pen," he said.

Jenny got him a stenographer from a secretarial service, because he didn't want to use a secretary from his law office, to come three times a week and take down his memories and type them up so she could put them in a binder.

One day, after having noticed that he was sometimes slurring his words, and that the effort to speak tired him, Jenny said, "Your language—it seems like you are having a little more difficulty speaking."

Harry hesitated. Then he nodded and spoke with deep pauses between phrases, "I am . . . I'm afraid it's going to get harder and harder."

"Maybe a speech therapist could help."

"Maybe," he said.

The speech therapist helped a little, but she was candid. "The disease is progressing. Soon it may be too difficult for you to have long conversations." She didn't say what was on their minds . . . that soon he wouldn't be able to speak at all.

That night Harry said, "Come talk to me, Jenny." Jenny pulled a chair up next to him. He didn't say anything for a long time.

"Is there something particular you want to talk about?" Jenny asked.

"Yes," he said. They were quiet again. He swallowed several times, breathed, used the propulsion of breath that the speech therapist had taught him to help get the words out clearly. "I have a confession to make." Again, he stopped.

"Yes?" Jenny felt her pulse racing. "What? What is it?"

He swallowed again. "There was a time," he said, "when I was . . ." breath "convinced that you were in love with Victor."

Stillness in Jenny. Harry's eyelid pulsed, a small twitch. Jenny opened her mouth to say something, but Harry continued speaking. "I felt . . . anguish. I was afraid to ask you, but I was so convinced it was true . . . I had an affair with one of the secretaries in my office."

Jenny's mouth stayed open, now in surprise.

"You probably . . . never even noticed," he said.

Jenny thought back, furrowed her brow. In truth she didn't know what he was talking about. She knew she should ask, *When? When did it happen?* But it seemed so irrelevant, so unimportant now. "I don't remember it," she said.

"Do . . . you care?"

Jenny saw it was harder for him to speak, the longer the conversation went on. She thought carefully. She got up, walked to the window and looked outside. The streetlights were on and gleamed through the windowpane. She had promised him the truth. She did not care that he had an affair, certainly not now. Maybe she wouldn't have cared then either. "Does it matter now? It was so long ago. What difference does it make?"

"Don't you want to know . . . how it happened? How long it went on . . . who it was with?"

Again, she searched. "No. I don't think so. Do you really want to go into all that now?"

"Only if it . . . matters to you."

He wants it to matter to me, Jenny thought. *He wants me to care who it was with and why he did it. He wants to dredge it all up.*

Suddenly he said, "Did you love Victor?"

This is so stupid, she thought.

"Did you?"

"What difference does it make now?" she repeated.

"It makes a diff... difference," he said. "Because it stands between us. How can we understand each other if we always hide things?"

"Everyone hides things." Jenny said.

"I don't want... hide things anymore."

"Okay." Jenny cleared her throat, pushing down the anger. She would tell him something. It was hard to talk. "When he first came to the house, when Papa first brought him, I had a crush on him. A terrible crush. Then he and Ruby got married, and after Joseph and Sarah were born, I had to help out a lot with their care because Ruby was so depressed. Victor and I were close . . . maybe I did love him then. But I didn't even know you, and I knew it couldn't turn into anything. I had to get on with my life. I met you, and you were wonderful and handsome. And we had our life, and they had theirs."

The stillness between them was immense, a thing that was there in the room. It encompassed all the events of all the years since she'd met Victor:

—the time she went to tell Victor not to marry Ruby because she was mentally ill

—the time after Joseph was born when she and her mother went to take care of him because Ruby was catatonic in a corner of the living room

—the time she touched Victor's wrist, looked at the fine silky black hairs on his arms, and knew she would betray Ruby if Victor wanted her

—the time she met Harry, a tall rugged lawyer who adored her and took charge of her life

—the summer days in the bungalow colony when Ruby had her spells and danced up and down the road with whoever would partner with her or stripped naked and tried to swim the lake and almost drowned

—the afternoon in the bungalow when Ruby slept drugged in the next room after Jenny and Pauline had pulled her, half drowned from the lake, and she and Victor sat watch

—the inevitability of their love affair

—the out-of-the-way motel rooms in Connecticut and New Jersey where they could have a quick lunch in a nearby diner and then slip into the motel room and out of their clothes to make hasty love

—the smell of sex that followed Jenny home and how she washed and washed herself, regretting that she couldn't hold onto the tangible fragrance of Victor's aftershave

—the final end of the affair when Irene barreled into her apartment and shouted, "This has to stop"

—the going on as if nothing had happened until finally it was so far in the past it was as if it never had.

Now Jenny kept still. She thought of the promise she had made to Harry to tell the truth. Well, she thought, I did tell the truth. I told as much of it as I could.

"So that was it then? A crush you had before we were married? You didn't love him then?"

His eyes, locked on hers were so deep, hypnotizing almost. Jenny licked her lips. A word stuck in her throat. Once. She didn't say it. She said instead, "I love you, Harry. You have given me a wonderful life." That, at least, was true.

They breathed together, synchronizing, in, out, in out, something they had begun to do since he was having more difficulty speaking and breathing. "I was so afraid," he said, forcing the words out. "All these years since Ruby died, I was afraid that you would leave me for Victor."

Jenny felt desolate. She suddenly remembered how after Ruby died Harry had doted on her, brought her unexpected presents, spent more time at home with her. She ached for him, reached out and took his hand. "I'm so sorry," she whispered.

The moment passed. "I'm tired, Jenny," Harry said. "I think I'll go to bed now."

They went on with their lives. There were more changes. Harry couldn't eat real food. He went on a liquid diet, but swallowing became more difficult, and he would choke on his own saliva. He lost weight. The doctor talked to him about a feeding tube, but Harry was resistant.

"ALS is the cruelest disease," Jenny said to their son George and his wife, Anni, one evening when they came to visit. They were sitting at the dining room table, drinking tea. Harry was asleep. "He's locked in his body now. His eyes show he understands everything but talking is so hard for him. Most people can't understand him."

George nodded. "He seems to want to tell me things, ask me things. He apologized for not spending enough time with me as a kid, and when I said that wasn't true, he got mad. 'The truth. I want the truth,' he said." George shook his head. "I'm not sure what he wanted me to say. I told him he was the best dad ever. I reminded him of how when he found out I was interested in music, he got me the best clarinet teacher we could find. That he loved to listen to me play. As I was talking, he started to cry . . . not loud, but silent. You know the tears just sliding down his cheeks." George shook his head. "It made me want to cry too."

"I don't know what to say either." Jenny looked at her son. He was only thirty-two and already a little overweight. Anni was as beautiful as ever, lithe as a cat with dark curly hair. They didn't have children, and Jenny had stopped asking about it, remembering her own trauma trying to get pregnant with George. Now she repeated what Harry had said that morning. "You're a good son, George. Your father told me that this morning."

After Anni and George left, Jenny went into the bedroom, undressed, and slipped into the bed she still shared with Harry. She had refused to sleep elsewhere since he was sick, even though he had told her she should. He was lying on his back, but pillows supported his upper body so he could breathe better. His eyes were closed; soon he would need a breathing apparatus, Jenny thought, so he could get enough oxygen. And then? She didn't want to think about then or afterward.

She lay on her side, her body pressed against his, and put her arm over his chest, feeling it rise and fall with each breath. She breathed with him. Slow and steady was his breath, and hers. She didn't know if he was really sleeping, but she whispered, "I thank you Harry, for the wonderful life you gave me. I love you. That is all the truth there is." Then she closed her eyes, and, breathing with him, fell asleep.

16

Jenny

1989

Later, Jenny wondered why she'd agreed so quickly to travel to India with Irene and Faye when it had never been on her bucket list. But somehow when Faye had suggested it at their celebration dinner for Irene's sixty-eighth birthday, Jenny had perked up.

They were sitting in Café des Artistes, an elegant uptown French restaurant, and had already shared a bottle of champagne. Each had also drunk a glass of pinot noir, which the sommelier had recommended to go with Jenny's succulent duck a l'orange and Faye and Irene's boeuf bourguignon. Jenny was feeling giddy and happy. The gorgeous Howard Chandler Christy murals of naked nymphs gamboling in the forest swirled around them, and she felt as if she were in Paris.

Jenny, too full for dessert, was playing with the chocolate decadence cake in front of her and watching Irene scrape the last bit of frosting off her plate, when Faye said, "Let's go to India together."

India, Jenny thought. *Now that would be exotic.*

Irene sat up as if startled. "India? Not Paris or London?"

"No," Faye said. "We've all been to Paris and London. Let's go to India. It will be an adventure—something entirely different."

"I don't know," Irene said. "Isn't it very dirty there? And poor? I've heard it's so poor. And how would we get around? We couldn't rent a car there—they drive on the wrong side of the road."

"We won't drive. I'll get us a guide and a car. I'll plan the whole trip. I want to do something really different." Faye looked from one to the other of her sisters.

Jenny watched Faye get more excited as she spoke, her words coming faster. "The three of us, all widowed, no ties. It will be really fun. And it will be good for you, Irene. Lots of things to paint."

Jenny let the words sink in. She wondered how it would be to travel with her sisters. She'd never done that before.

"I don't know," Irene furrowed her brow. "I sort of told Ellie and Karen I would take them on a trip. With Karen graduating from college, it's probably the last chance I'll get to vacation with a granddaughter."

"Well maybe we can take them too . . . I'd be great if Karen came. I love her. She's my favorite grandniece. Ellie used to bring her to me for tutoring in math, and we'd spend half our time looking at pictures from my different trips around the world." Faye laughed. "Imagine. If Ellie and Karen came, we could be a tour group."

Irene stared, openmouthed. "I didn't know that."

"What?"

"That you tutored Karen in math. Ellie never told me."

Faye shrugged. "Well it's true. She brought her every Sunday afternoon. It was very convenient. It was after they moved to Larchmont. They lived right near us. Sometimes I would go to Ellie's house instead."

Uh oh, Jenny thought. *Irene looks miffed, like Faye got one up on her.* Jenny turned her eyes away from them.

"Well," Irene said. "You can't ask them to come. I know that Ellie would have a fit if we took Karen to India—I won't do that. Ellie thinks she's reckless enough as it is. And Ellie would never go. Never."

Faye sighed. "So, we won't take them. Anyway, why are you so afraid of what Ellie thinks?" She laughed. "She's just your daughter."

"You don't have kids, so you just don't understand what it's like to dance around them . . . trying to say everything right . . . not to be too overbearing . . . you know what I mean, don't you Jenny?"

Jenny, although she heard them, was trying not to pay attention to the bickering and instead was admiring the slim, dancing nudes in the Fountain of Youth painting behind Faye and musing about it. *It would be nice to actually have a Fountain of Youth. Then I could do away with all the face creams and the beauty parlor appointments and worrying about whether my roots show.* Her eyes rested on Faye's head, opposite. *Why does Faye let her hair go so gray? She's only fifty-nine, and it makes her look older than me. At least Irene colors her hair, although why she picked that blond is beyond me.* Jenny liked her own warm brown color much better.

"Jenny?" Irene said. "Earth to Jenny. Where are you?"

"Oh, sorry. Just daydreaming."

"Never mind," Irene said. "Can I have the rest of your dessert, if you're not going to eat it?"

Jenny pushed the plate toward her. "You shouldn't eat it, Irene. You need to watch your sugar. You know Mama got diabetes."

"I know. I know I shouldn't eat this, but I love chocolate and it's my birthday."

"Oh, give yourself a break," Faye said. "Stop dieting and enjoy life. Not all of us can look like Jane Fonda—or Jenny for that matter."

"Is there something wrong with me for wanting to keep fit? And healthy? Or look good?"

"No, of course not. I wasn't criticizing you, Jenny. You look great. I just meant what difference does it make if you put on a few pounds? I've been fighting that losing battle my whole life. As long as you're healthy, weight doesn't matter."

But her sugar does, Jenny thought. *And weight contributes to it.*

And Faye is overweight too, but it isn't worth arguing over. Her sisters could pack on the pounds and look like old women if they wanted to, but she would keep on going to the gym and watching her weight just as she had when Harry was alive. The thought of Harry caused a spasm of pain, and she looked across the room and focused on the *Girl with Parrots* painting, a slim nude with two red parrots on the tree behind her—she didn't want to cry.

"It's not that I don't like to travel," Irene was saying. "You know I love traveling. And I guess it's colorful . . . India. But it's so far away. Sitting in this restaurant makes me want to go back to Paris. But India . . . I don't know." She looked at Jenny. "What do you think?"

Jenny took a breath. "India. It might be interesting—fun." But she wondered if she was telling the truth. Faye, with her exuberance and energy and Irene with her fears and cautions. Maybe she would be refereeing between them the whole trip. That wouldn't be fun.

"I think we'd have a great time together, the three of us. We'll be the Merry Widows," Faye said.

"I don't feel very merry," Jenny said. "Harry's only gone six months."

Faye took Jenny's hand. "I'm sorry. That was a stupid thing to say. But I do think it would be good for all of us. None of us have ever been there, so no memories, no repeats." Faye turned from one sister to the other. "What do you say?"

After a moment, Jenny said, "Yes."

Jenny and Faye turned to Irene. It was a while before Irene said, "I guess so."

Faye clapped her hands. "This is so exciting. I'll take care of everything."

That October, Jenny found herself stepping out of the plane into the heat and humidity of New Delhi. The first thing she noticed was the air—yellow and smoky, thick with a sweet, pungent odor. The highway was full of trucks, their bumpers painted with requests to "Blow horns, please."

"What does that mean," Jenny asked, pointing to the signs.

The taxi driver said, "The trucks are so high, their drivers cannot see the cars overtaking them. So they must be alerted by the horns."

Jenny could see that. The trucks were piled high with bundles and boxes making the rearview mirror useless, and many did not have side view mirrors either, so blaring horns blasted the air. Cars and motorcycles wove in and out. Sometimes four, five, six people rode on a bike. Occasionally, bony white cows wandered along the side of the road, and the cars honked at them too.

Irene was coughing. She said, "My eyes sting."

"It's the cars and the coal," Faye said. "I'm sure we'll get used to it."

"How can you 'get used' to air pollution," Irene said. She made quotation marks with her fingers. "We'll probably wind up wearing face masks." She coughed for emphasis. Faye looked away.

On the first morning, Faye arranged for a bicycle rickshaw to ride through the old city market. Everyone used the rickshaws—men in business suits, school children in blue-and-tan uniforms, women shopping, vendors carrying goods, young couples, families.

Jenny could not imagine how the bicycle *wallah* was going to drive them. He was impossibly skinny with every sinew in his legs showing as he pumped the pedals. He wore torn and dirty clothes and was missing his front teeth. But he smiled, and kept nodding his head, evidently very satisfied at the sum of money Faye had agreed to pay.

The three sisters crowded into the rickshaw. Irene clutched the side of the seat, white-knuckled, her eyes darting around, trying to find something familiar. "I feel terrible making him drive us," she whispered. "It must be so hard."

"He's earning a living," Faye said. "Can't you see he's happy?"

"I think they're used to it." Jenny said. Irene pressed her lips together.

Beggars were everywhere. Jenny saw them under the bridges and on the sides of the road. They slept on the street, on gunnysacks, in bicycle rickshaws. A man with no arms balanced a huge bag on his back. A woman holding a naked baby appealed with sad eyes as she moved her hand to her mouth in the gesture for food.

"Look at that poor woman," Irene grabbed Faye's arm. "I should give her something."

"No, don't! I told you . . . you can't go dropping coins in the hats of all the beggars, the way you do at home. The way Ruby always did."

"I know," Irene said. "It's just so hard. I keep remembering how Mom always told us not to forget the poor people."

Jenny patted her hand. "I don't think she meant beggars in India."

Jenny noticed a man on all fours, so deformed he couldn't stand up, held his hand out. "Look at him. What do you think is wrong with him?"

Faye said, "I read that they can distort their bodies on purpose. That's how they earn their living."

It was difficult for Jenny to believe that the contortion was deliberate, but Faye seemed to know. "We shouldn't give him anything," Jenny said to Irene.

Irene seemed to want to argue. She hesitated and then, as if her hands had a life of their own, Jenny saw her reach into her pack and surreptitiously tossed a handful of coins to the children running alongside. Instantly, more scrawny children materialized. "Please, madame, please." Their hands grabbed at Irene's arm, and she recoiled, her conflicting feelings of compassion and revulsion so plain on her face that Jenny almost laughed at her.

"Irene, what are you doing?" Faye asked. "I told you not to give anything to them."

"They're so poor. We have so much," Irene whispered.

"You don't have so much you can feed them all."

Jenny found the poverty heartbreaking, too. The gutters were strewn with plastic bags, rotting cucumbers and tomatoes, wilted marigolds. People ate, spat, talked, laughed, lived on the very pavement of the city. But it was beautiful too. There was color all around—in the rainbow silk saris of the women, in the gleaming displays of eggplants, carrots, apples, and greens in the vegetable and fruit markets, in the piles of orange marigolds sold everywhere for wreaths and offerings, and in the faces of the people.

"Don't you want to sketch, Irene? Everything is a painting."

Irene shook her head. "I can't seem to get past the dirt and the poverty."

They left the bicycle rickshaw and picked their way around the streets, following the map that Faye carried. Jenny and Irene were full of questions, but even Faye, who had done most of the reading beforehand, couldn't answer them all.

Jenny wondered about the black marks in the middle of women's foreheads. Irene asked what they did with the cow dung on the streets. "And why don't they put the people to work picking up the garbage? They don't have any other jobs."

"The beggars have jobs," Faye said. "Begging is their job."

"Some job," Irene said and made a face.

Over the next two days Jenny, Faye, and Irene went all over Delhi—to monuments and museums and the market where they bought red skirts and purple scarves. They bought gauzy blue blouses and bangles for their wrists.

When they got back to the hotel, they went into the two-room suite they were sharing and put on their new clothes. Irene seemed delighted. She giggled at her reflection. "Do you think I look silly in this?" she asked, twirling in a flouncy red-and-gold cotton skirt.

"You look young," Jenny said.

Irene was pleased. "You look gorgeous, as usual," she said to Jenny, who had bought a blue silk sari and was trying to arrange it over her slim figure.

Faye, too, was admiring herself in the mirror. She had bought a flowing rose-colored blouse that draped over her large breasts and flattered her. "India is so beautiful. I love it," she said. She looked at Jenny. "You like it, don't you?"

"It's complicated," Jenny said. "I like some things and I don't like others."

"You can say that again. The part about not liking some things," Irene said.

Faye rolled her eyes. "It'll be over soon. We'll be home before you know it."

"Ten days," Irene said.

"Oh God, look at her. She's counting the days. I'm sorry I brought her."

Jenny watched her two sisters, torn between them. She felt Faye's irritation with Irene, but she also understood Irene's discomfort. She wondered how it would all turn out. She knew that Harry would have told her not to worry about what other people felt or did. But it was hard to stop.

They had a car, a driver, and a guide to take them from Delhi around northern India. Their guide, Amit, was a dark and handsome Indian who spoke English well.

He bowed to them, his hands in prayer position. "Namaste," he said. "It means I greet the spirit within you. It is a sign of respect." They bowed back to him and from then on, they said "Namaste" to everyone they met.

Amit was a delight. He laughed a lot and made jokes in a lilting voice about the crowded roads, the peasants, the world they were passing through. At every sight that disturbed them, he shrugged and said, "It's India."

As they drove Jenny saw a woman in a hot pink sari walking alongside the fields carrying water on her head. A man, out in a field, squatted between furrows to relieve himself, his legs spread, covered by his white kurta—like an egret, wings outstretched.

Irene pointed. "Oh, my God. Is he doing what I think he's doing?"

"There is no running water, madame," Amit said, apologizing. "No plumbing. It's India."

Irene looked appalled. "Not even outhouses?"

"I guess it's more natural this way." Faye said. "Why waste the fertilizer?"

Irene shook her head and covered her mouth as if to keep from speaking.

When they reached the village, the car slowed through the crowded streets. Jenny watched a man sweep the garbage into neat piles, and immediately dogs, goats, and a cow rooted in the debris and scattered it again.

"Look at that," Irene said. "Why does he even bother?"

"Irene, that's enough," Faye said, looking at Amit to see if he was reacting. But Irene didn't stop. She stared at the men peeing in the road, and deliberately covered her nose in the crook of her arm. Faye glared.

Amit took them to Agra where the Taj Mahal appeared to float, a white specter in its reflecting pool. They went to Jaipur and the Red Fort with its mirrored ceilings and then to the healing calm of Ranthambore National Park, where fluorescent blue peacocks and aqua kingfishers flashed, and flocks of green parakeets swooped overhead. They sat beside a lake for over an hour, gazing at the ruins of a rajah's summer palace and waiting for a glimpse of a Bengal tiger, and when it came, all they saw was a splash of orange moving behind the leaves. Irene held her sketchbook in her hand, but Jenny saw that she didn't draw anything. She seemed in a constant state of agitation.

Finally, at the end of their trip they went to a festival in Varanasi at the Ganges River.

"We're going to the Ganges River twice," Faye told her sisters. "Once at sunset and once at sunrise. At sunset they put the river to bed and sing it to sleep. At dawn they welcome it and pray to it. It's supposed to be so beautiful and inspiring."

That evening they walked down to the river with hundreds of other pilgrims. They took two bicycle rickshaws. They got as close to the river as they could, and then left the rickshaws and walked to the *ghats*, or steps, that sloped to the river. Each ghat was an address on the river.

"Stay close and don't worry," Amit said. "It isn't dangerous, and everyone is very peaceful. But I advise you not to make eye contact with the beggars; otherwise they will bother you."

To Jenny it felt dehumanizing to walk past people who were talking to you and not look at them. She trailed a little behind her sisters, taking in the hawkers who pushed strings of shiny elephants, bracelets, postcards, and beads in her face. The trinkets were so cheap, Jenny couldn't resist, and she bought some little elephants and four packets of postcards from one of the boy hawkers. Immediately she was surrounded by ten more.

"No," she said in a stern voice to one boy who was pushing more postcards in her face. Jenny saw Irene waving frantically and bowed a hasty "Namaste" to the boy who, surprised, bowed back as she moved toward her sisters.

Irene was shaking with relief when Jenny reached them. "I was so worried."

Jenny waved her purchases to show them. "Calm down. It's no big deal. I'm fine. We're all fine." To Jenny, even though the crowds were large, they seemed benign. Everyone was celebrating. People were carrying garlands of yellow and orange marigolds to give to the river. The odors of the frying bread and incense crowded Jenny's nose.

At the river, Amit engaged a boat, and they glided upstream facing the ghats on which the people sat and prayed. Priests rang bells, and drums beat. They passed a crematorium where flames of orange and scarlet defined the pyres on which there were burning bodies. Chanting mourners surrounded them.

When the last bells were rung and the river was put to sleep, Amit took the sisters back to the hotel, telling them he would pick them up at dawn so they could watch the river awaken.

In their room Irene flopped on the bed. "I don't think I can move," Irene said.

Faye frowned. "What is your problem, Irene? You're acting like something awful happened. You'd think you'd never been anywhere in the world before."

Irene sat up. "I've never been anywhere like this. You didn't prepare me. You never told me how it would be."

"Why was it my responsibility to prepare you? You could have read some books. You've never acted like this when we traveled together before."

"That's because we went to normal places—France, England, Italy."

"God, Irene. You're giving me a headache."

Irene shook her head and looked at Jenny for support, but Jenny did not want to get in the middle of this ridiculous argument. She said nothing.

In the morning they rose before dawn. Jenny and Faye were excited to go back to the river and see it in daylight, but Irene seemed reluctant. They walked through the dark, quiet streets with the other pilgrims who were silently making their way to the river to do their morning prayers. Jenny felt peace descend on her. It was hard to believe the chaos of the night before.

They boarded a long shallow rowboat and glided again past the ghats. All around them the city was awakening. Jenny watched as pilgrims bathed and performed their sun salutations, immersing themselves in the river, throwing the water up to watch the first rays of the sun reflected in the droplets. The laundrymen beat their wash on the rocks. She saw a body drift by . . . it was a chanting, meditating holy man, floating on his back. In niches of the buildings that lined the river, other holy men meditated, looking like statues. Everywhere there was sound, smell, color and people. Jenny thought it beautiful.

This time, as they passed the cremation ghat, Irene pointed. "Oh, my God, look," she moaned. "There's a man's foot sticking out of the flames." She covered her eyes with her hands. "God, that's disgusting."

"Irene, that's an awful thing to say," Faye snapped. "It's their religion."

"I can't help it," Irene said, and her voice got louder and more urgent. "They're burning people and dumping their ashes in the river and then they're washing themselves and their clothes in the same water and they're probably peeing in it too. I wouldn't be surprised if they drank it."

Amit turned away, his face reddening.

"What's the matter with you?" Faye said. "It's their holy river."

"It doesn't seem holy to me," Irene whispered. "It's just dirty."

Faye glared and leaned over to touch Amit on his shoulder. "I apologize for my sister's rudeness." Then she turned her back on Irene and began to snap photos of everything. As the boat moved through the water Jenny saw that the sun had painted the water yellow and gold.

They left the boat and wandered back up through the streets where the shops of the ancient city were opening now. Cows wandered with them and meandered into the shops. Dirt and garbage and cow dung were everywhere. Jenny stepped carefully to avoid it. By the time they reached the main street it was morning rush hour, and the streets were streaming with cars and motorcycles and cycle rickshaws and carts pulled by oxen. The heat was beginning to cook the dung on the street, and Jenny had to cover her nose with her handkerchief and breathe through her mouth.

Dusty beggars approached again, following them, moving hand to mouth. Jenny and Faye shook their heads, but the children pursued them. Irene pulled her shoulders out of the way as they grasped at her. One little boy plucked her hand. He had scabs on his face, and he smelled of sweat and dirt and urine.

She cringed. "Don't touch me," she said, shuddering and throwing his hand off hers. She grabbed Jenny's arm. "Oh God, I can't stand them."

Behind the boy came a tall woman in a purple sari. She blocked the street in front of Jenny and Irene. She was dancing, moving her hips and waving her arms as if pulling them toward her. Her gold bracelets and bangles tinkled, and though her hands were decorated with henna, her nails were grimy and her neck sooty.

Jenny was mesmerized. The way the woman was dancing, shimmying her shoulders and wriggling her hips, the purple color she was wearing, the way she trilled her voice, her tongue flicking in and out—it seemed to Jenny that she was looking at Ruby when she was a young woman, before the medication she took for her mental illness had turned her into an automaton. Jenny stared, forgetting what Amit had said about making eye contact with the beggars.

Irene, too, seemed transfixed. She stood open-mouthed, her eyes so wide the whites seemed enormous. Faye was in front of them, and turned to see what was keeping them, but she didn't seem to take notice of the woman.

The woman came close to Jenny and Irene, holding her hand out. "Help me feed my children," she sang. As if on signal the children who were surrounding the woman began plucking at Jenny and Irene's skirts, murmuring, "Madame," and making the gesture of hunger.

"Get away, get away," Irene said, flailing her arms in front of her.

The woman touched Irene and her hand lingered on her arm. "We are hungry, madame."

"Let me go. Leave me alone!" Irene shouted. She flung the woman's arm off and then began to push the beggar, to move her away and give herself more space. And just as Faye came up yelling, "Stop it!" Irene gave a final shove and toppled the beggar into the street.

Faye grabbed Irene's arm. "What are you doing? You can't do that!"

With a face contorted with anger, her eyes wild, almost rolling in her head, Irene turned and pushed Faye so hard that she, too, tumbled into the street and under the wheels of an empty bicycle rickshaw coming alongside. The rickshaw teetered and fell, tangling Faye and the dancing woman somewhere beneath.

Jenny shouted. "What did you do, Irene?" As she scrambled to try to help, she could just make out the arms and legs of Faye and the beggar.

Irene stood transfixed, her hand covering her mouth, her face a map of shock and disgust.

The beggar woman was screaming, "Aiaah!" and the crowd surged toward them. Faye was moaning. As the people yelled, two men lifted the bicycle off the beggar and helped the wallah up from where he had landed, while Amit tended to Faye.

Irene reached her hand out, but did not touch Faye, whose skirt was covered in cow dung. "I'm sorry," she whispered. "I didn't know it was you. I thought it was her."

Amit helped Faye stand. "Are you all right, madame?"

"Yes," Faye said, her voice shaking. She immediately turned her back on Irene.

Amit talked to the beggar, the bicycle wallah, and the crowd, trying to calm them. The beggar woman pointed to a gash on her arm, which was bleeding a little. Jenny fished a tissue from her pocket and pressed it against the cut. She watched the bicycle wallah show them a dent in his bike, but it was hard to tell the new dents from the old. Everyone on the street talked and shouted.

"They want money," Amit said. "I don't think the woman is badly hurt, but she wants money. And the bicycle wallah too."

"How much?" Faye asked.

"One thousand rupees."

Jenny did a quick calculation. "That's forty dollars."

Irene stood, her face collapsing with a sob. "Give it to him."

"Too much," Faye said.

Amit nodded. "I'll offer him five hundred."

"I want to give it to him," Irene repeated. Then, abruptly, Jenny saw her tear open her fanny pack and peel off the notes from her wallet, giving them to the woman and the bicycle wallah. As fast as they could, they bowed, said "Namaste," and limped away, afraid Irene would change her mind and ask for the money back.

Faye stood for a moment and then bowed to their disappearing backs. "Namaste," she whispered. "Namaste." Jenny did the same. Irene just watched.

The crowd dispersed, still muttering at them as they made their way to the car. Jenny saw that Faye was furious. Her skirt, leg, and sandals were smeared with dung. She smelled terrible.

Irene kept murmuring something. She turned to Jenny. "I'm so ashamed. I'm so ashamed. I'm not like that. I'm not that kind of person." Then she unzipped her fanny pack and took out all her money, which she began to distribute to the hawkers and beggars who followed them.

Amit took her arm. "No, no, madame. That is not necessary."

Faye said to Jenny, "She's nuts. You stop her. I don't want to have anything to do with her."

Jenny agreed. "Don't do that, Irene. Stop it."

But Irene didn't stop. By the time Amit hustled her into the car she had given away all of her rupees, and her dollar bills too.

In the hotel Irene pushed past Faye, almost running toward the bathroom. Faye grabbed her arm. "Where do you think you're going?"

"I have to shower. I have to. I feel so filthy."

"You feel filthy? I'm the one covered in shit. What's the matter with you? Are you out of your mind?"

Irene stood shaking. "I'm not the one out of my mind. You are. Why did you bring us here? I hate this place. I hate everything about it. The dirt and the pollution and the beggars and the poverty. I don't like the smells . . . and . . . and the food. I hate curry. And why doesn't the government do something about all the poor people? They must all be untouchables! They're so disgusting. They pee in the street." Her words rushed out one after another so that Jenny could barely understand what she was saying.

Faye stared open-mouthed. "You have no idea what you're saying, Irene. Untouchables aren't beggars, they're a caste. Where did you learn that crap?"

Irene was sobbing. "Where did I learn it? Where did you learn it? How do you know about untouchables? You're so goddamned smart all the time. You know everything. I know nothing. Except that they just make me sick. It all makes me sick." Her shoulders heaved. "I'm scared I'll catch something awful . . . leprosy."

"Oh, my God. When did you get so screwed up?" Faye was yelling. "They're just people."

"But not people like I know . . . that woman, that beggar, she looked so crazy."

"You think she looked crazy? You should see what you looked like. You were practically frothing at the mouth. You're as crazy as Ruby ever was."

Irene stopped short. "You don't know what you're talking about." She had stopped crying now and her face was hard. She stripped off her skirt and blouse and threw them in the garbage. She stood in her

underwear, short and pudgy, hands on her hips. "Ruby was a lunatic
. . . She almost killed you."

"What are you talking about? When did she almost kill me?"

"All right. Stop it both of you," Jenny said. "Ruby did not almost
kill Faye."

"She could have easily. She took her out in a thunderstorm in the
middle of the night because her voices told her to. And how many
times did she take Faye out to the park and forget she was babysit-
ting? Accidents happen. Like with Mama and her baby sister, who
died. The one Faye is named for."

Faye looked from Irene to Jenny and back again. "I have no idea
what you're talking about."

"No of course not. You don't know a lot of things. You were the
baby. Everyone protected you, starting with Bubbie Ida. She protected you. She never told you about the people who murdered her
family, and her town."

"Mama told me about that when I told her I was going to marry
Angelo. But she never told me about a sister who died. She never told
me Ruby almost killed me." Faye stripped off her dirty clothes and
sat on the bed, her hands on her knees. Her flesh sagged over her
underwear. "Tell me now."

Jenny's head was spinning. How had they gotten from pushing
a beggar woman into the street to their mother's dead baby sister?
Irene looked at Jenny, questioning.

"You brought it up, so you better tell her," Jenny said.

So, Irene told Faye the story of how their mother's baby sister,
Fanny, had been scalded by boiling water when they first came to
America and died of burns and pneumonia. "Mama was supposed to
be watching her, but she was distracted, and Bubbie Ida almost didn't
live through it. Especially after losing the rest of her kids. And years
later, when you were born, Mama and Papa named you Feige for the
baby who died. Mama had to work with Papa in the store, and she

gave you to Bubbie Ida to take care of. That's why you were always so close to her.

"And Ruby, she knew about the pogroms in Europe and the family who died. And when she was having her crazy spells, she would imagine she was there, hiding from the murderers. And she would take you and hide with you the way Bubbie Ida and Mama did with the baby in Europe. And once she took you out in the middle of the night and disappeared in the rain for hours . . . you both could have died of pneumonia."

There was a long silence. Faye stared at the floor. Then she got up, walked to the window, looked out, and turned around, glaring. "Who the hell cares what Ruby did? She's dead. It's what you did today that disgusts me. You make me sick. I don't want to look at you anymore." Faye went into the bathroom and slammed the door.

Irene sat on the bed, tears sliding down her cheeks. Jenny wanted to tell Irene to stop feeling sorry for herself. Nothing bad had happened to her. But part of Jenny also wanted to comfort her, to fix this. Irene looked so forlorn sitting on the bed, her plump body sagging. She looked old and young at the same time.

After a few minutes Irene wiped her eyes with her bare arm. "I never saw her so mad. I wonder if she'll ever speak to me again."

Jenny wondered too. But then she thought, *Of course she will. She didn't mean what she said. She couldn't have. We're sisters. She'll get over it.* But Jenny couldn't get the words out. She walked to the window and took her time watching the traffic on the street and thinking of what happened. What would her mother have said? Family—something about family and sticking together. *But,* Jenny thought, *sometimes family isn't enough.*

What should she say? She just didn't know. So, she said nothing at all.

17

Irene

1996

After Irene's stroke, Ellie wanted her mother to move to Larchmont to live with her and her husband, Aaron. Their daughters, Karen and Janet, were grown, their bedrooms were empty, and the house was plenty big.

Irene thought about it. It wasn't that she couldn't take care of herself—it had been a small stroke, and she was left with almost no after effects. But the doctor said that because of her atrial fibrillation and her diabetes, she was at risk of another stroke, and she was terrified that she would have one when she was by herself.

She was also lonely. She was seventy-five, and she was no longer comfortable driving in the city. The family members were scattered now. Her son, Franklin, lived in Denver. Jenny and Victor lived together in Jenny's apartment on the upper West Side, and Faye, who Irene had reconciled with after their trip to India, was in New Rochelle. Morris and Pauline were the only ones left in Brooklyn. Even Charles Conyers, the young man Sam had saved from drowning, only visited once or twice a month now that he had a life partner.

So Irene agreed and moved into Karen's empty bedroom. She gave away or sold her furniture along with the house and stored her paintings in Ellie's basement. She only hung up two paintings: an old portrait of Sam, which she had done when they were first married and the big oil of Charles Conyers, in black and gray and red, a symbol of pain and loss, which she had painted of him right after they met. The portrait of Charles had won a prize at the Art Students' League, and because of that she had many commissions for portraits in the years afterward. In Ellie's house she took over Janet's room as a studio in case she still wanted to paint. The hall bathroom that the girls had shared became Irene's.

Irene was pleased with the arrangement. "It's like a suite," she told Ellie. "I really like it here." She settled in. But then Irene didn't seem to know what to do with herself. She went shopping with Ellie. She went to the movies with her. When Ellie was at work, Irene stayed home and watched television. When Ellie came home, Irene sat in the kitchen watching her prepare dinner, commenting on everything.

Ellie said, "You're driving me nuts, Mom. Why don't you go to the Community Center? They have lots of activities for seniors, and you could meet people."

"Old people," Irene said.

"You're old."

"Seventy-five is not old," Irene sniffed. "And I don't look my age." Even as she said it, Irene knew it wasn't true. She'd been pretty once, but now she had mousy brown-gray hair, which she no longer dyed, a pudgy double chin, and upper arm flesh that swung when she gesticulated. She looked like Bubbie Ida had in her last years.

After a minute Ellie said, "They have a very active painting class there. I've heard it's great."

Irene made a face. "They're all amateurs. I've been painting my whole life. And I'm not going to paint with people who don't know which end of a paintbrush to use. If I want to paint, I'll do it here."

Ellie sighed. "How about calling Aunt Jenny. I'm sure she'd drive out to have lunch with you."

"She's too involved in her new life with Victor. I swear, since she and Victor got back together again, she's a different person."

"What do you mean got back together again?"

Irene didn't answer for a moment. Then she said, "I meant moved in together."

"No, Mom, you didn't. What did you mean?"

Irene took a deep breath. She knew she should not say what she was going to say, but she couldn't help herself. "I guess it's okay to talk about it now. It was so long ago." She hesitated, then rushed ahead. "Victor and Jenny had an affair when Ruby was in the hospital for a major breakdown. Nobody knew about it, except me."

Ellie's mouth was open in shock. "Really? I never would have believed that of Aunt Jenny."

Irene smiled. "Still waters and all that," she said. "And the worst of it was that Ruby suspected. She always had a sixth sense. I often wondered if that was the reason she committed suicide at the end. She never believed Victor loved her after that."

"That's really awful."

"Yes, it is. And you can't say a word to anyone else about it. We never talked about it, Jenny and me, after that first time, when it happened." Irene was quiet for a minute, and then said, almost bragging, "I was the one who made her stop."

"How'd you manage that?"

"I told her if she didn't stop, it would tear the family apart. It would destroy her own husband, Harry . . . and you know she loved him too. We all loved Harry. And I never liked Victor that much anyway . . . you know he left his sick wife with his parents in Germany right after Kristallnacht. He got out, and the Nazis murdered them all. When I told Jenny that, she broke it off with Victor."

Ellie was staring at Irene. "It's amazing what things go on in families. You just never know."

"You can't tell anyone . . . not even Aaron. You have to promise."

"All right, I promise."

"I shouldn't have told you," Irene said, fidgeting with the silverware. "I feel terrible that I said anything."

"I'm not going to say anything to anyone," Ellie said.

Irene nodded and was silent for a few minutes. Then she took a deep breath. "Maybe I'll call Faye. She's always game for lunch together. Do you want to join us?"

"No," she said. "I'll pass. I'm still working, remember?" Ellie turned her back and busied herself wiping the kitchen counter.

"I know you're mad at Faye for giving Karen the money," Irene said.

"I don't want to talk about it. Faye's your sister, so you go to lunch with her."

"It's a shame. Faye was always your favorite aunt."

"*Was* is the operative word," Ellie said.

Irene pinched her mouth together to keep from speaking. Everything would have been fine if Faye had not given Karen the money to go to India when Ellie and Aaron didn't want her to go. And now Karen was tramping around India with a girl named Shakti Richmond whom she had met in an ashram. God only knew when she'd be home.

Irene was sitting at the kitchen table drinking coffee the morning that Shakti Richmond called from India and, expecting a call from Charles Conyers who usually telephoned on Saturday morning, she picked up the phone.

The voice on the phone sounded like a little girl. "Mrs. Whitby. I'm Shakti Richmond. I'm the one who was traveling with Karen from the ashram."

"Yes, Shakti. I know who you are. This isn't Mrs. Whitby. It's her mother. I'll get her." Irene called for Ellie who was in the living room, to pick up the extension, but she did not hang up the phone. She wanted to hear what Shakti was about to say.

"Shakti, this is Karen's mother. Is everything all right?"

The line went quiet. "No," Shakti said finally. "No. It's not all right. Karen fell off the train."

"Karen what?" Ellie asked.

"Karen fell off the train." Now her voice rushed. "Karen and I were riding to Delhi. The trains in India are so crowded and people were fighting for space, with their suitcases and their bundles of food and their children. Everyone was pushing . . . ."

"Yes?" Ellie said into the silence.

Irene gripped the phone in the kitchen. She knew she should hang up, but she couldn't. Her heart was pounding.

"An argument broke out between a Muslim family and a Hindu family. They both wanted the same seats. The men started punching each other and other people joined in too. Karen and I were shoved and pushed until we were standing between two cars, but there was still fighting and pushing . . . and the train was swaying, going around curves; we were hanging on, but then—then Karen fell off the train."

Irene was trying to picture it . . . Karen falling off the train and getting up and running after it. Or Karen rolling down an incline and being helped by a peasant. Or Karen lost, wandering somewhere in India. She heard Ellie say, "Where is she now?"

There was a long silence. "Mrs. Whitby, Karen fell off the train. She fell under the wheels. She's dead."

"Dead?" Ellie asked. "She's dead? Dead?"

"Dead?" Irene repeated.

Irene couldn't hear as Shakti's voice went on and on. Irene got up to go to Ellie and there was a loud rush in her ears. Her head pounded and the phone dropped from her hand. It dangled by its long curly chord, hitting the floor with a thud. She started to walk toward Ellie, but her leg gave out and she fell. She cried out Ellie's name. The sound was garbled. She heard Ellie's footsteps, and looked up from the floor. She could only see out of her left eye. The blue flowers on the wallpaper in the kitchen danced in front of her and she said, "What happened?" but it didn't sound right to her ears. The words weren't words, they were sounds. Her brain felt scrambled. Irene was holding on to a drumbeat in her head: Karen's dead.

Time was a blur. Irene saw Ellie speaking, but didn't know what she was saying. Then everything went black.

18

Ellie

1996

"Mom, Mom," Ellie shouted. She held the phone with one hand and shook her mother with her other. Then she shouted into the phone to Shakti. "Call me back in ten minutes." She dialed 911 and waited, making sure her mother was breathing. All the while there was a thrum in her head, *She's dead. She's dead.*

She heard sirens and waited while the paramedics tended to her mother, lifted her and strapped her on the gurney, and trundled her out the door.

Then she pushed Aaron's phone number into the keypad. She could barely get the words out. Which first? Her mother? Karen? She was sobbing. Aaron couldn't understand her. She repeated, "Karen is dead. My mother had another stroke."

There was a long silence, then his hushed voice. "My God. I'll be right there."

"No." Ellie's voice was raspy. "You have to go to the hospital. I have to wait here for Shakti to call back. Oh God, Aaron, oh God. Just go to the hospital—White Plains Hospital. Go. Call me when you get there."

She slammed the phone down to wait for Shakti's call. She was cold, shivering. Her mind whirled. Karen, Karen. Dead.

The telephone rang. She snatched it up. Even before Shakti spoke, Ellie said, "Tell me again. Tell me what happened to Karen." As Shakti repeated the story, Ellie nodded her head, closed her eyes. She was screaming inside, but outside she just asked questions. "Who pushed her? Where were you? What happened after she fell? Did the train stop?"

And finally, when she had exhausted herself and Shakti and all her questions, she asked, "Where is she now, Shakti? I have to bring her home. Where is the body?"

There was an interminable silence and then Shakti whispered, "There is no body."

"What do you mean, no body? There has to be a body."

Shakti began to cry. "I didn't know what to do, Mrs. Whitby. It's so hot here. We were in the country. There wasn't even a hospital. Just farmers and huts and the local temple." Her voice got tangled in convulsive gasps. The words were muddy.

Ellie's stomach was churning, her heart was pounding. She was yelling. "What? What do you mean? I don't understand."

"I didn't know what to do. They kept saying I had to. They can't keep a body here. Everything rots in the heat. We . . ." She was whimpering. "We cremated her."

Inside Ellie a long, hot wail began, but it took minutes before it reached her throat and came out in a howl. "Nooooo!" Then there were just sobs.

In the days that followed, Ellie and Aaron clutched each other and their younger daughter, Janet, going from raw anguish to confusion to helplessness. "There is no body," Ellie wept. "I can't see her. Never."

They spoke again with Shakti. At least she had the ashes in a box. They consulted their congressman about how to bring the ashes home. It was a complicated process with bureaucratic requirements that they could not immediately fulfill. Shakti did not have an official death or cremation certificate, and without it they couldn't bring Karen's remains home on a plane. Ellie was distraught. She had to bury Karen. Her mind was a jumble. She remembered how her mother described seeing the cremations on the Ganges River, seeing the feet of a dead man sticking out of the pyre, how it had frightened her. How she hated India. Now Ellie did also.

"Cremation isn't allowed," Ellie moaned to Aaron. "Will the rabbis even let us bury her in a Jewish cemetery?"

"Of course, they will. It wasn't her fault she was cremated," Aaron said. "And what about all the Jews who were burned at Auschwitz. No one blames them."

"Just check. You check with the rabbi. I'm scared to ask."

When Aaron checked there was no prohibition against burying Karen in a Jewish cemetery. The rabbi explained the laws. He told them much more than they needed to know, but he reassured them, too. Ellie was comforted by the fact that she had the ashes to bury.

What did people do when family members drowned at sea, where there were no bodies found, she wondered. What did the families do to remember their loved ones? She thought about her own father drowning in the Hudson River. At least they had recovered his body.

Ellie paced the house. The photographs of Karen were spread all over the kitchen table. There was a photo of her in a group on the summit of Kilimanjaro surrounding the sign that marked 19,341 feet. It had been her first adventure trip, and after that she was hooked. There was one of her on some unnamed mountain pass in Ecuador and another of her in Peru, standing in Machu Picchu, a yellow pack strapped to her back, her reddish-brown hair, frizzed and flyaway. Ellie kept moving the photos around on the table like the pieces in a jigsaw puzzle, thinking about how she had really lost Karen the day she took her first trip.

It had started with Kilimanjaro, which Karen had climbed with the man who was her boyfriend at the time. Then Karen got the adventure bug and came back from Africa more excited than ever about traveling the world for a year.

Ellie had been upset. She didn't like the idea. She wanted Karen to get the whole thing out of her head, go to graduate school, get married, have a family. She didn't understand her daughter's desire to traipse around the world to exotic places, travel on dilapidated buses with peasants holding chickens in cages on their laps, collapse with other unwashed bodies in hostels and cheap hotels.

Karen couldn't explain it to her mother. All she could say was, "I don't want this," while flicking her hands around Ellie's beige-and-blue-flowered living room. Ellie didn't get it. What was wrong with her house? It was just like the house she'd grown up in.

In the end Ellie couldn't stop her. Karen was an adult. She had her own money. Ellie settled for the occasional postcard or e-mail from an internet café. But she was afraid for Karen. After Kilimanjaro she seemed to like the most foreign, exotic places best—places where she couldn't drink the water and where she couldn't always identify the food that she bought from street vendors. Ellie would warn her. She could get sick or raped or kidnapped. Karen never took it seriously. She told Ellie with shining eyes all about her adventures in backwater towns in Ecuador and Peru. She was incandescent when she talked about it.

Then a little miracle happened. Karen had used up all her money and came home, begging her parents for a loan. "I'll pay you back, I swear I will. I just want to travel for another year . . . go to India, Nepal."

Aaron, knowing how his wife felt, refused. Ellie breathed deeply and said, "No. You can get a job, save up the money, pay for it yourself. I'm not going to pay for you to fritter away your most productive years. You're almost thirty, for God's sake."

"I'm going to ask Grandma, then."

"Just try it. She won't give you any money if I tell her not to."

Ellie was right. Irene refused her granddaughter.

That was when Karen went to visit Aunt Faye. When she came back, she announced she was going to India.

"I thought you had no money," Ellie said.

Karen pressed her lips together. "I asked Aunt Faye," she said.

"Did she know we wouldn't give it to you?"

"Yes, I told her."

Even now, moving the photos on the table, all Ellie could think was that Faye had betrayed her. The words went around in her head while she waited for Aaron to tell her that they could bring Karen home.

Finally, they arranged for the death certificate to be issued in India, and Karen's remains were properly transported to New York. They had a small, private burial in the cemetery and planned a memorial service for later, when things settled down and they could bring Irene home.

Meanwhile the family gathered around Irene in the hospital. Franklin flew in from Denver and stayed at her bedside. Faye or Jenny or Morris and Pauline came and went, taking turns holding her limp cold hands, wiping the drool from her lips, talking to her and hoping that their voices penetrated through her closed eyes and mumbled words.

Ellie came when they weren't there. She could not speak with anyone. She felt that her mouth was stopped up, except when she was with Irene. She laid her head on her mother's stomach and silently talked to her, the words forming in her head. She remembered the heat of her mother's grief when her father died so suddenly. Ellie hadn't understood it then, but now she thought she did, and she told her mother so.

"Oh, Mama, how did you go on after losing Daddy? I don't think I can live without Karen." She listened, her ear pressed to her mother's rising and falling belly. She pretended she could hear her mother's voice. What would she say? *Everyone loses someone. My Bubbie Ida lost her whole family except my mother. She kept on living. I did too— after Daddy died.*

"But how? How did you go on?'

There was no answer. Just the steady in and out of her mother's breathing, Ellie's head cushioned on the up and down movement. She thought that must be her mother's answer. Breathe. In. Out. In. Out.

Irene went to rehab and then came home, able to move her arms and legs, but not yet able to walk. Ellie felt her mother needed to be near her, so she was determined to see if they could manage her at home. Irene was speaking a few words then and seemed to understand everything they said. She could be moved from the hospital bed to a wheelchair, and the hallways of the ranch house were wide enough for a chair to be pushed through. They had an aide every day and a visiting nurse and physical therapist three times a week. Irene seemed to be improving.

Ellie planned Karen's memorial service.

The service at the chapel in their synagogue was full. Aunts, uncles, cousins, their children, and their friends crowded all the pews. The rabbi spoke about Karen's care and concern for the poor of Ecuador and Peru. Aaron spoke of her love of travel and her uninhibited laugh. Janet spoke about growing up as the pesky little sister who followed her big sister as she grew into a tall, beautiful woman. Ellie could not muster the words or the strength to tell the stories that whirled in her brain. She still could not say Karen's name without crying.

They invited the people who came to the service back to their home for a meal. After a while it was only the family that was left. Faye and Jenny were sitting next to Irene, holding her hands, and wiping her tears. Faye was crying too.

It was the first time Ellie had seen her Aunt Faye since Karen had left for India. Unable to help herself she turned on her. "Why are you crying Aunt Faye? It's your fault she went to India. You told her to go."

"I didn't. I didn't tell her to . . . to go to India. She told me she wanted to go."

"But you paid for it. I trusted you. I named you her godmother. I picked you above my mother and my sister to be her guardian if anything happened to Aaron and me." Ellie felt her face getting red and her voice getting louder. "You knew I didn't want her to go to India, but you encouraged her to go, and you knew that she couldn't pay for it, so you gave her the money. I wouldn't give it to her, but you did!"

There was a sharp intake of breath and then Faye stood up, "She was twenty-nine years old, an adult. She had a right to do what she wanted to do."

"Not with my money."

"She didn't do it with your money. She did it with mine."

"Yes. With your money. And look what happened. She died. She died. And it's your fault."

The silence was thick in the room.

Faye's face was drained of color. "I'm sorry, Ellie. I would never in a million years have hurt Karen. I loved her."

Aaron touched Faye's arm. "Leave it alone, Faye. You'll make it worse."

"Worse?" Ellie yelled. "How can it be worse? There is nothing worse than what happened."

Irene was mouthing something, but Ellie couldn't pay attention to her. She was shaking with rage. "I hate you," she said to Faye. Her eyes lit on Charles Conyers, standing near her mother with a glass of soda in his long delicate fingers. "I hate you too! It's because of you that I lost my father!" She was sobbing now.

Jenny came toward Ellie. "Don't do this Ellie." Jenny touched Ellie and pulled her into an embrace. Ellie put her head on Jenny's chest for a moment, letting her aunt comfort her. Jenny said, "Shush. It will be all right."

Ellie pulled her head up. "All right," she shouted. "How can it be all right? Karen's dead. Dead. And it's Faye's fault." Ellie shoved Jenny away.

"You can't blame Faye for an accident. These things happen."

"They don't just happen. People make them happen . . . and who are you to tell me these things happen? After what you did? You're so busy with your old boyfriend you have no time for my mother. Mom told me about it. You and Victor. Back together again."

Jenny opened her mouth and shut it quickly, shook her head and looked across the room to where Victor was standing with Morris and Pauline.

Aaron took Ellie's arm and shook it. "Stop it," he said.

Ellie pulled away. "My mother told me about him too." She pointed to Victor but continued talking to Jenny. "You betrayed your own sister, and he left his first wife and parents to be killed by the Nazis. You're quite a couple."

Irene was shaking her head, making sounds like, "Nah, nah."

Jenny recoiled, horrified. "Your mother told you that?"

"Yes. She told me. That's probably why Ruby committed suicide!" Looking at Jenny's stricken face, Ellie suddenly screamed, "Leave me alone, all of you. Just leave me the hell alone."

'We have to get out of here," Faye said to Jenny.

"Go, then. Go." Ellie turned her eyes blazing. "You too, Aunt Jenny. I don't need any of you. It's not as if you help me take care of my mother."

Irene moaned, but Ellie ignored her. She watched her two aunts and Uncle Victor bend down, kiss Irene's cheek and walk out of the house together. Everyone was staring at her, but she didn't care. She didn't care at all.

Charles Conyers sat beside Irene stroking her hand. Irene's

mouth moved making incomprehensible sounds. Ellie crouched beside her and touched her arm. She looked over at Charles, her eyes spilling tears. "I'm sorry," she said. "I shouldn't have said that about my father. She forgave you. I do too."

She turned to her mother. "I'm with you, Mom," she whispered. "I'll take care of you." She put her head on her mother's lap and took a breath. "We'll do just fine without them." Ellie closed her eyes and a deep shudder went through her body. But she wondered how she would go on with her life.

19

Morris

2002

The day in early June that Morris gave up the pearl handled cane and started instead to carry an umbrella was the same day he gave up driving his black Buick.

Pauline, sitting beside him in the front seat, said later that she watched in horror how the car slid through the red light and then how Morris slammed his foot on the brake and stopped in the middle of the crossroad. Morris said later that he had been looking at a green light and then it was red. What he didn't say is that for those minutes, he had no understanding of what a red light or a green light meant. And, as he sat, his whole body shaking with terror, he had no idea how to get out of the way of the traffic careening around them.

Morris and Pauline argued bitterly later about whether it was an omen or an accident. They sat at the blue Formica kitchen table in their apartment in Brooklyn waiting for their daughter to come. For once, Pauline had not wanted to call Linda and report what happened, but Morris insisted.

"Your father got into a little accident," she said on the phone. "He's upset."

"Tell them to come," Morris said, and then sat, staring at the wall, smoke curling upwards from the cigar clenched in his fingers.

At coffee that evening, Linda, her husband, Nat, and seventeen-year-old Peter all crowded around the kitchen table with Morris and Pauline. Everyone was shouting except Morris.

Pauline was adamant. Her face had a set look, the skin creased in fine wrinkles on her cheeks. "We can't give up the car. We couldn't go anywhere without it. If he doesn't want to drive anymore, I will."

The room fell silent. Pauline had been a good driver but, being short, sat perched on the driver's seat with a pillow behind her and a pillow beneath her. She had always had to crane her neck to see over the steering wheel. Morris never felt comfortable letting her drive when he was in the car with her.

"You're going to start driving again?" Linda asked. "You haven't driven in ten years. I bet your license has expired."

"No, it hasn't. I renew it every time." Pauline's face was set.

"What about your glaucoma?" Nat asked. His voice was quiet. "I thought that was why you stopped driving in the first place."

Pauline seemed to deflate. She turned away. "I hate getting old," she said.

After a few minutes of silence, Linda spoke again. "There's great public transportation in Brooklyn," Linda said. "That's one of the advantages of living in the city. You can take the bus or the subway wherever you want to go. And taxis too,"

Pauline said nothing. She stood at the window, her back like a rod. The voices swirled around Morris like the smoke that furled from his cigar. They were loud and argumentative, but he paid no attention. He was musing, looking around him. They'd lived in this apartment for almost twenty years, ever since they'd downsized and sold their house when he had retired from the police department.

They never had gone on that extended RV trip around the country after he put in his papers. Pauline wouldn't hear of it after that crazy Vietnam vet had kidnapped and almost killed him, and he didn't argue with her. Instead, they'd come back home. He'd taken a year's course in counseling at the John Jay College. Then he'd worked with troubled teenagers at the Children's Aid Society, a huge social service agency in Manhattan. A lot of his old buddies laughed at him. "You always were a goddamned social worker," they said. "That's why we always called you the rabbi." He'd quit the social work two years ago. He figured that at eighty-three, he was old enough to just relax.

As he looked around, he noticed the kitchen needed a paint job. Years ago, he would have gone to the hardware store, bought a bucket of white paint, and sloshed it on the wall in one Saturday afternoon. Now he wondered who would do it, and then the thought drifted away with the cigar smoke.

His eyes turned to the coffee table in the living room and the vase of dried flowers Pauline kept there. "Why do you have paper flowers?" he had once asked her. "Buy real."

She shook her head and said, "Real ones fade too fast."

He wondered if that was true of people as well. It was true of Pauline, he thought now. She was wrinkled now and dry, where once she had looked, to him, like a beautiful, exotic orchid. Then he was so in love with her that he could barely breathe around her. She had shiny black curls, which she piled high on her head. She walked in high-heeled shoes, somehow maintaining her balance on legs so shapely he used to say she could be a pin-up girl. Even after she had the children, she was shapely. When men whistled at her as she walked down the street, he felt a mixture of pride and rage. *She's mine*, he would think. *Keep away.*

"Pop," Nat said, touching his arm. Morris jumped. "Pop, you haven't said anything. What do you think?"

"What do you think he thinks," Pauline answered. "He won't give up the car. We need it." Morris saw that Pauline was on the verge of tears.

"Mom, let Pop talk," Nat's voice was controlled. Morris had always liked that about Nat. He was kind and considerate.

Morris reached into his pants pocket, took out his car keys, held them for a long moment, and then handed them to his grandson. "You take the car, Peter. I won't need it anymore."

There was a stunned silence and then everyone talked at once, with Pauline's voice wailing the loudest, crying out as if she had lost something very precious.

For a moment Morris watched with an almost detached curiosity, and then, with great effort, he reached behind him for the pearl handled cane that leaned against the chair and pushed himself up. *My body doesn't respond the way it used to*, he thought.

"Why are you doing this, Morris? Why?" Pauline's voice sounded strangled.

"Mom, listen to Pop. He knows he can't drive anymore. He doesn't feel comfortable driving. His reflexes are slow. The arthritis makes him so stiff."

"Stiff. Ha. Everywhere but where he should be. There he's limp." Pauline was crying. Linda looked away.

Morris ignored Pauline, moved slowly through the apartment into the living room. He stood gazing at the wall of photographs and awards in the living room. There were photos of him in the army, and his war medal was framed behind glass: a Silver Star medal. There were pictures from his days as a cop, in his formal police uniform, dress blues. There was a picture of him with Frank, his best buddy from the war and for so many years after—funny, fast-talking Frank, gone now for six years. He missed him. There were photos of him with Pauline, dressed up in suits and hats with their two kids in front of Radio City Music Hall, and one of them on either side of her now dead parents at their golden wedding celebration.

There was one photo of him that he especially liked, taken when he was about thirty years old, posing in the sunlight of a summer afternoon. He wore a white jacket and blue trousers, and his dark hair glistened in the sun. In his hand was the pearl handled cane, not for support, but for show. He had bought it in a pawnshop on the Lower East Side, and the mother-of-pearl handle was shaped like the head of a monkey. He loved to carry it when he dressed up, and in the photo, he was smiling out at the camera, strong and virile, a man to stop and admire.

Before last year he had never really used the cane, only taken it out as part of a costume—a look, he would say. Pauline called him debonair. But last year he started to notice that it was harder to get up from a chair. Oh, he could still walk, but no doubt about it, the cane helped.

Now, with Pauline's words still stinging, he made a big show of putting the pearl handled cane into the closet. He took a large black umbrella with a curved wooden handle from inside the closet and slammed the door shut. Then he turned and walked carefully away. But he didn't lean on the umbrella.

To their surprise, Morris and Pauline did very well without the car. Sometimes at night they ordered delivery from Mama's Pizzeria or chow mein from Fong's China House. Morris had his shot glass of schnapps, snapping his head back as the amber liquid shot down his throat. They ate at the blue Formica kitchen table, the familiar implements at hand—the glass salt and pepper shakers, the cutting board with the half loaf of rye bread, the large bread knife. When they had Chinese food, they always used the wooden chopsticks that came in the bag, and they laughed at each other when the rice dropped on their plates. Pauline saved their paper fortunes in a little glass jar and every now and then took one out and read it.

"Your fortune will double and redouble," she read to Morris, laughing. "Ha. What are you waiting for? You don't have much time left."

They watched the television news, commenting on this or that, wondering about the state of the world and the violence all about them. It was just one year after 9/11. Morris often had dreams about what he would have done if he were still on the force when those planes flew into the World Trade Towers. He had dressed in his blue uniform and gone to as many police and firefighter funerals as he could, to pay his respects to the fallen heroes.

Linda had suggested that they move to be closer to her in Great Neck, but Morris and Pauline loved living in Brooklyn and wanted to stay. They could take the bus to the Brooklyn Museum or the Botanical Gardens. They knew the shopkeepers and the neighbors on their street, and the cops on the beat, who treated them with respect. Morris was one of them. It was easy for them to get around. Each day they walked, arm in arm, dragging the shopping cart and filling it with their purchases: fresh seeded rye bread and cinnamon rolls from the bakery, fruit and vegetables from the Korean greengrocer, and chopped meat from the butcher. Morris carried the black umbrella with the curved wooden handle, rain or shine, and Pauline didn't seem to mind his using it as much as she had minded the cane. Once a week, they went to Linda's for dinner. Of course, Linda or Nat or, more often, Peter, now that he had Morris's Buick, had to pick them up and drive them home afterward.

One afternoon, with the heat of early July filling the apartment, Morris awakened from an afternoon nap and heard Pauline crying softly. He got up, stumbled out of the bedroom, and found her lying on the floor, thumping her hand against the carpet over and over saying, "Help me, help me."

He rushed to her, almost toppling himself. "Pauline," he said. "What happened?"

"I don't know," she cried. "I got dizzy."

He extended his hand, but he couldn't pick her up. As she pulled on his arm, he almost fell on top of her.

"Wait," he said. He pushed a chair right up to her and sat in it. With his balance assured, he reached down and, with great effort, lifted her to her knees so she was kneeling in front of him. She put her head on his lap and rested.

"Why didn't you come?" she whispered.

"I didn't hear you."

"I heard you . . . you were snoring."

"Are you hurt?"

She shook her head and rested her cheek again on his lap. He thought that she was in a perfect position to pleasure him as she used to when they were young, and he felt a vague stirring in his groin. He reached down and lifted her, moving her to lean against his lap. They stayed like that for a long time.

They did not tell Linda about the fall.

That summer in the afternoons, they sometimes sat on a bench in the playground behind the apartment building watching the children climbing, sliding, and swinging. There were still a few other elderly couples left in the building, people they had known for years, who sat on the benches too, and chatted in companionable bursts of conversation. The old people were mostly white, the children and their mothers Dominican, Haitian, Hispanic, African-American. It didn't bother Morris at all. He loved the kids.

He carried hard candies in his pockets, and he gave them out every afternoon to any child who came to talk to him.

He sometimes bought the kids ice cream from the Good Humor Man. He handed them a five-dollar bill and they bought Pauline a toasted almond bar, and got something for themselves—a red, white, and blue rocket ice or a fudge pop. Then they brought Morris the change. He didn't get ice cream for himself. The cold made his teeth ache.

In late July their son, Kenny, was visiting New York from Seattle on a business trip. He sat on the bench with his father as Morris watched the boys throwing basketballs on the cement court behind the playground.

"These boys remind me of you and your friends when you were that age," he said. "Remember how we went camping at Twin Lakes?"

"You had your flask of 'fire water.'" Kenny made a quotation mark sign with his fingers as he said firewater and then laughed. "And you used to start the campfire with the blowtorch from your truck. Everybody thought you were the coolest Scout leader in Brooklyn. A cop. But now I would never join the Boy Scouts."

"Why not?" Morris asked.

Kenny gave him a look. "You know how the Scouts treat gay men and boys. They wouldn't want me."

"Oh," Morris said, and nodded. They were quiet for a few minutes, and then Morris asked, referring to the roasted potatoes they used to eat, "Remember mickies? They were always raw, no matter how long we left them in the ashes."

"Watch out," Kenny said. "That's not politically correct any more."

"What's not?"

"Mickies. It's a slang word for Irish."

"Ah, people are too sensitive nowadays. It was just something we all said. I was called plenty in my day. It didn't hurt me. It made me tougher."

They were silent for a few minutes and Morris was feeling content. Then Kenny spoke.

"Names hurt. I was called plenty too," he said. "Queer. Pansy. Fruit. Fag. And it hurt me plenty."

Morris looked at him, nodded and sighed. "We were all pretty dumb then about a lot of things. Especially about gays. But it's changed now."

"It's better," Kenny said. "But not changed."

"Little by little, Kenny. Little by little . . . but I sure am sorry for any hurt I caused you." It seemed to Morris he'd been saying those words to Kenny for years now, ever since Kenny had first said he was gay. "You know I love you. And I like your . . . partner. Jerry."

Kenny laughed. "Still don't know what to call him, do you? I hope someday you'll be able to call him my husband."

Morris didn't answer. He couldn't imagine that, but he knew better than to say anything.

"I don't know why you still live here," Kenny said suddenly.

Morris felt his throat tighten. "We like it here. We're used to it."

"It's a tough neighborhood now, Pop. It's not like it used to be. I noticed you don't even put the chain on the door when you go inside."

"I can take care of myself," Morris said.

"What do you think? You're still a kid? Still a cop? You can't go fighting people who get in your face the way you used to. You're an old man now. You punch someone now and you'll get yourself killed."

"I can take care of myself," Morris repeated.

Kenny shook his head. "You should move to Long Island, near Linda and Nat. It would be easier if you were near them."

"Easier for who?" Morris asked. And Kenny dropped the conversation.

In August two neighbors died in the same week and Pauline and Morris went to one wake and paid one shiva call. They tried not to let it depress them, but at night, in bed, Pauline whispered, "Morris, are you awake?"

"Yeah."

"I wonder what's next?"

"What do you mean?"

"You know. Bad things come in threes . . . what's the next bad thing?"

"All of a sudden you're superstitious?" Morris said.

"Don't you ever get scared?"

"Of what in particular should I be scared?"

"Of getting sick. Of lingering. Of dying."

"Leave it to you to invent things to worry about." Morris turned to face her and stretched out his hand, sliding it under her nightgown, knowing his hand was rough and cold and knowing that she used to tell him how she liked his rough hands on her smooth skin. He hoped she still liked it. "None of us have a contract with God."

"Don't be such a smart aleck," she said. But she moved closer to his warm body, and soon he heard her rhythmic sleep breathing—'snorthing' he called it—a cross between snoring and breathing. Morris lay awake for a long time thinking.

One Saturday night in late October, after their weekly dinner at Linda's, Peter drove them home. He was very happy. He had turned eighteen two weeks before and was legally able to drive alone at night, even when, as now, the night fell early. He had a date with a new girl and had been urging them to leave Linda's earlier than usual, because he didn't want to miss the start of the movie.

Normally Peter walked them upstairs to their apartment. But Morris, sensing his grandson's anxiety, said, "Just drop us at the back. There're no stairs there. We'll take the elevator."

"You sure you'll be okay?"

"What do you think, we're cripples? I can take care of us."

Peter laughed. "Okay," he said. "But don't tell Mom."

Morris and Pauline stood waving to Peter as he pulled away and made the right turn onto Ocean Parkway.

They had just turned to go into the building when Morris glanced to the side behind a row of bushes. It was very dark out, but he thought he saw a movement, a shadow. Anxiety flashed through his head. He took Pauline's arm and tried to hurry her into the building, but she was walking slowly, carefully, because of the dim light.

There it was again, a movement. Then a boy, his pants slung low on his hips, jumped in front of them. Pauline gasped in fright. Morris looked at the boy's face. He didn't know him. Pauline clutched his arm, her bony fingers digging into his flesh.

"Gimme some money," the boy said.

Without thinking Morris said, "You want money, go to work."

"You deaf, old man?" the boy said. "Gimme your money." The boy's eyes were darting around fearfully.

"No," Morris bellowed. "Get out of here!" And with all his strength he began to swing the black umbrella, first one way, then the other, smashing the boy on his arms.

"Help," Pauline screamed, her loud peals echoing in the air. "Help. Help. Help."

The boy tried to grab the umbrella, but Morris was swinging so fast and furiously that all the boy could do was dodge the blows that landed first on his shoulder and then on his head. And with Pauline's screams and the headlights of a passing car, slowing to see what the ruckus was about, the boy ran away.

Morris held the umbrella, broken now, and stared at his hand. It was not, to his amazement, even shaking, although he was breathing hard. He turned to look at Pauline. She too was panting, still clutching his left arm. Morris took a tentative step forward, the useless umbrella dangling from his hand.

"Are you all right?" he asked her.

"Me? Of course I'm all right. I'm not the one who just got in a fight and almost got us killed. You should have given him the money."

"Let's go in," he said, pushing the door open.

In the elevator they stood silently. Morris was aware that Pauline was looking at him out of the corner of her eye. He thought he saw a faint smile on her lips. He imagined the phone conversation she would have with Linda as soon as they got inside.

She'd say, "You should have seen your father—he was a lion. And me, I screamed like a banshee." As he mused, Morris wondered if the word "banshee" was politically incorrect. It was hard to find ways to talk nowadays, he thought.

He could hear his kids too. He was sure that Linda would tell her friends, with fear in her voice: "You won't believe what my father did last night . . . and he's eighty-three!" And Kenny, would yell at him, and tell him that he could have gotten killed, but then he would shake his head and say to his friends, "My old man is some strong bastard. Can you believe he beat off a mugger with an umbrella?"

The kids would probably start talking about their moving again. Kenny would say, "You see, it's a bad neighborhood. I was right," and maybe he was.

Morris took the keys from his pocket, opened the door to the apartment and double locked the door, putting the chain on for good measure. He put the broken umbrella in the center of the kitchen table next to the salt and pepper shakers and the bread knife and went to the closet to get his pearl handled cane. He felt a measure of pride. He had acted quickly. He hadn't hesitated, the way he had two other crucial times in his life—once in Sicily and once with that crazy Vietnam vet. He'd taken care of Pauline, taken care of himself.

Pauline watched him for a moment, saying nothing, and then went to the telephone to call Linda.

"Wait," Morris said. "Don't call. It will only cause trouble."

She nodded. Morris sat down beside her at the table and fingered the umbrella, hefted the bread knife, fingered the umbrella again.

Pauline started to speak, but he shook his head to signal silence. Then he peered into a dark corner of the living room and said to no one in particular, "Don't worry. I'll take care of us."

20

Abby

2006

It was early Friday afternoon and Abby Strauss sat peering at her three-day-old niece, Shayna. A wispy red curl lay like a comma on the baby's forehead. She was another redhead, like Grandma Ruby had been. Her name was Shayna, which meant beautiful.

Abby's brother Michael, who now called himself Moshe, was standing in the doorway between the living room, where Abby sat, and the dining room. The table was already set for the Sabbath meal—just two places—one for him and one for his wife, Golda, who was taking a nap in their bedroom while the baby slept.

They were not at all alike, Abby and Michael. Abby was dark haired and small like their mother. Michael was tall, slim, with light auburn hair, like their father, Joseph, their Aunt Sarah, and their grandmother Ruby. Right now, a large black skullcap covered most of his hair. He had grown a beard recently, and it covered the pockmarks from a bad case of adolescent acne, the scourge of his teenage years.

"She's beautiful, isn't she?" he asked, gazing at the baby.

"Beautiful. She favors the redheaded side of the family."

It was quiet for a minute, but then he said, "I wish you would stay. There's enough food and we would love to have you."

"I can't, Michael."

"Moshe," he corrected, his face coloring slightly. "Then there're only one or two more buses that will get you into Manhattan on time for Shabbos."

She stared at him, a little surprised. "You know that doesn't matter to me."

"It matters to me. If you leave here late then I'm responsible. I would love to have you stay over. Maybe you would like to experience a real Shabbos. It would be so nice to have you."

Abby wondered what it would be like to stay over in their small apartment, but the prospect of spending a Saturday with prayers and rules about what she could and could not do, and worries about some infraction she might commit, was very unappealing. And then too, Daniel was waiting for her. She hadn't told Michael anything at all about Daniel, whose last name was Chu, from his Chinese father.

Daniel, on the other hand, knew all about Michael. They'd talked about him and Golda, and when she went home, she would tell Daniel about her visit, and Daniel would press her again to meet Michael. Now Abby said, "I can't stay. I'm sorry, Michael."

"Moshe," he corrected again. After a minute he shrugged, "Then you have to go."

She got up, put on her jacket and went to the door. Tentatively she reached over and kissed her brother's cheek. He allowed the chaste peck. They always used to hug goodbye, full body hugs, but they didn't anymore. That was not allowed.

"I'll call Sunday," she said, "and see if there's anything Golda needs before I come over . . . and I'll try to remember . . . Moshe."

Moshe nodded, a small smile on his face. "Thank you. But you don't have to come again on Sunday. We have lots of help from our community."

"I want to help," she said. "Golda's my sister-in-law, and her mother lives in Florida. When is she coming in, by the way?"

"Tuesday."

"Okay, well I'll help out until then." Abby didn't wait for an answer, but just waved goodbye and let herself out of the house.

It was fall, a crisp October blue and gold day. It looked, in Monsey, New York, where Moshe now lived, very much like it did in Great Neck where they grew up, with maple trees dripping red and orange leaves. She walked the six blocks to the bus stop and waited until the bus came. There was a window seat and she put her head against the cool glass and stared. *Well,* she thought, looking out at the people bustling along the sidewalk as the bus moved out, *maybe not exactly like Great Neck.* There were men here with long beards, black coats, and big fedora hats, children with side curls and fringes hanging out of their shirts, women with long skirts and covered hair.

Moshe would say he had moved up from his life in Great Neck to Monsey. To Abby, Moshe's path from their comfortable suburban home in Great Neck to Monsey felt like a precipitous slide, slow in the beginning, and then faster and faster.

It had started when Moshe first came to her apartment in Manhattan wearing a skullcap; it was exactly five months after their father Joseph had died of a heart attack. Abby didn't notice until Moshe turned to hang his coat in the hall closet. It was a very small knit skullcap, light blue with a black border, which he wore on the back of his head pinned with a clip.

"What is that?" she had asked.

"What?"

"That thing on your head."

"It's a *kipah—a yarmulke.*"

"I know that. But why are you wearing it?"

"I just want to see what it feels like."

Abby was standing with her hands on her hips.

Moshe had laughed. "You look just like Mom when she was mad at me." Then he mumbled something.

"What?" she asked.

"I said you look just like Mom, *alav ha-shalom.*"

"Alav ha-shalom?" Abby's voice squeaked. She knew that it meant "of blessed memory." It was something religious Jews said about those who had died, whenever they mentioned their names. She had heard their grandfather, Opa Victor, say it every time he mentioned Grandma Ruby, or any of the other people in their large family who had died. She knew what it meant but she had never heard her brother say it about their mother, who had died nine years before of cancer.

"What are you so mad about?" Moshe went into the living room and sprawled on the sofa.

"What's with you?"

There was a long silence, and he shrugged. "I don't know. Look, Abby, I'm just trying something out."

"What? What are you trying out?"

"I want to see what it feels like to remember all the time that I'm Jewish."

"Why?"

"I always wondered what it felt like to be a part of a group that everyone could identify. To deliberately look different—all the time. To belong."

Abby's heart was pounding. She sat down heavily next to him and after a minute said lamely, "I don't know what to say."

"I've been saying *kaddish* for Dad at the shul."

She took a deep breath. "Since when?"

"Since he died."

Their father had died in July. It was February now. How could she not have known? "Every day?"

"Not every day, but almost."

There was a thickening of the silence. "I can't imagine," Abby said. "All that mumbling. Do you even know what they're saying?"

"Only some of the time," he admitted. "It just makes me feel good. Like I'm protected or something."

"Protected from what?"

"I don't know. I was always so anxious. I couldn't sleep. And I mostly don't feel like that anymore. I don't even bite my nails now . . ." Suddenly there was an edge to his voice. "I don't think I want to talk about it right now." He shifted on the couch. "Could we just let it go? I'll talk about it when I'm ready."

She stared at him. He was biting his lip, and his eyes had shifted to a point behind her. He didn't want to look at her. Even though there were so many questions she wanted to ask him, she nodded. "Okay. But don't go getting weird on me."

"I won't," he promised, but she didn't believe him.

And from then on, she watched her brother's life change. He began to study twice a week with a Rabbi Lipinski so that he could be more familiar with the prayers. He began to lace his conversations with Yiddish words and stories of people Abby didn't know, families with whom he would spend Friday night and Saturday, singing at their Sabbath tables.

He refused to go to their Aunt Jenny's for Passover Seder or eat in Abby's house because they weren't kosher. He found an apartment in Monsey so, he said, he could attend morning and evening prayers at his new *shul*. And when, in September, a little over a year after their father died, Moshe called her with such excitement in his voice to tell her he was going to be married, it was hard not to be happy for him.

The wedding was a blur in her mind. She wore a modest dress as Moshe had instructed and didn't kiss him in public. Because both of their parents had died, Abby and Opa Victor walked Moshe down the aisle.

Abby had gone to the wedding alone, without Daniel. She sat with all their family members: Opa Victor, Aunt Jenny, Uncle Morris and Aunt Pauline, Aunt Faye, their cousins and spouses. Even little children were invited. There were circle dances, women with women, men with men. She watched her brother dance with wild abandon in a sea of black suited men, such joy on his face that it stunned her. There were scores of children running around, little boys with side curls, little girls with fancy party dresses, all from the large families of Moshe's new friends, and Abby realized that he and his new wife Golda, also a recent convert to orthodoxy—a *Ba'al Teshuva*—could easily have a huge family like these one day.

And here they were, Abby thought now, barely one year later, celebrating Shayna's birth.

When Abby got to her apartment in Manhattan, Daniel was already there, preparing a stir-fry, listening to the Bach Double Concerto and drinking a smooth red wine. He poured her a glass and they kissed.

Daniel and Abby had met at her friend's share house in the Hamptons in early July. She laughingly told everyone that they locked eyes across a crowded room and fell in love. Daniel was tall, with straight black hair, which came from his Chinese father and a hilarious way of telling a story, which came from his Irish mother. He was smart, funny, and handsome.

She'd been to his parents' house in Queens, and she reveled in the easy banter between Daniel and his parents. It seemed to Abby that his two sisters and their husbands were there constantly, and they sat around the table, drinking tea or coffee or beer, telling stories and laughing all the time. It was a very long time since Abby had been in a house like that. Maybe she never had.

"Good visit?" Daniel asked.

She shrugged. "The baby is beautiful."

"I can't wait to meet her."

"Don't hold your breath."

He looked steadily at her, his black eyes holding hers. "I'm coming with you next time," he said.

She shook her head. "Not yet."

"What are you afraid of?"

"I don't know . . . That he'll be rude, embarrass me." Even as she said it, she knew how silly it sounded.

"I don't care if he's rude."

"What if he shuts me out completely? I promised my mother when she was dying that I would take care of him."

"I don't think she meant take care of him for the rest of his life. She was talking about helping him get through the few years after her death. You know . . . his adolescence."

Abby closed her eyes. "I couldn't bear it if he shuts me out . . . I always took care of him. He's my little brother. My only family."

"Then be part of mine," he said quietly. Her heart flipped over. After a minute he added, "I want to go with you on Sunday."

"You can't. I haven't told him one word about you. How can I just show up with you?"

"You're going to have to face it sooner or later, Abby. So he won't approve of me. So what? Maybe I won't approve of him either. My mother had all kinds of problems when my father brought her to meet his parents. You think traditional Chinese parents wanted their only son to marry an Irish girl? They came around. It happens all the time nowadays." Daniel planted a kiss on her mouth. "He better get used to me, because I'm going to be around for a long time." Abby kissed him back, then reluctantly pulled away, smiled at him and sipped her wine.

Daniel tested the rice, declared it perfect, and spooned it on a plate with the vegetables and chicken. The aroma of garlic made Abby's mouth water. "Where did you learn to cook like this?" she asked.

"Don't change the subject. We're going."

On Sunday morning she called her brother before they left, and, incredibly relieved, got the answering machine. She said, "Mi . . .

Moshe, I'll be over around eleven o'clock. I'm bringing bagels and lox from the kosher deli. If you need me to pick up anything else, call me on my cell. And I'm bringing my friend, Daniel . . . Daniel Chu. I want you to meet him."

Daniel and Abby took the bus to Monsey and walked to the small garden apartment where Moshe and Golda lived. Besides the bagels they brought Danish pastries in a box that prominently displayed the kosher label. Daniel had also insisted on bringing a bouquet of flowers, yellow and purple asters, a riot of color. There were lots of children playing on the squares of grass; tricycles and balls, and baby carriages and strollers were all up and down the sidewalks.

Moshe opened the door on the second ring, and she could see the startled look in his eyes as he took them in. Daniel looked exotic, Abby realized. Not totally Asian, but not Caucasian either. She wondered what Moshe was thinking.

Moshe hadn't lost his manners and he extended his hand as Abby introduced them. "Daniel," she said. "I'd like you to meet my brother . . . Moshe."

"I'm happy to meet you, Moshe," Daniel said. "And Mazel Tov. Congratulations, on your baby."

Moshe nodded. "Abby surprised me. I didn't know she had a . . . friend. Please come in."

Abby saw that there wasn't anything wrong with the visit. It was perfectly civil. Golda smiled at Daniel but didn't shake hands. Abby had warned Daniel about that, and he knew Golda wouldn't touch a strange man's hand. Daniel made a fuss over the baby and talked about his two-year-old niece. Moshe asked Daniel about his work.

Abby was busy watching Moshe's face, realizing that there was nothing in it to remind her of the little boy who used to stay close by her side when they were kids. She was always there protecting him. Didn't she once pull him out of the water when he was swimming to the raft at the lake at the bungalow colony where their father's family summered? He had almost drowned. She had saved him.

Moshe was lost too, when he was sixteen and their mother died of ovarian cancer. He never left Abby's side during the three days they sat shiva. The promise she made to their mother weighed heavy on her. Moshe had paced the halls of their house, peeking into room after room as if looking for someone or something, but when she asked him if anything was wrong, he said, "Nothing."

So she went back to Cornell to finish her sophomore year. *He'll be all right,* she told herself and when she graduated and came back to the city to go to law school at NYU, Moshe was at Columbia and they began to spend more time together. They were close then, she thought. But not now.

Moshe got up to get the food from the kitchen. "Come help me, Abby," he said. She knew right away that it was just a pretext. The tiny kitchen was painted yellow, just like their kitchen in Great Neck. She concentrated on the checked curtains at the window over the sink and winced when he whispered: "How could you do this, Abby?"

She felt like she had been punched in the stomach. She wanted to say, *Do what? What did I do?* But of course she knew what he was talking about. So she answered him with as even a tone as she could manage. "I wanted you to meet him. He's important to me."

"Abby, he's not Jewish."

"Tell me something I don't know. You know I don't care about that."

"But I do." He rubbed his beard. "Especially now that I have a baby. You know how I feel."

Abby was determined to act naive. "I know how you felt about going to our cousin's wedding when she married a Protestant . . . but I'm your sister."

"Abby," Moshe said patiently. "If my Rabbi told me I shouldn't go to my cousin's wedding when she married a Protestant, what do you think he would say about my own sister with a Chinese man?"

She was in a rage. "He's not Chinese, he's American. And I don't care what your Rabbi says about it. Why are you asking your Rabbi permission, for god's sake? You really hurt Aunt Rita when you didn't go, and she's Mom's only sister."

"I don't approve of a Jewish girl marrying a gentile. And I sent her a letter, explaining my position."

Abby groaned. "Yeah, that was well received. Aunt Rita said what you wrote was a lecture, not a letter. And did you even call her to tell her about the baby? When I called her, Aunt Rita said, "Good luck to them. I'll wait to send a present when he tells me himself.""

Moshe turned away. "We haven't sent out the birth announcements yet. She'll get one."

Abby was disgusted. "That's not the point, Michael, and you know it."

"Moshe," he said and waited a moment.

"Moshe," she said.

"Look Abby," he went on. "I don't know if I can be all right with my only sister going out with a Gentile, bringing him to our house."

"What, do you think he's polluting your house or something?"

"No, no. Of course not. Just that we should be separate. Keep ourselves separate."

"Where did you learn that?" she asked. "What kind of stupid idea is that?"

"It's not stupid. It's what has kept our people together . . ."

Abby knew she was going to get the lecture again. She made the 'blah, blah, blah' sign with her hands, and Moshe stopped talking.

"Look, Moshe." She took a breath, making sure he noticed that she had used his new name. "You know that's not how we were raised. Dad was in the Peace Corps. Mom and Dad marched on Washington for civil rights. The ACLU was like our bible."

"Maybe that was the trouble. They were so busy marching for other people they never taught us about our own religion. Someone else had to teach me who I am."

"What are you talking about? We went to Hebrew school. We had Bar and Bat Mitzvahs."

"Yeah. We had big parties. But I could barely read Hebrew afterward. I had to start learning all over again when I met Rabbi Lipinski."

He put the lox on a plate, the bagels in a breadbasket, while Abby stared at him, wanting to scream, *Who are you? I don't know you anymore.* But the words were stuck in her throat and she followed him when he carried the food out to the dining room where Daniel was sitting alone at the table. Golda had taken the baby and gone into the bedroom to nurse her. Silently, Moshe went to get his wife.

Daniel smiled reassuringly at her. "Buck up," he whispered. "It's not so bad." Abby shook her head. *It is,* she wanted to say. *It is.* But she said nothing.

When Moshe brought Golda back to the table Abby took the baby and held her close to her breast. Daniel, to Abby's great shock, had taken a skullcap from his pocket and placed it respectfully on his head. She wondered where he had found it. The sweetness of the gesture was piercing, and she had a lump in her throat when she looked at him.

Moshe said the prayer over bread, and they ate. Then the silence was heavy. Golda answered Abby's occasional questions about the baby's sleeping and eating. Daniel asked Moshe about his job in a large software company. Moshe answered. Abby's throat was getting tighter and tighter. She had a deep ache in her chest. When they were finished eating, Moshe got up to clear the table. Abby handed Shayna back to Golda and followed Moshe into the kitchen.

Abby put the plates down. "Moshe. You are my only family. You have to be all right with this. I love him."

Moshe shook his head. "I don't know. I don't know if I can."

"You have to be. You have to be." Abby was shaking. She could feel tears coming. "What would Mom say? Her last words to me were about you. Take care of him, she said. I always took care of you." Abby knew if she spoke more, she would burst into tears.

For a while the only sound in the kitchen was the clanking of silverware. Moshe was careful not to let the spoons and forks touch the sink but placed them in a white plastic drainer on the counter. Abby knew there was an identical red one for meat. After a minute he said, "No, you didn't. No one took care of me after Mom died."

Abby felt defensive. "I did so. I did."

"No" He turned his face implacable. "No. Not you. Not Dad. Not Aunt Rita. No one. Not even Aunt Jenny. I was so scared. When Mom was sick and you were at Cornell, I was terrified. I couldn't stand to watch her. She was so skinny, and she had these sores on her lips, and bedsores too . . ."

Abby shook her head and put her hand up to stop him talking, but he didn't stop. "I went out every night. A friend in high school got me beer and vodka, and I drank. I wanted to die. I thought about Grandma Ruby and how she was in so much pain and had ended her life jumping off a building. I thought about it all the time, about how I could do it. Mom knew. She tried to talk to me, but she was so weak. That's why she told you to take care of me . . . that's why."

Abby's heart was beating so hard she thought Moshe must hear it. What had her mother said to her? *Michael needs you. He needs you.* Something like that. Abby closed her eyes and turned away from him. But he was not finished.

"Do you remember the day we ended shiva for Mom? You came into the garage to put the garbage in the cans and found me in the car?"

"What are you talking about? When?" But in that instant, she remembered. He was sitting in the garage, in the car, with the motor running. She could see him, a figure almost shrunken on himself, wearing a black tee shirt.

"You said, '*What are you doing, Michael? Don't you know you could kill yourself by sitting in a car with the motor running?*' You made me come inside with you. Do you remember?"

The kitchen was still. Time had stopped. She nodded, remembered. The garage stank. In one corner were piles and piles of old clothes her mother had put aside to give to Salvation Army before she got sick. The garbage bins overflowed with the trash from all the paper cups and plates they had used for the people who went in and out during the formal shiva mourning period. And the exhaust from the car filled the air with the smell of spent gasoline.

She had stared at his face, pitted with adolescent acne, and, focused on one big pustule on his chin. "Turn off the motor and come inside," she had said and waited while he did.

"We never talked about it," he said. "You never asked me what I was doing. Why didn't you ask me, Abby?"

She opened her mouth to answer, to say, *Yes, I did, I asked if you were all right, I did.* But she couldn't say the words, knew they were not true. She tried to recall why she didn't ask him, or talk to him, but she could not remember. She only knew that she needed to get back to school. She had felt that fiercely, the need to get away.

He sighed and repeated. "You didn't take care of me, Abby. No one did."

There was a deep weight on Abby's chest. "I'm so sorry, Moshe," she said, and shook her head, tears slipping down her cheeks. She reached out her hand and touched his face, and it was wet, too. "I'm sorry. So sorry."

Moshe reached out and patted her back. Then he let go and moved away, reset his yarmulke on the back of his head, folded the blue and white dairy dish towel over the drying rack. With no hint of irony he said, "It's okay, Abby. You don't have to take care of me. *HaShem* takes care of me."

She was still crying as she watched him go into the dining room. She knew she must go out there, kiss them goodbye and act like nothing had happened. But words had been said that could not be taken back. She was starting to remember things, like the summer she was fourteen and Michael was ten. They had come back from camp and were spending the week with Aunt Jenny at the bungalow colony. Their mother was in the city working. That August the sun gilded everything. Their young bodies, the water, the very air they breathed. She saw him laughing at the lake. She dared him to swim out to the raft in the deep water. He jumped and started to swim, a choppy stroke, a dog paddle. He kept his head up, his chin just above the water. She followed and for a while they glided together through the silky water.

But then he said, "Abby, I'm tired," and turned to reach for her. At first, she backed away, treading water, fearful.

"You can do it, Michael," she said.

"No," he said, "I can't. I can't."

"Come on Michael, come on," she said. He was thrashing and churning the water. He swallowed some.

She reached out her left arm to him and said his name, "Michael." He grabbed her and started climbing up her arm, just what they told her in her lifesaving course that drowning people do. For a minute she thought she would go down with him, but she didn't. She said, "Michael, kick." She locked eyes with him. She pulled with her right arm, a wide sidestroke. She pulled and pulled. "Kick." she said. And he kicked and she pulled and together they struggled safely back to shore.

Now she looked through the kitchen door. She saw Daniel shaking Moshe's hand, Moshe standing stiffly beside Golda and the baby. As Abby thought about the distance to reach them, her body felt the way it did in the lake all those years ago—volumes of water pressing against her. Dense. Cold. She took a breath, and, as she willed herself then to pull and kick, she willed herself now to put one foot in front of the other and walk the few steps through the door. When she got to them, she took Daniel's hand.

21

Faye

2008

Faye sat shivering in the tub. Her pendulous breasts dipped below the cooling water. Her skin was goose bumped, her fingers puckered, her lips trembled. She tried several times to raise herself out of the bath, but her arms had no strength. They slipped off the side of the tub. She imagined getting on all fours and climbing out that way but feared she would slip and crack her head. She remembered that more accidents happened in the bathroom than anywhere else in the house. She whispered over and over, "Sophia, come. Please come, Sophia."

Faye knew Sophia would come. She came every Tuesday and Friday morning, but this Tuesday it seemed she was late. Or was it just an illusion? Faye had no clock in the bathroom. Her heart pounded and fear filled her. Had she gotten the day wrong? Was it Monday, not Tuesday? She hated being so alone, hated getting old even more. Sometimes when she was by herself, she lost track of the time, day or night, weekday or weekend. Was she getting senile?

She should not have bathed by herself. She should have waited until Sophia came. But it was ridiculous that she, who had always been so independent, should be dependent on another person because of a little arthritis. Faye closed her eyes. And a little diabetes. And high blood pressure. Tired, so tired. It would be easy to slip under the water. She gripped the side of the tub hard. Her hands were shaking as they did when she was cold and stressed. Benign essential tremor, the doctor called it. Mild and non-progressive. Don't worry about it. Unless, Faye thought, you're sitting so long in a bathtub the water turned cold.

All right, she wasn't in such great shape. She had been ignoring the arthritis for months, the flare-up in her hips and her knees. She was finding it harder to raise herself from the easy chair in which she watched television, and she struggled getting out of the car. At least she lived in a ranch house. Climbing stairs would have been difficult.

It seemed to be getting worse. For years she'd kept herself fit playing tennis with friends and taking brisk walks around the track at the high school. But a few years ago, one tennis partner had moved to Florida, another had gotten sick and then died, and a third had moved to be near her daughter. She'd never managed to replace the people who'd been a part of her adult life. And her family . . . she closed her eyes. She didn't want to think about them just now.

She heard something and listened. It was the sound of the key in the lock and Sophia's voice calling her name as she had for the five years she'd cleaned Faye's house. Sophia's quick footsteps came down the hall, pausing at the bedroom door. "Faye. Faye." The grandfather clock chimed nine o'clock in the living room. It was Tuesday and Sophia was not late after all. The footsteps continued down the hallway and stopped at the door to the bathroom, which Faye had left ajar. The door opened and Sophia appeared, shock registering on her face.

"*Ah, Dios! Dios!*"

"I couldn't get out," Faye whispered; she was so cold her teeth chattered.

Sophia got a huge towel and pulled the plug from the tub, so the water swirled down the drain. She tugged and lifted with all her strength holding on to Faye's slack, spongy arms. With gratitude, Faye saw how Sophia averted her eyes, looking only at the flat link gold necklace on Faye's neck, so she would not focus on the colorless nipples on her swaying breasts, the folds of belly flesh, the sparse pubic hair.

"I'll call doctor," Sophia said when Faye stood, enveloped a towel. She led Faye with small baby steps, to the bedroom.

"No. No doctor."

"We should call doctor," Sophia repeated.

"I just felt a little weak. It's the arthritis. That's all. I'll be fine in a few minutes." But it occurred to Faye that she was not fine. When Sophia pulled the plug in the tub, Faye had wondered why she hadn't done that or at least added more warm water to the bath so she wouldn't be so chilled. Two years ago—even last year—she would have done that. She was slipping. Definitely slipping. But now she said, with more energy, "I'm all right."

Sophia didn't answer. Faye sat on the side of the bed, her legs dangling, as Sophia wiped her dry, dressed her in underwear, a flannel gown, a woolen bathrobe that she found in the closet, and socks from the bureau drawer. She helped Faye down the hall to the dining room and then said, as she went into the kitchen, "I will make chamomile tea." She brought it to the table and Faye watched her spoon two packs of Splenda into the cup, stirring it well. Sophia knew about Faye's diabetes.

She put the cup to Faye's mouth, but Faye insisted on holding it herself.

The teacup clattered against the saucer. Faye's hands trembled. "You do it."

Sophia fed the chamomile tea to Faye with a teaspoon and Faye slurped the liquid again and again until the cup was empty. "Like I did for you," Faye said. "After Alex."

Sophia nodded. She closed her eyes.

"I'm sorry," Faye said. "I know you don't want to remember."

"I don't forget."

"Of course not."

How could Sophia forget. She had come to the United States from Colombia with her son after her brother was killed in a drug war. "Fleeing my fate," Sophia had told her. "But it didn't help. Everything is destined. Your fate pursues you." Faye didn't believe in fate, but she said nothing—just listened.

Alex had been killed in a drive-by shooting while he stood on the porch of Sophia's two- family house in the Bronx. He was holding his baby Alicia in his arms. Sophia had told Faye how she saw him turn his back just at the instant the black Lincoln drove down the street, taking the bullet below his left shoulder so that it pierced his heart. He spiraled down, cradling the unharmed baby in his right arm, his blood pooling under and around them.

Sophia had picked up the squalling Alicia, so covered in blood she only knew the baby was alive because of her cries. When she bent to touch her son's face, pressed against the wooden slats of the porch, his eyes were wide open, and his brown hair waved over his ears. "Just that morning I told him he needed a haircut."

On Sophia's first day back to work two weeks after Alex died, she was unable to do anything but sit at the mahogany dining table drinking the chamomile tea that Faye made for her. For two hours Sophia wept for her lost boy, her eyes swollen from crying, while Faye sat with her and patted her hands. Faye remembered her saying, "You are so kind, the only one of my people who paid my wages for the time I didn't work."

Now it was Sophia's turn. She touched Faye's hand and said, "More?"

"No." Faye picked at the tablecloth with chipped fingernails.

"I can give you manicure," Sophia said. "It will look nice."

Faye shook her head. After a minute she said, "I don't know what to do. All my friends are gone."

Sophia stared at the photos that covered the mahogany buffet against the wall. She made a sweeping gesture with her hands. "Your family. Call them."

Faye wondered who was left? And who would come if she called? How had it come to this . . . to being so alone? She felt as lost now as she had when Angelo died. At least then she'd had her mother and Irene and Jenny, Morris and Pauline. Now Irene was dead, and Jenny . . . why didn't she see Jenny much anymore? Faye found it hard to explain. Why was there no one left of their close, bustling family— the ones who came on Friday nights for dinner at Bessie's house, who summered together at the bungalow colony when their children were little, who gathered in the hospitals and the funeral home when, over the years, one by one, they died.

As if reading her mind, Sophia said, "Your sister, the nice one, the one I used to meet here sometimes—where is she?"

"Jenny?" Sophia nodded. "She lives in the Bronx, at the Hebrew Home."

"Oh, that's a good place," Sophia said. "Is she sick?"

"No. But she's getting old. Last year she broke her hip."

Sophia picked up a photo of Faye and Irene and Jenny in India and gave it to Faye. "You all look so happy here," she said.

Faye took the picture and put it face down on the table, remembering. "Could you come and live with me? I could pay you well."

Sophia pulled back. "No. No. I have the baby—Alicia—now. "

Faye nodded, was silent for a while and then said, "Where is her mother? Why doesn't she take her back?"

"Lilly. She's no good. She uses drugs."

"Your son's wife is an addict?"

"She's not his wife!" Then her voice softened. "Maybe not an addict, but she uses drugs. Heroin, coke. I don't know. She did not even come to his funeral. . . ." After a moment of silence, Sophia said, "You had no children."

Faye shook her head. Not for lack of trying, she thought. She got pregnant easily enough—it was keeping the pregnancy that was the problem. Five miscarriages, hope and joy each time she missed her period, the early months when she felt she was holding her breath to keep the fetus within her, then the day she noticed that her underwear was smeared with a rusty color, then the cramps and the blood and the devastating pain clutching at her abdomen and her heart. They had held each other, she and Angelo, each time, comforting one another with promises that next time it would be all right. But finally, when she almost died from hemorrhaging, the doctor told her she should not get pregnant again, and she had agreed to a hysterectomy.

Faye had tried not to be morose or to sweep the rest of the family into the depth of her sadness. Jenny and Irene and Pauline called and visited frequently during the two weeks she was in the hospital, and for once her mother, Bessie, had been there for her, bringing dinner and desserts when Faye finally came home, so Angelo didn't have to cook. It was true Bessie usually had Ruby with her, and that was a mixed blessing. After Faye's hysterectomy, Ruby had sat beside her, held her hand, and said, "It's probably just as well. You wouldn't want to bring a child up Catholic, would you?"

All these years later, Faye could almost laugh at the memory. Especially because after her hysterectomy, she and Angelo had thought about adoption, but one of the problems they encountered with the agencies was the need to choose a religion. And they weren't sure what to do. They never had to decide, as Angelo, who had been a heavy smoker, became ill with lung cancer the following year and died a year later. They'd only been married seven years. That was the end of the line for the Benedetto family.

Now, after a moment of silently shaking her head, Faye said aloud, "No. We never had children."

Sophia picked up another photo. "Your wedding?"

Faye nodded. She and Angelo stood in the middle of the picture. She wore a white suit and a hat, not a wedding gown. Her Bubbie Ida and her father, Abe, had died the year before, and Angelo's family was all gone. Bessie stood beside the wedding couple, only agreeing to be there because they got married at City Hall. Angelo had asked Faye's brother Morris to be his best man. Feeling that her sisters, who were all around forty, were too old, Faye asked her three nieces to be her bridesmaids.

Faye pointed at them in the photo. "My nieces Sarah, Linda, and Ellie—she was the youngest. Thirteen." It was hard not to smile at them. They were all dressed in baby blue satin, all grasping their bouquets in the exact center of their waists and all beaming. "I was very close to Ellie. She was like my little sister."

"So, call her."

"We don't speak any more."

Sophia looked shocked. "Why?"

Faye didn't want to talk about it. "Old family stuff. It's just the way it is."

Sophia gave her a look, narrowed her eyes. After a minute she said, "Then call your other nieces." As if it were settled, she got up and took the cups into the kitchen. Just then Sophia's cell phone rang. She glanced at the number and ignored it.

"Why don't you answer?" Faye asked.

"It's Lilly—the same thing every day. She says, 'I want to come to see my daughter.'"

"Maybe you should let her. It's her daughter, after all. Give her a chance."

"A chance? I give her a chance? So she can take baby?" Sophia clenched her fists, hid them in her lap. "I told you it's her fault Alex died. Her fault."

Faye remembered what Sophia had said—how Alex had gone to

Lilly's apartment and found her high and Alicia crying in her crib. How he had thrown the packets of cocaine that were on the table into the toilet and taken the baby home to his mother. Later the drug dealers came to him for the money Lilly owed for the coke. He didn't have it, and they had killed him.

"Lilly sent them to Alex." Sophia was furious. "So don't say she can come to me. She can't. She says she's in rehab. I don't care. She can't come."

Faye murmured, "I'm sorry. You did tell me. I'm sorry."

She watched Sophia struggle to calm herself as she took deep breaths and pressed her lips together. Before Alex was murdered, Sophia had been a cheery, optimistic woman. She sang as she went about her chores; her brown eyes sparkled, and her mouth was in a perpetual grin. Now she seemed shrunken even from her usual tiny stature, and Faye detected threads of gray in her curly black hair. Faye wondered how bad things happen to some people, the chain of events that led from a simple mistake to disaster. Lilly used drugs, Alex threw them away, the drug dealers wanted to be paid, Lilly sent them to Alex, he had no money, and they killed him.

"It's the butterfly effect," she said to Sophia.

"What?" Sophia stared, wide-eyed.

"It's called the butterfly effect. It's a theory in physics. I used to tell my students that small things, like the beating of a butterfly wing, could cause a hurricane on the other side of the world. You do one thing, make one mistake and it causes another to happen, and another, and before long you have catastrophe."

Sophia shook her head. "I don't understand."

"No, I don't either."

The house was still. Faye got up. She felt stronger now. She walked to the kitchen and got Social Tea Biscuits from the cupboard, made more tea. She wondered if the girl, Lilly, had changed, now that she was sober, and understood that her mistakes had led to Alex's death.

She wondered if Sophia would ever give Lilly a chance to say "sorry" and see her baby again. She wondered if Ellie would ever give her another chance.

She looked around at the yellow-and-blue kitchen. It was exactly as it had been after she had painted it when she and Angelo moved into the house. The only other thing she'd done was to remove the pictures of Jesus and take the crucifix off the wall behind their bed.

She gazed at the phone hanging on the kitchen wall. Maybe she should call Jenny. She hadn't called Jenny in almost two months. But then, Jenny hadn't phoned her either.

The last time she saw Jenny, they had met for lunch in a café in Manhattan, and Jenny told her that she and Victor had gone to Ellie's grandson's bris. "They named him Karim in Hebrew, in memory of Karen. They call him Kenneth. It was a huge celebration with everybody there."

It felt like a knife had pierced Faye's chest. "Everybody wasn't there. I wasn't," she said. Then she added, "I hate circumcisions anyway. I think they're barbaric."

Jenny looked down at her plate and pushed the salad around with her fork. "I probably shouldn't have said anything. I know it hurts you."

"Hurts me? What about you? How could you go, after what she said to you? That you betrayed your sister and that was the reason she killed herself."

"That was seven years ago, Faye. And she only said that because she was really upset—remember Karen had just died." Jenny reached out and touched Faye's hand. "Don't go on like this. Ellie and I talked, and she told me how sorry she was. And I accepted her apology."

Faye sat back in her chair. She felt deflated, like someone had stuck her with a pin.

"You could call her," Jenny said. "Maybe apologize."

"For what? I didn't do anything."

Jenny looked at her for a long time and then shook her head. They ate the rest of their lunch in silence, and although they pressed their cheeks against each other when they left, acting like nothing was wrong, they hadn't spoken to each other since then.

Now Faye looked away from the telephone and brought the biscuits and tea to the dining room. She and Sophia sat and dipped the biscuits in the tea, and the cookies dissolved on their tongues.

After they had been sitting for a few minutes, Faye said, "I understand about Alex. Terrible things happen in families. Even ordinary deaths—like my sister Irene's stroke when she was seventy-five—seem very sad."

"You must have felt very bad when she died."

"I did. After our husbands died, we used to travel together. We called ourselves 'the Merry Widows.'" Faye looked away. It was hard for her to think about Irene's death, all mixed up as it was with Karen's. "We weren't so close to each other by the time she died, but she was my sister, and I still loved her. And I was very close to her daughter Ellie . . . and her granddaughter Karen. I was Karen's godmother. She was like the daughter I never had." Faye reached up and touched the chain around her neck. "I always thought I would leave this gold necklace to her. My grandmother brought it from the old country and gave it to me just before she died."

"It is beautiful," Sophia said. She thought for a minute. "I don't understand then. Why you don't call Karen?"

It hit Faye with the force of a punch. Sophia didn't know. Faye licked her lips. "Karen died."

Sophia breathed the words out. "Oh. No." They sat in silence. Sophia took Faye's hand. "What happened?" she asked.

Faye forced the words over the lump in her throat. "Karen wanted to go to India. While she was there, she had a terrible accident. She was pushed off a train and she died. Irene and Ellie blamed me."

"How could that be your fault?" Sophia asked. "How could you know she would fall off a train? It was not your fault."

Faye was quiet. She fidgeted with her teacup. "I sometimes feel it was. Her mother didn't want her to go. Karen asked my advice and I told her she should live her own life. I told her I thought she would love India as I did." She stared at the table. "Karen had run out of money in South America. When she came home, she asked her mother and grandmother to lend her enough so she could go to India. They refused. She asked me, and I gave it to her."

"You could not know that her mother said no to her."

Faye swallowed, hesitated and then said, "But I did know. I knew, and I gave it to her anyway. And I didn't talk it over with them first." Then she spoke very fast wanting to get the rest of the story out. "Karen took my money and went to India and fell off a train and died. When Irene heard Karen died in India, she had a big stroke and died a few weeks later. Ellie lost her daughter and her mother in one month. That's why she hates me. We haven't spoken to each other since."

Sophia turned away. The minutes ticked in silence. "Why did you do that?" she asked finally. "Go against your sister's wishes?"

"I don't know exactly." Faye's words were halting. "I was happy that Karen went to India. I think I wanted her to listen to me and not her grandmother or mother." Her face reddened. She took a deep breath. "It was a stupid, selfish thing to do."

"Yes," said Sophia.

The word reverberated in Faye's head. She felt ashamed.

Sophia stared at the table. She said, "You know why these things happen? *Es su destino.*"

Faye shifted in her seat. "Destiny? I don't know about that. More like luck. Coincidence. The choices we make—the things we do."

"Si, destino," Sophia insisted.

The big grandfather clock ticked on and on. It was twelve thirty.

Suddenly Faye was famished. "I'm starved," she said and started to get up to go into the kitchen.

Sophia jumped to her feet. "I'll do it." She looked in the refrigerator. "There are eggs," she said. She scrambled them in the kitchen and brought two plates to the dining room with buttered toast and more tea. "Eat," Sophia said, setting the plate in front of Faye.

Faye picked up a fork and ate her eggs. The words destiny, fate, choices, were whirling in her head. She wondered if Sophia really thought it was Alex's destiny to die at the hands of drug dealers and not some random event. Faye thought it was Lilly's choices and actions that caused Alex's death. Was that what Sophia meant by "*destino*?"

It was all too confusing. She pushed her plate away. "I'm finished."

Sophia began cleaning off the table. "Sophia," Faye said, stopping her. "Do you really think Lilly was destined to cause Alex's death? Is that what you meant by "Es su destino?"

"Si." Sophia took the plates into the kitchen. "Lilly invited in the devil."

"What do you mean, devil?" Faye asked.

Sophia didn't answer. She filled the sink with soapy water, swirled the dishes in it, and set the plates in the dish drainer. She wiped her hands on a towel. "I go do the bedrooms and bathrooms and then I leave. I have to pick up Alicia. I will finish Friday."

Faye nodded. She sat at the dining room table listening to the sounds of the vacuum cleaner down the hall. Sophia had not answered her question. It was ridiculous. She felt rebuffed, anxious. Did Sophia, too, blame her for Karen's death? All she had done was to give Karen money for a trip. She hadn't pushed her off the train . . . or even told her to go on the train. She closed her eyes, listening to the vacuum cleaner, listening to the clock, *tick-tock, tick-tock*.

Sophia came into the dining room. "I'm finished now. I will come back Friday."

Faye followed her to the door and stood on the porch watching Sophia get in her car. She wanted to say, *Let Lilly visit. At least try.* But the words wouldn't come. Who was she to advise Sophia to speak to the girl who had invited in the devil, when she herself may have done the same thing? Faye watched Sophia drive away.

She went back into the house. Empty. She wondered why she had never moved to an apartment after Angelo died. This house was too big for her. She could move into one of the apartments at the Hebrew Home in Riverdale. They had these arrangements. When you needed more help, you moved up to the next level of care. Or maybe move back to Brooklyn, near Pauline and Morris, or Florida where her best friend lived. She had choices. She didn't have to stay here alone and isolated.

She looked at the photos on the buffet in the dining room, and then walked into the living room to look at the ones on the long, low bookcase opposite the sofa. What had Sophia seen? Laughing faces. Loving faces. Family faces. It was a long time since Faye had looked at them. A long time since Faye had talked to any of them.

Her fingers drifted along the backs of the books. It was a lifetime of reading. She and her sisters used to share books, lending each other the ones they loved, sometimes forgetting to return them to their original owner. She knew she had Jenny's copy of *Gone with the Wind* somewhere on the shelf.

When Faye was eleven, she had spent precious birthday money from Bubbie Ida to buy her own copies of *Little Women* and *Anne of Green Gables.* There they were, dog-eared and much thumbed. She had lent them to Ellie when she was a little girl. Ellie had loved them with the same devotion as Faye, reading them over and over, even at the breakfast table on weekends when she could pore over them for hours. She had once smeared jelly on page 51 of *Little Women.*

Faye took the book out and turned to the page. There was the stain, faded and brown now, but unmistakable. Faye remembered the day years later, when, sitting at Ellie's kitchen table, she had given Karen the book to read.

"Be careful never to get any food on it," Ellie had said to Karen, winking at Faye. "Especially not jelly."

Faye and Ellie laughed as Faye opened the book to page 51 pointing to the jellied fingerprint. "Your mother was really scared to show it to me, but I told her not to worry." Faye looked at Ellie and they said together, "Jelly stains are the mark of a well-loved book."

Faye held the old copy of *Little Women*, and her hands shook with her tremor and the knowledge of what she had lost. Suddenly she was crying. She dropped down on the sofa. Wave after wave of sobs engulfed her, and she was overcome with sadness and with shame. All she ever wanted in her life was a family. When she couldn't have children of her own, she was given the precious gift of surrogate daughters—first Ellie and then Karen. And she had thrown it away because of envy. Because she wanted Karen to love her more than she loved her own mother.

She did not know how long she sat on the sofa crying, but it was a long time. Finally, she got up and replaced *Little Women* on the bookshelf. She walked into the kitchen, her heart pounding a little with apprehension. How would Ellie respond if she called her now?

The telephone hung black and silent on the kitchen wall. Faye took a deep breath. She realized that she was afraid to call Ellie. But maybe she could call Jenny. Maybe Jenny could help her find a way to say, "I'm sorry."

She picked up the receiver and listened to the buzz of the dial tone. Then she punched in Jenny's number.

22

Jenny

2012

"Victor, wake up," Jenny said. She touched his shoulder. It was ten in the morning, and they had both overslept.

He had awakened her in the middle of the night with one of his recurring nightmares. "Feel my heart," he had whispered. Jenny placed her hand on his chest and felt it fluttering so fast she was afraid it would kill him. She lay beside him, stroking his arm as his voice trailed off, making delicate shushing sounds with her mouth next to his ear, quieting him to sleep again with the rhythm of her breath. But she couldn't sleep for a long time afterward. Now they were going to be late for his hundredth birthday celebration at noon today.

"I dreamed it again, Jenny," he said, sitting up in bed. "The whole thing. Kristallnacht. Dachau." He never remembered that he had told it all in the middle of the night. In the morning he wanted to talk about what had happened: how he and his older brother and father had been arrested and sent to prison in Dachau for a month, how sick they were when they were released, how afterward, his brother didn't get well fast enough and Victor, the only one who had obtained a visa, had abandoned him and his whole family to save himself. He never mentioned that he had abandoned his dying wife as well, but Jenny had discovered that years ago.

She was tired. She didn't want to hear the story again. She placed her finger on her mouth and whispered, "Victor, we're not going to talk about it now. Today is your birthday celebration. We are going to be happy."

I hope. The thought intruded. *I hope it will be a happy day.* There were so many family issues, old business that interfered and upset. It seemed everyone came to Jenny to make them right. *Would Sarah come to the party? Would Ellie and Faye be talking to one another? Would George be there?* At the thought of her son, George, she felt a riffle of anxiety. Lately he'd been so angry with her. She pushed the feeling away.

"It's time to get ready," Jenny told Victor, and she called the bath aide at the Hebrew Home, who came each morning to help Victor get washed and dressed.

For the past two years, Jenny and Victor had lived in the Bronx in a two-bedroom apartment in the Hebrew Home. It was elegant and well kept, and downstairs there was a large community room where even now, Victor's granddaughters Didi and Abby and their families were hanging all the photographs that they had collected. There would be flowers and music and food, and a video by a professional photographer.

Jenny was mostly looking forward to the party, to seeing the family—the children and grandchildren and great-grandchildren—but underneath the excitement was a lump of anxiety. She wondered again if George would come and how he would treat her if he came. She'd last seen him almost a month earlier, and he'd been angry and upset because of what he'd found in the apartment.

When she and Victor had moved to the Hebrew Home, she'd

given George the apartment she had shared with Harry her whole married life, and later lived in with Victor. It was a large apartment, and Jenny left most of the furniture as well as boxes of photos and papers. She told George, "It's yours now. Keep everything, give it all away, or throw it out. Whatever you want. We have no room here."

George and his new wife, Barbara, gradually redecorated the apartment and finally, in the last two months, George got around to the spare room in the back of the apartment where Jenny had stored boxes of papers and odds and ends. George methodically went through them and found Harry's letters and journals.

George read them all. At first, he told Jenny how proud he was of what his father had done in the war and afterward. Then one day, after he hadn't called her for a week, he asked Jenny to meet him in the lobby of the Hebrew Home. He said he wanted to talk to her alone.

Jenny was waiting for him when he came, and she watched him walk toward her. He was not tall like Harry had been, but he was trim now from his yoga practice and running. He was carrying a manila folder, and he sat beside her on the sofa and handed it to her.

Jenny took the folder. "What is it?"

"Read it."

Jenny opened it and skimmed the pages.

"Now I understand why you were in such a hurry for Victor to move in with you after Dad died," George said.

Her heart hammering, Jenny read on. She had forgotten about this. If she'd remembered, she would have thrown it away. It was Harry's journal from 1954, the year Jenny and Victor had their affair, the year that Ruby spent so much time in the hospital. The papers described the suspicions he'd had about Jenny and Victor and how he was sure Jenny loved Victor. There was nothing in it about the brief affair he had told her he had with his secretary.

Jenny looked at her son. He was scowling, his eyes half closed in a squint. She took a deep breath. She didn't know what to say.

Admit her betrayal? Say, he did it too? I thought you knew. Forgive me? Jenny stared ahead. In the lobby where they sat, a maintenance worker was taking long slow swipes at the marble floor with a wet mop. He had put up a yellow sign: CAUTION. WET FLOORS. After a long time, she said, "It was so long ago."

"So, it's true."

"Your father understood. I loved him very much." It wasn't clear if she meant she loved Harry or Victor.

George shook his head. "When I first read it, I thought it was just conjecture or suspicion. I didn't believe it. But then I remembered how Victor moved in with you so soon after Dad died. It was after you came back from India. I was so upset at the time. I didn't understand why you let him." His voice rose.

"You never said."

"What could I say? I told myself you were just two old people finding comfort together. But now—now I understand."

Jenny put her hand out to touch him. "It was so long ago. I was so young. What does it matter?" She realized those were almost the exact words she had said to Harry when he asked her about Victor.

"It matters because you betrayed them—Dad, your sister. Did Aunt Ruby know? All my life I thought you were the perfect wife, the perfect mother. Selfless. Always taking care of other people. And now I don't know what I think."

Jenny squared her shoulders. "You forgave Anni." She regretted the words as soon as she said them. Jenny remembered how George had collapsed when his first wife, Anni, left him. His face was bruised with grief, his body expanding under the weight of the food he shoveled into his mouth to fill the emptiness. Anni had come back to him and they had lived together for six more years until she'd died of pancreatic cancer, but Jenny knew it had never been the same between them.

Jenny had suffered with him. You are really only as happy as your unhappiest child, Jenny thought, and she had only George. All her life she had felt the pain of every disappointment he faced. Children had no such connection to their parents' misery.

George looked away. The silence went on for a long time. "I forgave her, but I never quite trusted her again. . . ." His words trailed off and he looked deliberately at his mother. Jenny wondered. Was he telling her he would never trust her again? He took the manila folder from Jenny and left her sitting on the sofa.

That was almost a month ago. Jenny had been sick with anxiety and regret ever since. But she was also angry. She'd called George twice on his cell and left voice mails, but he never called back. Now she wondered if George would show up at all. Jenny was so tired of managing them all—her sisters, their children, her own son. She swallowed, feeling her anger like a block in her throat. She'd pushed it down most of her life, only becoming acquainted with it in the last year of Harry's life.

After Victor was washed and dressed and seated in a chair, Jenny got herself ready. She wore a deep maroon silk dress, which set off her pure white hair. She put on a little rouge and lipstick and was pleased with her reflection in the mirror. People said she didn't look her age, but she wasn't sure what a ninety-year-old should look like. She had always taken care of herself, eaten well, and exercised—even now—to keep her bones strong. After she'd broken her hip five years earlier, she'd worked very hard at that.

She stood before Victor to get his approval and he said, his European courteousness coming to the fore, "You look lovely, *mein Liebling*. Like the young woman I met all those years ago."

"How many?" Jenny did the arithmetic in her head. "Seventy-one! You were twenty-nine, and I was a baby, nineteen." She kissed the top of his head. "It's time. Shall we go down now and be there before the guests arrive?"

Jenny stood before Victor and put her hands under his armpits to help him move out of the chair and into the wheelchair they used to get him through the hallways and down the elevator. She grunted as she tugged on his arms. It was getting harder for Jenny to pull him up or help him to walk to the bathroom.

They took the elevator down to the main level, and she pushed him through the hallways to the community room, where she helped Victor out of the wheelchair and gave him his cane. He was determined to stand up when he greeted his guests.

Didi saw them and came to kiss Jenny on the cheek and hug her grandfather. "Doesn't everything look beautiful?"

There were blue and yellow balloons on all the tables, and irises and yellow chrysanthemums in tall blue glass vases. Jenny saw Abby and her husband, Daniel, in a corner of the room setting up a camera for group pictures. All around the room were huge, old-time photos of the family, which Didi had blown up to poster size.

"It's wonderful," Jenny said. "I don't know how you did all this with your busy practice. How did you make time?"

"The Frau doctor can do anything," Victor said beaming with pride.

"I had lots of help," Didi said.

Jenny looked at Didi. "You look beautiful." And it was true. Didi looked a bit like her mother, Sarah, and her grandmother, Ruby, but in a quieter way. She was dressed in aqua, which complemented her auburn hair and green eyes. She was glowing with happiness.

"Look, Aunt Jenny," Didi said. She touched the gold necklace which hung around her neck. "It was Bubbie Ida's. It's the one she brought from Europe. Aunt Faye gave it to me. She said Grandma Ruby always thought it should have belonged to her as the oldest child, and so Aunt Faye said I should have it."

Jenny reached out and touched it. "Yes, I think that's wonderful. You were the oldest great-granddaughter. It should be yours."

"And now, Opa," Didi said. "Let's get you over to the chair of honor."

Victor walked slowly with his cane saying as he went, "Have you heard from her?" He didn't need to say Sarah's name. Didi and Jenny both knew who "she" was.

"I called yesterday and left a message on her cell to remind her," Didi said. "She never told me what flight she was on, but the last time I spoke to her, she said she'd come. And she told you she would come when you spoke with her."

Jenny said to Victor, "Don't you remember? You even asked her if she still had the cameo pin you gave her, and she said she would wear it today."

Victor nodded. "I just want to see her once more before I die. I don't care about that pin."

"I know," Jenny said. "She'll come. You'll see."

Victor said, "I'll believe it when I see it."

Jenny could see that Victor was worried. They always worried about Sarah, as they had always worried about Ruby—just in a different way. Sarah wasn't mentally ill like her mother, but she was impulsive, untrustworthy, difficult to pin down.

Sarah had disappeared after the family's shiva for Ruby. They thought at first that she just wanted some space from the family so she could forget her mother's suicide. But when none of them—not Victor or Joseph or Didi or Jenny—heard from her, they began to panic.

They went to Sarah's apartment. The rooms had an eerie stillness. In the bedroom the closet stood open, empty of all Sarah's clothes. Didi pulled out the dresser drawers, and they too were bare. "She's taken everything!"

It was hard for them to stop the flutters of fear. Sarah seemed to have vanished. For months they didn't know where she was. Finally, Victor got a postcard, all palm trees and sunshine: *I'm traveling for a while, don't worry about me. I'll be in touch soon.* "Soon" turned into a year, and then she called. "I'm settling down in Southern California," she said. "I'll send you my address when I have it."

After that she called them irregularly. She gave them her address in Imperial Beach, California, a small city five miles north of Tijuana. She said she couldn't come for a visit because she didn't have the money. Victor sent her the money. She still didn't come. Finally, Victor said, "Enough," and he, Didi, Jenny, and Joseph went to California.

It was December 1989, five years after Sarah had left New York. Didi was on her winter break from her first year in medical school. They found Sarah's house easily. It was in a small development, a few miles north of the border and not too far from the beach, with square bungalows, all painted pastel colors. Many of them were decorated with Christmas ornaments—wreaths and colored lights. Jenny thought it was very incongruous to be in sunny, summery weather with Christmas trees.

They hadn't told Sarah they were coming, fearing that she would tell them not to come, so when she opened the door and saw them, she gasped, and her face turned white. Her mouth hung open. Sarah had let her hair grow out to its natural color. It was dark auburn, heavily streaked with gray, and it was cut in a pixie again. She looked good—young for her forty-three years. She was wearing cut-off jean shorts and a red-and-white polka-dot halter top, and she was barefoot.

She stared at them for a long time. "You came."

Victor and Jenny didn't speak. Didi finally said, "Mom. I missed you so much," and she fell into Sarah's arms.

There was a kind of scrabbling sound behind Sarah. Jenny looked and saw a little boy, around four, with a tabby cat spilling out of his arms. The boy had a round face, tanned skin, and a shock of reddish-brown hair that fell over his forehead. He came and stood by Sarah's side, staring at Victor, at Didi, at Joseph, with solemn eyes. Then he yanked Sarah's shirt to get her attention.

"Who is that lady and why did she call you Mom?"

"She's your big sister," Sarah said.

"And that's how I found out I had another grandson," Victor told everyone when they came back.

"And I found out Adam was my little brother," Didi added.

It was painful to remember. Sarah had been afraid to tell them that she was pregnant when she moved to California right after Ruby died. She had decided she wanted to raise another child. That was why she hadn't come back to New York. There she was, perfectly happy, supporting herself by teaching art in a local elementary school. She said she had reinvented herself and liked who she was.

Sarah's house was filled with colorful paintings hanging on the walls; it was small and clean with a flower garden in the back. In New York, Jenny thought, she couldn't keep a houseplant alive, and now she had a garden.

They actually had a pleasant visit. They stayed at a nearby motel and went out to dinner. They bought Adam presents. Victor set up a new toy train set in the living room, Joseph bought Adam a blue tricycle, Didi got him a yellow plastic baseball bat and whiffle ball, and Jenny filled a bookcase with picture books. Adam was very sweet. He seemed hungry to know them. And when they left, Sarah told them she would love to see them again, but not in New York. She didn't want to return to New York. It had bad memories.

"She was true to her word," Jenny remembered. She sent Adam to New York alone to visit the family. They all went out to California to see her. But she did not come East for visits. Sarah had stayed disconnected. Although she came to Didi's wedding she hadn't shown up to her graduation from medical school. And there was always the fear that she would disappear, not follow through or do what she said. Now, of course they were worried that she would disappoint them again.

Jenny looked around. People were arriving. The guitarist and keyboard player, who had set up against the wall, were playing soft music. Didi sat Victor in a big chair in front of them. The guests came up to greet him; they bent low and touched his arm, said their names as they kissed his cheek. Victor nodded and smiled at them, making small talk, but then after a while he seemed irritated. Finally, he put up his hand. "Give me the mic, give me the mic."

Jenny hurried to him. "What's the matter?"

"I want the mic," he said. She took the microphone with its long black chord toward Victor and as she handed it to him, he muttered, "They think I have no memory." Almost shouting, Victor's amplified voice boomed into the room. "You don't have to keep telling me who you are. I know who you are!" There was a moment of stunned silence, and then laughter and one voice after another said, "I did that. I told him my name too." Victor smiled with glee at everyone's surprise.

At that moment Jenny saw George come in with Barbara and her children and grandkids. She put up a tentative hand and waved. He only nodded. Other arriving guests distracted her. Abby hurried over to her and kissed her. Moshe and his children were there too. She saw Morris and Pauline and their kids. Morris's son Kenny and his partner had even come in from Seattle for the occasion. And Faye and Ellie avoided each other on opposite sides of the room. Jenny had tried so hard to get them to make up, but it hadn't worked. Maybe some things were just not forgivable.

All the generations were there—doctors and lawyers, teachers and engineers—educated and successful people. It seemed impossible that everyone here came from that one woman, Bubbie Ida, whose large photo on the wall dominated the room.

Didi had hung other family photos all around the room, some enlarged to poster size. There was only one picture of Victor's family—his parents and brothers—which he had carried with him when he fled Germany. All the other photos of Victor showed him as part of the Weissman clan. There was a big photo of Victor and Ruby at their wedding. He was slim and handsome, and Ruby looked like a movie star with her wedding gown spread around her feet like a fan. There were the five Weissman siblings—Ruby, Morris, Irene, Jenny, and Faye—laughing together at a party; there were the men in uniform during WWII; there were pictures at the lake where they all summered together when the children were growing up.

Jenny stood in front of her own wedding photo. There she was in her white satin wedding gown, a circle of flowers crowning her brown curls. Harry stood beside her, a marine major in his dress blues, his chest covered with bars and medals, holding his cap under his arm. There was something about him—the strong jaw, the squared shoulders—that signaled he was a man to be listened to, trusted.

"He was quite a guy," a voice said behind her. Jenny jumped. It was George.

She turned. He was not smiling. She could see he had not made peace with her yet. Jenny breathed deep. "You're like him. Very principled," she said.

"I'm not half the man he was."

She stared at her son. He was fifty-eight. Why was she nervous? Why should she have to worry about how he felt about something that happened more than forty years ago? She was sick of people judging her, expecting her to behave a certain way.

"Maybe you're right. You're not like him after all," she said. "I don't know what to tell you. If you're still upset about what happened all those years ago, I think you should . . ." She searched for the words she wanted to say. *Get over it? Forget it? No. Keep it to yourself. Yes.* "Keep it to yourself." She turned and walked back to Victor, who remained vigilant, watching the door. George did not follow her.

And then Adam appeared. His skin was burnished from the sun, and he wore a blue jacket and tan slacks. He was the kind of heart-stopping handsome that made young girls swoon. Behind him was Sarah. She was sixty-six years old now—four years older than Ruby had been when she died. Her hair was a shining silver cap around her head. Jenny had somehow thought she would wear purple—that's what Ruby would have done—but she was wearing pale gray, a soft jersey material that fit her small figure beautifully and complemented her hair. She did not look like Ruby—flamboyant with bright red lipstick and rouge. She was only wearing a little pink lipstick and small earrings and no jewelry at all on her dress. She was a lovely woman.

Sarah came toward them, Adam behind, carrying a square wrapped package. They leaned down on either side and kissed Victor's cheeks.

"What is this?" Victor said. "We said no presents."

"It's not a present," Sarah said. "It's a loan to you for now. And then later it will come back to me and then to Didi or Adam." Adam unwrapped it, and Jenny saw it was a painting. Sarah turned the canvas toward Victor and placed it on his lap.

It was a painting of Ruby, shining in all her beauty. It was from a black-and-white photograph taken on her honeymoon. She had been wildly happy that night, twirling, singing in that glorious silver voice of hers, and Sarah had imagined the color, her sparkle, her green eyes, her shining red hair, and the purple jacket with the velvet collar and the cameo he had pinned on it.

Sarah crouched beside him. "The cameo is gone, Papa. It was stolen from me a long time ago." She took a breath. "But I painted it for you."

Victor reached up, touched Sarah's cheek. "I always thought you were the image of your mother," he said. "But you don't look like her at all."

"Everybody always told me I did," she said.

"Maybe in the beginning," Victor said. "But no more. "You are not your mother. You are you."

"Yes, I am," she said. "It took me a long time to know that. I think I finally believe it. But thank you for saying that."

Victor smiled. "I am so glad you came."

Jenny leaned over and kissed his cheek. This family problem, at least, was okay.

Didi announced that she wanted to start the video. People were moving their chairs so they could get a good view of the screen. Didi pulled up a chair, and with Jenny on the other side of Victor, they watched the family scroll across the screen. There they were having weddings and babies and graduations and bar mitzvahs, laughing and dancing, swimming and playing ball, traveling around the world and growing old.

There was Faye, waltzing with Angelo; there were Sam and Morris slamming a little black handball on the court at the bunga-low colony, their strong muscled bodies gleaming with sweat; there were Jenny and Pauline and Irene, bustling around a barbecue. And always behind them all was Ruby, dancing and swaying and singing. Jenny could hear the silver voice in her head singing, "Somewhere Over the Rainbow," as she had when they were young in the family's little apartment in Brooklyn.

And each time a picture came on the screen of Bessie and Abe, of Ruby or Jenny, of Victor or Harry or Morris or Irene or any of their children, someone would say, sometimes loud and sometimes in a soft whisper, "Look how lovely they were—all of them so young and beautiful."

Reading Group Discussion Questions

1. *How to Make a Life* is a book about a large family, and it has many characters spanning four generations. Which, if any, characters did you find particularly appealing or interesting? Why? Did any of them remind you of your own family members? How so?

2. How one generation's choices and actions affect the next generation is an important theme in *How to Make a Life*. In what ways is this expressed in the book through the generations? Have you experienced or seen generational themes being repeated in your own life and family?

3. Most families have secrets. What are the secrets the Weissman family members keep from one another, and what impact do these secrets have?

4. The matriarch of the family, Ida, and her daughter, Bessie, experience unimaginable losses in their lives. How do they cope with their losses?

5. In what ways does Ruby's mental illness affect the family? Is there someone in your life whose mental health or physical health needs have impacted your family's functioning? In what way has this affected your family?

6. Bessie and Abe make a bargain with Victor to get him to marry Ruby. Do they think this is a fair and just bargain? What are the family's feelings about it? What are the consequences of this agreement?

7. Jenny is the self-described "Watcher" of Ruby. How does this responsibility frame her life? Who benefits from this arrangement? How?

8. Morris has struggled his whole life with making decisions and taking action quickly. How does this affect him and his self-esteem?

9. Jenny's betrayal of Ruby has an impact on the family. Do you think Ruby knows—and if so, what does it do to her? Who else in the family does it affect?

10. Sarah struggles her whole life with the fear that she is like her mother, Ruby. How is she similar to Ruby? How is she different?

11. Why do you think Irene is willing to take responsibility for Charles Conyers, and how does that help her?

12. Faye, in many ways, is the rebel of the family, as shown by her marriage to Angelo. But her decision to give her niece Karen money for a trip to India, against Karen's parents' wishes, has enormous consequences. Do you understand Faye's decision and think you would have made it? What is the impact of the decision on the family, on Faye, and on her sisters?

ACKNOWLEDGMENTS

I loved listening to family stories from the time I was a small child, sitting quietly in the kitchen and absorbing the details of the lives of my aunts and uncles as they drank coffee together and shared tales. Later, in my professional life as a clinical social worker and family therapist, I saw, up close, the conflicts and mysteries of family life in their astonishing range. These experiences impacted me and as I began to write, inspired me. So first, I want to thank my large, extended family, who, while not the Weissman clan, was my frame of reference for family; second I thank my many clients who bravely shared their lives and problems and taught me that each person has a unique story. Although I started out to write about individual people, the stories began to string themselves together and soon they became a novel about family itself.

For this novel, my thanks go out to the many people who helped me on my journey. First to my writing group, Marc Coppen, Lyn Halper, Marsha Jamil, Virginia McKenna, Sharon Picard, and Pamela Stemberg, who read many iterations of the novel as I developed it over six years, always offering encouragement and advice.

I want to thank those writing teachers who worked with me on early drafts of the novel: June Gould, a gifted teacher who inspires imagination and creativity with every assignment and Pat Dunn,

Jimin Han and Tessa Smith McGovern from the Writing Institute at Sarah Lawrence College, whose guidance was inestimable. I am deeply grateful to Stephanie Lehmann, who worked with me at the Fairfield Country Writers' Studio and whose wise insights and advice helped me craft the third and most important draft of the book.

To my beta readers of early and later versions of the book, I send my everlasting gratitude: Jill Edelman Barberi, Nina Shilling, Nora Stonehill, Virginia Weir and Gail Reisin who read the novel twice with the critical eye of a talented English teacher. To my family members who also read and critiqued drafts of the novel, you have my love and appreciation: Dawn Kraut, Michael Appel, Mark Reiss, Joan Reinhardt Reiss, Elizabeth Nahar, Hannah Nahar, and my daughter Ruth Kraut who not only read the novel but crafted the family tree that appears in the front of the book, and my son, Jonathan Kraut, for his legal advice. Finally I thank my beloved husband and partner, Allen, whose several and careful readings of the book caught many errors and inconsistencies.

I am very grateful to the staff and editors at She Writes Press for their unique and supportive work with me and other women and emerging writers. Brooke Warner, Shannon Green, Samantha Strom, and Jennifer Caven, your professionalism is appreciated. To the sister writers in the She Writes Press Facebook Group, thank you for your wisdom and unfailing support.

I have learned so much from my publicist Andrea Kiliany Thatcher of Smith Publicity, and also Meghan Orciari, my web developer. Because of them I have a website and a start in social media.

To all of you, I can never thank you enough.

ABOUT THE AUTHOR

© Allen Kraut

Florence Reiss Kraut is a native New Yorker, raised and educated in New York City. She holds a BA in English and a MSW in social work, and she worked for thirty years as a clinician, a family therapist and finally CEO of a family service agency before retiring to write and travel widely.

Her intense interest in family comes from growing up in a close family of 26 aunts and uncles and 27 first cousins where, listening to stories at kitchen table coffee klatches and family parties, she learned about the conflicts and mysteries of family life. Those stories became the inspiration for many of the stories and essays written and published from the early years raising her three children throughout her career as a social worker. She has published stories for children and teens, romance stories for national magazines, literary stories, and personal essays for the Westchester section of the New York Times. She has three married children and nine grandchildren. How to Make a Life is her first novel.

Learn more about Florence at www.florencereisskraut.com

SELECTED TITLES FROM SHE WRITES PRESS

She Writes Press is an independent publishing company founded to serve women writers everywhere. Visit us at www.shewritespress.com.

Odessa, Odessa by Barbara Artson $16.95, 978-1-63152-443-1
A multigenerational immigrant story of a family, joined by tradition and parted during persecution, that remains bound by a fateful decision to leave Odessa, a shtetl near the Black Sea in western Russia, to escape anti-Semitism.

The Belief in Angels by J. Dylan Yates $16.95, 978-1-938314-64-3
From the Majdonek death camp to a volatile hippie household on the East Coast, this narrative of tragedy, survival, and hope spans more than fifty years, from the 1920s to the 1970s.

Portrait of a Woman in White by Susan Winkler $16.95, 978-1-938314-83-4
When the Nazis steal a Matisse portrait from the eccentric, art-loving Rosenswigs, the Parisian family is thrust into the tumult of war and separation, their fates intertwined with that of their beloved portrait.

An Address in Amsterdam by Mary Dingee Fillmore
$16.95, 978-1-63152-133-1
After facing relentless danger and escalating raids for 18 months, Rachel Klein—a well-behaved young Jewish woman who transformed herself into a courier for the underground when the Nazis invaded her country—persuades her parents to hide with her in a dank basement, where much is revealed.

The Sweetness by Sande Boritz Berger $16.95, 978-1-63152-907-8
A compelling and powerful story of two girls—cousins living on separate continents—whose strikingly different lives are forever changed when the Nazis invade Vilna, Lithuania.

Tasa's Song by Linda Kass $16.95, 978-1-63152-064-8
From a peaceful village in eastern Poland to a partitioned post-war Vienna, from a promising childhood to a year living underground, *Tasa's Song* celebrates the bonds of love, the power of memory, the solace of music, and the enduring strength of the human spirit.